BURIED

BURIED

Lynda La Plante was born in Liverpool. She trained for the stage at RADA and worked with the National Theatre and RDC before becoming a television actress. She then turned to writing and made her breakthrough with the phenomenally successful TV series *Widows*. She has written over thirty international novels, all of which have been bestsellers, and is the creator of the Anna Travis, Lorraine Page and Trial and Retribution series. Her original script for the much-acclaimed *Prime Suspect* won awards from BAFTA, Emmy, British Broadcasting and Royal Television Society, as well as the 1993 Edgar Allan Poe Award.

Lynda is one of only three screenwriters to have been made an honorary fellow of the British Film Institute and was awarded the BAFTA Dennis Potter Best Writer Award in 2000. In 2008, she was awarded a CBE in the Queen's Birthday Honours List for services to Literature, Drama and Charity.

✉Join the Lynda La Plante Readers' Club at
www.bit.ly/LyndaLaPlanteClub
www.lyndalaplante.com
⦿Facebook @LyndaLaPlanteCBE
◉Twitter @LaPlanteLynda
#BuriedBook

Lynda La Plante

BURIED

ZAFFRE

This is a work of fiction. Names, places, events and
incidents are either the products of the author's
imagination or used fictitiously. Any resemblance to
actual persons, living or dead, or actual
events is purely coincidental.

Copyright © La Plante Global Limited, 2020

All rights reserved.
No part of this publication may be reproduced,
stored or transmitted in any form by any means, electronic,
mechanical, photocopying or otherwise, without
the prior written permission of the publisher.

Typeset by Scribe Inc., Philadelphia, PA.

First published in Great Britain by Zaffre in 2020
This edition published in the United States of America in 2020 by Zaffre
Zaffre is an imprint of Bonnier Books UK
80–81 Wimpole Street, London W1G 9RE

10 9 8 7 6 5 4 3 2 1

Trade paperback ISBN: 978-1-49986-246-1
Hardback ISBN: 978-1-49986-243-0
Canadian TP ISBN: 978-1-49986-244-7
Ebook ISBN: 978-1-49986-242-3

For information, contact
251 Park Avenue South, Floor 12, New York, New York 10010
www .bonnierbooks .co .uk

BURIED *is dedicated to Variety, the Children's Charity.*
Before you read the book, please do take a look at the
wonderful work they do at www.variety.org.uk.
I'm very proud to be one of their ambassadors
and to give my support to them.

PROLOGUE

1994

In the soft light of the flickering candles, the room looked like a film set: five women enjoying a celebration dinner. As the clumsy maid leaned in to overfill her glass, no one caught the strange glint behind the watchful eyes of the guest of honor. Smiling and nodding graciously, she seemed to be enjoying every moment of this strange, unexpected reunion. In reality she was waiting. She knew they wanted something and on this, her first night out of prison, Dolly Rawlins' suspicious mind was in overdrive.

She had not expected anyone to meet her when she left Holloway that morning, but a black Mercedes had been waiting outside the main entrance. As the chauffeur opened the door, he had handed her an invitation to join "friends" for dinner at The Grange, a large manor house. It had been handwritten by Ester Freeman, who had briefly been in the same cell block as Dolly, so, against her better judgment, Dolly had got in the car. After all, she had nowhere else to go.

As the car pulled up on the graveled driveway, the outside of The Grange was in darkness, while the inside exuded a welcoming glow. It looked warm, inviting. Typical Ester, thought Dolly, to reach for dramatic effect. As she headed for the front door, she realized it was intended to distract from just how dilapidated the mansion actually was. Typical Ester, indeed!

The door was opened by a young girl dressed as a maid and, behind her, theatrically poised at the foot of the sweeping staircase, stood the glamorous Ester Freeman.

"Darling!" Ester exclaimed in her husky voice, opening her arms wide. "A few old friends, indebted to your kindness, have gathered to celebrate your freedom."

She turned to the maid.

"Angela, tell the others our guest has arrived. Dolly—" she turned back to Dolly—"come with me . . ."

Upstairs, in the candlelit master bedroom, a stunning velvet gown hung on the outside of the wardrobe door, draped with an accompanying shawl. On the dressing table was an array of paraphernalia relating to hair and make-up; a dressing gown was laid on the bed. In the adjoining room a bath was already drawn.

Ester handed Dolly a glass of champagne.

"No rush, Dolly. You have all the time in the world now."

An hour later, Dolly was seated at a large dining table boasting a banquet of meats and vegetables, breads and sauces, and enough wine to keep them all happy for days. Once again, the dim lighting did its magic. The blazing fire and a bank of candles on the mantel and the grand piano made the run-down room look fabulous.

As the maid worked her way around the table, pouring the delicious chilled wine, Dolly took a moment to look round at the "friends" who had gathered for this welcome dinner.

At the far end of the table sat Ester Freeman, seductively touching the rim of her champagne glass to the glass of the woman sitting beside her. "Any port in a storm," thought Dolly. Ester was the sort of prisoner who set her sights on a suitable sex toy within seconds of being booked in. Her latest conquest was Julia Lawson, who had also been in Holloway. Julia was a doctor, imprisoned for prescription fraud. She was also, Dolly knew, a heroin addict.

On Dolly's right was Gloria Radford, another former inmate. Loud and uncouth, she was dressed tonight in a tight mock leopard-skin dress and was midway through telling a dirty joke, screeching across the table to Kathleen O'Reilly in a coarse voice. Kathleen was overweight, in her mid-forties, and, as far as Dolly could recall, had been convicted of fraud. Her long hair was tied back unfashionably and her crumpled satin blouse was scattered with food stains and bursting under the pressure of her ample breasts.

Lastly, Dolly's eyes fell on the very pretty woman sitting to her left. Dolly recognized her face, but she couldn't remember what Connie Stevens had been in for, although she did recall that she had always been in tears, claiming to be totally innocent. Connie was very curvaceous, her bleached blonde hair reminiscent of Marilyn Monroe, and she had perfected the movie star's sultry pout. Dolly guessed prostitution.

As Gloria finished her dirty joke, everyone laughed a little too loudly. In the silence that followed, Ester raised her glass to their guest of honor and the others followed, looking at her expectantly. Dolly looked round the table and smiled. She had no idea what they wanted, but she could wait. She was used to waiting.

CHAPTER 1

Present day

Rose Cottage had been empty for eight months. It was a neat, two-story white stone building with thick, black wooden lintels above the central front door and each of the five small windows—three up, two down. On the more sheltered west side of the front wall, the ivy had completely taken over and was lifting the slates from the roof, but on the exposed east side, the stonework was bare and had been flattened by centuries of strong winter winds swirling down from the hills. From some angles the cottage looked as though it was leaning to the left.

As the cottage was rural, with stables and a hay barn, the land surrounding it had been fairly unkempt even before it was left empty, but a small area directly outside the front door had been landscaped into narrow, winding footpaths circling rose beds. The wild roses, left to their own devices, were still fighting against the changing seasons, but today they looked particularly beautiful. In fact, they were the only real reminder of how lovely the cottage had once been.

Inside, the furniture had been moved into the center of the room, just in front of the hearth. A heavy wooden chest of drawers and two bookshelves surrounded a two-seater horsehair sofa, which had four side tables piled high on top of it. Some of the books from the bookshelves had been forced into the gaps of this makeshift bonfire, and the rest had been thrown into the hearth on top of a huge stack of paper.

Suddenly, the small downstairs windows to the left and right of the front door exploded under the immense pressure from the heat inside, sending glass and wood showering into the rose beds. Flames quickly took hold of the wooden lintels and, within seconds, smoke had blackened the white stone wall.

The small room was soon consumed by flames, which rose to the ceiling beams and traveled to the wooden staircase and up the stairs. They eventually pushed their way out between the slates from the wooden ceiling beams beneath, and it wasn't long before a spark leapt across to the hay barn, still full of bales of hay for horses long gone. The barn went up like a Roman candle and, from that point onward, there was no stopping the fire.

* * *

A quarter of a mile away, in a small housing estate, the first of the 999 calls was made. Neighbors watched as dark brown smoke billowed into the clear blue sky. When the house had been occupied, the smoke from the chimney had always been the expected wispy light gray, but this was different. It looked heavy and rancid, and just kept coming.

Speculation was rife as to how the fire had started. Was it a tramp trying to keep warm? Was it kids taking their games too far?

Fourteen 999 calls were made in total, sending two fire engines racing toward Rose Cottage from Aylesbury Fire Station. By the time they arrived, the interior of the cottage had almost gone and the hay barn was a pile of rubble and ashes. However, the stables, which were furthest away from the cottage, were still fully ablaze.

When the fire brigade arrived, they split into two teams—one to tackle the fire inside, and a second to the stables to prevent the flames from jumping to the woodland beyond. It was easier to gain control of the stables because, once the wooden frames had gone, there was nothing left to fuel the fire. The interior of the cottage, however, kept re-igniting as the fire found new fuel on the upper floors and from the wooden roof beams. It didn't take much to give the flames a new lease of life.

By nightfall, the grounds resembled a muddy swamp and the rose beds had been completely destroyed by hours of heavy fire boots. What was left of the furniture had been thrown into the front garden, to avoid further re-ignition inside the property, so the once beautiful rose garden looked like a garbage dump.

"Stop!" the sub-officer shouted as he emerged through the hole that used to be the front door. "Nobody goes back inside!"

He reached for his phone and dialed Sally Bown. It was late and the phone rang for quite some time before it was finally answered.

"Sal, this one's for you. We've got a body."

* * *

Fire Investigation Officer Sally Bown arrived at the scene at eleven o'clock. From the neck down, she was kitted out in her wellworn fire officer's uniform, but from the neck up, she was immaculate. Her long brown hair was in a loose, low braided bun, held in place by an antique hairpin of white beads and silver leaves, and her light make-up enhanced her natural beauty. The whole crew fancied her on an average day, so her arrival was definitely making their arduous night better. She didn't mind. They respected her position, so them watching her arse every now and then didn't bother her in the slightest.

"It's way better than men *not* watching my arse," was her response to any woman who objected to the glib sexism that came from the male firefighters. And Sally looked at them, too, so she thought it only fair.

At Sally's side was a child of a SOCO with puffy eyes and bed hair. He carried a case almost as big as himself, and he stuck to her like glue. He wasn't quite used to shift work yet, but if he'd been called by Sally Bown, then he was good at his job. He'd learn the rest.

In the lounge of Rose Cottage, the pile of heavy wooden furniture was now destroyed. The brass hinges and handles from the chest of drawers lay on the floor just in front of the hearth and, on the obliterated sofa, part-melted into the springs, lay a dead body, charred and blackened beyond recognition.

"Jesus," muttered Sally as she got out her camera and filmed the scene, starting at the front door and moving methodically toward the center of the lounge and the dead body. Her young SOCO waited outside until instructed to do otherwise.

"Sally, stop!" Sub shouted. She stopped dead. Sub was a man of very few words and everyone who worked with him knew that he only spoke when he had something important to say. "Retrace your steps, Sal. Now. Please."

Sally started walking backward, toe to heel, following exactly the same path as she'd taken to come in.

There was a deafening crack from directly above Sally's head. A hand grabbed her belt and she flew backward with the force of a recoiling bungee rope, to be caught by Sub's waiting arms. Once he had a firm hold on her, he fell backward onto the floor, taking

Sally with him. In the next split second an iron bed frame dropped through the air and landed right where she had been standing. A cloud of ash and debris flew upward and took an age to come back down. When visibility returned, Sub was still on the floor, Sally held between his legs, his arms gripping her tightly round the waist. The two legs of the bed that were closest to them had smashed deep holes through the lounge floorboards, and the other two were straddling the remains of the sofa and the charred body, which was still, miraculously, in one piece.

Sub momentarily tightened his grip around Sally's waist before letting go. That tiny squeeze reassured her that she was safe. As she gripped Sub's raised knees to lever herself to her feet, and he eased her forward with his hands politely in the small of her back, she couldn't help thinking what a massive shame it was that he looked so like her dad.

* * *

When he arrived on the scene, Detective Inspector Martin Prescott was frustrated to be held back from entering Rose Cottage until the risk assessment had been done. He couldn't imagine three more infuriating words in the English language than "risk fucking assessment."

Prescott had been senior officer to Sally Bown's older sister for more than twenty years, and the families were close. This was not unusual for rural Aylesbury, or for the local emergency services. Sally knew he'd be impatient so, while the fragile ceiling and crumbling walls were made safe, she kept him occupied by showing him the video footage of the interior.

"At first we thought he could be a vagrant," Sally told Prescott.

"He?"

Prescott smiled as he corrected Sally's assumption. It was clear from the video that there was no way of knowing the gender of the charred remains at this point. Prescott made Sally smile without even trying. She thought his thick Yorkshire accent made him sound happy, even when they were disagreeing with each other.

"Sorry," Sally corrected herself. "We initially thought that the body could be that of a vagrant unlucky enough to have set fire to themselves after lighting candles to keep warm. There's no electricity in the cottage, and we found several tea lights scattered around the lounge—on the mantelpiece and in the hearth—but when I looked more closely at the debris on the floor directly next to the sofa, it looked like the furniture had been piled up around him. I mean, around the body."

"So, the body was there first?"

"That's for you to decide, Martin."

"Accelerant?"

"Undetermined as yet."

Prescott was disappointed when the video footage ended.

"That all you got?"

Sally started to play a second video, which began by showing the iron bed frame sitting squarely astride the sofa. Prescott closed his eyes and sighed heavily at the sight of his crime scene buried under a double bed. The quiet breath he exhaled formed the words "Fuck me!"

Prescott took a moment to gather his thoughts. When he was thinking, his eyes flicked from side to side as though he were seeing the various scenarios flashing past inside his head. He appeared to be a very laid-back man, but there was an intensity bubbling away underneath the surface. Mildly dyslexic, soon after joining the force he had made the decision never to write anything down in public. Instead, he'd decided he would remember everything, and in a brain that full, it could sometimes take a little longer to process what he was seeing. Although he hid his intellect under Northern glibness, Prescott was a clever man, and it was always worth waiting for him.

"Right, well, you know the rules, Sal. It's a suspicious death, so I have to assume murder till the evidence tells me otherwise." He walked away from Sally before she could reply and headed for the cottage to see if he could at least peek in through where the window had once been. "And if it's murder, then I'm wasting valuable time standing out here doing naff all!"

Sally raced ahead and stood in his way, forcing him to stop.

"This may be your crime scene, DI Prescott, but you are *not* going in until I say it's safe for you to do so."

Prescott looked down at Sally. She was at least four inches shorter than him, but she was a feisty woman and she wasn't going to back down.

"And anyway," Sally added, "I hadn't finished."

She fast-forwarded the second video, stopping it at seven minutes and thirty-two seconds. On the wall above the hearth the word PERVERT could be seen scrawled in red paint. It was mostly covered in a thick layer of black soot, but the letters could still just be made out.

"It looks like you could have a dead sex offender. And I doubt he got here on his own."

Prescott got his vape out of his left-hand jacket pocket.

"I know that should make me feel better about having to wait to gain access to me crime scene, but it just annoys me more. I don't know if that word relates to this dead body or not, do I? So now

I'm more frustrated than before you showed me." He dragged on the vape, but couldn't for the life of him get it to work. He put it back into his pocket and, from the other jacket pocket, got out a packet of cigarettes and a lighter. "You follow your rules and get that place scaffolded up asap and I'll be over there shortening me life."

* * *

It took six hours before Martin Prescott could don a blue paper suit and shoes. His white paper face mask sat round his neck as he watched Sally pointing at the partially collapsed roof and muttering to Sub. When Sub nodded, Prescott immediately pulled up the mask. The man of few words had spoken.

Inside Rose Cottage, scaffolding held up the charred ceiling beams and the loose stones from the walls had been removed, leaving behind a relatively solid and safe structure. Visually, the scene was as Prescott expected, based on the preview he'd got from Sally's videos, but nothing ever prepared him for the smell of a body. The stench of burnt flesh and bones overpowers every other sense and, even through his face mask, he could smell and taste the distinctive miasma of "long pig."

"'Long pig' is what cannibals call human beings," Sally had explained on their first ever meeting at a crime scene, more than fourteen years ago. "By all accounts we taste like barbecued pork and, as we cook, we definitely smell like it."

"Fuck me," Prescott had mumbled through his face mask. "No wonder you're single."

Now, Prescott and Sally paused just inside the jagged hole in the wall that used to be the front doorway of Rose Cottage and watched the dog handler lead her spaniel through the rubble. The dog wore tiny red canvas boots, Velcroed in place around the ankles and with thick rubber soles that protected her paws from smoldering embers and sharp debris, allowing her to work safely and comfortably. The single repeated command of "Show me, Amber" was all that could be heard inside Rose Cottage.

Amber's handler kept her off the sofa, as the charred body was still there. The dog worked hard, sniffing and moving around the remnants of furniture. Her tail wagged, her tongue lolled, she jumped and rummaged, but she didn't make one single indication that an accelerant was present.

"Maybe the fire burned intensely enough to destroy any accelerant?" Sally speculated. "Or maybe a less common one was used. The dog only knows the most common ones, such as petrol or household flammables. Your forensics people might still find accelerant on the items you collect."

"I'll make sure I've got a tennis ball in me pocket if they do."

Sally giggled at the unstoppable image that popped into her head, of an entire forensics team being trained to seek out evidence with the promise of a ball as a reward.

"I think the ball only works with Amber."

Prescott signaled for his blue-suited SOCOs to descend on the scene. He pointed at the sofa.

"There's a body in there, fellas, but it's goin' nowhere, so don't rush and don't compromise evidence just to get it out."

A sea of nodding blue paper heads dispersed around the room and set about collecting anything and everything that might be useful—wood, brass hinges, plaster, bed springs. All items were individually double-wrapped into nylon bags to preserve any traces of accelerant.

Now that Prescott was inside his crime scene, he had the patience of a saint. He could see the wheels of the machinery turning, see his officers working and progress being made. He followed his SOCOs deeper into the mess, allowing them to clear and preserve the way in front of him, and Sally followed after. This was *his* scene now, and she totally respected the shift in authority.

Eventually, and in relative silence, Prescott and Sally made it as far as the sofa. The iron bed frame, which had now been removed, had missed the body when it fell. Even so, the body was massively damaged. The face was not only burnt down to the skeleton, but the cheekbones and lower jawbone were smashed and many of the teeth were missing.

"Could that damage to the skull be from falling debris?" Prescott asked.

Sally leaned in to get a better look. "The ceiling was largely gone by the time we arrived, so God knows what might have fallen through and landed on the sofa. The cleaner-looking skull fractures around the temple area could be heat stress. The skull can sometimes just pop, depending on the intensity of heat."

"Damn shame this fella's teeth are so damaged," Prescott commented, almost to himself. Then louder, "Look at the bloody mess your lot have made of this place!"

Sally was just about to tear a strip off him when she looked at his partially hidden face. His eyes were crinkled at the edges and she knew he was smiling.

"Bloody fires," Prescott continued, avoiding her gaze. "If the flames don't destroy the evidence, the water does." He scratched his head through his blue paper hood and his eyes flicked about again as he thought through everything he was seeing. "If this is murder, we might be looking for someone who's savvy about forensics, you know. I mean, you can't print burnt wood and you can't find shoe prints under water."

He was suddenly distracted by the contents of the hearth. The water from the fire hose on the floor in this area of the room looked like thin black paint—a result you might expect to get after paper is burnt, creating a fine, soluble ash. Further back in the hearth, untouched by the water altogether, were the remnants of what looked like stacks of dry, charred paper. The paper was now nothing more than tiny fragments of its original form, but the volume was confusing.

Prescott picked up the longest of four fire pokers, and gently nudged the top layer of paper away in the hope of getting to some less burnt samples underneath. He tried not to damage any of the delicate paper. Eventually he spotted a single intact piece, no more than one centimeter in length, showing the instantly recognizable pale blue-green pattern from the bottom left-hand corner of an old five-pound note. Prescott carefully picked up this fragile piece of evidence and placed it in the palm of Sally's gloved hand.

"It's cash, Sal. These stacks of paper . . . it's all cash."

* * *

Jack Warr was a strikingly attractive man. Thick, dark hooded brows hid the deepest brown eyes. He had a cleft chin which showed the permanent shadow of impending stubble and, when he smiled, two long dimples appeared on either side of his mouth, running from his chin to his cheekbones. He had a naturally athletic physique that looked great in anything.

Maggie, his partner, always said it was a good job that his body was so amazing as he made no real effort with the clothes he dressed it in, but she fancied the pants off him no matter what he wore.

It was those eyes that had got her in the first instance, though. Eyebrows down, Jack's eyes would express such incredible intensity that if he told you he could take on champion boxer David Haye and win, you'd believe him. Eyebrows up, he looked like a delicate, innocent soul that any woman would love to care for. This balance between man and boy was why Maggie loved Jack so much. He was her protector and her lover, her rock and her friend.

"Where's the jacket that goes with this shirt you've put out?" Jack shouted from the master bedroom. He liked to call it the "master" bedroom, regardless of the fact that it was exactly the same size as the spare bedroom. The view over Teddington was what made it masterful, according to Jack.

Maggie didn't answer, so Jack was forced to go into the kitchen to find her. On the breakfast bar were a bowl of cereal and a cup of tea that she'd put out for him. On the back of his chair was his jacket and underneath were his shoes. Maggie's crooked smile said, *Why do we do this every morning?*

Jack kissed and hugged her tightly. He never tired of just holding Maggie in his arms. She felt the same today as she had when they first met. Jack would maintain that Maggie kept her exceptional figure effortlessly, but she tried her very best to go to the hospital gym during every lunch break and, when Jack had the car for work, she'd leave herself enough time to walk to the hospital. For Maggie, this daily exercise was not only good for her body, but also hugely therapeutic, as it took her away from the stresses, pressures and horrors of being a medical resident. Neither Jack's nor Maggie's job was easy. Shift patterns and heavy workloads dictated that junk food was sometimes on the menu and, when they did get a rare day off together, they loved nothing more than going out for drinks, dinner, and a movie.

Maggie exercised to stay beautiful for Jack, and Jack did absolutely nothing to stay fit for Maggie. She was a health-conscious 34-year-old and he was a slobbish 36-year-old. Maggie, in stark contrast to Jack's "Heathcliff" look, had blonde hair and blue eyes. Jack adored the way she looked when she rolled out of bed in the morning, with her hair ruffled and her pale, flawless skin unhidden by make-up. She was the most beautiful woman he'd ever seen, and would ever see. He had eyes for no one but her.

Maggie had just come off a night shift on the orthopedic ward at the New Victoria Hospital. She was three weeks into her new rotation and, despite always coming home exhausted, she still got Jack ready for work before she went to bed. By the time he got home that night, she'd be gone again, so this hug had to last him at least twenty-four hours. Jack nuzzled Maggie's neck. He normally hated the way she smelt when she came home from work—the horrible combination of alcohol hand sanitizer, that chemical smell that hangs in the air in hospitals, mothballs and, occasionally, vomit— but this morning he was running late, so she'd already had time to shower and, therefore, smelt of tangerines.

Fourteen months previously, Maggie and Jack had agreed that moving from Devon to London was the right thing to do for her career. His career, in his words, wasn't as big a deal as hers. Maggie knew she wanted to be an orthopedic surgeon, whereas all Jack really knew for sure was that he wanted to be able to go and watch Plymouth Argyle Football Club whenever they played at home. He wasn't lazy, but he was restless. Or, as he put it, at a crossroads.

At 36, Jack should, by now, have been a detective inspector at least, rather than a lowly DC. When Maggie had asked him if they could move to London for her career, he'd said, "Sure. Gang wrangling will be a bit like sheep wrangling, I expect. Only with knives."

Maggie had asked Jack what it was he truly wanted, and all he could come up with was "you," which, although lovely, wasn't very helpful. Then he'd answered more seriously.

"I want that look I see in your eyes when you put that stethoscope round your neck. You're proud of what you do, Mags. You're excited. I want to feel excited."

London was, in fact, a huge risk, both emotionally and financially, but Jack's commitment to Maggie made it the right decision. They knew no one in the South-east and, although Maggie could make a lifelong friend in a supermarket line, Jack was more standoffish. He didn't care about friends—he had Maggie—but the money was a worry. They went from having both time and cash to spend at the end of the month, to being skint ships that passed in the night. And they had to plan two months in advance for any extra expenditure—such as the car's inspection fee. Maggie dealt with all of this, though. She was the organizer, and she was the one who never panicked when the account turned from black to red.

Jack had agreed to make the life-changing move because he'd always known that Maggie was destined for greater things, and he didn't want his indecisiveness to hold her back. As it happened, Jack's current boss, DCI Simon Ridley, had heard about his transfer on the grapevine and had done a little digging. Jack's reputation in Devon was as a solid foot soldier with an exceptional eye for detail and a natural ability to talk to people, read them and work out the best way to get what he needed from them. His interview technique was greatly admired, although it had never been pushed to its limits in Totnes. Ridley had decided to give Jack the opportunity to find his path with the Serious Crime Squad, but very quickly worked out that Jack's not being stretched in his previous role was less to do with the location and more to do with his lack of ambition. However, he was diligent and got on with his work, so Ridley had kept him on . . . for now.

* * *

It was Jack's turn to have the car that morning which, as he sat in a tailback on the A3 near Battersea, he was deeply regretting. His work mobile danced on the passenger seat, pinging and vibrating away as message after message came through from the app version of HOLMES. HOLMES was the bible for police case-related information and was normally installed and issued on tablets for use in court or on cases. But the technology was unreliable, so many officers invested in top-of-the-range mobile phones and installed HOLMES on them instead. It was allowed—just about.

As the pinging and vibrating continued, Jack smiled and shook his head as he imagined DCI Ridley's messages, all perfectly spelled and punctuated instructions for the day. Ridley was in meetings all morning, which was why being a little bit late was no big deal. Jack would make the time up at the end of the day, seeing as Maggie would be on her next night shift and he'd be going home to a cold bed.

Ridley led a divisional team of twelve Serious Crime officers. The case that Jack was currently working on had started out with one young dad, who happened to be an engineer, realizing that the baby monitor in his daughter's nursery was sending a signal to three devices, rather than the two he expected. The monitor had been hacked and an unknown person or persons were watching his daughter sleep.

Once the police had the geography of the rogue signals pinned down, the legwork had begun. Hundreds of hours tracing, interviewing, ruling in or ruling out every known pedophile and associate in the area. Over several months, they had discovered hundreds of hacked baby monitors, all within the same fifty-mile radius. They visited 756 pedophiles, their friends and their families, and narrowed the field to thirty-two. Then to one, a Donal Sweeney, who shared a cell with a man whose never-convicted pedophile nephew sold baby monitors to high street stores.

It was 8:45 by the time Jack walked down the battleship-gray corridor toward CID's shared office. There was nothing remotely dynamic about this part of the station. He paused in the canteen doorway, inhaled the coffee-bean air and diverted inside.

Jack slowly worked his way through all of his text messages and emails over an espresso and a croissant dipped in honey. He only drank coffee at work, because Maggie hated the smell and taste of it when he kissed her, and seeing as kissing Maggie was more important than caffeine, he did without coffee when he was at home. But Jack needed caffeine to get him through this bloody case.

The canteen was bustling with uniformed officers. Some ate heavy meals, some light breakfasts, depending on where they were in their shifts. As Jack made himself a to-do list from Ridley's text messages, he snorted through his croissant, sending a fine spray of loose puff pastry across the table. Ridley had written:

Laura's post-8 p.m. report overwrites yours, rather than adds to yours from yesterday morning. Please amend in the system. Print in triplicate and leave on my desk.

Ridley was the only man in the world who texted in full sentences. Jack sat back in his chair and, wiping the stubborn, buttery crumbs from round his mouth with the back of his hand, looked around the canteen. He could hear snippets of conversations as officers talked about the cases they were on, the arrests they'd just made, the raids they were about to make. The amount of adrenaline and testosterone flying around Jack was dizzying—but none of it was his. He knew that his team would be at their desks, focused and driven to find the dirty bastard who was watching other people's kids sleep. So why was he late and sitting by himself in the canteen? The truth was that, no matter how friendly and welcoming Ridley's team was, Jack still kept them at arm's length.

Jack had gone from being a normal-sized fish in a normal-sized pond, to being a very small fish in the biggest pond in the UK— the Metropolitan Police Service. And he felt out of his depth. After fourteen months of working at the Met, he still hadn't found his calling, his passion, his heart in London and, as the months ticked by, he honestly feared that he never would.

* * *

When Jack finally walked into the squad room, he froze in the doorway. *Shit!* Ridley was *not* in meetings all morning and Jack being a little bit late was a *very* big deal.

Ridley didn't acknowledge Jack's presence, and no one in the team dared look away from him while he was talking. This was an impromptu briefing, in response to a phone call from DI Martin Prescott over in Aylesbury.

"We've just been handed a house fire, in which the charred remains of an unknown person have been discovered, together with approximately two million pounds in old money—also burnt. This is being treated as murder, arson and robbery. It's come to us because it's looking like it could be connected to one of our old cases from '95—the biggest train robbery this country has ever seen. As I'm sure you remember, no one was ever arrested and thirty million plus vanished without a trace. We're heading to Aylesbury this afternoon, after we've been to Donal Sweeney's."

Then, and only then, did Ridley look at Jack. His dark eyes were a frightening combination of anger and disappointment.

"You're with me," he said, then headed into his office and slammed the door shut.

The team shuffled uncomfortably in their seats, wondering what the hell Jack thought he was playing at by being so late. As Jack bowed his head in disgrace and wondered how this day could possibly get any worse, he spotted a blob of honey sliding down the front of his trouser leg.

CHAPTER 2

DCI Simon Ridley was organizing files in his glass-fronted office. He was a slender, almost sinewy 50-something man who did everything standing up: reading, eating, phoning. He could walk a couple of miles up and down the room in a single meeting.

In the shared squad room, Jack, DS Laura Wade and DC Anik Joshi waited patiently along with the rest of Ridley's team. They knew that when Ridley finally emerged, his handover would be short and straight to the point but, by God, watching him prepare was painful!

Ridley was known around the station for getting things done quickly, but that was because no one outside this squad room saw the upfront, focused effort he put in. Once he was organized, there was no stopping him, that was true; but this part—the part where he was getting himself organized—was like pulling teeth. It stemmed from his aversion to delegating. He overcame this by hand-picking and training his own team, giving precise commands and keeping a very close eye on each and every one of his officers.

"Do you think he's like this in the bedroom?" Laura whispered to Jack. "Prepping at the speed of a tortoise and delivering at the speed of a train."

By the time Ridley finally emerged from his office, Jack and Laura were in silent, shoulder-shaking hysterics. True to form, Ridley was quick and to the point.

"Our target is Donal Sweeney. Yard in twenty. DC Joshi, you're with me."

And Ridley was gone.

Jack got to his feet. "I wonder what he'd do if, one day, none of us followed him?"

Laura retracted her head into her neck, giving herself a double chin, and looked sideways at Jack, eyebrows raised, as if to say, *You try it first!*

She then led the way out of CID and down into the yard.

* * *

Donal Sweeney lived on a council estate just outside Dagenham. He was a 36-year-old former computer engineer who, after being made redundant three years previously, went off radar. No job, no signing on, seemingly no income. And now they knew why. He was a big man, according to a mugshot taken after a drunken brawl the week after he lost his job where he had pulled a couple of knives, so they were going in hard and loud. He was clearly volatile, and a dozen coppers arriving to arrest him could be dangerous.

This council estate was a typical high-density social housing experiment from the 1960s, duly forgotten about and now looking after itself as best it could. Petty criminals were rife, but crime wasn't too bad as they tended not to "shit on their own doorstep." More serious crime, such as murder, was restricted to people who were known to each other.

Anik sat in the passenger seat of Ridley's car, watching Ridley give orders to an Armed Response Unit—they all wore holstered Glock 17 pistols strapped to their thighs, and two of them held on tight to a short-strapped Heckler & Koch MP5 submachine guns. They stood with their legs unnecessarily wide apart, encased head to foot in Kevlar. Anik had always thought that armed officers must be both brave and crazy; it certainly wasn't for him. He'd started the training last year, but as soon as the first simulated hostage scenario began, he lost his nerve. The idea of taking a life was something he could just about get his head round, but the idea of someone trying to take *his* life was impossible to accept. It takes one hell of a special person to race toward a crazed gunman to save a total stranger—and Anik wasn't that special. He could handle himself well for a smallish man, but he'd never faced a gunman and never wanted to.

Jack and Laura leaned on the bonnet of Ridley's car, arms folded, chatting and laughing. Anik couldn't hear what they were saying, but he envied how their experience made them so relaxed in situations like this. He wished he wasn't having palpitations; he wished the sweat wasn't running down his spine and he wished his stab vest hadn't ridden up so high underneath his chin that it chafed every time he turned his head. Eventually he decided to get out of Ridley's car, so he could pull his vest down; sitting in a stab vest was clearly an acquired art.

Ridley's "slow and steady" prep had been done in a quiet side street about half a mile from Sweeney's estate, away from prying eyes. Now they were in position, the next bit would happen fast.

* * *

The "Big Red Key" was swung back for a third time and slammed into the base of the front door. The bottom had more than one bolt fitted, so it was holding its own against the 16 kg metal battering ram. Each second of delay was giving Sweeney time to destroy evidence—Ridley was visibly frustrated. The fourth hit did its job and the door finally gave way. The officer wielding the "Big Red Key" quickly stepped to one side, allowing the armed officers to enter.

"Armed police! Armed police! Get down on the ground! Get down!" Then a pause. Then a little mumbling. Then, "Secure!"

Ridley led the way in, closely followed by Jack, then Laura, then Anik, then a team of uniformed officers who would be tasked with searching the premises. In the lounge was an elderly man in his mid-70s. He sat in a Mobility riser recliner with his feet up on the elevated footrest.

"Donal Sweeney?" Ridley asked.

"Yes, sir," the man wheezed. "You might be after my boy though, I reckon."

Ridley showed Sweeney Senior a warrant to search the premises. "Jack . . ." was the only word he uttered before leading everyone else out of the room.

Sweeney Senior asked Jack to pass him his reading glasses, which he did.

"The little shit!" Sweeney said once he'd read the warrant. "I said he could use my address to open a bank account and he does this? Am I under arrest?"

"Until we can establish the facts," Jack explained, "you'll have to come to the station."

"Right, then. I'd better start moving, 'cos it takes a while."

Sweeney Senior reached down into the pocket in the side of his Mobility recliner. The Armed Response Unit instantly raised their weapons and pointed them at the old man.

"Don't move! Stay still! Show me your hands!"

Sweeney Senior slammed his hands over his eyes and waited to be shot.

"The remote! Jesus Christ!" Jack shouted. "He's just going for the remote!"

He took the remote control from the side pocket of the chair and pressed the "down" button as the overexcited ARU team lowered their guns. The footrest on the Mobility recliner started to lower, the seat started to tilt, and the back started to push Sweeney Senior very, very slowly onto his slippered feet. As he became more upright, a catheter bag half-full of urine dropped out of the bottom of his trouser leg. The old man stood there, hands over his eyes, crying and trembling in fear, pissing into his bag. This was a whole new low for Jack.

* * *

Prescott and Sally watched as two of his SOCOs attempted to move the charred body from the sofa into the body bag waiting on the ground, ready to be lifted onto the undertaker's trolley, which was parked just outside the front door. The undertaker, employed by Thames Valley Police to transport bodies to the mortuary for postmortem, was playing *Candy Crush* at full blast on his mobile.

"Turn that down!" shouted Prescott. "If I hear another stupid fucking noise from outside, there'll be two dead bodies being driven to the mortuary, not one. Idiot . . ." he muttered. He turned to Sally. "What do you think of 'Sheila'?" he asked through his white paper mask. Sally frowned. "We got to call him something till we find out who he is."

"I get that. But why 'Sheila'?"

Prescott suddenly realized that the twenty years between them meant his joke was about to fall flat. He plowed on regardless.

"Sheila Ferguson? The Three Degrees? I know he's got six-degree burns, but there isn't a group called the Six Degrees." Sally was still looking very confused. "I pity you," Prescott mumbled. "You're too young to appreciate how bloody funny I am."

The melted underside of the charred body was tangled in with the sofa springs and each time the SOCOs wriggled an arm free, a leg would get caught, and vice versa. In the end, one of Sally's firefighters decided to cut the springs so that any pieces of metal embedded in the melted skin could just stay there until the body reached the postmortem table, where the pathologist could remove them in their own time. Getting the body off the sofa was like peeling a label off a jar—no matter how carefully you tried to keep the paper in one piece, it would inevitably tear, and you'd then have to decide whether to push the pieces back together and try again, or just leave some bits behind. Finally, the firefighter lying on his back beneath the sofa with wire cutters said, "That's the last spring gone, you're good to lift."

The undertakers lifted the charred body and placed it in the body bag.

As the fluids and dirty fire hose water from the blackened corpse slowly seeped out, it was abundantly clear that something was missing. In the springs of the sofa, the rubber sole of the left shoe had melted like glue and its hold on the foot inside had proved much harder to break than the ankle joint above it. Prescott shrugged his shoulders and walked away.

"Valiant effort, lads."

Sally stared down through the shell of the sofa at her despondent firefighter on the floor.

"If you could bag the left foot, please, he'd be very grateful."

* * *

Forensic pathologist Abigail Coleman laughed so loud that it disturbed her assistants in the next room.

"Ha! 'Sheila'! Martin, you are funny!"

Once the laughter had died away, she got down to business. Sheila lay on the postmortem table in the fetal position.

"Well," Abigail began, "it's definitely a boy. The pelvic measurements tell us that. But, more importantly, I'm almost certain that he was murdered—there's a large fracture at the back of the skull. This isn't a stress fracture caused by the intense heat of the fire, and it's not an impact fracture caused by the ceiling falling down because, as we can see from his very badly damaged jaw and cheekbones, 'Sheila' was face up on the sofa. The back of his head, if anything, would have been protected as the fire took hold and debris fell. No, I'd say that the fracture to the back of the skull is a good old-fashioned blunt force trauma. But I won't be able to tell you until tomorrow. His postmortem is scheduled for 9 a.m."

"What's wrong with today?"

Prescott wanted the victim's cause of death and he wanted it now.

"Well, I could do him today." Abigail glanced across the lab at a postmortem table in the corner of the room. On the table was a sheeted body, no taller than three foot five. "But you'll have tell the parents of that 6-year-old boy that they have to wait another 48 hours before I can tell them if their son was raped before he was strangled."

Prescott left without saying another word.

* * *

Prescott's office was minimalist to say the least. His desk, under normal circumstances, had a metal lattice cup for his pens, a desk diary, a phone and a small tray for the junk he'd pulled out of his pockets and needed to drop somewhere safe. This tray contained chewing gum, a USB stick, headache tablets, his wallet and a set of keys, complete with a miniature screwdriver for tightening the arms on his glasses. The desk itself was standard, but his chair was magnificent; Prescott liked to think in comfort.

Today, his desk was littered with crime scene photos from Rose Cottage, and Sally's video evidence played on a tablet propped up against the phone. He sat, enveloped in his huge leather office chair and took in all the images. Prescott's visual memory was legendary—when he looked at a photo, he could also recall what was just out of frame. It was as though he was back at the scene. The stacks of cash in the fireplace of Rose Cottage were a puzzle to him because the money dated from before May 2017, when the cotton fiber five-pound note went out of circulation and was replaced by notes made of polymer. His eyes flickered as he thought.

There was a quick knock on Prescott's door and two of his officers, knowing he was waiting for them, entered without being asked. They were each armed with a tablet and a notebook. Gerrard and

Miriam made themselves comfortable and waited for their cue to speak. After a second or two, Prescott leaned forward over the array of images and gave Miriam the nod.

"Rose Cottage was on a long-term lease to Norma Walker until eight months ago, when she died of cancer. Norma was an ex-mounted officer . . ." At this point, Prescott sat back in his chair, as for him, this was the most effective position in which to think as well as listen. "She kept our working horses in her stables when the need arose, and most of them retired there. She was diagnosed with breast cancer back in 2013 and, since 2016, she was pretty much house-bound. She was well respected, had lots of friends. For the final eight months of her life, there was a steady flow of off-duty coppers in and out of Rose Cottage making sure she had everything she needed. Her partner moved in with her toward the end, I think. She had no family, which is why all her possessions were still there."

"Norma Walker? Norma Walker? Why do I know the name?" Prescott seemed to expect Miriam to know the answer to this. But she didn't. Gerrard took over. Prescott loved listening to Gerrard's gentle Cork accent so much that an unconscious little smile crept over his face every time he spoke.

"Speculatively, if all the paper in the hearth at Rose Cottage was old money, we're looking at somewhere between £1 million and £1.8 million. It depends on how much was in £5 notes and how much was in £10 notes. Forensics haven't found any intact serial numbers—and they say they won't, by the way—so we can't date the money more accurately than pre-May 2017. I've got a list of robberies longer than me arm, with hauls big enough to be the Rose Cottage money—"

Prescott jumped to his feet, slamming his palms down on his desk.

"Norma Walker was interviewed about an armed robbery . . ." Prescott's eyes flicked around the room as he tried to find the memory he needed. Gerrard searched his notes whenever Prescott added more information into the search filter. "Early nineties. Maybe mid-nineties. And Bill . . . Bill . . ." Prescott clicked his fingers repeatedly at Gerrard.

"I was born in '92, sir."

Prescott ignored Gerrard and turned to Miriam. She was only one year off retirement. She would be more helpful.

"Bill . . . Mounted officer, must have worked with Norma . . . Talked your ear off—"

"Thorn!" Miriam yelled in an excited outburst.

"Bill bloody Thorn!" Prescott slumped back down, exhausted. "In '95, the Aylesbury mail train was robbed by a gang of five or six blokes, not half a mile from Rose Cottage. £27 million they got away with. Bill Thorn was in the Thames Valley search team that partnered up with the Transport Police. They reckoned it was outsiders—no local names had it in 'em to pull something that big. The roads were closed within minutes and hundreds of officers searched the entire area. Found nothing."

Prescott put his elbows on the desk, wrapped his right fist in his left hand and leaned his chin on his clenched fingers.

"If Sheila and the Rose Cottage cash are connected to a £27 million train robbery from 1995, it'll be an open Flying Squad case, I reckon." He pointed at Gerrard. "You—dig up everything you can on the '95 train robbery. And you"—he turned to Miriam— "dig up Bill Thorn."

CHAPTER 3

By the time the two-car convoy had reached Watford, Anik was feeling sick. He sat with his head leaning back against the headrest, his eyes closed, and his fingers clenched together on top of the file on his lap. The handwritten words on the front of the file read ROSE COTTAGE, AYLESBURY.

"I can't read in cars, Laura. I'm sorry, I just can't. From what I can gather though, the worst-case scenario is that the body's a sex offender, burned to death in an abandoned cottage. And the best-case scenario is that the body's connected to a twenty-four-year-old train robbery."

"You're defining 'best' and 'worst' by how exciting you think the investigation is going to be, are you?"

"Yes I am," Anik replied defiantly, opening his eyes and lifting his head. "It's better than arresting a 70-year-old man with a bag of wee strapped to his leg, anyhow."

Then he gagged a little as Laura changed lanes too quickly. She pulled into Sainsbury's petrol station, so they could swap places.

Ridley glanced in his rear-view mirror and watched Laura pull off the M1. At the same time, Jack's mobile pinged. Message from Laura:

Anik needs to puke. L x.

"Toilet break," Jack lied to Ridley. "Laura knows where she's going, so they'll catch us up."

Jack continued to flick through the file on his knee.

"We've got statements from hundreds of people from back in '95. DI Prescott's highlighted the ones we need to focus on." He read out loud in bullet points for speed: "Former mounted officer Norma Walker—last rental occupant of Rose Cottage. Dorothy Rawlins, also known as Dolly—last owner of nearby manor house, The Grange. She and five other occupants all interviewed. John Maynard—builder working at The Grange in '95. James Douglas— railway signalman on duty on the night of the train robbery."

Ridley allowed Jack to finish his list before speaking. "Check Dolly Rawlins."

Jack logged into the HOLMES app. A moment later, he glanced at Ridley in astonishment. Ridley was looking smug.

"Dolly Rawlins," Jack read out loud. "Convicted of the murder of her husband, Harold Rawlins, also known as Harry. Shot to death on August 27, 1995, by Ester Freeman. She sounds like she could have known an armed robber or two."

"Who was in charge of the investigation back then?" Ridley asked. "Newman. Deceased. But we've got access to a retired mounted officer called Bill Thorn. He knew Norma Walker personally and was on the front line of Newman's investigation." Jack closed the file. "So, back in the day, this gang got away with £27 million pounds. They burn one point eight million in old fivers and tenners 'cos they can't spend it legally anymore, leaving them with twenty-five-ish million in legal tender. And whatever they plan to do, they've got to do it fast—because next year, the new twenty's due to come into circulation."

For the first time in ages, Jack felt his heart beat a little faster at the prospect of a new case. He thought back to poor old man

Sweeney gripping his arm as he shuffled toward the police car with his trouser leg pulled up and a catheter bag in his hand. This felt different. He thought of how he'd said to Maggie that he wanted to feel excited by his job, just like she does, and here he was . . .

Ridley noted Jack's wide eyes, raised eyebrows and relaxed posture and congratulated himself. This was the look of an officer who was alert and ready to investigate. He'd been right about Jack, after all.

"What are you doing about the sergeant's exam?" Ridley's question snapped Jack out of his daydream.

Jack didn't want to talk about this now, but trapped in a car with Ridley he had no choice.

"I'm discussing it with Maggie as soon as we can get time off together. Our shift patterns are . . . well, you know how it is. And she's still trying to impress her bosses so they keep her on after this rotation."

Ridley twisted his ten-to-two fists on the wheel in frustration. "Maggie's career is important, I appreciate that, but so is yours! And I'm not sure what's to discuss. There's a sergeant's post open, you're a solid officer, you've got your qualifications, and you meet the Met's criteria. Either you or DC Joshi is going to get the sergeant's position. You've been at this far longer than him, but . . . Look, you plateaued in Devon, but you can't get away with that here."

Jack's mobile vibrated silently in his hand and he sent his mum to voicemail. He could hardly pause a bollocking to take a call from his mum.

"I'm not saying 'go for it,'" Ridley continued. "But I am saying 'decide.' Some people are DCs for the whole of their careers and that's fine. But *my* DCs have ambition. Do you understand? Make a decision."

For the remainder of the journey, they traveled in silence.

Jack's first decision was to throw himself into the Rose Cottage case 100 percent and help Ridley bring an armed gang to justice after twenty-four years in the wind. Possibly with a murder conviction thrown in for good measure. He also decided to nurture the newly acquired excited feeling he had in the pit of his stomach. He'd allow it to guide him in the hope that, by the end of this case, he'd know whether to either leave the force with his head held high, or shatter Anik's hope of promotion and beat him to the sergeant's position.

CHAPTER 4

DI Martin Prescott and DCI Simon Ridley had met several years ago on the College of Policing's Senior Investigating Officers course, and had bonded over polystyrene-tasting coffee and a mutual love of golf. They were chalk and cheese; Prescott was a man's man who treated colleagues, male and female, like his mates until they proved him wrong—whereas Ridley was more formal in his approach, liking to keep a professional distance. However, when it came to police work, they were both sharp, methodical and rarely wrong. Although these men would never choose to spend their down time with each other, they shared great mutual respect. Ridley was very grateful to have been brought in on this case at such an early stage.

Prescott walked Ridley and his team round the outside of Rose Cottage and into the back garden, where dozens of uniformed Thames Valley Police officers were scattered about doing a finger-tip search of the grounds to make sure they'd not missed anything. Prescott got everyone up to speed as they walked.

"All the information from '95, and my recent conversation with Bill Thorn, suggests that this could be the Met's open train robbery case. All of the evidence we've gathered so far is being organized for transfer. We'll carry on at this end if you like, or do you want to bring your boys in to take over?"

Before Ridley could answer, the dog handler popped up from the other side of a hedge.

"Sir!"

Amber was sitting to attention, pointing her nose to the ground, tail wagging. Her handler moved the low branches of the hedge to one side and revealed a short piece of garden hose, which was the same color and design as the garden hose in the back garden of Rose Cottage. In the soil was an intact toe print from what looked like a trainer.

"Amber's indicating that this hose smells of petrol."

"Could Amber have missed a petrol accelerant inside the cottage?" Prescott asked.

"At this scene . . . yes, sir," Amber's handler explained. "The fire had already been burning for a long time when we arrived, so all traces of accelerant could have burned away. And the smell of the body could have overpowered the scent, too."

Prescott waved to a SOCO carrying a digital SLR camera as he reassured Ridley.

"We've bagged samples of every piece of debris from inside, so if petrol was used, forensics will tell us. And we'll get a cast of that toe print."

As the SOCO took pictures of the cut hose in situ, before bagging it as evidence, Anik was mesmerized by Amber bounding around the neighboring field with her tongue flapping about from beneath the tennis ball.

Ridley replied to Prescott's earlier question. "I'm more than happy for your men to continue at this end, DI Prescott. Thank you."

With that, Prescott led the way back round to the front of the cottage. Jack paused, made notes on his mobile and pondered "intent" as he looked at the clearly improvized piece of cut hose. Whatever had happened here, the fire might not have been planned. Something could have just gone very wrong, very quickly.

In the front garden, everyone stood amid the muddy mess of trampled roses and fire-damaged furniture as Prescott continued with his heads-up.

"After Norma died, a supermarket approached the owner of the cottage within weeks and made him an offer he couldn't refuse. There's a newish housing estate about a quarter-mile away, built on the land where The Grange used to be, so a supermarket here'll make a killing. Demolition's paused now, of course. This place'll stay exactly as-is till you say otherwise. And the postmortem's paused an' all. I'll get Abbi's preliminary findings to you, along with all the evidence and statements we've collected so far. Collecting the cash has been a bloody nightmare. Most of it crumbles on contact, but we're getting video and photographic records of every step we're taking. 'Ave I missed anything, sir?"

"Do the witness statements for the fire give us anything?" Ridley asked.

"Nah. No direct witnesses. No CCTV. We've got dozens of housing estate residents giving you an accurate timeline for when the fire started, though."

"Thank you, DI Prescott."

Ridley looked at the carnage that surrounded him. He dreaded to think what the inside looked like.

* * *

Anik frowned over the top of his blue paper face mask as he watched everyone else milling around the now-empty lounge of Rose Cottage. They all wore their blue paper suits well, whereas his was far too big and made him look inflatable.

"How come everything police issue never bloody well fits me?" he thought to himself.

Ridley, Jack, Laura and Anik had each been given a tablet so they could flick through crime scene photos as they moved. Jack stood in the center of the room, where the sofa had been, and looked at images of the burnt body melted into the springs. The fire must have raged with real intensity to obliterate the body, down to the bone in places. Jack was overwhelmed by the need to know who this man used to be—was he one of the bad guys or was he an innocent victim? Was he a "pervert," as the faint red paint on the wall suggested? Or was he just in the wrong place, at the wrong time, with the wrong people? His train of thought was broken by his mobile buzzing in his pocket. His mum had left a second voicemail.

Ridley was across the room listening to Prescott talk inter-station politics. Prescott was explaining that he wasn't going to get in Ridley's way, but that he did want to stay close to the investigation; after all, Norma was one of their own and the mystery of a dead body in her old house was definitely something they wanted answers to. Jack took the opportunity to quickly nip out into what used to be the front garden and listen to his mum's voicemail, as he wouldn't be able to do it in the car back to London with Ridley.

"Hello, darling. It's Mum." As though he didn't know. "Can you visit? Soon, I mean. Only me and your dad need to have a little chat with you. Nothing for you to worry about, just . . . we'd love to see you."

The words "nothing for you to worry about" clearly told Jack that there *was* something for him to worry about. Without thinking where he was and who might be listening, he called straight back.

"What's up?" Jack asked quickly, not bothering with any of the usual pleasantries.

Initially he heard nothing in reply, as his mum held her breath on the other end of the phone; then he heard that very distinctive slow exhale that comes with letting overdue tears flow. Jack's voice was all it took for Penny to be overwhelmed by pent-up emotion.

"I'm going to come to you as soon as I can. OK, Mum? It might not be today, but I'll try my best. Is Dad OK?"

Again, Penny didn't—couldn't—answer immediately. After what seemed like an age, she managed to whisper, "No, sweetheart."

Jack kept his voice calm. "I'll be there tonight. Don't worry. I'm coming."

He hung up, regained his composure and looked at Ridley, who was now lording it amid his temporarily extended team, dishing out his anally retentive orders, checking and double-checking that everyone knew their role.

"Guv," Jack said politely. This wasn't going to go down well. "Could I have a word in private, please?" He and Ridley stepped away from the bulk of the people. "I have a family issue, guv. I'm sorry, I know it's bad timing."

"Now?"

Ridley wanted confirmation before he decided just how disappointed he was going to be with Jack.

"It's my dad. I think. I mean, Mum called and . . . something's wrong."

Ridley sighed a long and heavy sigh, making Jack wait for his decision.

"We've just found a dead body, at the scene of a fire, next to approximately £1.8 million in non-legal tender, inside a cottage whose last occupant was a mounted police officer." Jack knew exactly what Ridley wanted him to say but he couldn't; his subsequent silence told Ridley, loud and clear, that his dad was more important. "Take the rest of today, Jack. This lot will take an age to process and transfer across to us anyway. I want every one of my team to be on their best game, and if you're fretting about what may or may not be happening with your parents, then you're a million miles away from your best game."

Before Jack could thank him, Ridley had walked away and got into the driver's seat of the car they'd shared to get there.

Fuck, Jack thought to himself. *This is going to be one shit drive home!*

CHAPTER 5

Maggie got up at her usual time of three o'clock and went into the kitchen to make herself a cup of tea. On the breakfast bar was a scribbled note:

Gone to Mum and Dad's. I'll call you when you're up. Don't worry. Jack xx

And then Maggie's phone rang.

"Hello, lovely," Jack whispered. "I'm on a train so, if I lose you, I'll call you back. I brought the car back to the flat for you."

"What's happened? Are Penny and Charlie OK?"

"Not sure. I'm two hours away, so I'll call you when I know."

Jack wasn't being standoffish, and Maggie knew it. He just hated talking on trains, surrounded by strangers who couldn't help but listen in. And this—especially this—was nobody else's business. So Maggie did the talking.

"OK, honey. Well, I'm in work from four, but I'll keep my phone on vibrate and, if you need me, you call me. I may not be able to pick up, but I'll get to somewhere quiet and call you back as soon as I can. Was it your mum who called?"

"Yes."

"So, it's Charlie?"

"Yes."

"OK. Well . . . whatever it is, we'll be fine." Jack's phone pinged as a text message came through—which he ignored for the time being.

Maggie continued, "We can cope with anything, you know—the four of us. And if you need me there, you ask, OK? Don't think I can't come, Jack, because I can. I'll make work understand—"

And then the phone went dead and Jack lost signal.

The text message was from Laura—

Ridley told me. Hope you're OK. L x.

Jack texted Maggie—

love you xx—

and then watched it fail to send. Seven times. On the eighth attempt, it finally went through. He spent the rest of the journey looking out the window, thinking about how to react if his mum told him that his dad was dying.

* * *

Charlie and Penny Warr always knew that they couldn't have children of their own; it was something to do with Charlie, but they never dwelled on the details. Adopting had been a very quick and easy decision for them.

It was June 1987. Jack was four years and seven months old when Lillian, his social worker, walked him across the village green toward the little Devonshire pub where they'd all agreed to meet. Penny and Charlie watched for what seemed like an age, because Jack was constantly distracted by the world around him—he'd pause, look round, change direction, sit down—and all the while,

Lillian gently encouraged him to keep on track. Little Jack smiled the entire time, his wide brown eyes taking in every detail.

"She's wearing the same pedal pushers as me," Penny whispered. Charlie looked at his wife, noted the tears welling in her eyes, and they both burst out laughing.

"What a ridiculous thing for me to say! I'm just so nervous. Look at those amazing brown eyes, Charlie. Look at him looking. He's so smart."

Charlie put his arm around Penny's shoulder and she slid along the pub bench, closer to him. They sat there, sipping lime and soda, watching their boy toddle toward them. And by the time Jack had covered that small patch of grass, they loved him.

Jack didn't clearly remember any of this first-hand, but, like many memories that actually belong to someone else, this one had oddly started to feel like his own. As the train continued toward Devon, he could even recall the color of Penny's pedal pushers and the smell of Charlie's aftershave as he fell asleep in his big, working man's arms.

* * *

At Rose Cottage, Laura watched the last of the evidence, including the cut hose pipe, being bagged and loaded into the back of a police van. She checked her mobile for the umpteenth time, but Jack hadn't texted her back. In her heart of hearts, she knew he wouldn't; but, like many women in love with the wrong man, she couldn't bring herself to give up hope.

* * *

Ridley stood with forensic pathologist William Fox, as the grumpy Aylesbury undertaker opened the back of his white van and the overwhelming smell of over-barbecued pork hit them both. The transfer journey to the London mortuary had only taken an hour and a half, but still, the driver clearly hated moving around the capital and couldn't wait to get home.

Will backed away from the smell, slipping his jacket off as he moved. "Bloody hell, Simon. You didn't say it was a fire. That smell sticks to everything and this jacket's new, you know!"

Ridley smirked to himself.

Will was only in his late thirties, but he was one of the foremost forensic pathologists in the UK. His mind was as sharp as his dress sense, he was loved by everyone and he showed an unrivaled passion for his profession. His sense of justice had originally taken him toward the police force, but his height, or lack of, his small frame and his aversion to physical confrontation forced him toward a behind-the-scenes job. And from the second he chose forensics, he shone brighter than anyone else in his class.

Will, or Foxy as he was sometimes called, played the sexy *Silent Witness* pathologist card on women all the time—and it worked. He referred to himself as "The Death Detective" and made out that the police couldn't make a move without him. Ridley didn't mind; it wasn't entirely untrue and, besides, all he cared about was his team being exceptional. And Foxy was exceptional.

The Aylesbury undertaker handed Foxy a large evidence bag and pushed the gurney indoors. Ridley explained.

"His left foot came off when they picked him up."

* * *

The walk from Totnes railway station to Charlie and Penny's bungalow was visually quite an ordinary picture of semi-rural life, but emotionally, for Jack, it was borderline enchanting. Every step was a memory: the pub where he'd had his first underage drink; the back garden where he'd first touched a girl underneath her clothes; his first fight, his first heartbreak and the pub where he first saw Maggie. She was horrible to him. But they were both drunk and were showing off with their respective groups of friends.

The day after, Jack had gone to the café where Maggie worked and apologized. He'd stayed for four hours until she finished her shift and then taken her for a drink ... Three hours later, they knew everything there was to know about each other. Jack wasn't Maggie's first love, but she was his.

Of course, he *thought* he'd been in love before, but he hadn't really—he'd been in lust. Love was calm, lust was frantic. Frantic because Jack never knew exactly how long it would last, so he had to make the most of it while he could. But with Maggie, he knew immediately that he had all the time in the world. She was going nowhere.

*　*　*

Jack stared at the bungalow he'd grown up in. Every light was on. Every light was always on. He smiled and shook his head. He watched Penny fussing in the lounge through always-open curtains, then in his old bedroom—she was fluffing his pillows, probably for the twentieth time. He was sure she was checking she'd put every toiletry under the sun in his en suite, just in case he'd forgotten anything—which would be handy on this occasion because, in his rush to get here, he'd forgotten pretty much everything.

From the second Penny opened the front door, she never once stopped talking.

"Tea, darling . . .? Oh, the trains are a nuisance, aren't they . . . ? How's Maggie . . . ? Georgina's got herself a puppy, can you believe it . . . ? There's a chicken in the oven, but the veg isn't on yet . . . Would you like a whisky to tide you over?"

Charlie smiled at Jack and rolled his eyes, gently mocking his hyperactive wife.

Father and son hugged. Charlie held on for a moment longer than usual and, in that instant, Jack knew something was very wrong. When Charlie pulled away, the tears were welling—then he sniffed, shook his head and squeezed Jack's shoulders. In the background, Penny fussed between the sink, the oven and the drinks cabinet—oblivious to the fact that the dreadful news she was so frantically avoiding had just been silently shared.

When she finally turned around, holding two glasses of whisky and ice, Charlie and Jack were hugging again, and Jack was crying.

* * *

Penny carved the chicken as Jack and Charlie sat across the table from each other. Jack was frowning as he tried to get his head around everything.

"OK, so who's said it'll be no more than a few months from now?"

"Dr. Chakrabarti, his name is."

This was Penny's domain, as Charlie had never been any good with details.

"And what treatment has he suggested?"

Jack picked up his mobile and googled Dr. Chakrabarti.

"We've done it all, darling. Your dad was told just before Christmas and—"

"*Christmas?* You were with *us* in London at Christmas!" "Are you listening or shouting, darling?"

Jack fell silent. His mum faced away from him and started to tear the remains of the chicken to pieces with her hands. He knew she wasn't being rude, she was just terrified of breaking down before she'd said everything she needed to.

"Your dad was told just before Christmas, and in the new year he went straight into his first round of chemotherapy, which didn't agree with him at all, did it, my love?" Charlie shook his head. "So, we tried a second type, which didn't have as many side effects, but didn't really do much good—"

"I can't find Chakrabarti," Jack interrupted. "Does he work at Derriford?"

"Yes. The best in the West Country, he is. C—H—A—K . . ." "Found him." Jack read background on Chakrabarti at the same time as finding out everything that had happened while his bloody back was turned. "But there must be something else you can try. Isn't there? I mean, even if there's nothing right at this moment, new cures come along all the time."

Now, Charlie spoke for the first time.

"The word 'cure' was never used, son. Not from the very beginning. It was always only ever about giving me as much time as possible. And they've done that. We are where we are."

The pain in Jack's chest built as he squeezed the words out from between his pursed lips and the tears welled again.

"A few fucking months!"

Penny let the swear word go on this occasion.

"Yep," Charlie said. "So, me and your mum are going on holiday. If that's all right with you."

"For how long?" Jack asked. "Do you need money? Where are you going?"

Charlie beamed as if he didn't have a care left in the world.

"Everywhere. We've cashed in the pensions and the bungalow's on the market."

Jack couldn't believe what he was hearing. "You're selling? That makes no sense at all. Where are you going to live when you come back?"

Penny gently, lovingly, stroked the back of Charlie's head.

"Why don't you boys nip to the pub?"

* * *

Although it was way too late to be starting the full postmortem, Foxy did need to make certain that there was no evidence on the body which simply couldn't wait until the morning. The preservation of any dead body was a delicate process at the best of times, but Sheila, as he'd now been universally christened, was extra vulnerable and brittle due to the fire.

Sheila still lay on his side, in the fetal position. This was a common death position for people exposed to extreme temperatures—partly as a natural yet futile defense against flames and smoke, and partly because as the body dried out, the joints would naturally curl. However, this body had been found on a small two-seater sofa and so the curled position could equally be because he'd been too long for it.

Foxy flicked through Abigail Coleman's very thorough preliminary observations and tentatively agreed that the large fracture to
the back of the skull could be a blunt force trauma and therefore
the cause of death.

Tomorrow morning, when he cut Sheila open, the first thing
Foxy would look for would be signs of smoke inhalation. If there
were none, then Sheila would have already been dead when the fire
started. Which would be some consolation.

As Foxy refrigerated Sheila for the night, he smiled. He loved a
good mystery.

* * *

Jack and Charlie sat in the window of the King's Head, looking out
over the patch of grass that the locals proudly called the "village
green." Charlie told the story of their first meeting and, although
Jack had heard it a thousand times, he didn't mind at all hearing
it again.

On that day back in 1987, Charlie had got up from the garden
bench and knelt on the grass to greet his potential new son. As Jack
got within touching distance, he'd instinctively turned his back to
Charlie, reversed, and sat down on his waiting knee. And there he'd
stayed, while the women tutted about how inexplicable it was that
someone had chosen to walk away from such a stunning little boy.

Reluctantly, Jack brought the conversation back to the present.
"You're selling the bungalow 'cos you're not coming back, aren't
you?"

Charlie took his time in answering. "A friend of my brother's
has reserved a short lease on a one-bedroomed flat in a wardened

complex for your mum. She can have it for as long as she likes. She's said she doesn't want . . ." Charlie stumbled over his words for a second. "She doesn't want to be in our bungalow on her own."

"You might come home though, eh, Dad? I mean, you hear about people surprising doctors all the time. A few months doesn't have to mean a few months."

Charlie took a slug from his pint and even managed a smile, as he lied to his son.

"Maybe. You know us builders, lad . . . if we're given six months, we always take twelve."

* * *

The rest of the evening was like old times. Jack moaned about how badly Plymouth Argyle were doing this year; Charlie asked about Jack's job, about Maggie and whether there were any kids on the horizon.

"The jobs have got to come first at the moment, Dad. Mags has not long started at the New Victoria and she's doing really well— impressing all the right people, you know. Maybe in a year or two."

"Ah, Jack, once she gets where she wants to be, she'll not want to leave to do parenting."

"She might not be the one who leaves."

Jack realized that he'd said this almost without thinking. He wasn't even sure where the thought had come from—him being the one to give up work and look after kids—but, once he'd said it, he really didn't mind how it sounded.

"Mags skips to work—I don't. It's my fault. I need to focus and get into the swing of things in London. Don't tell Mum right now, she'll only worry and, in all honesty, there's nothing to worry about. Me and Mags are strong. It doesn't matter who does what, as long as we're together."

* * *

Charlie took an age to get his key in the front door, partly because he was pissed and partly because it was 11:30 and he was tired from all the meds he was currently taking. They sniggered like naughty schoolkids, thinking they were being completely silent when, in fact, they were making a terrible racket.

Two cling-filmed plates of food sat on the kitchen top, already pierced and ready for the microwave. The kitchen table was set, complete with two glasses for water and two glasses for whisky. Charlie heated the food and Jack filled all four glasses. While the microwave was on, Charlie said, "I've got something for you, lad," before disappearing. By the time he came back, the piping hot food was on the table.

Charlie put a dog-eared file down in front of Jack. At first he thought it was probably filled with the legal stuff that would have to be dealt with after Charlie had gone; but this file was as old as Jack, by the looks of it. He opened it up and, inside were several yellowing pieces of paper and tons of old photos. Charlie ate in silence as his son slowly took in the enormity of what he was looking at—a birth certificate, adoption papers, photos of a young woman holding a baby. Jack slammed the file shut. Charlie spoke before Jack could.

"You're my son. You took my name, you have my mannerisms and I'd swear that you've got my nose, even though that's impossible."

"I'm not interested," Jack snapped, before stuffing his mouth full of chicken.

Charlie laughed for a second. "And when you sulk, I'd swear on my life that you've got your mum's frown." He suddenly seemed to sober up. "You've never asked where you're from, Jack, and you don't have to ask now. Just know that you're not disrespecting me or your mum if you choose to find out."

"Why would I want to, Dad? I don't need . . . You think I'd want to call someone else 'Dad'? You think I want anyone else calling me his lad?"

"People come and go, that's life—and we make the most of them while they're here. If you want to look into your past, all I'm saying is . . . you have my blessing."

* * *

Jack lay on his fluffed-up pillows, on his childhood bed, and listened to Maggie's phone send him to voicemail. He didn't leave a message. She'd know no message was the same as saying, "call me back when you have a second." Jack waited for the screen of his mobile to light up silently, because tonight of all nights, he knew that Maggie would call him back within seconds.

It was actually three minutes later when his screen eventually lit up.

"Hey, Mags," he whispered.

Maggie got straight to the point. "How are things there?"

"He's been given a few months. It's in his lungs and his liver, but they're both secondaries, they don't actually know where the primary is."

"Oh, Jack, I'm so sorry."

"That can't be right, can it, Mags? Not knowing where it started? I mean, it can't have disappeared, can it? Why can't they find the primary? If they find the primary, maybe they can fix it. Do you think . . . ?"

"Do you need me there?"

By changing the subject, Jack knew that Maggie had no answers to his barrage of questions.

"No, I'll be home first thing." He sounded almost bitter in his reply. "I was only given one day off and, anyway, they've got it all sorted here. They knew before Christmas, so they've already got their heads round everything and they're off on a world cruise, if you can believe that."

"So, no more treatment?"

"It won't do any good."

"Jack . . . you have to let them do this in the right way for them."

Maggie could hear Jack holding his breath, then that slow exhale as he stifled the noise of crying.

"What about me?"

"This isn't about you, love."

Jack took deep, heavy breaths and regained his composure. Once his breathing was back to normal, Maggie continued.

"Don't be angry for long. The most important thing in times like this is to have no regrets. Give them your blessing. We'll Skype every day, and we can even meet them on one of their stops if you like."

Jack's voice suddenly perked up, just a little. "They go to St. Lucia."

"There you go, then. We'll meet them there and stay on for a few days. I can even book the same hotel we stayed in when we did that extravagant holiday we couldn't afford. It's nearly two o'clock, Jack. Go to sleep. I love you."

* * *

By five o'clock, Jack was up, showered, dressed and heading out the front door to catch the 5:45 train back to London. As he leaned into the hallway to close the front door, he saw Penny standing in her dressing gown in her bedroom doorway.

They shared the tightest, saddest of hugs. Penny kissed his cheek. And Jack left.

* * *

If Jack hadn't walked into the squad room carrying his overnight bag and looking as if he was running on fumes, he'd have been in big trouble. As it was, Ridley took one look at him and immediately assumed that Jack had had very bad news from his parents. Ridley wasn't going to inquire further, and he allowed Jack a free pass for rolling in at ten o'clock rather than 8:30. Laura, on the other hand, was desperate to inquire further and see if Jack might need a friendly shoulder to cry on. Jack joined the briefing and Ridley continued.

"William Fox is doing the postmortem as we speak. What we know is that the body found in Rose Cottage is definitely male, but dental records are a no-go due to extensive, seemingly accidental, facial damage. We'll get DNA from bone marrow so, when that's through, Laura, I want you to lead a couple of uniforms in checking it against all databases. Anik, the money?"

"Our forensics have picked up from where DI Prescott's left off and are trying to find a serial number or part serial number for comparison. It's very unlikely, they say."

"Keep on them, Anik. And in the meantime, I want you checking all known sex offenders. Start close to Aylesbury and work outward."

Anik clearly wasn't happy with such a menial task on a murder case, but Ridley didn't care about that. "The word 'pervert' was painted on the wall for a reason. Actually, Anik, check local vagrants as well."

"Sir," Anik mumbled obediently as he opened a brand-new file to record his part in this investigation. Jack glanced at his overnight bag and recalled that the file Charlie had given him was lying atop his clothes right beneath the zip.

Jack got an empty file from his desk, just as Anik had done, and wrote on the front cover: AYLESBURY ARSON / MURDER. JUNE 23, 2019. He then reached into his overnight bag, pulled out the dog-eared file containing information on his birth parents, and put it inside the Aylesbury file. As Ridley waffled on, none the wiser, Jack read his birth certificate.

He had always known his birth mother's name was Trudie Nunn and his birth father was James Anthony Nunn. There were no photographs in the file of James Nunn. Just Trudie. Looking at the photos, she had a petite frame, bleached blonde hair and a naturally sexy look about her. Jack wished that the word "sexy" hadn't popped into his head, but he couldn't change that now—it was a fact: his birth mum had been a sexy woman in her day. Jack then found Trudie's death certificate. It was dated 1998 and the cause was a brain tumor.

Jack didn't hear Ridley say his name the first time.

"Jack!"

He slammed the file shut on his desk and looked up. An elderly man—early seventies—was standing next to Ridley, leaning on a cane.

"For your benefit, Jack, as you missed the opening of the briefing, this is retired DS Bill Thorn from Aylesbury. He's kindly agreed to help us with some background information as he was part of the investigating team on the mail train robbery and knew Norma Walker, last occupant of Rose Cottage."

Jack smiled his "hello," as Ridley gave Bill the floor.

"I chatted with DI Prescott first and he directed me your way—this could be one hell of an open case you've picked up." Bill Thorn was clearly a copper to his very core. He was in his element at the front of Ridley's squad room, all eyes on him. "I worked with Norma in the mounted division till I moved to CID in the late nineties—but it's 1995 that you need to hear about. Bottom line is, I don't know anything about your murder, DCI Ridley—but I think I know plenty about your money. Back in '95, Aylesbury had the biggest train robbery this country's ever seen. As you already know, £27 million was taken from a mail train by a gang of masked gunmen. It was bloody smart, I can tell you. One was on horseback, posing as a mounted officer, and there was definitely one in a speedboat on the lake next to the tracks, 'cos the two train guards distinctly recalled hearing the engine. They all disappeared like ghosts. But it had to have been a decent sized gang based on sheer volume of cash. I mean, a million is a fair weight, so twenty-seven million would need some muscle to shift it *and* hide it in less than forty minutes. That's how long they had before we started closing all the main roads into Aylesbury. And we were searching properties by the early hours of the following morning."

"How well did you know Norma Walker?" Jack asked.

"She wasn't the armed robber on horseback, if that's what you're asking." Bill was adamant. "Norma was as honest as they come. I think someone took advantage of her property, nothing more than that." He paused. "May she rest in peace. Cancer's a bloody horrible way to go."

Jack flinched, but pushed on. "Took advantage in 1995 when Norma still lived there, or took advantage once it became empty after she died?"

"I don't know about that," Bill said. "But I can tell you, whatever happened, and whenever it happened, Norma was *not* involved with the mail train robbery."

Despite Bill's vehemence, every member of Ridley's team noted down Norma as a potential suspect for the armed, mounted rider who had brought the train to a halt so that it could be robbed. She was an experienced horsewoman, and she lived on the spot, so it didn't make sense to rule her out.

Oblivious, Bill continued. "Imagine . . . imagine if you've found where they hid the cash from that train robbery after 24 years!"

The room didn't quite share Bill's enthusiasm. It seemed too unlikely that train robbers would have left the stolen millions untouched for so long—especially in the cottage of an ex-copper who "allegedly" was as honest as they come.

Ridley politely humored the ex-copper. "Who were your suspects at the time, Bill?"

"We didn't have any firm suspects if I'm honest. We pulled in all the local names, but it was none of them. We raided all the local properties within hours. The first place we went was The Grange—that was the big old manor house that stood on what's now the housing estate. We had to go there first 'cos it was occupied by a bunch of ex-cons, but it wasn't them either. They were all women. When we showed up in the early hours, they were in their nightdresses, and we woke a load of kids, too. There's a lot about those women in the files DI Prescott's sent you. The cops—not my division, mind you—but the cops made a fair few mistakes back then. They raided The Grange numerous times on nothing more than rumors. They accused those women of stashing guns on one occasion. Oh, DCI Craigh was certain he'd got 'em bang to rights, but he hadn't. Sure, they were all ex-cons but, according to Norma, they were on the up-and-up. Starting a kids' home or something, and I'm far more inclined to believe Norma than Craigh, who I always found to be a bit hot-headed. The only one of them Craigh arrested was Kathleen O'Reilly, and that was on a poxy 'failure to appear' charge. And besides, like I said, twenty-seven million in mail sacks is bloody heavy—so a bunch of women pulling it off is fairy stories. They were all investigated anyway, of course. No connection."

Ridley persisted a little longer for his own satisfaction.

"Can you tell us anything about Dolly Rawlins? She owned The Grange at the time of the train robbery, didn't she?"

"And before that, it was owned by Ester Freeman, who ran it as a brothel." Bill laughed. "Although if you ask the Neighborhood Watch crowd from back then, they'll tell you she ran night classes. Load of old shit. She was closed down as soon as the ages of the girls started to dip below legal."

Laura couldn't hold her tongue. "Running a brothel isn't legal, no matter how old the girls are."

"You know what I mean." Bill shrugged. "It was the nineties." Blaming the decade for the abuse of vulnerable women was clearly a good enough excuse for Bill, so Laura didn't say anything more on the subject.

"So, Ester was a madam," he continued. "Kathleen, as I recall, was a forger. Julia was . . . I'm not sure what Julia was. Connie was a prostitute, and Dolly shot her husband. I've missed someone, I think. Ester, Kathleen, Connie, Dolly—"

Ridley interrupted. "It's fine, Bill. As you rightly said, it's all in the files."

"Those women didn't rob that train," Bill repeated. "It was a smart, savvy bunch of professional men who, I reckon, came from your neck of the woods. I tell you, when you find those train robbers and, more to the point, when you find that missing money, you'll be a bloody hero, DCI Ridley."

An additional thought popped into Ridley's head.

"Anik, I want you to cross-reference all the sex offenders that end up on your list with known patrons of The Grange when it was a brothel. And Jack, use Bill's files to locate all of the surviving women from The Grange."

"That'll be a waste of his time," Bill interrupted.

Ridley remained polite, calmly explaining that everyone around at the time of the train robbery needed interviewing again, as potential witnesses at least, and so they could be eliminated from the current inquiry. He then swiftly, and very politely, ended Bill's visit.

"Thank you so much for coming down, Bill. You've been very helpful. May we call on you if we have any more questions?"

"Please do, sir, please do." Bill still exuded enthusiasm. "It's exciting to think I might finally get to see this case closed."

Ridley nodded at Jack.

"May I take you to the lift?" Jack asked, rising to his feet and opening the door.

They walked at Bill's slow pace.

"This bleedin' paint's a depressing color," Bill sneered. "Who chose gray?"

"Someone who doesn't have to walk this corridor. The top floor's painted sky blue."

"Course it is! Sky blue for the suits upstairs, depression gray for the workers down here. You're not from London, are you? Your accent's further west."

"I was brought up in Devon. Although I worked hard to get rid of the accent." Jack paused. There was something he wanted to ask. "I hope you don't mind me asking, Bill . . . but did you see Norma when she was ill, toward the end?"

"At least once a week." Bill looked Jack in the eye. "Cancer's a shit illness, I won't lie. But you know, even when the outside didn't look anything like Norma anymore, she was still there. She had a wicked sense of humor—even at the very end. Cancer kills the body then, eventually, the spirit. So, you pay close attention and when you see them flagging, you remind them how loved they are. That's your only job, really."

Bill didn't ask who Jack was losing, and Jack didn't tell him.

* * *

The rest of Jack's day and early evening was spent tracing the women from The Grange. He was a heads-down kind of officer with tasks like this one; whereas Anik, who sat opposite him trawling through a depressingly long list of Aylesbury sex offenders, couldn't stand this part of the job. Anik was young and enthusiastic, so he saw policing as being "out there" and not in here.

As Anik waffled on about how disgusting it was that more than five hundred sex offenders allegedly under surveillance were actually off-radar, Jack was discovering all he could about the Grange women.

He learned that Kathleen O'Reilly had been arrested at The Grange in 1995 during the disastrous "arms deal" raid led by DCI

Ron Craigh. No guns were found, Dolly Rawlins sued Craigh for damages and Kathleen was arrested for failing to appear in court. She was immediately sent back to prison to serve out her sentence on a forgery charge. By the time Kathleen was released, her three girls were in care and none of them wanted to see her. She opted for a very slow death by turning to the bottle, until in 2009, her liver finally gave up and she died alone in a hospital corridor.

Gloria Radford, Ester Freeman, Julia Lawson, Connie Stephens and Angela Dunn were all last arrested on the same day, August 27, 1995—just days after the mail train robbery in Aylesbury. Ester was arrested for the murder of Dolly Rawlins; the other women were arrested as a matter of procedure because they were present at the scene. Once any kind of conspiracy was eliminated, they were released.

Ester's statement to the police was a rambling, venomous spewing of hatred for Dolly Rawlins. She screamed about being doublecrossed and about being treated like a piece of shit on Dolly's Italian leather shoes.

The statements from the other women supported the fact that these two alpha females had always rubbed each other up the wrong way. It seemed that their mutual disdain had started when Ester conned Dolly out of £200,000 to buy The Grange without divulging that it used to be a brothel; and it ended when Dolly accused Ester of sabotaging her dream of turning it into a children's home with the help of the other ex-cons. Tens of thousands of pounds' worth of funding had rested on one unannounced spot check from the board of councilors and, when they'd turned up, Ester was caught hosting an orgy in the sauna. In that split second, Dolly's dream had shattered into a million irretrievable pieces.

On the morning of the shooting, DCI Craigh had visited The Grange to bargain with Dolly about the amount of money for damages she wanted from his misguided arms raid. Ester, quite wrongly, had heard them making "a deal," and thought that Dolly was setting her up to be arrested on some trumped-up charge. The red mist descended, Ester spectacularly lost her senses, picked up a gun and emptied all six rounds into Dolly.

Craigh had been standing right next to Dolly at the time. He retired shortly afterward.

Ester was released in 2017, after serving fourteen years for Dolly's murder and a further eight years for the attempted murder of her cellmate. According to Ester's parole officer, she now lived in Seaview on the Isle of Wight. Jack noted down her current address.

Gloria Radford had a record for gunrunning with her husband, Eddie. They both died in the same car crash in 2004. They'd been out celebrating Eddie's release from prison and came off worse in a headon collision with the median. It was a blessing that the crash occurred at 3 a.m., as the road was clear of other drivers.

Connie's last known location was Taunton, where she'd applied for various safety assessments in connection with running a B&B; but, from there, Jack was struggling to pin down an actual address. And he lost track of Julia Lawson and Angela Dunn around 2010 and 2015 respectively so, for tonight, he gave up.

Jack glanced across at Anik. He looked miserable, but also pre-occupied enough not to notice that Jack was about to misappropri-ate the HOLMES database. James "Jimmy" Nunn had a mediocre juvenile police record for drink driving, TDA and similar car-related crimes. Then, in his mid-twenties, he moved up to being a getaway driver for hire. Jack was so disappointed, and hoped to

God that if this "wheels-man" was the Jimmy Nunn on his birth certificate, there was more to him than that. He turned to Google to fill in the blanks.

Jimmy Nunn, for a short but glorious time, had been a racing driver. Something undocumented put a sudden end to his blossoming career when he was just twenty-three years old, and that's when things started to go wrong. Jimmy had worked as a mechanic to pay the bills, but the money was terrible and this, seemingly, was when he got into more serious crime.

Jack read article after article, mentioning Jimmy in association with some of the all-time greats: Niki Lauda, James Hunt, Jackie Stewart and Mario Andretti. Jack shook his head.

"What a fucking waste," he whispered to himself.

"What's a fucking waste?" Anik asked.

Jack took a second to think up a lie. "One of these women lost her kids while she was in prison and then drank herself to death."

"That's not a waste. They're better off without a mum like that."

"Probably," Jack agreed, just to bring the conversation to an end.

By the time he was ready to pack it in, Jack had created a timeline from Jimmy's birth in 1945, through his wayward teens, his short-lived Formula One career, and on into his adult criminal years. In 1984, however, the timeline ended abruptly. One of the recurring names from Jimmy Nunn's Formula One years was Kenneth Moore, an engineer now in his mid-70s and living in Hackney. With the digital trail at an impasse, the next step would be to start talking to people who'd actually known Jimmy Nunn . . . Packing his various files into his overnight bag, Jack headed home.

* * *

Jack was surprised to see that Maggie had taken the night off; dinner was in the oven and the wine was poured. This was the first time he'd seen her since he'd told her the news about his dad. She hugged him, handed him his wine and waited for him to talk about Charlie. She wasn't expecting to hear him talk about a man she'd never heard of before.

Jack started in the middle, rather than at the beginning.

"Jimmy Nunn could have been right up there with the likes of Jackie Stewart, but then something changed the course of his life and he ... Well, he just carried on doing what he was good at really—driving." Maggie stared at the contents of the dog-eared file, tipped out and scattered across the living room floor. "Dad said that, if I wanted, I could learn about my past. I snapped at him, Mags, and said I didn't need anyone but him and Mum. But, well, by the time I got to work, I was curious." He picked up Trudie's death certificate and showed it to Maggie. "Dead end."

"She was beautiful," Maggie commented as she sifted through the old photographs.

Jack shrugged. "Yeah, maybe ... But I'm going to find Jimmy Nunn. I've tracked down one of his old work colleagues and Aunt Fran must know something about him."

Frances Stanley was Trudie's sister, and her signature was on Jack's foster care paperwork, dated 1984. On the floor in front of Maggie and Jack were several birthday and Christmas cards from Fran, but these seemed to have stopped around the time Jack was five or six years old.

"I think I remember speaking to Aunt Fran on the phone once. I'd won something at school and I asked Mum if I could phone her. She was proud of me. Said she'd send me something for being so clever ... but she never did."

"Love," Maggie said gently, "why do you want to find Jimmy Nunn?" Jack looked at her blankly, as though the answer should be obvious. "I mean, you can," she continued, "and I'll gladly help you. But why?"

The oven pinged and dinner was ready. Maggie kissed him and took her glass of wine into the kitchen. By the time she came back, he'd gone. The hallway door was open and she could hear him talking on the phone.

"I'm sorry to call so late, Aunt Fran." Jack checked his watch: 11:45. "Oh—I'm really sorry, I didn't realize what time it was. Yes, I'm fine. I know, it's been ages . . . London now. Yes, we moved with Maggie's job . . . I'm a police officer." Jack laughed politely. "I do like it, yes. It's challenging, you know."

Maggie sat down on the sofa to listen.

"The reason I'm calling is that I was wondering what you knew about Jimmy Nunn." Jack fell silent except for the occasional "hmm," "OK" and "I see." "Well, do you know anyone who might know anything about him . . . ? Yes, I know it's old ground but . . . No, I understand. OK then, well, thank you for your time and apologies again for calling so late. Mum and Dad are fine, yes, thanks for asking . . . I'll tell them you said hi."

Jack came back into the living room and started to gather up the scattered papers and photos and put them back into the file. He looked dejected.

"Don't worry, love, you'll find him without her," Maggie reassured him, and went back into the kitchen to dish up their dinner.

CHAPTER 6

Jack was first in the squad room the next day. Not because he was being keen; he just hadn't slept well after the dead-end phone call with his Aunt Fran. He was frustrated by her apparent indifference to his request for help, and it had made him suspect she might have something to hide. For the first time in a long time, he'd had a "copper's hunch," and now he was more determined than ever to find out more about Jimmy Nunn. But he'd have to be careful: if Ridley thought he was slacking, he wouldn't hesitate to send him back to Devon.

By the time Ridley and the others walked in, the evidence board displayed photos of all the women from The Grange along with notes to date.

"Dolly Rawlins . . ." Jack started as they all settled to their desks. "Murdered in 1995 by Ester Freeman. Freeman was released in 2017 and now lives on the Isle of Wight with a guy called Geoffrey PorterLewis, a retired solicitor. No record. Kathleen O'Reilly died from alcoholism and Gloria Radford died in a car crash, along with her husband, Eddie. Connie Stephens had a B&B in Taunton, but I'm not sure that she has any more. The tax office has got an old address for her, as has the Licensing Authority, Building Inspectors, local fire safety assessors and so on. I'll keep looking. Nothing on Julia Lawson and Angela Dunn as yet."

Ridley looked at Jack, clearly hoping he had more to say—and in that split second, Jack went from being pleased with himself to being deeply disappointed. Ridley could do that with a single look—like a parent who is used to being let down.

"Right," he said, "tomorrow I want you in the Isle of Wight . . ." He paused. "Seeing as Freeman's the only lead you've got."

Jack winced, sat down and the floor was handed to Anik.

"Did you know, sir, that we don't actually know where around five hundred of our community-based sex offenders are?" Anik sounded like he was about to give a lecture on police shortcomings. "They're meant to stay at the halfway houses we put them in and . . . well, they don't."

"We'll tackle that disgraceful statistic another day, Anik. For now, let's hear what we do know rather than what we don't."

"Yes, sir. I'm working through a list of 45 sex offenders from the Aylesbury area and—"

"What do you mean by 'I'm working through'?" Ridley asked. Anik clearly didn't understand the question. "Get on to the Vulnerable Persons' Unit and ask for a couple of PCs to do the donkey work for you. You take what they report and collate it into a document that we can use."

Anik grinned from ear to ear at the thought of "commanding" a team of PCs.

"I'll do that, sir. Thank you. And I found an arrest report for a Daniel Green. He's a vagrant who's been picked up a couple of times for squatting in Rose Cottage. He used to nick tea lights from the village church, food from the Co-op and then break into the cottage for a kip. Last time he was picked up, he had a load of printed kiddie porn images from the internet, so he could be the 'pervert' we're looking for. He did two and a half months for that. The local bobbies know him by sight—they're keeping their eyes open. If they don't find him, he could be Shirley."

"Sheila," Jack corrected, childishly hoping to make Anik look as stupid as he felt.

Anik took no notice and added Daniel Green's mugshot to the evidence board. Laura then picked up the reins.

"The total amount of cash being transported in the train back in '95 has been confirmed as £36.7 million; but a number of sacks were left behind during the robbery. It was all in used, untraceable notes. So we've stopped trying to find any serial numbers, seeing as they won't help us link any of the burnt cash to the robbery anyway. But it's got to be from that, hasn't it? I mean, if it was legitimate, who wouldn't at least *try* to change one point eight million in old money at a bank? No way you'd just burn it . . ."

Jack concluded Laura's thought: "Unless you had another twentyfive million stashed away in legal tender somewhere else."

"Exactly." Jack and Laura were now talking as one person. "One point eight million becomes pocket money when you look at the bigger picture. This haul has to be from the train robbery."

Ridley kept the brainstorming going. "The other thing we now know is that the accelerant used was petrol. And it has to have been siphoned from a vehicle driven there, as there were no vehicles at the cottage. Laura—track down all the CCTV you can. There won't be much, but I want you to identify all cars using that top road. Most cars will belong to residents from the estate, but that doesn't automatically rule them out. Check them all, please." Laura nodded her understanding. "The rest of you, use the pathology report that Jack's about to bring you, to find 'Sheila' in missing persons. Any questions? Jack . . . with me."

And, with that, Ridley was gone.

* * *

As Ridley and Jack walked the corridor toward Foxy's lab, Jack waited for the bollocking. And here it came.

"How come you only managed to trace three dead women, and the one living woman who was piss-easy to find because her probation officer's name was in the files sent across by DI Prescott?" This was rhetorical, so Ridley left no space for Jack to answer. "New DCs like Anik should look up to you, Jack, but he doesn't. You're just a bloke he works with."

"I'll talk to Maggie about the sergeant's post—"

"Don't bother unless you really want it," Ridley ended as he pushed his way through the heavy rubber doors into Will's stark, white, sterile labs beyond.

Foxy was oblivious to the tension between Ridley and Jack. In his domain he barely even noticed that other people were in the room when he was on a roll. Without bothering to say hello to his visitors, he pointed to Sheila, lying flat on his back on the table in front of them.

"The DNA sample I took from his bone marrow hasn't turned up any matches in the national database. So, if you can find me a direct or familial DNA sample to match it to, I'll tell you who Sheila is. What I can tell you is that he was dead before the fire started, because there's no smoke in his lungs." Foxy flicked the wall-mounted light box on, backlighting an X-ray of the man's skull. "The blow to the back of the head is what killed him. The fracture itself is extensive and this darkened patch directly beneath the fracture is the resulting intracranial hemorrhage. He'd have died quickly. What's left of his teeth tells me that he's late thirties to mid-forties. I broke his hips and knees to straighten him out, so I can also tell you that he's five foot ten on the right side and a foot shorter on the left."

With a howl of laughter, Foxy threw the severed, bagged left foot at Jack—who instinctively caught it before dropping it onto an empty mortuary slab once he realized what it was.

"Prick," he mumbled, trying not to laugh in case Ridley was still in a bad mood.

But Ridley was laughing, too. He seemed different with Foxy— far more casual. Perhaps because there was no crossover between them, no stepping on each other's toes. Ridley couldn't do Foxy's job if his life depended on it, and vice versa. All that left room for was pure, mutual admiration.

Foxy carried on talking. "Based on what's left on the bones, I'd guess Sheila was 160 to 180 pounds, something like that. And he's white. So, no ID, but a great starting point for missing persons. You're most welcome."

"Take that description back to the squad room and get them to put it into Missing Persons. Off you go."

Ridley dismissed Jack with a wave of his hand.

* * *

It was a long day of desk and phone work, but on his way home, Jack took a detour through Hackney to drop in on Kenneth Moore, the Formula One engineer who had worked with Jimmy Nunn back in the seventies. Jack had an address, but no phone number, so he had his fingers crossed that Ken was in.

Outside the tower block, he called Maggie and left her a voicemail.

"I'm going to be working late, so if you fancy a takeaway around midnight, I'll bring one back with me. Text me if you can and . . . well, if you can't, I'll see you in the morning. Love you Mags."

The lift in Kenneth Moore's block was out of order and, as his flat number was 22, Jack figured he had to be on the eleventh floor. God, he wished he'd had the man's phone number. He looked at his watch: 9:30. Across the street was a social club. He'd check there before tackling eleven flights of stairs. Jack's "gut" was playing a big part in these two cases—the Rose Cottage fire and the search for Jimmy Nunn. He liked this change in himself and hoped it would be permanent.

Jack walked into the club and silence fell while everyone sized him up. They seemed to guess he was a copper.

"Is Ken Moore here?" he asked. "I think he might have known an old friend of my dad's," he lied. "Jimmy Nunn."

From the far end of the bar, a round, heavily bearded elderly man shouted, "I'll only talk to you if you pay me the seventeen quid he still fucking well owes me!"

Jack turned to the barman. "I'll have a Beck's and whatever Ken's drinking, and one for yourself."

The barman obeyed silently and the club instantly relaxed back into its previous conversations.

By eleven o'clock, Ken had drunk four pints compared to Jack's two bottles, he'd not drawn breath, and had said absolutely nothing of interest about Jimmy Nunn. The old man had no sense of personal space and no awareness of how bad he smelt. Jack was squashed into the corner of the room trying to keep a safe distance, but it wasn't working. Every now and then, Ken's knee would brush against Jack's and he'd pull away, fearful of what the brown stain down the front of Ken's beige trousers might turn out to be. Eventually, Ken started a story that was actually interesting. He momentarily slapped his hand down on Jack's knee, and Jack could feel the clammy dampness of his fat palm.

"I remember once, Jimmy was showing off to a couple of birds . . . You know that people say being in a rock band gets you all the women you want? You should try Formula One, Jack. Stone me!" He opened his mouth wide and howled a hot air combo of beer and beef crisps into Jack's face. "Me and Jimmy quickly decided which bird we were gonna 'ave—and then, for some reason I'll never fathom, he decided that the quickest way into her knickers was to climb the massive fence between them and us, instead of opening the gate . . . which was right there, by the way! Not locked or anything. Course he fell on his arse, didn't he? Them women walked away laughing their beautiful tits off and Jimmy lay on the ground screaming at the top of his voice, 'Me arm! I bust me arm!' And he had. I thought he'd dislocated his shoulder, but he'd actually managed to chip the socket and snap his . . . You know, this bit . . ." Ken prodded Jack in the clavicle. "What a prick. This was just days before the most important race of his life. Jimmy could have been a big name in Formula One, but instead, he vanished without a trace."

"People don't just vanish, Ken."

"His name popped up a couple years later in connection with the Fisher brothers—you know them? Big names down Soho way." Jack shrugged. The name "Fisher" meant nothing to him. "That's 'cos you're a baby. I'm going back a good forty or so years. When proper gangsters ruled the streets, not skinny kids with guns who shout the odds at each other from opposite ends of the estate. That don't take balls."

"How was Jimmy Nunn connected to the Fishers?"

"Well, all Jimmy could do was drive cars and fix cars, so it must have been one of those two things."

Ken necked his pint and then looked sideways at Jack. Jack took a £10 note from his wallet and dropped it on the table.

"I've got to go, but you . . ."

Jack's mobile pinged. And before he could finish reading Maggie's text, Ken was at the bar buying another pint and a cheeky chaser before Jack left.

"Keep the change!" Jack shouted.

* * *

Jack and Maggie sat in the canteen, eating noodles from a non-specific takeaway right by the hospital's entrance. It wasn't a Chinese, or an Indian, or a chippy—but cooked all three amazingly well. As Maggie shoveled the last king prawn into her mouth and listened to Jack, she felt guilty for not being on the rowing machine instead. But he needed her.

"So, yeah, he was a right prick, by all accounts. Smashed his shoulder and his dreams, all because he was showing off to some woman he fancied. And he must have been with Trudie at the time, so he was an adulterer as well. Nice guy."

"It's not 'by all accounts,' is it?" Maggie reasoned. "It's one account from a man who, by the sound of things, will turn up in the ER with liver failure by the end of the night!"

Jack looked so disappointed in the man he could have ended up calling "Dad." Maggie reached across the table and stroked his arm.

"Jimmy must have been, what, late twenties in Ken's story? Of course he was showing off to women. That doesn't make him a prick, it makes him a boy. He could be a professor of engineering by now. And, if he's not, who cares? You've got to remember, Jack, that this man you're looking for isn't your dad. Your dad is the man who's off on a world cruise tomorrow."

"Jesus, is it tomorrow?"

Jack had been told the date they sailed, but hadn't expected it to come around so quickly.

"They sail at two, so they'll need to check in by midday. The cruise is for four months, love, so . . ."

The missing words from the end of Maggie's sentence were . . . *this could be the last time you see Charlie.*

Jack's mind drifted off for a moment as he contemplated his dad dying at sea.

"Do they have coffins on board cruise ships?"

"Dozens." Maggie smiled gently. "Most passengers are well over 70. You know, Jack, you've been given a unique opportunity to get everything right, for the rest of his life. Take them for lunch and tell them that you love them. They both need to hear that, I expect. Penny and Charlie will have a wonderful time . . . until the moment it stops."

CHAPTER 7

Jack stared in awe at the gigantic cruise ship in front of him. It was seventeen decks high, the top six of which tapered off into the sky like a pyramid. From where Jack stood on the dockside, he could see palm trees, water slides, a climbing wall and a zipwire on the top decks. It was staggering. Hundreds of Asian-looking men and women scurried up and down each of the decks, brimming with purpose and commitment. They would wait on his parents hand and foot, making them feel like they were the most important people in the entire world—not because they cared about his parents having a good time, but because they, and their families back home, would rely almost entirely on the size of the tip left at the end of the cruise. But Jack balanced that cynical thought by wishing them all well, as he was certain how hard it must be sucking up to strangers 24/7.

This ship was taller than Jack's apartment block and wider than the M25. It was like Vegas and Florida all rolled into one selfcontained dream holiday. His parents would *love* it. He could see them now—they'd walk the decks each morning, drink champagne with breakfast, lose nightly in the casino and eat themselves silly.

Jack checked his ticket to the Isle of Wight for the umpteenth time. Still there. He had only loosely planned his line of questioning for Ester Freeman. He wasn't one for being boxed in by pre-emptive thinking, and would rather let Ester's answers guide how their meeting went. He'd be late sailing, but he had his excuse planned for when Ridley asked; he was going to say that he'd been dragged into helping the Port Authorities to control a problem passenger. Ridley wouldn't be able to bollock him for that.

Jack's mobile rang.

"Where are you, darling?"

"Look up, Mum. See the massive white cruise ship?" Jack joked to Penny. "Head for that."

He smiled as he slid his mobile into the inside pocket of his leather jacket. As Charlie and Penny ambled toward him, they looked as though they hadn't got a care in the world.

"We're here!" Penny laughed.

* * *

There were numerous high-end restaurants in and around Southampton Docks, but Jack took his parents to a small pub. Charlie and Penny were not complicated people, and nor was the food they liked to eat.

Charlie and Jack both ordered steak and chips, and Penny ordered chicken and mushroom pie. She always ordered pie when she went out because she'd never been able to master the art of making pastry—"I like to order something I'd never have at home, otherwise, what's the point?" They shared a bottle of red and talked and talked, but not about anything important. Nobody mentioned Charlie's cancer, or the fact that he might never set foot on English soil again.

After they'd eaten, Jack left his parents in the pub, while he nipped to Penny's car to collect their suitcases. Penny had parked in the longstay car park, in the furthest space of the furthest zone— this was because she was of the firm belief that car thieves only steal from cars close to the exit in order to make a quick getaway.

Jack said goodbye at the check-in desk; the hugs were extra tight and extra long, and everyone said those underrated, underused words: "I love you." The things that we assume go without saying but that should be said every day.

Charlie took Penny by the hand and her thumb automatically stroked the back of his hand. Penny would be Charlie's rock . . . until the day she came home alone, and Jack would then be her rock. Penny kissed Jack's cheek and led Charlie onto the cruise ship.

From the dockside, Jack searched the thousands of faces across all of the open decks. Eventually, he saw them. Charlie and Penny were leaning close to each other against the rail, with a glass of champagne in one hand and a tiny Union Jack in the other.

Jesus Christ. Jack laughed to himself. *They're going to be pissed before they've left Southampton.*

Suddenly, his laughing turned to crying and he had no idea how to stop. Safe in the knowledge that he was surrounded by strangers, he let the tears roll. The maniacal, mass waving went on for at least forty minutes until the ship's horn finally blared and, painfully slowly, the ship started to move away from the dockside. Penny blew a thousand kisses down to Jack, and Charlie repeatedly gave him the thumbs-up. Jack walked the dockside as far as he could, waving and smiling. He could no longer distinguish his parents from the people around them, but he hoped they'd be able to spot him—seeing as he was the only person following the ship out to sea.

Jack checked his ticket to the Isle of Wight for the umpteenth time.

"Shit!"

He turned tail and raced for the ferry . . . which turned out to be the second ship that day he watched disappear without him.

CHAPTER 8

The facilities on the Isle of Wight ferry came a very poor second to the cruise ship that was currently heading toward St. Lucia with Charlie and Penny. Jack imagined that, by now, they'd be in an open-deck restaurant eating as much shellfish as they could—the extravagance of it would be too much for Penny to resist, and as long as Charlie had a drink in his hand, he'd do whatever kept her happy. Jack smiled at the thought of his parents trying to "fit in" with the other posher passengers ... then he wondered how many more passengers had gone to sea to die. And his smile disappeared.

Jack had researched the Fisher brothers, using various police databases and Google. The name of Fisher had been slurred by Ken Moore toward the end of their evening together; the mention had been brief, but it was the only lead Jack had for now.

Arnie and Tony Fisher had run a club in Soho, which had been the subject of numerous failed drug, gambling and underage prostitution raids. Arnie Fisher was clearly the smart one, keeping his criminal activities well concealed. He was slick and charming with a penchant for young men, but he was also known to be ruthless and brutal when the mood took him. Arnie was a slimy character, with eyes like a shark—unreadable and terrifyingly soulless. He never got his hands dirty but, throughout the seventies and eighties, the police suspected his orders had resulted in numerous unsolved robberies, assaults and murders. Tony Fisher, on the other hand, was an out-and-out thug. He loved being hands-on, loved fast cars and tarty women, loved terrorizing and torturing—Tony was a dangerous psychopath and had a rap sheet to prove it. Jack had to scroll three times on his mobile screen to get from the top to the bottom of Tony's police record.

One newspaper article from 1984 covered the brutal murder of a man called "Boxer" Davis. It seemed Boxer had been a low-level, gullible dogsbody whose loyalties tended to shift toward the biggest pay packet. He was loosely connected to both the Fishers and to Harry Rawlins—and he was murdered in the spring of 1984. According to police reports at the time, Boxer had been in a Soho alley when a car crushed him against a wire fence, backed up, drove over his body twice more, then drove away. Nobody saw a thing. Boxer was found among the rats the following morning by a chef throwing out the slops.

This was the seedy world that Jimmy Nunn had frequented once his Formula One career went down the pan. Jimmy stuck with the only thing he knew how to do—driving—and he must have done it well, because he never served any substantial amount of time in prison.

Jack called Laura.

"Would you do me a favor, mate? Would you get hard copy police records for Arnie and Tony Fisher?"

"Course," Laura chirped. "Who are they?"

Laura was so smitten with Jack that she blindly misinterpreted how he called her "mate." She thought it was an endearment—when in fact, from Jack's perspective, it was just easy, non-committal and leveling. Everyone was "mate" to him.

"I'm digging about in the pasts of the women from The Grange, and Dolly Rawlins's husband was a big-time crook back in the seventies and eighties. The Fisher brothers were around at the same time and . . . I dunno. Might be something, might not."

"Ester gave you those names, did she?" Laura asked.

Jack looked up. Ahead of him was the stunning Cowes harbor, with its motor cruisers, yachts and tall ships. Laura jabbered away in his ear.

"I bet she's a rough old hag by now, isn't she? I mean, she was bloody ropey in her younger days, so, Jeez . . . Did she try it on with you? Old habits die hard and all that."

Then she giggled.

"She wasn't in," Jack lied. "I'm waiting—"

The ferry tannoy screeched and the announcer told passengers to make their way to their cars and get ready for disembarking in East Cowes. Laura clearly heard.

"Oh, my God, Jack." She glanced around the squad room and lowered her voice. "You're still at sea?"

"Don't let Ridley know."

Jack sighed heavily and he was sure she could hear the tension in his voice. She probably thought that Charlie had died unexpectedly suddenly, so he felt he had to correct her.

"No, Dad's fine. Well, he's not fine, but . . . They left on a world cruise this morning and, seeing as I was in Southampton anyway, I bought them lunch before they set off. It might be the last time I see him. I can't tell Ridley that though, can I?"

"I reckon he'd understand, you know," Laura empathized.

"I'm not taking the risk. I'll be at Ester's within the hour, and back by early evening."

"He said to be back by end of shift."

Anik entered the squad room. He guessed Laura was talking to Jack.

"Well, he won't hear it from me," she continued. "I'll dig out the Fisher brothers' records for you, it's no problem—I'm on Missing Persons, but I can do both. You take care and I'll see you tomorrow."

Laura hung up. She didn't need to glance up to know that Anik had a disapproving look on his face.

"If you know what's good for you, you'll just get on with your work," she said.

"You sure it's me you should be saying that to and not Jack?" Anik quipped, rather pleased with himself. Laura spun her chair and glared at him.

"I'm positive, DC Joshi. You know, being a sergeant is about understanding your team and how to get the best from them. With that in mind, I'm going to put the kettle on and make you a green tea to help you do the boring bits of the job, such as sitting at your desk trawling through Missing Persons."

Laura stood and headed out before she said something she'd regret.

* * *

Jack had to double-check Ester's address when he finally arrived, because the house he was now looking at was a stunningly beautiful beachside property in Seaview, just south of Ryde. How on earth could an ex-con afford this place? The road he'd come in on had brought him past a yacht club, brimming with blazered gents and Pimm's-supping ladies all showing off their knees regardless of the fact that it was cloudy with a stiff breeze. Every other building was a hotel or B&B and the beach was a characterful combination of fine sand and rock pools. Boats were sprinkled throughout the calm sea, pushbikes outnumbered cars, grown-ups wore deck shoes whether they owned a boat or not, and children mostly wore no shoes at all. People sat on the sea wall with fish and chips, or a pint of beer, or both. On one stretch of sand, canoes stood up on their ends in what looked like a revamped bike rack. The houses were sensibly spaced, not crammed in like in big cities, and there was green space in between them. Seaview was allowed to breathe. Jack took in the stunning scenery, the calm, quiet feel, and the crisp clean air. *I'd be bored shitless within minutes*, he thought to himself.

Jack knocked at number 34 and the door was opened by a short, balding man. He had a wealth of hair in a semicircle that didn't go higher than the top of his ears. He had a large gray mustache that left his mouth entirely to the imagination and he wore round, wire-rimmed glasses, as well as a tight white muscle T-shirt over his less-thanimpressive abs, black shorts that stopped just above the knee, a black maid's apron complete with white frill around the bottom edge, and pink slippers. A pair of bright yellow washing-up gloves poked out of one apron pocket and there was a bulge in the other apron pocket that—if Jack didn't know better—was the size and shape of a pair of handcuffs. The short man stood and looked at Jack, seemingly with no intention of speaking first.

"Sorry." Jack suddenly realized that he'd been staring for some time. "I'm looking for Ester Freeman."

"And you are?"

"My name's Jack Warr. I'm a DC with the Metropol—"

The small man's face suddenly beamed. "Oh, come in, love. She's in the orangery."

Ester was lounging with a copy of *Marie Claire*, a cigarette and a glass of red wine. A half-empty bottle of McGuigan Classic Cabernet Sauvignon sat on the table next to her, as did a well-thumbed copy of *Men's Health*. In the corner of the orangery was the box that the wine had arrived in—it was a bulk-buy deal, a dozen bottles for £49.99, delivered free to your doorstep. Jack and Maggie shopped for wine in exactly the same way. They'd sign up, get the first case at a third of the actual price, then cancel the subscription. Looking round, Jack saw Ester had clearly done this with at least four different companies. He smiled to himself. *I like her!*

Ester's hair and nails were immaculate, although the tips of her fingers were stained yellow from decades of smoking. She wore a long tan-colored cardigan that, when she was standing, would come below her knees; underneath, she wore a pair of loose cotton trousers and a vest top slightly too low for her 74-year-old cleavage. The cardigan hung provocatively off one shoulder as she read. She slowly closed her magazine and looked up, silently indicating that the short man could now speak.

"DC Jack Warr from the Met, no less," he announced. He turned to Jack. "Tea or wine?"

"I'd love a cup of tea. Thank you." The short man made for the door.

"Geoffrey, darling." He paused. "Find some biscuits. No. Cake! Find some cake. And make a pot, I'll indulge as well."

Once Geoffrey had left, Ester focused on Jack. She looked him up and down, admiring every one of his youthful lines and curves—and she made no bones about it.

"Sit anywhere, darling."

Jack sat directly opposite Ester in a huge, overly cushioned, wicker garden chair.

"How can I help you, Detective Constable?"

"I'd like to speak to you about your time at The Grange, if you don't mind."

"The time I whored young girls out to wealthy businessmen? Or the time I emptied the contents of a handgun into Dolly Rawlins? You'll have to be more specific."

Ester's face remained deadly serious as she stared at Jack, but her eyes twinkled.

"1995 please, Miss Freeman."

Jack wasn't going to be intimidated by an old madam like her.

"You'd have been, what, ten years old? Why do you care about what happened so long ago?"

"You may have read in the news about the fire at Rose Cottage in Aylesbury?"

Ester sat forward in her seat. "I don't read any news relating to the world outside Seaview ... but I'm intrigued by Rose Cottage burning down. And I'm even more intrigued by why a DC from the Met has come all the way to Seaview to chat to me about it. Why not just send a local plod round?"

Jack didn't answer; instead he continued with the questions he needed to ask.

"Can you tell me about the time you lived at The Grange in 1995, please?"

Ester sat back again. "Fucking disaster waiting to happen. I mean, a murderess, a fraudster, a gunrunner, a druggie and a couple of whores trying to open a kids' home! I assume you know everything about each of us already, so I doubt I'm telling tales. Julia and Gloria might have been looking for a new start to their shitty lives, I suppose. Connie and Kathleen were looking for someone else to make the decisions—useless bloody pair. I was looking to scam Dolly Rawlins out of her cash."

Geoffrey entered with what looked like afternoon tea for two on a silver tray. He handed Jack a garish, flowery side plate with scalloped embossed edges and instructed him flirtatiously to help himself to anything he liked the look of. He then poured two cups of tea, handed Ester her plate and left the room.

"Delightful, isn't he?" Ester grinned as she loaded her tiny side plate with three different types of cake. She ate with no regard for the fact that she was also talking. "He was one of my first customers at The Grange back in the eighties. He would only see me, which was very flattering. He's supremely loyal. Thirty-odd years on and he still adores me."

"This is his place?"

"Well, it sure as shit ain't mine, is it, my darling? Have some cake, Jack—I've decided I'm going to call you Jack."

"That's fine," Jack replied as he put his side plate down and sugared his tea.

"Geoffrey's a Switch. Do you know what that is, Jack?" Again, Ester didn't pause for a response. "It means that sometimes he likes to be the Dominant and sometimes he likes to be the Submissive. Clearly, he's a Sub this week—which is the only time I get the housework and baking done, so you're lucky there. If you'd popped round last week, you'd have found me shackled to the bed . . . You wouldn't think it to look at him, would you?" And she filled her mouth with a pink square of Battenberg.

Jack hid his snigger in his cup, which made Ester laugh out loud.

"We can't hide who we are, Jack. So why bother trying?"

"You said that Dolly Rawlins gave you cash?"

"She bought The Grange from me for £200,000, which was £100,000 less than it was worth, but it released me from some big debts and gave me the freedom to do what I wanted to do. Only problem was that I didn't know what I wanted to do, so I stayed at The Grange until I decided. I ate well, drank well, fucked Julia. And then, one day, four suits from the council rolled up unannounced to do a spot check. They wandered down to the basement and caught me and Julia going at it in the sauna—not the sort of image they had in mind for a kids' home, so they pulled Dolly's funding. She blamed me entirely and told me to get out."

"So, you shot her?" Jack asked cautiously, certain there was more.

"Wouldn't you?" Ester said, as though her reaction of murder had been a perfectly sane one. "No? Well, lucky you to have always had something to live for, Jack. It was the second time in my life that I saw red and thought, 'Fuck this.' She betrayed me first, Jack. She screwed me on the money because she knew I was out of options. Dolly Rawlins was a prize bitch. How she'd survived into her forties without being shot by someone is beyond me."

Jack's next question was not on his list, but he felt compelled to ask, "When was the first time you saw red and thought, 'Fuck this'?"

Ester smiled. She didn't mind Jack's overly personal question and she even liked the fact that he was brave enough to ask.

"When I was twelve and my uncle Derek forced himself into me for the first time. I thought, 'Fuck this, Uncle Derek,' and I stabbed him in the ball sack with a pair of scissors." Ester howled with laughter. "'What doesn't kill you . . .' as they say."

"Do you remember the train robbery of '95, Miss Freeman?"

"If you don't call me Ester, I shan't answer another one of your questions."

"Do you remember the train robbery of '95, Ester?" Jack repeated obediently.

"I remember your lot tearing The Grange apart at some ungodly hour. We didn't know what it was about at the time, but I was flattered when I found out! I've never been accused of anything so clever before."

Jack went on to ask a few more questions, but Ester's recollection aligned with Bill Thorn's, and the statement she had given back in 1995. He was already getting the feeling that interviewing all of The Grange women was going to be a waste of time, but it had to be done.

"I don't suppose you know where Julia Lawson, Connie Stephens and Angela Dunn are now, do you?"

"Have you tried prison? They're probably there. Too stupid to stay out, those three."

"They're not in prison."

"Oh. Well then, Julia will be in a gutter or a mortuary somewhere— just can't leave the 'nose candy' alone or, more accurately, it can't leave her alone. Connie will be lying on her back underneath some violent, possessive dickhead—it's all she knows and she's never had an original thought in her life. And . . . who else?"

"Angela."

"Oh yes, her. I don't know. I recall her being a worse maid than Geoffrey, so I doubt she'll be doing anything that requires intellect. Thick as pig shit, and that's being rather unfair to pigs."

* * *

Jack sat on the sea wall with fish and chips and a pint. The sea was out and some of the closer boats now lolled on the seabed. He looked at the horizon and tried to imagine where his parents were and what they were doing. He smiled as he pictured his dad losing in the casino, and his mum placating him with a cocktail in her hand that she didn't even know the contents of. She'd have simply chosen a name she liked—she did exactly the same with the horses in the Grand National.

He checked his notes on the three remaining women from The Grange. He considered Ester's opinion of Connie as a woman who'd never had an original thought in her life and he wondered . . .

He called Laura. "Do me another favor, please?"

"'Hi, Laura. How are you?'" she interrupted sarcastically, then quickly added, "Go on."

"Connie Stephens. Can you see if there's a B&B in Taunton called The Grange?"

Jack could hear Laura tap-tapping away on her keyboard. She spoke the words as she typed them, which was a habit of hers that he hated.

"Oh, by the way," she said as she waited for the search results to show up, "Arnie Fisher died in 2012 from AIDS. And Tony Fisher's in Pentonville for manslaughter. He's got four years left." Then more tap-tapping.

Before Jack could thank Laura for her help, he heard Ridley's distant voice at the other end of the phone.

"How are the Fishers connected to our murder victim at Rose Cottage?"

Leaving Laura to stumble her way through a half-remembered response about the Fishers' connection to Dolly Rawlins, Jack leapt off the sea wall, binned his fish and chips and grabbed the first person he came across.

"Where would I find a taxi, please?"

"Ryde train station's your nearest taxi rank—an hour's walk that way. But John at the post office sometimes . . ."

Jack raced toward the post office, phone clamped to his ear.

Ridley was asking about B&Bs in Taunton.

"Jack had a hunch that Connie's B&B in Taunton might be called The Grange, so I'm seeing what's registered and cross-referencing . . ." Jack heard her tapping the keyboard.

Ridley interrupted her. "Why's Jack got you doing it? Is that him?"

There was a muffled sound as he snatched Laura's mobile.

"Jack?" Ridley boomed before realizing that he was shouting.

"Jack," he said more quietly, "when you get back, I want a full debrief in my office."

"Yes, sir," said Jack, trying not to sound out of breath.

Should he explain to Ridley about the importance of buying his dying dad a prime fillet steak for the last time and hope he cared enough to be lenient? Or should he stick to the lie he'd planned about helping the Port Authorities with an invented disruptive passenger? Would Ridley believe he was a dutiful policeman? In reality, this thought process only took one second, and before he could begin his lie, Ridley cut in.

"You running? Where are you?"

Jack braced himself for a bollocking.

"Um . . ." he began, but Ridley interrupted him again.

"Hang on, Jack. Laura says there is a 'Grange B&B' in Taunton with the registered owner showing as Connie Stephens. How did you get to that?"

"It was something Ester said about Connie never having an original thought in her life, sir."

Jack could hear a change of tone. "Well done. I'll see you when you get back later. What time do you expect that to be?"

Jack looked at the post office up ahead. Maybe he'd be lucky.

"Public transport's a bit of a pain, sir, but I'll be back as soon as I can."

* * *

Ridley handed Laura back her mobile.

"That boy thinks I was born yesterday," he mumbled. Then louder, "Right, you lot! Let's face front for a minute, please." Ridley's team turned toward him. He picked up a whiteboard marker and wrote underneath the photo of Connie Stephens, THE GRANGE B&B, TAUNTON.

"Missing Persons is an arduous task, so thank you all for your hard work so far. Our murder victim is in there somewhere, he has to be, so keep at it. Laura, what do we know about the kids' home Dolly Rawlins was planning?"

"It's legit, sir. There's a paper trail of loan applications, building inspections and quotes, legal documents from social services, and a background check on Dolly Rawlins. The prison warder at Holloway gave her a glowing report, saying she was a model prisoner who helped guide the young mums. Rawlins frequently talked about opening a kids' home when she was inside. Half her wing wanted her to take their kids on till they got out."

"Right, so it seems The Grange women weren't in Aylesbury under false pretenses. Anik?"

"'Sheila' isn't Danny Green. As of last night, Danny's in lock-up downstairs for flashing at a girls' hockey team. So the word 'pervert' painted on the wall probably does relate to him and not 'Sheila.'"

"And Jack's on about the Fisher brothers. Why?" Ridley turned to Laura.

"Because they're part of Dolly Rawlins's past. Arnie's dead and Tony's inside. I think the connection is more to do with Harry Rawlins than Dolly. The men all shared the same patch back in the eighties, so ran in the same circles. Harry Rawlins was the one behind the Strand underpass robbery in '84. I think Jack's looking at how involved Dolly might have been."

"Well, if Jack was here, we could ask him, couldn't we?"

Laura didn't like being spoken to as though she was in cahoots with Jack, although it was true.

"Right," Ridley continued, "the priority is still to identify our murder victim so, tomorrow, it's straight back on to Missing Persons, please, for all of you. We're running his DNA against the Misper database, aren't we?" There was a sea of nodding heads. "Good."

Ridley went into his office and closed the door.

Ridley's door was always open until that time of day when he wanted no more conversations, no more questions and no more work to cross his desk. It was the moment his team knew they could wind down, finish what they were doing and slowly filter out over the next hour or so. Ridley would be last to leave. He always was.

* * *

It was nine o'clock by the time Jack got home and Maggie was curled up on the sofa with a glass of red wine from their very own bargain box.

"How did it go?" she asked.

"Why aren't you at work?" Jack asked, as he sat down next to her with an empty glass and an expectant look.

Maggie filled his glass for him. "I took the night off to be with my lovely man, after his very tricky day."

Jack let his head flop onto the back of the sofa.

"Very tricky . . ." he said. "Between the pervy old weirdos and keeping Ridley off my back, I'm exhausted."

He glanced at Maggie with a tired smile on his face. She wasn't smiling back.

"I was talking about saying goodbye to Charlie and Penny."

Jack put his hand on Maggie's knee. His day had been so hectic, he'd almost forgotten how it had started.

"Sorry, love. I bought them a pub lunch, we shared a bottle, I waved them off. They had huge grins on their faces the whole time." Jack glugged half his wine down in one go and rested his head back again. "I know they know what's happening, Mags, but it's like they're in a world of their own."

"Best place for them, I expect." Jack loved that Maggie was so wise. "Go on then. Tell me about work."

"Nah, it's too late for work talk." Jack rubbed his eyes hard. "I've got a couple new leads on finding Jimmy Nunn though. One of the women I'm tracking down lives in Taunton, so when I go to interview her, I'm also going to call on Aunt Fran. She fobbed me off the other day on the phone, so I'm going to sit her down and make her tell me what she knows. And a guy called Tony Fisher apparently knew Jimmy really well, so I'm going to see him as soon as I can sort the visiting order."

He couldn't see Maggie's face as he was still rubbing his eyes, but she was now scowling.

"So," she said, "the only man you can find who knew your birth dad really well is in prison. Dare I ask what for?"

Jack looked at her with his bloodshot, watery, very tired eyes. He slowly sipped the remains of his wine. She didn't need to know that Tony Fisher was in for killing someone.

CHAPTER 9

Laura was at the vending machines deciding how much sugar to have for breakfast when Jack walked past.

"How was the Isle of Wight?"

She hadn't noticed that he was on his mobile. He raised a finger.

"Yes, OK, well, will he be back on the wing tomorrow? Ah, day after . . . Yes, it's in relation to a current investigation. It has no bearing on any conviction he's in for, no, just background stuff on an old acquaintance . . . If you could, please. Great."

"Tony Fisher?" Laura guessed.

"The guy's a pensioner and he took on some 20-year-old wannabe."

"And I bet he won. You should read his file, Jack. He's a genuine, old-school psycho."

Laura collected her chocolate, crisps and can of pop.

"Apparently Tony pinned the kid down and snapped both of his middle fingers so that, and I quote—" Jack put on a gruff, cockney accent—"'You won't be able to wank proper for a munff !'"

Laura let out a loud screech. "Is that what Tony sounds like?"

"Probably."

Jack laughed and they both headed for the squad room. As they walked down the corridor, Anik ran to catch them up.

"What's the joke?" he panted.

"You had to be there." said Laura dismissively.

Anik's face fell.

* * *

There were two evidence boards at the front of the squad room now, gradually filling up with information dating all the way back to 1984. Ridley sat at Jack's desk while Jack led the room. He pinned up three photos with their names scrawled underneath—Harry Rawlins, Joe Pirelli and Terry Miller—and a black silhouette with a big question mark on the face. Pirelli's and Miller's photos were mugshots, but Rawlins's photo was an old newspaper cutting from the opening of a Soho art gallery back in the early eighties. He had a champagne flute to his lips, his head tilted back and his shoulder toward the camera. In truth, it could have been anyone.

"... see, on the first Strand underpass job, everyone initially thought that Harry was one of the robbers blown to smithereens, but he wasn't 'cos he was shot by Dolly Rawlins just over six months later. Speculation was that Harry Rawlins was probably behind the second Strand underpass job, and he was definitely behind the diamond heist. Now, if Dolly Rawlins planned to convert The Grange into a kids' home, she had to have had at least some capital. I know she was going for funding to do the place up, but she gave Ester Freeman £200,000, *in cash*, to actually buy the place. Where did she get that from, less than one month out of the nick?"

Ridley raised his hand to bring silence to the room. "Where is all of this going, in relation to our murder victim?"

Jack paused for a moment to think, which Ridley allowed.

"Well, sir, we know the cash found at Rose Cottage is likely to be the cash from the train robbery back in '95, because of the age and volume of the notes. And because of where it was found. Every police report from '95 suggests that there's no way the armed robbers could have got that amount of money out of Aylesbury before the roads were closed and the searches began. At the moment, I'm trying to eliminate the women from having anything to do with the train robbery or our murder victim—but I can't definitively. Equally, I can't connect them either. It's far more likely that they'll end up being potential witnesses to something, rather than being involved."

Anik exhaled a sharp, short stream of air from his nostrils, as though mocking the non-committal comment Jack had just made.

"Something to add, Anik?" Ridley asked.

He knew Jack was dawdling on this investigation, which was something he'd deal with when he was good and ready; but the one thing Ridley hated more than anything else was one copper disrespecting another. That's not what his team stood for and he wouldn't tolerate such bad manners.

"Get up there, Anik, and tell us what you've got to add."

Anik slowly stepped up to the front of the room, next to Jack.

"Erm . . . Well, Missing Persons has still not given us anything, but I found a . . . erm . . ." He went back to his desk, grabbed his file and raced back to the front of the room. "I've been doing some background on John Maynard, the builder who started the conversion work on The Grange for Dolly Rawlins before she died—obviously— and he's still living in Aylesbury. Also, Jim Douglas, the signalman on duty on the night of the train robbery—I've got his current address too. Both of these men have no criminal record and no obvious long-term connection to each other or the women, so, you know, as independent witnesses, they might be useful for us to speak to and see what they recall from the night of the robbery."

Ridley stood up and, as he walked to the front of the room, Jack and Anik parted like the Red Sea and made room for him to take center stage.

"I'm going to arrange for us to go back to Aylesbury tomorrow to see the scene again. Anik, arrange for us to interview Maynard and Douglas while we're there. Jack, I'll get the local station down in Taunton to go and see Connie Stephens. I think you traipsing up and down the country is not a good use of your time."

Jack's brain silently went into overdrive. *Fuck!* He had to go to Burnham-on-Sea to see his Aunt Fran.

Ridley continued, oblivious to Jack's dilemma. "Today, I need you all back on Missing Persons please—expand the search radius from Aylesbury. Jack, my office."

* * *

Jack shut Ridley's office door behind him. This was the only other time Ridley's door was ever closed—when he was in a private meeting. Ridley stood by his expanse of windows, with his back to Jack.

"I don't need to know exactly where you are all the time, Jack, but I do at least need to know what island you're on." Ridley moved behind his desk, stuck his hands deep in his pockets and held Jack's gaze. "I mean, that's just about respect, isn't it?"

Jack had no choice. "My parents set off on a world cruise yesterday. It's unlikely Dad will come back."

"And you didn't tell me this, because . . . ?" Jack didn't answer. "I won't tolerate officers who try to pull the wool over my eyes and don't take the job seriously. I don't think you do take this job seriously, Jack, that's one problem me and you have got." His tone softened. "How long's the cruise?"

"Four months."

"That's no time at all, is it? I'm sorry, Jack, I really am. You OK to be here?"

"Yes, sir. I want to work. In fact, I'd like to be the one who goes to Taunton and interviews Connie Stephens. If I hadn't seen Ester face to face yesterday, I'd never have figured out that Connie's B&B was probably going to be called The Grange. That came out of a bit of chat over a cuppa. I'm getting to know these women one by one and so, I'd like to keep control of all the interviews if that's OK with you, sir."

Ridley took no time at all to change his mind completely and agree that Jack could go to Taunton to interview Connie. His focus and commitment was all Ridley ever wanted. And now he felt as though his protégé finally had it.

"Thank you," Jack said. "I get the strong feeling, sir, that on this one, we have to go backward in order to go forward."

Even as the words left Jack's mouth, he wasn't sure if he was referring to the Rose Cottage case, or to his own search for his birth dad.

CHAPTER 10

On the evening of the diamond raid, Dolly's only plan had been to make absolutely certain that Harry went down for the crime. She hadn't even considered where the diamonds might end up—she certainly had no intention of putting herself at risk to steal them. No, this was pure revenge.

But when she learned of Shirley's involvement, things started to go horribly wrong. No one Dolly cared about was meant to be at the event, but Shirley, when asked by her new boyfriend to model the jewelry they were intending to steal, had agreed, not knowing that Micky Tesco was one of Harry's gang.

As soon as Dolly learned that Shirley was at risk, her plan for revenge vanished in the blink of an eye and was replaced with a desperate need to protect her friend. She knew for a fact that Harry's gang would be armed.

By the time Dolly arrived at the event, chaos had already taken hold. Police were racing into the building and glamorous people in black ties and ball gowns were flooding out, heels in hand, fear in their eyes. But Shirley was nowhere to be found.

A gunshot echoed from inside the building. Before Dolly knew what she was doing, she found herself running down the back alley and in through the open kitchen door. Dolly had seen many sights she'd rather forget, but none was more harrowing than that of Shirley, dolled up to the nines and as beautiful as ever, lying dead on the kitchen floor in a growing pool of her own blood.

It took Dolly a good ten seconds to realize the horror of what she was seeing. Behind her, Shirley's low-life boyfriend was frozen to the spot.

As Micky recovered from the shock, he raced forward, pulled the jewels from around Shirley's neck and disappeared out the kitchen door. Rage filled Dolly's heart and she charged after him like a woman possessed.

As Micky ran, he stuffed a dark blue cotton bag into his leather jacket, along with the broken necklace, jumped on his motorbike and raced away. Dolly was right behind him as she launched herself into her car and sped after the motorbike.

As Micky took a sharp right turn, he lost control of his bike and careered into a parked car. Without thinking, Dolly jumped from her car, grabbed the blue bag and broken necklace from inside his jacket, and drove off, leaving him for the approaching sirens to deal with.

When it was safe to stop, Dolly pulled over. Her heart was pounding and she gasped for breath as the tears welled in her eyes. Her fists pounded the steering wheel as she tried to forget the sight of Shirley's body, but she knew she never could. It was what she deserved. It was she who had called the police and caused the chaos. She had been so consumed by vengeance that she hadn't given the bystanders a second thought. What had happened to Shirley would be an eternal torment that Dolly would take to the grave.

An ambulance roared past, siren blaring, and snapped Dolly out of her melancholy. She looked inside the dark blue bag and saw jewels sparkling back at her. Diamonds, emeralds, rubies, pearls . . . every gemstone you could think of, encased in gold and platinum. Dolly put the broken necklace—torn from Shirley's neck— into the bag, pulled the drawstring tight, put it into the glovebox and drove home.

* * *

The signal box at the old rural track crossing in Aylesbury was now abandoned. The lower half of the small oblong building was mostly wood paneling with two very small windows; it seemed to be entirely separate from the upper half, which was accessed by an external flight of wooden stairs. All of the wood panels were a creamy color, or used to be, and all of the trimmings were dark brown. Ridley stood in the middle of the disused railway tracks, looking up, oddly transfixed by the signal box. The upper half of the building was all windows, giving a 360-degree view of the surrounding countryside. Each floor-toceiling window was split into eight smaller panes of glass, separated by wooden beams in the contrasting dark brown wood. All of the glass panes had been smashed by stones, probably thrown from where Ridley now stood. He glanced down at the sea of heavy gravel beneath his feet and the temptation to see if he could hit a window was almost too much to bear. Laura frowned as she watched a very slight grin creep over his face.

"I'm not a trainspotter if that's what you're thinking, Laura. But I did have a train set when I was a kid. I saved up for two Christmases and two birthdays to buy a signal box just like this one."

Laura shook her head as Ridley reminisced. She couldn't imagine he was ever a child. Then Anik appeared at one of the broken windows—"stinks of piss in here"—and Ridley's beautiful childhood memory was shattered.

Anik stepped out at the top of the external wooden stairs.

"Stop there!" Ridley shouted. "What can you see?"

"Nothing." Anik shrugged as he glanced down at Ridley's stern face. He looked around again. "The trees would have been lower back in '95 but, even so, the bridge where the train was held up definitely can't be seen from here. Can't see the new housing estate either 'cos of the ... the ... erm ..." He made a wavy movement with his hand.

"Terrain?" Ridley guessed.

"Yes," Anik agreed. "The terrain's, you know, up and down. So, The Grange wouldn't have been visible from here either. Not much *is* visible from here, to be fair. Nice view though."

He walked down the wooden stairs, joining Ridley and Laura on the tracks.

The team then went their separate ways. Anik went to interview James Douglas, the signalman on duty the night the train was robbed. And Laura and Ridley went to interview John Maynard, the builder who had been helping to convert The Grange into a children's home.

* * *

Jack was halfway through a 1 hour and 50-minute train journey from London to Taunton. He had his notepad out and was scribbling names down as he searched for various people in the HOLMES database and also googled news articles from back in the day. Jimmy Nunn, Boxer Davis, Carlos Moreno, Joe Pirelli, Terry Miller: the same names kept coming up, over and over. The East End of London was definitely a different place back then. The criminal "underworld" was actually quite visible, with everyone knowing who the key players were, who to stay away from, who not to cross. There was a definite hierarchy and it was respected. Not like today. Criminals today never climbed to the lofty heights of "notorious."

Jack came across several old case files belonging to DI George Resnick who, back in the late seventies and early eighties, had seemingly been obsessed with tying the elusive Harry Rawlins to any of the numerous crimes he was suspected of. Resnick had been like a dog with a bone, ignoring all contrary opinions and faithfully following his gut. His name had been dragged through the mud by the gutter press; he'd been suspended, forced toward early retirement, denounced as an embarrassment to the force . . . Still, he stood by what he absolutely *knew* to be true—that Harry Rawlins was involved in the Strand underpass armed robbery on a security van. It was Resnick, and only Resnick, who'd claimed that Harry Rawlins had survived that otherwise deadly explosion. It was Resnick, and only Resnick, who'd chased a ghost with the absolute conviction of eventually being proved right.

Shit! Jack thought to himself. *That's what I want.*

That all-consuming passion for catching the bad guy. That unshakable knowledge you were right.

But Jack knew he was asking for the impossible—because to be that kind of copper, he'd require a nemesis like Harry Rawlins and they just didn't exist anymore. Each day on the job, all Jack was doing was hoovering up scrotes, wasters, druggies and lazy bastards who had decided that crime was easier than working. That's why the Rose Cottage case was so intriguing and why tracking Jimmy Nunn was so exciting: because he was being taken back to a time when being a criminal was a vocation and a crime could be a work of art. Jack couldn't quite believe he was yearning for "proper" gangsters, but the thought of his birth dad being part of this old-school criminal underworld was oddly exhilarating.

* * *

Jim Douglas was a timid, unassuming man who said very little, very quietly. He was round, in his early sixties and bald as a cueball. He had a large, rosy-cheeked face with wide eyes like those of a child.

"You OK being in the garden with me?" Jim asked Anik, "Only, the grandkids are coming for tea and I want to get these trees planted before they arrive."

He knelt on a flowery gardener's knee-pad and dug the last hole, as Anik slurped tea from a chipped mug.

Jim's house sat at the heart of the housing estate that had been built on the grounds once belonging to The Grange, and it was a clone of the rest of the street. But this garden had been lovingly landscaped and was clearly Jim's domain. At the far end of the garden was a shed and, through the window, Anik could see the top half of a bike with a child's seat on the back. Scattered about the lawn were numerous footballs, a miniature football net, some plastic toys and stray pieces from a giant Jenga. Kids were obviously welcome here and any ensuing mess was most definitely allowed. There was even a home-made tree house in an old, sprawling oak that must have been around for centuries longer than any of the buildings which now surrounded it. The oak would have known the Grange women and all of their secrets.

"Do you remember the night the mail train was robbed, Mr. Douglas?"

"Jim, please. Yes, I remember. Well, I remember my bit. All those police loading the money sacks into the carriage at the crossing, then me sending the train on its way. About a minute later, I heard a massive crack of thunder, then saw the lightning and that was it. Course, it wasn't thunder at all—it was dynamite on the tracks. Very clever, that."

"Clever?" Anik asked.

"Well, the explosion made the carriage leave the rails, making it invisible to my track monitoring equipment. The equipment is very accurate but it can only 'see' a train if its wheels are in contact with the tracks."

"So . . ." Anik mused. "The robbers would have to have known that?"

"Every trainspotter in England knows that. It's common enough knowledge."

Anik couldn't see Jim's face, but it had gone from rosy cheeked to deathly white; he'd started sweating and struggling to control his breathing.

"Was there any aspect of the robbery that did require insider information?"

Jim closed his eyes in silent panic. "What do you mean?"

"I'm not suggesting you had anything to do with it at all, Jim," Anik assured him. "We know that you were privy to the normal running schedule of the mail train, but we also know that the schedule changed on the night the train was robbed—and you wouldn't have been told about that till the last minute."

"I might have been on the front line, but I was always the last to know anything."

As he headed toward a panic attack, Jim knew he'd not be able to hide it; he knew he'd have to disguise it as something else. He brought the trowel down hard and fast onto the back of his hand. He yelled in pain and sat his bottom down into the fresh pile of soil he'd just dug. Anik raced over.

"Sit still. Crikey, you're as white as a sheet. Don't panic, Jim, you're OK. Try to control your breathing." Anik covered the cut on the back of Jim's hand with a hanky, so that the seeping blood didn't make him feel worse. "When you're ready, we're going to go into the kitchen and run this under the cold tap. Then we'll

see what the damage is. OK?" Jim nodded, slowed his breathing, calmed himself down and Anik could see the color gradually
returning to his cheeks.

As Anik hunted for the first-aid kit in the bathroom upstairs,
Jim's hand was slowly going numb under the cold water from the
kitchen tap. Diluted blood ran down between his fingers and into
the white porcelain sink, but Jim was miles away, recalling the
steamy nights he'd shared with Connie in the signal box. It was the
most daring thing he'd ever done and she was the most wonderful woman he'd ever known. He could still feel her hot breath on
his neck as she perched on the side bench, her legs wrapped tight
around his waist, panting in time with him. Her hands caressed
the top of his bare buttocks poking out from beneath his white
briefs and her nails dug into his skin as she urged him into her.
He had never in his life, before or since, felt so desired. Jim's wife,
Jean, who he loved dearly, was the opposite of Connie. She was
steady, loving and *exactly* the sort of woman Jim's friends and family would have put him with.

Jim had had no clue why Connie allowed him to love her
for those few short weeks back in 1995, but he had just been
eternally grateful for the time they shared. He hung his head in
heartbreaking pain. That was a lie. He knew exactly why Connie had allowed him to love her. She'd asked so many questions
about his job: about how he knew where the train was on the
tracks at any given moment; about the trackside alarm systems.
She'd flattered him and been impressed by all of his "oh, so
important" responsibilities—she'd told him how such a complicated job turned her on and he'd fallen for it. Jim didn't care. He,
honest to God, did not care a jot. Connie had made him feel like

he could take on the world. She'd been his beautiful secret and that's how she'd stay until the day he died.

Jim knew nothing for certain, but if Connie had been using him for information, that would make *him* the inside man Anik was asking about. How lucky he was to have been used by someone so wonderful and so lovely—any man would be jealous. And any man would have done exactly the same.

*   *   *

John Maynard almost coughed up a lung when Ridley asked him about the building work he'd done for Dolly Rawlins at The Grange. He squeezed every last ounce of air from his body, spat into the bin, gasped a huge lungful of stale air, sat back in his seat, and took an extra-large drag of his cigarette before answering.

"That happens every time I think about Dolly bleedin' Rawlins, that does. Always paid me too little, too late. Paid me just enough to keep me happy though—knew exactly what she was doing, looking back. I gave her the benefit of the doubt for far too long. I thought, 'Cashflow's hard on a job this size. She'll come good.' Never did. She drip-fed me just enough cash so that I couldn't walk away. I should have known she was broke."

John paused to finish the remaining quarter of his cigarette in one single drag. He then got up and headed into the kitchen.

Laura looked at Ridley and the sickly color of her face said it all.

"Step outside if you need to," Ridley whispered.

John's home wasn't small, but it was unfinished. From the outside, it was a four-story, terraced town house in the good end of Aylesbury; inside, it was a building site. The room they stood in was currently being used as a lounge and, they speculated, a bed-room. The potential for this property was endless, but John was well past being able to do the work. Laura indicated to Ridley that she'd be OK to stay, just as John returned with a beer and a fresh packet of cigarettes. He was dressed in gray joggers, worn thin at the knees and at the crotch, a black T-shirt with tiny holes all over it, and black socks. He smelt of deodorant, but it couldn't hide the stench of the unwashed body underneath.

"Did Dolly Rawlins pay you in the end, Mr. Maynard?" Ridley inquired.

John smirked and glanced at Laura when he spoke. "Connie paid me. If you get my meaning."

Ridley responded, so that Laura didn't have to. "I think DS Wade got your meaning, yes."

"It's an absolute fact, DI . . . ?" "DCI Ridley."

"It's an absolute fact, DCI Ridley, that women fancy men who have physical jobs, like builders. Connie came out of The Grange on the very first day I was there, immaculate except for a tiny cobweb in her hair, holding a tap or a pipe or something, I can't recall. 'This just come off in me 'and. It's from the sauna.' Girly little Liverpool accent she had."

John laughed and rearranged his balls before he sat back down. Ridley got to the point before Laura passed out.

"What happened after the train robbery, Mr. Maynard?"

"The coppers searched my building yard and my house. They even poked about in my pond, if you can believe that. But that robbery wasn't done by anyone from round here. It was a bunch of outside fellas. They'd have had a barge or something, 'cos over land would have been impossible. Remote controlled maybe, so they could be miles away just in case it got seen. Or maybe they sank the money in waterproof bags, using weights, and came back for it later. That's what I would have done. I'm a bit of an engineer at heart, see—building and engineering go hand in hand and I can do both. So, yeah, I'd have put the cash into waterproof bags and sunk it. Could have stayed there for years, no bother. You should talk to Warren at the Dog and Gun. He's been here for centuries—knows everyone and everything. He'll have some ideas for you, an' all."

Ridley asked for John's opinion on a few more subjects, such as Norma and the other women from The Grange, but he had nothing useful to add.

Outside John's house, Laura gasped at the clean air, as though there wasn't going to be enough for her and Ridley to share.

"I'm really sorry, sir. I can't believe that Connie Stephens, that carbon copy of Marilyn Monroe, would let *that* touch her. Did you see his fingernails?"

"Call Anik," Ridley said as he unlocked the car. "Tell him to meet us for lunch in the Dog and Gun."

He dropped into the driver's seat and lowered his own and Laura's windows before she got in, to create a through-draft of fresh air for her.

"And I'll tell you what, sir," Laura continued as she fastened her seatbelt. "Women do like men who have physical jobs, but we also quite like personal hygiene . . . Oh, thanks for opening the windows."

*   *   *

Across in Taunton, Jack headed along Hazel Lane toward The Grange B&B. As he got close, the front door opened and a stunning, slender, 40-something, bleached blonde woman exited to water the plants on the front doorstep. Connie still looked like a glamour model. She wore far more make-up than in the 20-year-old photo of her on the evidence board, and comfy shoes instead of heels but, my God, she was still a head-turner. And she still had her figure. Jack tried not to look but she was side-on to him, so there was no chance of that.

The Grange B&B was one of five in a row, all connected, all displaying a three-star plaque. Jack speculated that each B&B probably had three or four bedrooms. The Grange had a hand-written sign outside boasting "Bed & Brekfast," which made him smile. He knew that Connie had no education to speak of, so he found this misspelling strangely endearing.

There was a large expanse of grass in front of this long row of buildings, with benches and picnic tables randomly scattered about, all approximately facing the bottom of the hill, from where you could just about see the start of the Blackdown Hills—an official "Area of Outstanding Natural Beauty."

A tall wooden signpost indicated that the Blackdown Hills were a twenty-minute drive, the village was a ten-minute drive, and the ruins of an old fort were a steep, ten-minute walk. And beneath the three directional wooden arrows, carved into the vertical wooden signpost was a cock and balls. Jack frowned. Even in such a beautiful place kids were still dickheads.

The front door opened wider and an elephant of a woman stepped outside.

"I'm off to the shops. Need anything?"

"We're out of butter," the bleached blonde answered, "and get some more pens for the bedrooms. Why does everyone nick the pens?"

The women shared a knowing chortle, before "elephant woman" squeezed herself into a Fiat Punto and drove away. The bleached blonde shouted after her.

"Ta-ra, Connie! See you at five!"

Jack stopped in his tracks. *Shit!* He'd just watched his interviewee drive away.

He sat down on one of the benches and got out his mobile to check the time; just gone midday. He opened Google Maps, typed in his Aunt Fran's address and discovered that she was no more than a twenty-minute taxi ride straight up the M5, in Burnham-on-Sea. Jack requested his Uber and waited.

He looked across at the Blackdown Hills and remembered how he and Charlie had walked the hills when he was in his early teens. Of course, they'd walked the Exmouth end, where the hills met the south coast, so all of this part was, in fact, completely new to him. But it felt the same.

Even though Dartmoor National Park had been right on their doorstep in Totnes, Charlie liked Jack to explore different places and see different things.

"Everywhere and everyone has its own beauty, Jack," Charlie would say. "You gotta find your spot."

Charlie loved the Blackdown Hills, because they had a tranquility to them, whereas Jack always preferred the rugged, unpredictable wildness of Dartmoor. But, right at this moment, he loved these hills and the memories they held, and he didn't want to leave.

CHAPTER 11

Frances Stanley didn't recognize Jack when she opened her front door to him; she'd only ever seen him as a small boy, not this impressivelooking young man who stood in front of her now. As she looked at him, not knowing who he was, she thought he dressed younger than his years, but that he carried it off perfectly—he was too smart to be selling something, too casual to be a copper, too young to be a Jehovah's Witness. Fran simply stared, unable to guess who Jack was or what he wanted.

"Aunt Fran? It's Jack."

He would have liked his Aunt Fran's face to instinctively relax at this point, to smile and to seem pleased to see him, but that didn't happen. Instead, Fran's face tensed, and it was only when she realized she must be coming across as cold and hard that she forced a smile.

"Jack, lad! Come in. Come in." They gave each other an awkward hug as he passed her and entered the hallway. "Why didn't you say you were coming? I've not tidied. And, look at me! I'm in my scruffs."

"It was a last-minute thing, sorry. I didn't know I was going to be in the area until it was too late to let you know."

Fran led the way into the kitchen, where she set about making some tea and searching for biscuits. She had to wash mugs from the overflowing sink as there were no clean ones. She rinsed them under the cold water and rubbed the inside with her fingers until the old tea stains had gone; then she dried them on a dirty, part-burnt tea towel that was obviously also used to take things out of the oven. When Fran opened the fridge to get the milk, a waft of onions filled the room and Jack just knew that the milk would taste of the same smell. He couldn't take his eyes off Fran. Her hair was dry and brittle from years of perming and bleaching. Her face was weather-worn, leathery, with smoker's wrinkles round her mouth.

Is this what Trudie would look like now? he wondered. *Shit, I hope not!*

All the while Jack was staring, Fran was making three mugs of tea and excusing her messy house. The front door opened silently and then loudly slammed shut. Seconds later, a skinny, unshaven black man walked in with the *Racing Post* under his arm and a cigarette in his mouth. The third mug was obviously for him.

Fran launched into an introduction before the man could ask.

"Clay, this is my nephew, Jack."

The men smiled at each other and shook hands. Clay was missing a couple of teeth in his lower jaw, but it didn't seem to be something he was bothered by. He kissed Fran on the forehead and sat down heavily at the small, sky-blue Formica kitchen set, dropping his paper, cigarettes and lighter on the table. It was only now that Jack noticed there were two dining chairs—which was fine by him, as sitting down in this house didn't really appeal.

"The reason I popped in was to chat about Jimmy Nunn," Jack started. "If you don't mind, just talk to me, say anything, regardless of how small or insignificant it might seem."

Fran put the three teas on the table, together with the milk carton and a sugar bowl which had a teaspoon already buried deep. Then she opened the kitchen window and picked up Clay's cigarettes and lighter. Clay grabbed the teaspoon from the sugar bowl and it lifted a solid lump of wet sugar up with it. He dissolved that into his tea before scooping up another spoonful of sugar. The motion of him stirring made the table rock just enough to create a tiny wave of tea inside each mug, that lapped over the edge with each rotation. He then put the wet teaspoon back into the sugar.

Fran took a couple of drags before she started talking.

"Your mum came to live with us when you were about eight months old. We'd just had our first and our second was on the way."

"Two babies," Clay echoed, rolling his eyes. "Full house."

"Jimmy'd gone without any warning," Fran continued. "Trudie had nowhere to live and no money. She didn't even try to sort herself out, instead she just knocked on my door. We did our best, Jack, but . . ."

Fran dipped the end of her cigarette into a water-filled cereal bowl and then flicked the butt through the open window into the back garden.

"The babies had the spare bedroom and Trudie was on the sofa," Clay added.

Jack was warming to him. Each time Fran made an emotive comment, he repeated it from a practical perspective, as though he was translating into "man speak."

"Your mum was . . ." She looked from Jack to Clay. "What's the word, Clay?"

"Needy. Not a very confident girl."

"Trudie needed to be taken care of and when Jimmy left her, she fell apart. She started drinking too much, going out too much and leaving you here with us too much. It wasn't fair."

Clay scraped his chair back and lit one of his cigarettes; he then stood next to Fran and smoked by the window. He was a good foot taller than Fran and half her width; they were an odd-looking couple, but the strength of their relationship was clear.

Clay looked straight into Jack's eyes as he spoke, making absolutely certain that he understood.

"Your mum was abusive to my Fran. She was rude, shouting—even hit her once." Jack was clearly shocked and Fran bowed her head, as if in shame. "He asked, love, so I'm telling him." Clay directed his words at Jack again. "Your mum's drinking got out of control and she became depressed. We were looking after three kids under one year old, and Trudie—emotionally and financially."

Fran took over. "Then she got sick. She had a tumor on the brain—you knew that, didn't you?" Jack did. Penny had told him when he was old enough to understand. "It was over and done with very fast. She didn't suffer for long. You were ten months old and we had to make a decision. We couldn't afford to look after everyone."

Jack smiled. He wasn't here to make his aunt feel bad.

"I have great parents, Aunt Fran. You don't need to worry about me."

"I'm so sorry for those first five years of your life, though, Jack." Fran spoke with genuine feeling. "If we could have kept you and done right by you, we would have. Do you remember it?"

Jack could remember moments from his childhood in unfamiliar places, so he assumed them to be from his time in foster care. Some memories were bad, some were OK. His first pleasant memory certainly had Penny and Charlie in it. He didn't have memories of anything horrific, although he did recall being hit on several occasions. Mostly he remembered care as being a dull and

LYNDA LA PLANTE | 123

soulless time—spending most days on his own, dreaming of the exciting things he was going to do when he grew up.

"Sounds like you did better without your dad," Fran suggested. "Jimmy Nunn was a lot of hard work for no reward. He was always letting your mum down. I don't know where he is now, Jack, and, if I did, I'm not sure I'd tell you. My sister loved you with all her heart, she just wasn't cut out to be a single mum—but Jimmy . . . Jimmy didn't love anyone but himself."

*　*　*

The food at the Dog and Gun was lousy. Ridley had very wisely chosen a ham and cheese toastie with chips, whereas Laura had mistakenly gone for something that needed actual cooking. Her burger was inedible, but fortunately Anik had the constitution of an ox and so finished off hers as well as his own.

"You eat like a teenager on a growth spurt," she said.

"Well, at least I don't stink of fags," Anik blurted out before he could edit his brain. "Sorry, sarge."

Laura sniffed her top and winced.

At the bar, Ridley watched his pint of Coke being poured while listening to Jack's answerphone greeting, then the beep.

"Jack, ask Connie about John Maynard, please. According to him, they had a sexual relationship, maybe as an alternative to cash for work done. That's it for now. Call me when you get a break."

The barman and owner, Warren, put Ridley's pint of Coke down next to the two pints of lime and soda. Warren was an old Londoner who'd moved out to Aylesbury about forty years ago.

"Dolly Rawlins? First murder we'd had round here in donkey's years, so too right I milked it. The Grange was only, what, a 20-minute walk away. Tourists would come in here first to get the background story on the murderous gunfight between the notorious 'London Madam' and the gangland 'husband-killer.' Then they'd go for a wander round the location, then they'd come back here for steak and chips, and a souvenir from the murder scene itself. Forty quid all in, excluding drinks."

"A souvenir from the murd—?"

"Don't worry, that bit was horse shit. We stuck a piece of old rubble in a food bag. It was like owning a piece of the Great Wall. Or Ayers Rock. Or the Moon. An actual piece of the most depraved whorehouse and bloodiest murder scene this side of the Watford Gap."

"And where was the rubble actually from?"

"My back garden. Law against that, is there?"

"Not that I can think of, sir, no." Ridley maneuvered the three pint glasses into a triangle, ready to be picked up. "You've got my card. If you remember anything relevant about the train robbery, I'd be grateful if you'd call me."

"Will do, guv. Will do."

Warren tapped the breast pocket of his shirt, where Ridley's card was safely tucked away.

* * *

By five o'clock, Jack was back sitting on one of the benches outside Connie's B&B, listening to Ridley's voicemail. As he put his phone away, Connie's Fiat Punto pulled up behind him.

Connie opened the car door, gathered her shopping bags and then took a minute or two to actually get out. She had to swing her legs round first, then wriggle to the edge of the driver's seat until her feet touched the ground; she had to grab the edges of the car door and heave herself out in a rocking one-two-three motion. Jack was so riveted by whether or not she'd make it to vertical that he forgot to offer to help.

As Connie swayed toward her B&B, Jack joined her.

"Miss Stephens? I'm DC Jack Warr of the Metropolitan Police. May I speak with you about your time at The Grange?"

Connie said nothing. She just handed him her bags and unsteadily led the way indoors.

The hallway to the kitchen ran the depth of the property, which was surprisingly big once inside. Jack couldn't help but watch Connie's ample backside sway from side to side as she walked. She still had an intriguing sort of catwalk wiggle and, although several sizes larger than Jack's personal taste, he could see the appeal.

In the kitchen, she poured two glasses of chilled water, handed one to Jack and then headed back outside to sit on the bench he had vacated a moment earlier.

Once Connie was settled and had glugged most of her water, she said, "Why are you interested in that? I don't think I'll remember much, but go on."

Her voice was soft, husky and very sexy, with the slightest hint of a Liverpool accent. Jack recalled the twenty-year-old photo of Connie on the evidence board . . . That was the woman who suited the voice he was listening to now.

"I'd like to know what you remember about the train robbery."

"Terrible, it was. I couldn't believe it had actually happened. We didn't know anything about it until the police hammered on the door in the early hours. I understand why they came to us first but, well, as soon as they walked in, they knew they'd made a mistake. Still searched the place though, inside and out. Dolly said, 'You damage it, you pay for it!'—'cos we'd had trouble before with some coppers taking the door off its hinges. Do you know about that?"

"I do, yes. The report says they were looking for guns."

"Another mistake. It seems that once you've got a police record, there's no leaving it behind." Connie finished her water. "I love this view. Don't you?"

"It's impressive," Jack agreed. Then he got back on track. "How did you end up at The Grange?"

"Ester Freeman invited me. She said Dolly Rawlins was getting released and she had a project she needed help with. She wanted to open a kids' home. We all knew each other from inside and, well, I suppose Ester thought we all needed an opportunity to be better. That's what it was, really. An opportunity to start again, give something back, look after troubled kids before they turned into us, you know." When Connie smiled, her dimples appeared, and her eyes sparkled. She dipped her gaze and looked up at Jack through her long black eyelashes. He couldn't help but warm to her. "We all got on really well . . . or at least, I thought we did."

"Why do you think Ester shot Dolly?"

"Money? Maybe even something less important than that. Ester lashed out at all of us at one time or another. Mostly verbal, but she couldn't half slap hard as well. She called me a whore once, so I said something back and she whacked me. Have you met Ester?" Jack's smile told Connie that he had. "She's a strange one, isn't she?

I mean . . ." Connie's face became serious as she thought back to the day Dolly died. "Dolly had made mistakes, but she'd paid for them. She was trying to do a good thing with the kids' home and Ester, because of money or whatever, took that away. Took it away from all of us." She reflected for a while and Jack didn't attempt to fill the pause. "You know when . . . like, something's the best and worst all at the same time? The Grange was that. For me, anyway, I can't speak for the others. It was exciting to be literally building our future—which is why it hurt so much when we lost it."

Jack nodded. "Talking of building, tell me about John Maynard."

Connie blushed slightly, but still chose to look him straight in the eyes as she responded.

"My, my, you have been doing your homework. I was a twenty-something woman stuck in the middle of nowhere with a bunch of other women so, yes, me and John had a bit of a thing. Have you got my mugshot from back then, DC Warr?" she teased. "I was a good catch, don't you think? Even in a photo taken under your harsh police station strip lights." Connie sat up straight and leaned toward Jack. "When a lady's got no one to look good for, Jack, this happens. John was nice. Before him, I was with Lennie—he'd beat me senseless, quite randomly. Training, he called it." She looked at him with her gentle smile and her dimples, and he could see tears pooling in the bottom lids of her striking, pale blue eyes. "What were those dogs called that were trained to think about food every time they heard a bell ring? Have I got that right?"

"Pavlov's dogs."

"That's them. Within a couple of months of being with Lennie, he'd stopped hitting me—but every time he walked into the room I'd shake, and sweat, and my heart would beat out of my chest. The memory of the beatings was enough by then, you see. That's what kept me in my place. The fear." A tear rolled down Connie's cheek. She put her hands flat on her knees and pushed down slightly, as if trying to contain her emotions. "That's why I like being here. Nobody knows I'm weak and nobody wants to take advantage of me—not now I'm past my prime and on the big side. I can just be on my own and be me and I like that."

As Jack watched Connie's chubby fingers wipe away the tears from her chubby cheeks, he thought she looked like a little girl. She stared out across the Blackdown Hills and tucked a stray blonde curl behind her ear. Her wet eyelashes glistened in the early evening sun and Jack felt that he should hug her, or put a hand on her shoulder, or something.

"I've not seen John since the day Dolly was shot. I don't miss him. I don't miss any of them."

Jack's mobile rang; he excused himself and stepped away to answer it.

With his back to her, Connie lifted her hands an inch or two off her knees. Her skirt was damp from where her palms had been, and her hands shook now that they were unsupported. Jack hung up and Connie quickly put her hands back down on her knees to stop the shaking.

"Thank you for your time, Miss Stephens. My boss is wondering where I am, so I'll have to go. And thank you for the water."

"My pleasure." Connie stood and picked up the two glasses. "Have you got a car somewhere or do you need a lift?"

"Actually, I'm going to walk to the edge of the Blackdown Hills and get a cab from there."

"That's a very nice way to end the day, Jack. Bye now."

With that, Connie waddled back indoors and Jack headed off down the hill toward the memory of teenage walking with his nowdying dad.

Connie put the glasses on the draining board, leaned on the edge of the sink and bowed her head to aid getting her breath back. She shakily poured herself a gin, added a pointless splash of tonic and a slice of lemon. Her mind raced. She took out her mobile and looked at the blank screen. She put it away while she silently drank the first of two gins and relived her interview with Jack. Connie took out her mobile again. And dialed.

"That copper from the Met's been round. I said exactly what we agreed, don't worry . . . I can still act the dumb blonde when I need to. I just wanted you to know that he might be heading your way."

CHAPTER 12

The call from Ridley had been another bollocking.

"Why am I calling *you*?" Ridley had asked rhetorically. "Tomorrow morning. Eight o'clock. You're first up."

It was now ten o'clock and Jack was standing in the center of his spare room, looking at his "evidence wall." It displayed dozens of photos of Trudie: some with him as a baby, some without; black and white photos of a very young-looking Jimmy Nunn, standing with Formula One heroes such as Jackie Stewart and James Hunt; his own birth certificate, change of name deeds and foster papers from the day he was signed away by his Aunt Fran.

On a separate wall, were three photos—Tony Fisher, Harry Rawlins and Dolly Rawlins. These three seemed directly connected to Jimmy Nunn's past. The photo of Harry Rawlins was the best of a very bad bunch—he was at a racetrack, shades on, standing behind a woman who hid the bottom half of his face.

Maggie walked in with two glasses of red wine and handed one of them to Jack. She looked around the walls and her eyes stopped on the mugshot of Tony Fisher.

"*He's* who you're going to see in prison? He's not an embezzler, you bloody liar! He's a . . . What is he?"

Jack faltered. "He's in for manslaughter." Maggie glugged her wine. "He used to run a club in Soho with his brother, Arnie." As Jack explained in more detail, Maggie couldn't believe that he actually sounded excited. "They took over Harry Rawlins's patch when he died the first time—the time he was supposedly blown up in the

Strand underpass armed robbery, not the time his wife shot him. They got forced out eventually and when Arnie died, Tony had no one to hold on to his leash, so he very quickly ended up inside."

"No, he doesn't look like the brains of the operation," Maggie remarked. "He looks like an awful man, Jack—those horrible beady eyes—and I don't like the idea of you going to see him."

"He's pertinent to the investigation."

"Which one? The one you're actually getting paid to work on, or the search for your birth dad?"

"Both."

He leaned in and kissed her. This affectionate act meant two things: "Don't worry" and "Stop talking." But Maggie wasn't going to do either. She wasn't sure she understood Jack anymore.

"So, the fact that your birth dad is connected to some of the worst gangsters London has ever seen doesn't bother you? Because it bothers me. And I'm sure it'd bother Ridley if he knew what you were doing."

Jack didn't look at Maggie because this wasn't a conversation he wanted to have. He just kept thinking, *please don't ask me why I'm tracking Jimmy Nunn*, because he honestly didn't know the answer, he just knew that he *had* to do it.

Maggie talked for a while longer about how Jimmy Nunn didn't seem to be a man worth knowing, about how Charlie should be their priority and about how she didn't want Jack to be hurt if Jimmy turned out to be even worse than he already sounded.

"These are dangerous people you're mixing with now, Jack. I know that's all part of your job, but when you're on a case, the dangerous people stay in the office. These ones are in my home and I don't like it. I don't like Tony Fisher, although I do like her— what's her name?—Dolly Rawlins. I think maybe I can empathize with her. Do you think perhaps she shot her husband because he was filling their spare room with his insane obsession?"

Jack suddenly laughed out loud. God, he loved Maggie! He threw both arms round her neck, pulling her head to his chest. She turned her head to the side and they both looked at his evidence wall.

"Just be careful," she whispered.

* * *

Jack stood at the front of the squad room and led the briefing. Ridley stood just outside his office, legs wide and arms folded— he was a mix of emotions. He was pissed off with Jack's disregard for his authority, but he was impressed with the information Jack was sharing now. As Ridley listened along with the rest of the team, he was deciding whether or not to give credit where credit was due.

Jack put a printed iPhone image of Connie up on the board.

"Crikey!" Anik blurted out, once again speaking before his brain had kicked into gear. "Look at the size of her!"

Laura threw him a stern look. "Nice."

Jack began his handover. "Connie Stephens talked about the train robbery in exactly the same way as Ester Freeman did. She said the first they knew about it was the following morning when the police arrived. This tallies with the statements taken at the time. Nothing's changed in 24 years."

"Suggesting she's telling the truth." Anik was trying to redeem himself with Ridley. "I mean, lies are hard to remember so there'd be discrepancies in their stories if they were lying, either then or now."

Ridley chipped in. "Sure. But 'I never saw anything' isn't that hard to remember."

Anik looked disappointed in himself. He needed patting on the head every now and then, and Ridley wasn't really a "patter." Ridley just looked back at Jack, indicating that he should carry on.

"Neither Ester nor Connie is living in a manner that suggests they've got thirty million lying around. Their bank accounts show nothing unusual, in fact Connie goes overdrawn at least once every month. Ester's slightly better off, but that's because the money she spends is Geoffrey's. I think the original investigation was right to eliminate them as suspects."

Anik's mobile rang and he stepped to the side of the room to take the call.

Jack continued, "I'll still track down and interview Julia Lawson and Angela Dunn, but I'd be surprised if they gave me anything different."

Anik bounced to the front of the room.

"Sir!" He beamed. "I expanded the Missing Persons search, like you said, and my mate at Paddington Green nick just called. A lady by the name of Susan Withey reported her estranged husband missing two days ago." Jack went to his desk to examine his notes as Anik continued, "Mike Withey is the same height and build as our murder victim from Rose Cottage. *And* he's an ex-copper from this station."

Ridley unfolded his arms quickly. "Anik, Jack and Laura. My office."

Without another word, he turned on his heels. On his way across the room, Jack got out his mobile and started to search through all the notes connected to this investigation so far.

"Anik," Ridley said calmly, once they were all assembled, "we need to be mindful of those around us when announcing information as potentially volatile as 'the corpse in our mortuary might be that of an ex-copper from this station.' Do you know when Mike retired? Do you even know if he retired? Or was he sacked? Did he work with any one of those officers out there?"

Anik understood his mistake. "I don't know, sir."

"Tell me what you've got."

"That was pretty much it, sir. My mate's sending me all the details now."

Anik got out his mobile, opened his emails and refreshed the app. At the same time, Jack was rifling through his own mobile, trying to find the notes he needed.

"I've heard the name, sir," Jack mumbled. "Mike Withey's already connected to this case somehow, I just can't . . . Bear with me . . ."

Anik was desperate for his email to come through before Jack could steal his moment of glory, willing the page to refresh.

"Ah, right," Jack said finally. "Mike Withey is the son of Audrey Withey and the brother of Shirley Miller, the model shot dead during a diamond raid in '84. That raid was planned and carried out by Harry Rawlins, husband of Dolly Rawlins, who bought The Grange back in '95."

Ridley rocked back in his black leather ergonomic chair and rubbed his eyes. Jack and Anik, both with mobiles in hand, looked at each other. Then at Laura. They all waited for Ridley to finish thinking whatever he was thinking.

"If our murder victim is Mike Withey," Ridley said after some consideration, "we need to tread very carefully indeed. Anik, seeing as this is your information, I want you to come with me to see Susan Withey. We need a DNA sample for comparison."

"Wouldn't Mike's DNA already be on file for elimination purposes?" Anik asked.

Ridley thought his question was logical, even if it was naïve.

"Not if he left before 2006, because it wasn't mandatory till then. Jack and Laura, while Anik's waiting for Susan Withey's home address to come through from his friend at Paddington Green, I'm going to request permission to see Mike Withey's service file. Once I've got that, I want you two, and only you two, to go through it with a finetoothed comb. Until we get a positive ID on the body, Mike Withey is just a person of interest . . . but let's find out a bit more about him. Tread carefully."

Anik's mobile pinged.

"I've got an address for Susan Withey, and one for Audrey Withey."

Ridley picked up his desk phone. "Anik, you'll lead when we arrive at Susan's home. Go and prep how you're going to handle it and you can run it by me in the car."

Anik couldn't believe it. He was going to lead the interview of a case-breaking individual, in the company of his DCI. He almost ran from Ridley's office, completely forgetting to say "Thank you" or "Yes, sir" or anything at all.

"I'll find a private room to view the file, sir," Laura reassured him as she closed Ridley's door behind them.

Jack and Laura sniggered as they followed Anik out.

Ridley pressed the top button on his phone and waited for no more than five seconds before it was answered.

"Ma'am, I need you to authorize the release of an officer's service file."

* * *

Ridley leaned forward in the driver's seat of his BMW and peered through the windscreen. Susan Withey's house was set back from the road at the end of a gated driveway. The gate was open and a white Smart car was tucked almost out of sight under a tree. Anik sat in the passenger's seat, using twice as many words as he needed to.

". . . if they're estranged, I'll ask her for Mike's current address. I'll also ask if Mike has any children and if we can get a sample of their DNA to check against the cremated rem—" Anik checked himself. "I won't refer to the body as cremated remains, obviously."

"Obviously," Ridley murmured.

"If there are no kids, then we'd need DNA from an object such as a hairbrush, or an old hat maybe."

"See how much their house was bought for," Ridley instructed.

The house was in the middle of a long, tree-lined street in Weybridge. Ridley guessed that the purchase price would have been around the £2 million mark and wondered how the hell an ex-copper could have afforded it—unless Susan Withey had been seriously rich before she married Mike. They knew Audrey Withey lived in a tower block in central London because Anik's mate from Paddington Green had told them as much; they knew she was a retired fruit and veg stallholder, from the numerous police interviews she'd given over the years. The main one being when her daughter was murdered. So, it was highly unlikely that the money for this property had come from her.

Anik showed the screen of his mobile to Ridley.

"One point five mill, sir. It's got a double garage, games room and covered swimming pool."

Ridley closed his eyes in momentary, silent despair. Not only was Anik seemingly under the baffling impression that Ridley wanted to buy the house—but Mike Withey paying for a mansion with the proceeds of a train robbery suddenly looked like a possible scenario.

"What will you tell her about the body?" Ridley asked.

"I won't mention the circumstances or condition of the body, sir. It's currently just an unidentified male whose physical description is similar to that of her ex-husband."

Ridley got out the car and headed toward Susan's house. Once he heard Anik's short steps scurrying after him, he locked his BMW.

* * *

Susan was an austerely beautiful woman—calm and almost serene in manner. Ridley thought she seemed like a person who'd seen bad times, but kept her emotions well concealed. Her jogging bottoms sat loosely on her hips and were rolled up once at the waistband; they looked more like Mike's than hers. She wore a tight white tank top over her athletic figure. She wore nothing on her feet and her tiny toenails were painted bright red. Ridley thought she must be in her early fifties, but she looked ten years younger than that. Being single and Mike-free seemed to suit her.

The lounge was minimalist in its décor, with off-white walls, a dark brown wooden floor and white blinds at the windows. No frills, no fuss. Color was introduced by the red embroidered cushions on the white sofa, and the abstract paintings on the walls. Among the paintings were framed pieces of artwork done by a young child or children. It was as though Susan had very kindly surrounded her children's artwork with that of adults who had little additional skill, so that all the paintings looked to be on a par with one other.

Anik carefully and delicately explained that they'd found an unidentified body that *could* possibly be that of her husband. He was tactful, respectful and, although long-winded, he was doing well, Ridley thought.

Susan's imagination, understandably, ran riot.

"How did he die?" she asked, putting her hand to her mouth.

"I'm afraid I can't divulge that at this stage, Mrs. Withey."

Just as Anik started to relax, his eyes fell to a newspaper on the table and the front-page story headlined ARSON AND MURDER IN FORMER POLICE OFFICER'S HOME. His expression immediately gave him away. There was no doubt, if Anik ever played poker, he'd lose his shirt.

"No . . ." she breathed quietly.

She picked up the paper, dropped to the sofa and quickly scanned the article.

Anik looked at Ridley for guidance. Ridley turned away and let him get on with it. He had to learn.

Eventually, Susan spoke. "Is this the case you're investigating?"

Anik had no choice. "Yes."

"Did he . . . ? Did the fire . . . ? Was he alive when . . . ?"

They both knew what she wanted to ask. Ridley took over.

"It's possible, based on physical description, that the body found in Rose Cottage could be your husband. And we are treating the death as murder."

Susan couldn't get her head round why Mike might have been in Rose Cottage in the first place. She couldn't think that he had any connection to the place, and this led her to hope that the poor, unfortunate dead man wasn't her husband at all. Ridley understood that denial is about selfpreservation at times of emotional distress, so he didn't try and dissuade her. From here on, Susan's demeanor became practical as she spoke about Mike as though he was very much alive, and just missing.

"Mike hasn't lived here for almost a year, and he does go AWOL quite often, but he's always in touch with me or the kids every couple of days, even if it's just a text message. That stopped about a week ago, which is why I called you in the first place. I'll write down the addresses of his flat and his office for you. They'll no doubt be in a terrible state, so apologies for that. The office is in a sort of compound shared with other units. There's a warden who can let you in. It was one of the first places I went actually, when Mike stopped texting. The warden hasn't seen him since last Wednesday. I've got a spare key to Mike's flat if you want to go there as well. Please be careful. I mean . . . I don't want him to think he's been burgled."

Whether or not Susan actually still loved Mike wasn't clear but, as she bowed her head and turned her back, it was obvious that the possibility of him being dead was very upsetting.

"Take anything you need," Susan muttered.

And then she jogged up the stairs to fetch Mike's flat keys.

The lounge fell silent. Ridley saw Anik open his mouth at least two or three times to speak, and then think better of it. He was clearly the kind of person who was very uncomfortable with silence; Ridley wanted to train this out of him because police work was more about listening and looking than it was about talking.

"What do you think of the house?" Ridley asked.

"Smart, yeah." Ridley turned to Anik, who instantly knew that his answer had missed the point. Then the penny dropped. "Mike Withey was a DC. I couldn't afford this house in a month of Sundays, so how could he?"

Ridley's slight smile told him that was the right answer.

Susan came back into the lounge carrying a single front door key and two scraps of paper. One was the address of Mike's flat and the other was a scrappy-looking business card with the unimaginative name "Withey Security."

"This is Mike's current mobile number?"

Susan nodded.

Ridley moved and stood in front of a wall of family photos, showing Mike and Susan with two girls at varying ages, from babies to young women.

"Mrs. Withey, in the interest of obtaining a comparative DNA sample for the purpose of identification, the best way would be to get a sample from a child. Would that be possible?"

"The girls don't live here anymore. They're grown. I . . . How would I explain what you're doing? How would I explain why you need it? No, I don't think that's . . . What else can we do?"

"We could use an item, such as a toothbrush . . ."

"Claire's got clothes and toiletries here for when she visits."

Susan left the room slowly, giving herself time to comprehend the magnitude of going to collect an item that would tell the police whether her husband was dead or alive. When she got back, Anik was waiting, evidence bag at the ready, gloves on. Susan dropped the sparkly pink toothbrush into the bag.

"Thanks, Mrs. Withey."

Ridley nodded to Anik, meaning it was back to him to question her about the house.

"You have a lovely home," he started . . . and the information he needed flowed easily from Susan. She wasn't thinking about Mike anymore; she was thinking about her girls and this made her talk without caution.

"Thank you. Audrey sold a villa in Spain some years ago and gave the cash to Mike. I said if he gambled it away, I'd leave him. So, he bought this." Susan shook her head as she remembered how unreliable Mike actually was. "From one extreme to the other. He had no idea what actually mattered to me and the kids. He thought this lovely house would solve all of our problems, but that's all it turned out be in the end—a lovely house. It wasn't ever a family home, regardless of the pictures on the wall. Nothing more than a façade."

"I'd suggest you don't tell Audrey that we've been to see you. Let's do the DNA test first," Anik suggested.

"She knows he's missing, but . . . Well, it's not unusual for Mike to go off for a while so she'll not be worried yet. She's concerned— but not 'worried,' you know."

"I know you mentioned that the text messages stopped but . . . was that the only reason for you reporting him missing this time?"

Ridley noted how Anik was starting to question intuitively.

"He'd been distracted. I assumed it was by work, or the lack of work. I don't know. He'd been . . . off. Mike wasn't the deepest of people so he was easy to read. Something had been wrong for a while."

The conversation was rounded off by Ridley asking the harder questions. Questions he knew Anik wouldn't think of.

"Mrs. Withey, could you tell me if Mike still wore his wedding ring?" And then came the biggie. "And do you have the contact details for his dentist, please?"

A single tear rolled down Susan's shocked face. The burnt body, whoever he was, wasn't visually identifiable.

*   *   *

Back at the station, Jack and Laura were huddled round the same desk in a small, rarely used break room. There was an ancient, unplugged coffee machine in the corner, which was why Laura had requested an urn of hot water, sachets of tea and coffee, disposable cups and a selection of biscuits.

Mike's extensive personnel file was scattered all over the table and Jack was randomly showering each sheet of paper with biscuit crumbs as he read. As Jack leaned forward, reading intensely while devouring a chocolate Bourbon, Laura sat back sipping her tea. Their knees just about met underneath the narrow table, and all of Laura's senses focused on the tiny area of skin at the tip of her knee that brushed against the tip of Jack's.

"Do you think he knew Norma?" Jack asked, snapping Laura out of her trance.

"I can't see how he could have. Mike was Met, she was Thames Valley. Their paths could have crossed on a security detail in London maybe, 'cos her mounted division was brought down for large events." Laura set aside her teacup and leaned forward across the table. If Jack looked up now, their noses would almost be touching. "But there's no record of their teams being on the same detail for anything."

"He was liked and respected for the majority of his career. Never reported. Never disciplined. Until 1995, when he was hauled over the coals for not revealing a personal connection to a case he was working on.

"The case was the retrieval of the stolen diamonds. Mike gave his boss, DCI Craigh, a tip-off that Dolly Rawlins knew where the diamonds were, and that she was going after them when she was released from prison. Turned out to be a load of crap, and the tip was nothing more than Mike's hunch based on his hatred of Dolly Rawlins. He blamed her for the death of his sister, Shirley, and wanted to see her back inside. Mike retired at the beginning of the following year." Jack let his hands and the sheet of paper drop heavily into his lap. "We're coming in late on what look like some very old scores being settled here, you know. Our 2019 arson and murder is linked to a 1995 train robbery and the murder of Dolly Rawlins, which is linked to a 1984 diamond robbery and the murder of Harry Rawlins. I just don't know how."

"Well, I've got enough to show that Mike's probably definitely dodgy."

"Probably, definitely? Ridley'll love that." Jack laughed.

"His phone records show that, in recent months, he's been in contact with his mum, his ex-wife, a guy called Barry Cooper and . . . wait for it . . . a burner phone."

Laura held her hand up, palm toward Jack and he high-fived her, ending with laced fingers.

"Definitely dodgy."

Jack stood up and headed off to make two celebratory cups of tea.

When Jack first arrived at the Met, Laura had thought he was moody and standoffish but once they became partners, she began to really like him. He was naturally tactile and, somewhere along the line, she'd become confused by that. She knew he was with Maggie, but she also knew that affairs happened all the time in stressful, potentially violent jobs. It was the uncontrollable adrenaline, the heart pounding, fight or flight situations, it was knowing that your life was in someone else's hands. Jack turned to her.

"Bourbon?"

Even mumbling through a half-eaten biscuit, Laura thought his mouth looked lovely.

Tea and biscuits were put on hold when Ridley called Jack's mobile and instructed them both to go and search Mike's place of work. There was a search warrant waiting for them to collect at the court building.

* * *

Withey Security was nothing more than a run-down modular office trailer in the middle of a gated lot. Fourteen such trailers occupied the space, overseen by an ancient warden who was key-holder to them all. The warden stepped into his own trailer to find the keys to Mike's. This trailer was more like a caravan, complete with a small TV, a tatty armchair that looked as if it had been re-covered several times, a three-shelf bookcase, and a selection of yachting magazines to pander to the warden's daydreams. A half-eaten packed lunch sat on top of a miniature fridge and there was a bowl of children's sweets on a salvaged coffee table. The bowl of sweets was momentarily confusing, until Jack saw the photos pinned to a wooden noticeboard. The warden had a football team of grandkids.

While the warden searched for the key that unlocked the box of keys bolted to the wall, Jack couldn't help but focus on a large hole in the top of the right arm of the tatty armchair. He quickly decided that this hole had been made by hundreds of beer bottles sitting in exactly the same spot, over decades of TV watching. Through the uppermost, flowery cover on the armchair, Jack could see snippets of all of the previous coverings—a couple of velour patterns, fake suede, tartan, monochrome stripes, solid black—years of wear and tear that mapped this man's life. Jack swore he could actually guess the moment that the warden started living with the woman he loved; that move from fake suede to velour was a declaration of his life-long commitment to her.

Laura watched Jack as he longingly stared, all gooey-eyed, into the trailer.

"*That's* what separates men from women," Laura whispered. "You see a man cave—I see a shithole."

As the warden led the way to Mike's trailer, Jack could see he had something seriously wrong with his lower back. He stooped almost in half and paused every now and then to look up and see exactly where he was heading. Jack had offered to just take the key and unlock it himself, but the warden had insisted on escorting them to the door because he took his job very seriously and refused to allow any keys out of his sight. As they progressed at a snail's pace, Jack got some background information.

"How long's Mike Withey had this office?"

"Since 2003." The warden had a surprisingly high voice with a North London accent. "Business took a serious dip in the 2008 recession and I hardly saw any of these businesses for almost a year. Mike still kept his partner on, mind—didn't lay him off or anything like that. I think they go way back." Jack was just about to ask about Mike's partner when the warden continued, unable to see Jack's expression because his eyes were turned down toward the ground. "Barry Cooper, his name is. Nice and easy to remember, 'cos of the legend that is Gary Cooper. Barry's been with Mike from the beginning. They're not partners, strictly speaking. Mike employs Barry, but they're clearly friends on account of the number of empty bottles I clear out of their bin. Proper boozers, both of them. Whisky's their go-to drink, and cheap crap it is an' all."

The Yale lock on Mike's trailer, and the wood on the door surrounding it, were both scratched from where the warden repeatedly missed the keyhole. Laura was pulling her hair out as he missed the lock with the key, time and time again. Once the door was open, he backed off, perched on the edge of a stack of tires and waited.

* * *

Across London, Anik was feigning composure as he instructed a uniformed PC on how the search of Mike's flat was going to go and what they were looking for. Ridley had gone back to the station, leaving Anik with this weighty responsibility. He waved the search warrant round ostentatiously and was a little bit disappointed that he had no one to actually serve it to.

Mike's flat was a typical, grubby-looking bachelor pad in dire need of a very deep clean. The carpet was worn thin in a T-shaped pattern, showing that Mike walked most frequently from the kitchen, to his favorite armchair, to his bureau. The bureau was stuffed full of paperwork in no kind of order—bills, bank statements, ownership documents for a Range Rover and some payslips for Barry. This bureau gave Anik two vitally important pieces of information— Barry's mobile phone number, and the only vehicle registered in his name.

Mike's expendable cash each month amounted to nothing more than pocket money which, judging by the four empty whisky bottles down the side of his armchair, was mainly spent on booze. There was a block of several years when Mike's bank transactions occurred in Spain rather than in the UK, so that was presumably where he was living.

The uniformed PC entered the lounge, holding an evidence bag containing an obviously well-used toothbrush with splayed bristles. Anik nodded his approval at the toothbrush being an appropriate DNA source.

"Can you also bag all of this paperwork, please?" Anik requested, waving his arm vaguely over the bureau before heading toward the kitchen.

As he left the lounge, he grinned to himself. He thought he sounded just like Ridley—authoritative, commanding, intelligent. Ridley was exactly the kind of copper Anik aspired to be. He wanted nothing more than to be able to dish out an order and then walk away from his subordinates, knowing that they'd do as he asked out of total respect . . . so it was a good job he didn't turn around or he would have seen the PC, who was twice Anik's age, making a "wanker" motion with his hand.

Anik knew Mike's kitchen would probably be grubby, seeing as they were now nine days into the investigation, but the food in the fridge was way older than that. He gagged as he opened the fridge door and the smell of the cheesy milk hit his nostrils. In addition to the milk, there was a heavily sprouting red onion, half a bottle of white wine, several bottles of beer and a leaking breast of chicken in an open food bag.

The sink was piled high with dirty mugs, each patterned on the inside with several brown rings of varying shades, dating back weeks. Mike definitely wasn't a man who could survive for long living alone. He needed to be looked after.

As Anik progressed through the flat, each room was a different degree of filth. There were no surprises and definitely no hidden millions. Less than one hour later, the tiny, one-bedroomed flat had been searched from top to bottom. Anik's final instruction to the PC was to bag all of Mike's shoes, so that their treads could be compared to any footprints found at Rose Cottage.

Then he bellowed, Ridley-style, "I'll be in the car!" and left.

Once on the pavement outside Mike's flat, he realized that "I'll be in the car!" would have been a far more impressive exit if he was the driver and actually had the car keys.

*　*　*

Mike's trailer office contained a gray metal desk with three drawers, a gray metal filing cabinet, two fake leather office chairs and a plastic yucca plant. The desk drawers were pretty much empty apart from the proverbial half-bottle of cheap whisky and two glasses. There was also a chewed pen lid and some paper clips, but nothing else.

Jack flicked through a desk diary, while Laura leafed through files in the cabinet.

"These are all clients. Low-end security, mainly night shifts. There's a packing factory, a private hospital, a bit of door work. Nothing exciting. His last few jobs might be worth a look into—see if they could have got him into trouble with anyone."

In the bottom drawer of the filing cabinet was a grubby old sleeping bag.

"He sleeps here sometimes."

Laura stepped outside. Round the back of the trailer was a set of deep, wide tire tracks.

"Excuse me!" she shouted to the warden.

"Range Rover," he said before she could ask. "Second-hand's my guess, 'cos new you'd be talking fifty or sixty thousand and Mr. Withey didn't have that. It sometimes sat back there all night, which isn't strictly allowed but I assumed he'd had another row with the missus and they both needed a little bit of space, so I let it go."

Laura smiled her thanks and stepped back inside Mike's Portakabin.

"He's on the ball for an old fella." She sat on the edge of the metal desk, facing Jack. "No laptop. You think he never had one or did he just work from his mobile?"

"This diary's mainly work related," Jack mused. "When he writes down jobs, he includes a lot of detail. Full names, addresses, phone numbers, an outline of what's needed. Which makes other pages with less detail stand out as maybe hiding something. On the day of the fire, he's written 'RC. 2am. Del.' RC could be Rose Cottage. Who do we think Del is?"

Jack's mobile pinged and a text message from Anik popped up. Jack read it out.

"No laptop at the flat. Must be there." Jack quickly typed something back and waited for the ping. "Anik says it's all paperwork at the flat. So I don't think Mike's got a laptop."

From nowhere, Laura suddenly got all personal.

"How's your dad?"

Jack suddenly felt very guilty for having not thought about Charlie all day, but he definitely didn't want to have a conversation about him now.

"He's going how he wants to go."

Laura put her hand on Jack's arm, looked deep into his eyes, gave him a sympathetic tilt of the head . . . but said nothing. He wondered what she wanted him to do—smile? Cry? Ask for a hug? Not knowing how else to get out of having an unwanted emotional exchange, Jack stood, scooping Mike's diary up and moving away from Laura.

"Is this all we're taking?" he asked.

He knew he'd been rude, but if he wanted a heart-to-heart about losing his dad, it would be with Maggie. He didn't know how to explain that, so walking away was actually the most polite response he could think of.

Outside, the warden still sat on the stack of tires with his head dipped and Jack couldn't tell if he was sleeping until he heard, "Ready for off?"

Jack and Laura thanked him for his time, made sure that they could return if and when the identification of Sheila was confirmed, and left Mike's sparse office in the warden's shaky, but otherwise very capable hands. By the time they had walked back to their car, the warden was still trying to get the key in the door of Mike's trailer to lock it.

"Sorry for making you feel uncomfortable," Laura said.

Jack didn't know what she was talking about. He stared at her, racking his brain, before deciding that she must be referring to when she put her hand on his arm. He shrugged and smiled a tight, fake smile.

"I wasn't uncomfortable. I just thought we'd finished."

* * *

When Anik returned to the station, the accompanying PC was carrying nine bagged and tagged pairs of shoes to compare to the footprints found at Rose Cottage. Five came from Mike's flat, and a further four from Barry's flat, which they'd also received permission to search.

Barry had not only been out, but his neighbors had confirmed that he hadn't been seen for just over a week, approximately the same length of time as Mike.

Today had been hugely productive with regards to information about Mike and, although the DNA comparison between the bone marrow and the toothbrush would take between twelve and twentyfour hours to process, most of the officers on Ridley's team now suspected that their murder victim from Rose Cottage was, in fact, Mike Withey. But Ridley knew that by answering the question of identity, a thousand more questions would need to be asked.

Why was Mike Withey in Rose Cottage? Did he know about, or was he involved in, the train robbery? Or did he stumble across the hidden money years later? Then the biggest of all the questions . . . who killed him? Ridley took Mike's personnel file into his office and shut his door.

He pored over Mike's file during this pause in the investigation, while they waited for DNA results. But he didn't look at Mike's case reports, as Jack and Laura had done. He looked at Craigh's. Craigh had been Mike's DI; therefore Ridley knew how his reports should have been written, so he was looking for anything out of the ordinary. Sure enough, around the time of the wrongful raid in search of weapons at The Grange, Craigh's reports started to feel clumsy. They lacked detail or seemed incomplete and Mike's name was often omitted altogether, making Ridley wonder if this was an attempt to distance him from the case. The information that led to the gun raid had come from Mike and was, after all, bogus. Maybe Craigh was protecting his own reputation by distancing himself from Mike? Mike's personal vendetta against Dolly Rawlins certainly seemed to have influenced his actions and—in Ridley's opinion—Craigh was covering his back.

The biggest alarm bell for Ridley was that Mike had retired from the police force eight months after the train robbery, spent some time in Spain and acquired enough money from the sale of a villa to buy a massive mansion in Weybridge. Or did he? Did Audrey's villa sale make anywhere near enough for Mike to buy his £1.5 million house, or did he have money from some other source to make up the shortfall?

From his desk, Ridley could see the two crammed evidence boards in the squad room, and all the faces and names that had so far been connected to one or more crimes dating back as far as 1984.

Did Mike Withey know Norma Walker? And, regardless of Bill Thorn's saintly opinion of her, was Norma the mounted rider who stopped the train on the night it was robbed? Did Mike help her? Did Barry? It certainly seemed far more likely that people with an inside knowledge of police procedure robbed the train, than a bunch of women setting up a children's home, even if they were ex-cons. Once Ridley had got his head around everything, he stepped back out into the squad room with his instructions.

"Anik, go back and speak to Susan Withey. I want a detailed timeline of every move her husband made, from the moment he left the force to the day she reported him missing. And I want to know how much they paid for their house and how much Audrey got from the sale of the villa. Jack, find out everything you can about Mike's family—Audrey, Shirley, and there's a younger brother, Greg. And find those missing women from The Grange."

The pace of this investigation had now increased—from this moment forward, Ridley knew that every little detail would have to be nailed down before he went to the Super accusing a possibly dead ex-copper of committing the biggest train robbery in UK history.

CHAPTER 13

Jack and Maggie sat unnaturally close on their sofa, champagne glasses in hand, fixed grins on their faces, staring at the open laptop on the coffee table in front of them. It was eleven o'clock. Jack wore a nicely ironed shirt, Maggie wore a smart blouse, as though they were going out to a smart dinner party—and both wore pajama bottoms. Their image in the top right-hand corner of the screen deliberately showed them from the waist up. Eventually the word "connecting" disappeared from the center of the screen.

"Hello, darling!"

Penny's overly excited voice crackled through the laptop speakers and Jack's head sank in momentary despair as Penny launched into her obviously rehearsed chatter.

"Mum! Mum, click the camera! Dad! We can hear you, but we can't see you. Click on the little icon thing that looks like a video camera!" Jack and Maggie could hear Penny and Charlie having a mumbled conversation, before their faces finally appeared on screen. "We can see you now!"

All four of them raised their glasses and said "Cheers."

Maggie and Charlie looked like typical Brits abroad—they had bright, shiny pink faces and looked drunk. Charlie's shirt was open down to his belly button, showing off his abundance of gray hairs that looked ten times grayer against his pink chest. Penny wore a halterneck dress but had clearly been wearing a spaghetti strap tank top throughout the day, so now her shoulders were an array of pink and white stripes. Jack couldn't stop grinning as she went on and on about what they'd been up to.

"Madeira has the most wonderful food, Jack, Maggie would love it. We've seen whales and dolphins, haven't we, love? And it's ever so green considering the heat. We're in Funchal—have you been to Funchal? It's Europe's most picturesque and cleanest capital, according to the guide books. It's famous for pirates. And do you know who was born here? Guess, Jack. Go on."

"No idea, Mum," Jack lied.

"Cristiano Ronaldo!"

Jack and Maggie stifled a giggle and sipped their champagne as Penny continued with her various tales of beautiful gardens, long beach walks, the thrill of eating at eleven o'clock each night and drinking cocktails with fruit perched on the rim of the glass. And all the while, Charlie watched every move that she made, listened to every word and laughed at every single terrible attempt at a joke. He was exactly where he wanted to be and Jack knew it. He almost cried because his parents looked so incredibly happy. His relief was palpable.

* * *

At ten o'clock the next morning, Jack was being frisked by prison guards on his way into Pentonville to see Tony Fisher. Tony and all of the other inmates wore yellow smocks to distinguish them from the visitors—not that that was really required. The cons in this wing were the kind of men you'd cross the road to avoid just because of how they looked.

Tony walked toward Jack with a scowl on his face that said *You'd better be worth getting out of bed for, boy.*

When he sat down, he didn't bother pulling in his chair and getting comfortable, suggesting that he had no intention of staying.

He had a natural sneer and, for 75 years old, he was still a frightening man. He had a split lip, a cut just beneath his left eye and a small wound to his neck, which Jack assumed was where his young assailant had tried to cut his throat. Tony was bigger than Jack, stockier and far more intimidating—and he knew it. Tony stared, motionless and silent. If Jack didn't speak within the next couple of seconds, he had the feeling Tony would get bored and leave.

"Thank you for agreeing to see me, Mr. Fisher. I appreciate it."

Jack knew that a man with such a big ego would prefer to be treated with respect, even if it was fake.

"I don't give a fuck," Tony growled.

Jack couldn't help but smile, because he sounded exactly like the impression of a stereotypical East End gangster Jack had done for Laura.

"I'd like to talk to you about the Witheys. If you don't mind." Tony's face softened just marginally and he scraped his chair under the table; he was staying after all. He grinned, showing his short, worn, yellowed teeth with blackened lines round the gums.

"I'll talk to you about Shirl. I'll talk to you about her all day long. She was proper tasty and fancied me something rotten. Great tits that just fit into the palm of your hand. Big blue eyes with zero brain behind them. Perfect woman in my books. She was a model, ya know. Pretended to be prim and proper but she was just a council slag underneath all that make-up and fancy hairdo. I reckon she saw me as her ticket out of there and to something better. I owned half of Soho back in the day."

Jack pandered to Tony's ego again by revealing everything he knew all about the Fisher brothers' social standing back in the eighties. It had been comparatively impressive; they were very well respected in the criminal hierarchy *and* they normally stayed one step ahead of the police, so Tony actually had a lot to be proud of.

"The rest of the family? Greg was a twat," he suddenly blurted out, so he'd obviously been thinking about the rest of the Withey family while Jack was talking. "Drugs and all that crap. Made him thicker than Shirl. And Audrey . . . Jesus Christ! She was an ugly cow. How she produced a stunner like Shirl, I'll never know."

"Did you know Mike Withey?"

"Not for long. He was a bugger when he was a kid, then he went into the army, which turned him into a pussy. People think the army turns boys into men, but it don't. It makes pussies who can follow orders, but who can't think for themselves. That ain't got nothing to do with being a man in the real world—that's institutionalization, that is. And there's no fucking point in being able to kill a man with your bare hands if you're not allowed to actually do it. Nah, the only thing Mike could have been when he came back from the army was a copper—from one bunch of sheep to another. No offense," he added with a grin. Oddly, Jack agreed. "My path never crossed with Mike's in a professional capacity, you understand. He came to the club a couple times, Shirl told me bits about him, then there was gossip from people he was into for a couple of grand. Mike Withey had one foot in your world and one foot in mine. He never quite had the balls to be bent, but he was definitely flexible, if you know what I mean."

Once Jack had asked all the questions he needed to about the Witheys, he moved on to his own investigation.

"I spoke to a bloke the other day who suggested that you might have known Jimmy Nunn."

Tony immediately wanted to know who had mentioned his name, and Jack thought there would be no harm in revealing that it was Kenneth Moore. He explained that Ken knew the Fisher brothers by reputation and had "great things to say." This seemed to placate Tony enough for him to answer.

"Jimmy Nunn was thick as pig shit," he said. "Best wheels man in the business though. How come you're asking about Jimmy Nunn? He ain't been seen for donkey's years. His missus pegged it, I know that. She was a proper slag—the only man I knew that never had her was my brother, and that's 'cos he was bent."

Jack had no memory of Trudie and he'd already heard bad things about her from his Aunt Fran, but to hear scum like Tony Fisher slagging her off in such a horrific way was more than he was prepared to listen to. An uncharacteristic temper began to boil up inside him which, for now, he kept a lid on because there was more he needed to know.

"Trudie would come to the club and hang around the biggest wallets till one of them took her home. If it was a quiet night and she got no takers, she'd wait around for me to finish work and we'd take a bottle of something up into Arnie's office. He had a great big leather sofa, but she liked me to shag her on his overpriced, antique, French-polished, poncey fucking desk. It was his pride and joy—he'd say, 'Don't touch my desk with your filthy hands.' And I'd think, 'I ain't, bruv, but Trudie Nunn's been all over it with her filthy arse!' *Ha!* He had no idea! God, I ain't thought about Trudie Nunn in years." And with that image in his mind, Tony grabbed his groin and left his hand there until the memory passed. "What a bleedin' shame she's dead. A visit from good old Trudie would go down a treat right now."

If looks could kill, Tony would have fallen stone dead right there in front of all the prison guards. As Tony grinned his horrific psychopathic grin, Jack glanced down at his own hands in his lap—his fists clenched tight and his knuckles white. He was filled with a simmering rage that he'd never felt before.

"And Jimmy Nunn . . ." Tony went on, oblivious to what was going on in Jack's mind. "The last time I heard Jimmy's name mentioned was in connection to that armed raid on a security van in the Strand underpass. That was one of Harry Rawlins's fuck-ups." He bellowed laughing. "Harry bloomin' Rawlins! I'd never seen my brother so overjoyed to see someone put six feet under. He spent a fucking fortune on the wreath." Tony mimed the size of it with his hands, then went on to explain how every criminal in London had felt the same way as Arnie did. "Harry Rawlins was the only man who could make my brother nervous. He'd never been arrested for so much as a parking ticket but, Jesus Christ, he was like an octopus with tentacles in everyone's business. There was nothing that man didn't know about the criminal world, and *that's* what made him so dangerous. If you'd ever worked for the son of a bitch, you'd never be safe again."

Jack really wanted to hear more about Jimmy, but Tony seemed determined to continue talking about himself and Arnie.

"My brother was a bit of an art expert—fenced loads of paintings for Harry over the years. That was his mistake. Like I just said, once you was involved with Harry, he had you by the balls. 'Cos if he went down, so did you. I never met the man personally, on account of him always doing business with the organ grinder and not the monkey—that's what he called me, the cheeky bastard. A 'monkey.' Fuck him! The newspapers made out Harry's funeral as being half of London paying their respects . . . It wasn't. They were making fucking sure the bastard was dead. Criminals *and* coppers. And we were all wrong!"

In a flash, Jack's mind leapt from the hatred he felt for Tony to an overdue penny finally dropping . . . *If Harry Rawlins was shot to death by his wife in the autumn of 1985—who did Tony and half of London watch being buried approximately nine months earlier?*

Tony was *still* talking—having a whale of a time—but at least he was back on topic now.

"Jimmy Nunn was a fucking nobody who did what he was paid to and then kept his head down, spending his cut on women and cars till the next job came along. So, I'll tell you something for nothing, DC whatever-you-said-your-name-was—if Jimmy's still got his head down after, what, thirty-somefink years, then he took one hell of a cut from his last job."

"You think he's got his feet up somewhere?"

"If there's one thing Jimmy Nunn was good at, it was running away. He was there for a good time, not a long time . . . as they say. He'd do a caper, then disappear. He'd do a bird, then disappear. I mean, if Trudie was mine—full-time I mean—I wouldn't have left her."

Jack noted Tony's last comment about Jimmy Nunn probably being on the run with a load of cash. But, as he stared at Tony, he could also see the very second that the dirty old man's mind strayed back to the good ol' days of shagging Trudie on his brother's French-polished desk. Jack's nostrils flared and his eyebrows dipped.

"Somefink I said?" Tony grinned. Jack pushed his chair away from the table and stood up. "Don't go yet, son. We're having a nice chat, ain't we?"

Jack paused. "I hear the man who attacked you is recovering well."

His tone was now very different. The sucking-up had stopped, the pandering to Tony's ego had stopped and he was suddenly playing a different game. Tony could feel the change in mood, although he didn't know what had brought it on.

"I also hear that you're on a warning. One more bit of trouble and you'll get a nice, long stint in solitary." Jack placed his fists squarely on the table, looked Tony straight in the eye and whispered, "I'm going to make sure you die in here. No one looked up to you then and no one looks up to you now—as Harry Rawlins said, you're just a big, stupid ape."

Jack waited for the second Tony's brain disengaged and animal instinct took over. It didn't take long. Tony leapt to his feet, dodged round the table and charged. Jack, being thirty years his junior, dodged his incoming fist with relative ease; but Tony swung again and again. He was strong and relentless but Jack was fast and that's all that mattered, because all he had to do was stay out the way. The alarms sounded within seconds and all of the other inmates started cheering for Tony. The guards ran across the room, Asps extended, and landed a couple blows on Tony's back but he didn't even flinch. The next three hits landed on his thighs and they took him to the floor. Once he was down, there was no getting up. With his face pressed against the cold blue lino, Tony spat out every threat he could think of while Jack walked calmly from the room.

* * *

In the incident statement Jack was asked to write, he neglected to mention that he'd called Tony an ape, and instead made something

up about bringing up the wrong person from Tony's past and stirring bad memories.

"He's got quite a temper, hasn't he?" Jack said innocently.

The prison warder reassured Jack that Tony would have plenty
of time to think about his actions in solitary confinement. Jack was
then given back his mobile, his wallet and his warrant card, and
he left.

Once outside the prison, he checked his phone. There was one
missed call from Ridley, with an accompanying voicemail asking
if he'd found Julia Lawson and Angela Dunn yet. *Shit!* Jack hadn't
even started looking.

CHAPTER 14

Jack sat at his desk with his trouser leg pulled up to just below his knee. When stumbling backward in an attempt to stay an arm's length away from Tony Fisher, he'd banged his calf on something and now a large bruise was forming. He could feel it as he'd walked up the station stairs and now, as he looked at the purplish-black circle on his skin, it reminded him of the satisfaction he felt in seeing Tony face down on the floor. It was as much of a power rush now as it had been at the time. Jack was by no means a violent man, but he loved the feeling of manipulating a thick shit like Tony Fisher into securing himself a stint in solitary confinement. It was the first cruel thing Jack had ever done in his life, but he felt no guilt.

Two hours and several cups of tea later, Jack sat plowing through the extensive police files on Harry Rawlins. Rawlins's actual file was surprisingly thin because he was too smart to be tied to most of his suspected crimes; it was the unproven files that were extensive. George Resnick had collated hundreds of case reports which, if they were all accurate, showed Harry Rawlins to have been one of the most prolific gangsters of the 1980s. No wonder Resnick had been like a dog with a bone—Rawlins would have been the catch of the century.

Jack flicked through the crime scene photos of the explosive Strand underpass robbery from 1984. Joe Pirelli and Terry Miller had been in the back of the van when it burst into flames. Pirelli had been identified from his dental records, as his hands were never found and he couldn't be printed. Miller was identified from a partial thumb and forefinger print from what remained of his left hand. And "Rawlins," assumed to have been the driver, was blown sky-high. All forensically identifiable parts of his body were too badly damaged to be of any use. However, a cadaver dog had eventually found a charred left forearm about seven feet from the van, not belonging to either Pirelli or Miller. This arm wore a gold Rolex watch with the inscription To Harry—Love Dolly—2/12/62. And so the mangled, unidentifiable third body—missing its head, both legs and one arm—was documented as belonging to Harry Rawlins.

Jack looked at the images showing this mammoth jigsaw puzzle of body parts. He understood why 1980s forensics had identified this man as Harry Rawlins—but the fact remained that Rawlins had been shot to death by his wife several months later, so the third man in the Strand underpass robbery actually remained unidentified. It could be one of a dozen known criminals from the time. It could even be Jimmy Nunn. Jack sighed heavily as he weighed up the possibilities. His birth dad could be in a thousand pieces, wrongly buried in place of Harry Rawlins back in 1984, or he could be hiding out on some paradise island spending stolen money. Maybe even the money from the train robbery. Jack couldn't decide which discovery would be more disappointing. Then again, neither might be true.

* * *

Jack woke at five o'clock in the morning. His body had molded into the shape of his desk chair, so for a good few minutes he had to sit motionless, waiting for the blood to start circulating back into his extremities. Jack stared at his computer screen—once again, he'd spent police time and used the police databases to research his own paternity case. If he was caught, he'd be sacked for gross misconduct, but that seemed to encourage him rather than anything else. He was working smart for the first time in a long time and it made him feel good.

The showers in the station reeked of lemon-scented bleach; the cleaners had been working into the early hours too. Jack watched the mass of shampoo suds slowly spiral down the drain and replayed the events of the previous day in his head. There were two key memories—Tony Fisher's face being squashed into the blue lino by four prison guards . . . and Ridley asking if he'd found Angela and Julia yet. One memory made him grin with a new-found sadistic thrill; the other made him turn the shower off and race back to his computer.

* * *

"Ester Freeman said that Julia Lawson would be in a gutter or a morgue somewhere," Jack announced to the attentive squad room.

Ridley stood in his office doorway leaning against the frame, arms folded, unblinking. He was like one of those paintings whose eyes follow you round the room. Since this investigation began, he had mainly communicated with Jack via voicemail—which Ridley hated. Jack knew that by the time he'd finished speaking, he'd need a damn good excuse for missing yet another one of Ridley's phone calls yesterday—and "I was in Pentonville, without your clearance, asking Tony Fisher about my birth dad" definitely wouldn't cut it.

It was a good job he was now redeeming himself by having solid leads on Julia and Angela.

"It seems Julia kept a low profile running a children's home. Most of the kids she cares for are in trouble with one or both sides of the law, so she doesn't advertise what she does. She registered as a safe house with the Manchester force, and she takes in the kids of parents who choose rehab programs instead of prison. And Angela Dunn got married, but didn't change her name. I have addresses for both of them now."

Behind Jack, the two evidence boards were almost full. They spanned 1984 to 2019, and the face of Tony Fisher had been added since the last time Ridley was in the office.

"Good work, Jack. And I'm glad you weren't injured when Tony Fisher attacked you."

Jack felt his face flush. From the corner of his eye, he saw a flicker of concern on Laura's face, but he didn't take his eyes off Ridley. Jack couldn't believe that Ridley knew where he'd been all along and had never said a word. Within seconds, it became clear that he wasn't going to elaborate—he just wanted Jack to know that nothing got past him.

As Jack's face slowly cooled down, he continued.

"You requested that I find out more about the Witheys, sir. Tony knew them all back in the day."

He told the squad room about Shirley and Greg, and how he'd decided that neither was of great relevance to this investigation. He also told them that Audrey Withey might well have known all the big players vicariously through her children, and that she probably couldn't be trusted.

Ridley waited until Jack had finished.

"Remember, Audrey must be kept in the dark about the corpse until a positive ID has been made. Now, write up all your notes from your visit with Tony Fisher, before you head off to Chester to interview Julia Lawson."

* * *

Sam, who'd just been delivered to Julia by the police and a social worker, was eight years old, with a face that bore witness to a life-time of horrors. In his soul, he was already a man—a hardened, streetsmart, thick-skinned, scowling man. His fists were clenched, his shoulders were tight and his jaw was pushed forward. He was fearless as he stood there, fully prepared to be slapped or punched or locked in a cupboard. What Sam was not prepared for was . . . Julia.

"I'm having cake for lunch," she said cheerfully.

She headed into the kitchen, leaving Sam in the hallway to either follow or not. The back door, directly behind him, was open and children played in the small, fenced-off garden. He was free to run if he wanted to.

Sam stood by the kitchen table, watching Julia cut a huge slice of chocolate cake and put it on a dinner plate. She surrounded it with two scoops of ice cream, added a spoon and put it on the table.

"Don't wait for me." She smiled.

Sam was in the chair before she'd finished speaking, scooping up a huge spoonful of cake and ice cream.

"I ain't fucking staying," he grunted as he stuffed his face.

Julia lifted herself onto the kitchen top and waited for the kettle to boil.

"I bet you ten quid you fucking do."

* * *

In London, on the third floor of a high-rise flat in Ladbroke Grove, Angela Dunn sat, legs crossed, on her corner sofa surrounded by fabrics and sewing material. Underneath the window was a sewing machine and, to the side of that, were dozens and dozens of transparent plastic boxes, stacked ceiling-high. Each box had a client name written on the outside and each was filled with multicolored fabrics, lace, buttons, cottons and various other embellishments. Angela had been a self-employed seamstress for more than ten years and she got enough work from her immediate community to keep her busy till her dying day. The wall behind the sofa was papered with family photos, so that not a square inch of wall could be seen. A vehicle horn musically blared three times and Angela raced down into the courtyard.

Rob was a hefty, muscular Jamaican man in his early fifties. His speckled gray beard and tightly cropped hair made him look like a tough nut but, as Angela's arms crept round his boxy waist, he smiled the broadest of smiles, revealing the gold cap on his left lateral incisor, his eyes wrinkled, his face softened and the gentle giant appeared. Angela moved round Rob's body without letting go, sliding underneath his armpit until she was by his side and his arm was round her shoulder. They looked at the second-hand bus he'd just driven back from the monthly auction in Wimbledon. Rob's voice was gruff, like that of a lifetime smoker, despite the fact that he'd never taken a single drag.

"The tires are solid. Seals on the fuel pump are a bit dodgy and the battery needs replacing. It overheated a couple of times on the way back, so the cooling system wants an overhaul. It needs some new bulbs for the brake lights and left indicator. And there's a horrible smell coming from the air con. Plus the spark plugs make her misfire every now and then—"

Angela asked the only question she cared about. "How many seats?"

"25," Rob confirmed.

"It's perfect, Rob! I'll call the girls and get things moving."

Rob paused the conversation to kiss Angela, long and tender. He loved the very bones of her and she adored him. Angela had had her share of useless men and when she found Rob she spared no time in telling him, straight out, that she'd do anything for him as long as he treated her right. Since then, they'd been totally devoted to each other.

"So, the SUV—" Rob stopped Angela mid-sentence with a peck on the lips.

"You've asked me this a dozen times."

Angela smiled, her beautiful brown eyes asking him to humor her one more time.

"The Chevy Suburban was delivered to Amsterdam yesterday morning, collected and driven to the hotel in Düsseldorf by Julia's lad and put round the back in the bus parking where, lo and behold, the CCTV don't work too well. So, as long as you're sure the lad's trustworthy, we're sound as a pound."

Julia's "lad" had been in Angela's care and, fifteen years ago, she'd saved his life when he slit his wrists. He'd been systematically abused by his family since birth and he finally snapped. When a boy like that finally meets an adult to love him, his gratefulness knows no bounds. Angela was confident that Julia's "lad" would kill for her, so hiding a car for her would be a doddle.

Jack was using his mobile phone torch to see the writing on the gravestones in the otherwise dark churchyard. As he moved through the beautifully kept grass, he hated the fact that Charlie popped into his head—a well-kept plot would be important to him. Jack thought about the cemetery just up the road from his mum and dad's bungalow in Totnes. It was on a hillside overlooking the sea and Jack used to shortcut through it to and from school— he and the lads would pause on one of the numerous benches to drink cider and smoke tabs. It hadn't felt disrespectful or naughty; it had felt fine. As though the residents really wouldn't mind them being there. Unlike tonight ... Tonight Jack felt very disrespect- ful, traipsing over grave after grave trying to find the name he was looking for.

Just then, a second torch light joined Jack's—but this one was bigger, brighter and was being held by a broad Glaswegian.

"Who you looking for?"

Jack couldn't see the man behind the light as his beam was blinding. He could, however, just make out that he was holding a round-head shovel over his right shoulder. Jack immediately got his warrant card from his pocket and held it in the light.

"I'm from the Met," Jack said. "Sorry if I'm not meant to be here. The gate was open."

The Glaswegian dipped his torch. He was a small man, wiry, young, tattooed to the hilt.

"Who you looking for?" he repeated.

"Harry Rawlins."

The Glaswegian started to walk away, so Jack followed.

"Ya drugs polis? I was nicked three years ago for intent to supply. Best thing that ever happened to me. Got put here for ninety
days of payback, picking up litter and dog shit—do you know how
many people just leave their dog's shit lying around? Properly boils
my piss, that does. When my ninety days was up, I got a job doing
exactly the same thing." The Glaswegian let out a short, sharp
belly-laugh. "Funny, right? This was meant to be a punishment and
it turned my life around. We buried a lady just after five o'clock and
the family left pot plants instead of bunches, so I'm planting them
up for her. She's got a sister landing from Canada in the wee hours
and I want the grave to look nice, you know."

"I'm glad you've straightened out. Good for you, mate, it's not easy."

"Everything's easy when you know why you're here. I never
knew why I was put on this earth until the day I got that community service. Boom! It was like that. Boom! I'm here to look after
your loved ones. Life's easy now I know. Clean, too. Not touched
drugs since, unless you call a wee nip 'drugs,' which I suppose it is.
Rawlins, Rawlins . . . Here you go. Harold Rawlins. One of two."

The headstone was ornately carved and rather grand compared
to those around it. The inscription read: MAY 12, 1941–AUGUST 12,
1984. ALWAYS LOVED, IN DEATH AS IN LIFE.

"Is he the one? There's another round the back. Weird. Funny
what you can tell about a person from their grave. Tall, nice headstone, pride of place. This guy was loved. The other 'Harry' . . . not
so much."

The second grave was marked with a small stone wedge and a
brass plaque simply engraved with Rawlins's name and his years
of birth and death; no months, no message. But this was where
Rawlins actually lay.

"Thank you," Jack said.

The Glaswegian nodded and backed off respectfully. Jack turned his phone torch on again. There really was nothing to see at this sad little graveside. Then . . .

"Excuse me!" Jack called.

Next to this small, untended grave was another small stone wedge bearing the inscription: Dorothy Rawlins. March 1941–August 1995. This grave had had a recent visitor, because fresh flowers lay on the grass.

"Do you know who visits Dolly Rawlins?"

"A wee girl. Only seen her a couple times. Young. Petite." The Glaswegian shrugged. "I stay out the way when people come visiting. Sorry."

"No, you've been really helpful. Thank you." As the Glaswegian walked away for the last time, Jack added, "Look after yourself."

The flowers on Dolly's grave were no more than a couple days old and had been taken out of their wrapping, so Jack wouldn't be able to trace where they were bought. He'd have to dig into Dolly's family history—but "young and petite" definitely didn't describe either Connie or Ester. Maybe the flowers weren't relevant at all.

Jack made his way back round to the first grave of "Harry Rawlins"— the one with the ornate headstone. This was the grave that held the most interest for him, because someone else was down there: someone who had been buried in Rawlins's place; someone who had been blown to smithereens in the botched Strand underpass robbery and misidentified. Someone wearing Harry's gold watch. And Jack was going to find out who that was.

CHAPTER 15

"You want to *what*?" Maggie asked.

They were standing in the middle of the spare bedroom, which now looked like a full-blown evidence room, with photos, notes, names and places all linked together with bits of different colored string. She wore one towel round her body, one round her head and held two glasses of red wine.

"You want a coroner's permission to dig up a coffin on the off chance that the body inside is Jimmy Nunn's?"

Jack took one of the glasses of wine from Maggie. He knew not to disturb her when she was in full flow.

"How you going to manage that exactly . . . ? 'Oh, guv, you know that grave that half of London thought belonged to Harry Rawlins? Well, can we dig it up please 'cos I think my dad might have been the getaway driver in an unsolved raid on a security van?'"

"I didn't say Jimmy was dead. In fact, if Tony's right, Jimmy walked away clean with pockets full of cash. But someone's in there, Mags, and it definitely isn't Rawlins."

"Who cares? Genuinely, Jack. Who cares which deadbeat gangster got buried 35 years ago?"

Jack looked at her with his beautiful, wide eyebrows-up eyes. *He* cared. Maggie put down her wine and cradled his face in her warm, water-wrinkled hands.

"You confuse me so much," she whispered. "I see the excitement in your eyes when you talk about this case and about your birth father and I love it, but, Jack, you have to think straight. For

35 years, the police haven't given a toss who's really in that grave. How are you going to make them care now?"

"You're right," Jack conceded. "I'll need to think of a far more compelling reason than just some missing gangster. Thanks, Mags. What would I do without you, eh? Did you leave the water in?"

And he headed for the bathroom.

Maggie looked around the spare bedroom in despair. Jack had finally found his passion, his focus, his smile—and it made her deeply worried. Instead of being the making of him, she worried it might actually be the breaking of him.

* * *

Jack had been parked outside Julia's home for about an hour, watching the comings and goings. What he first thought was a small mid-terraced two-up, two-down was actually three small terraced houses knocked into one. He discovered this when a little black girl with braided hair and a bright pink hoody went in one "house" and, moments later, came out of another.

This part of Chester was middle income, and Jack reckoned Julia owned a good £300 k of property between the three terraced houses. He knocked on the front door nearest to where he'd parked. From inside, Jack could hear a woman's voice shouting instructions about not doing anything else before she got back, then the door was opened by a tall, slim woman, wiping her floury hands on a souvenir tea towel slung over her shoulder.

"Julia Lawson?" Jack asked. He couldn't help the tone of the question: he could see she'd spotted him for a copper.

Julia blocked the doorway, as if protecting every living soul beyond it.

"You have to call first. If you don't call, I have the right to turn you away. These kids don't like surprises."

"I'm not here to see any of the children, Miss Lawson. I'm here to see you."

A crash from deep in the house forced Julia to step back and Jack followed her into the kitchen. The floor was covered in cake mix and two young boys stared up at Julia like butter wouldn't melt. She handed the older one a five-pound note.

"Tidy up. Go and buy a cake."

Then she headed into the conservatory.

Numerous kids played in the back gardens, which, just like the houses, were all knocked into one. The ages ranged from about 6 to 16 and they spanned numerous ethnicities. The conservatory was like half a goldfish bowl and, from here, Julia could see every inch of the garden. Nothing was getting past her. The low windowsill that ran around the edge, only stopping to accommodate two sets of double doors, was filled with picture frames of various kids. Some photos were sun-bleached with age, other were newer—but all were displayed proudly. One wall in the lounge they passed through was also floor-toceiling pictures. Julia had pointed to them.

"Some of the kids can't be photographed, but those who can are in a frame somewhere in the house. It's important for the new kids to see that they're not the only ones. It can feel lonely, thinking everyone else's life is better than yours."

The older kids in the garden eventually noticed Jack and instinctively moved closer to the conservatory in case Julia needed them.

"I'm DC Jack Warr from the Met."

Julia stood silent, waiting for him to explain further. But he didn't.

"How many kids do you look after here?"

"I thought you weren't here for the children."

Julia clearly didn't trust the police and nor did the kids in the garden.

"I'm not. I . . ."

Jack looked through the window at the happy children and finishing this sentence suddenly became very hard. Julia recognized a lost child when she saw one and guessed that he had started life in a place like this. No one said anything for a moment.

Jack smiled as he started again. "I hear you work wonders with the kids. I spoke to a colleague in Manchester and she was certainly impressed."

Another silence. Julia waited.

"I could have been in that system," said Jack. "But I was lucky enough to be placed relatively quickly. I was 5."

And with that one sentence the atmosphere changed completely. Ten minutes later, he was drinking tea and listening to Julia talk about how, to date, she'd helped more than 370 troubled or unwanted children.

"We go to West Kirby near the Wirral every month and, once a year, we head a bit further north to Formby beach and nature reserve. The kids love it—some pretend not to, of course, but that's just to save face. Tough men can't enjoy donkey rides."

Jack spotted one photo on the windowsill of a young girl, maybe 9 or 10, jumping a small fence on horseback. He made a comment about that child progressing far beyond donkeys on the beach.

"That's me." Julia spoke with a long-forgotten pride. "I hardly recognize her now. Horses are such trusting beasts—they teach children respect and kindness."

Jack used this casual memory to segue into the reason for his visit. "The Grange would have been a wonderful place for a kids' home, then."

Julia looked directly at Jack. "Is that why you're here . . . ? Good God! That was a lifetime ago." She didn't seem unsettled by the change of topic. "The problem you've got, DC Warr, is that I was using back then. I may not be able to help you, not because I don't want to but because it's all a bit of a blur."

As Julia began talking, she repeated much of what Jack had already heard. That they were a group of women brought together by Ester Freeman to welcome Dolly Rawlins back into the real world. Then the children's home idea raised its head and they all decided to stay on and help Dolly with that. They were ex-cons with nowhere else to be, so they jumped on the back of her ambition and went along for the ride.

"It doesn't take long at all to get into your blood. Dolly disappeared from my life in the blink of an eye, but the kids' home idea . . . that refused to leave. I would like to have seen The Grange come to fruition, horses and all." Jack asked whether Julia had known their nearest neighbor, Norma Walker. "Vaguely. She kept retired police mounts. Now, they're amazing animals. Country horses can get skittish at a leaf falling, but police horses . . . nerves of steel. I'm sure you know."

"I've seen them work. They're trained to remain calm around loud noises and crowds, all that sort of thing. I've never even been on one, if I'm honest. They scare the life out of me."

Julia smiled a sweet, understanding smile. "Once you make friends with a horse, you'll never be scared of them again." She glanced into the chaotic garden. "Friendship's so important. I think Dolly would have liked this place. She was the strongest person I've ever met. I asked her once if anything ever scared her and she told me about the night she shot Harry, her husband. She said that after doing that, nothing scared her. She said, 'I'm not like my husband. I'm better. I always was. I was just clever at making sure he never knew it.' How ballsy is that?"

"Can you tell me about the night Dolly was shot?"

"It was ridiculous! Craigh was standing right next to her! Ester rushes in and, no hesitation, she pulls the trigger. What the fuck she thought she was doing, I will never know. We were all arrested, kept overnight, then Craigh let us go the next morning. Ester's got a screw loose. Have you met her? I assume you're speaking to all of us?"

"I have met Ester, yes. And Connie."

"Now she's a nice girl. Haven't seen her since the shooting. Thick, mind you. I don't suppose that's changed."

Jack gave no indication of his opinion on Connie or Ester.

"Three houses knocked into one," he said, sounding impressed. "That must have cost a bit."

"I don't own this place, I just run it. Dolly once said, 'If you've got money, Julia, you can be whatever you want.' Money meant a lot to her. She liked people to see that she was someone. But I always thought there was something missing from her life that no amount of money could buy. Something fundamental. Kids, I suspect." Julia glanced out of the conservatory at the children playing in the garden. "Most of these will never know where they're from, so it's vital for them to know where they're going. Do you know where you're from?"

Jack liked Julia, and talking about the subject of childhood with someone experienced actually felt quite therapeutic.

"As I say, I was lucky." And then he lied. "I never felt the drive to find my real parents because I don't need them. I know who I am and I know where I'm from. My foster parents taught me."

The way Julia looked at Jack made a deeply buried memory pop right into the front of his mind. He suddenly recalled a moment when he was about six. He'd stolen the last of Charlie's diabetic chocolate brownies and, when Penny asked him about it, he'd lied straight to her face, even though he had chocolate-covered hands and lips. He'd just done the same to Julia and she saw right through him, just as Penny had done.

"But the kids here," he concluded, "are very lucky to have you."

"I'm lucky to have them. I need to be needed, you see. Always have.

I think that's why I became a doctor all those years ago, before I royally fucked it all up. I'm a recovering addict and I'm weak, especially when I'm on my own. I have to have someone to live for and the kids give me that. But every day I walk a tightrope between success and failure. I'm only ever one step away from falling off the wagon and ending up dead. That's what would happen if I took drugs again . . . I'd die."

* * *

Ridley could see Superintendent Maxine Raeburn sitting at her desk through the wall of glass that separated her from the corridor. She was on the phone, nodding and humming in all the right places. Max had seen and acknowledged Ridley, but he had to wait outside regardless—he guessed that the call she was on was above his pay grade. Max Raeburn was one of the best superintendents Ridley had ever worked under, a quiet, patient, but surprisingly intimidating woman. She was so slight, she looked as if she could be knocked down by a feather, but she'd be nipping at your ankles the moment she hit the floor. When she was promoted, she'd refused the big office on the top floor and insisted on being in this huge goldfish bowl of an office next door to Ridley. She wanted her officers to see her daily; she wanted them to know that she was first in and last out; she wanted them to know where she was at all times; and she wanted them to feel free to knock on her door. Not many people did, of course, on account of the chain of command. CID officers knocked on Ridley's door (even when it was open), Ridley knocked on her door—that's the way it was.

When Ridley was eventually allowed in, he held up the DNA results in his hand.

"It is Mike Withey."

Raeburn couldn't hide her bemusement. "So, Mike Withey, an ex-police officer from this station, was murdered and then disposed of in an arson attack at Rose Cottage, surrounded by an estimated one point eight million in burnt fivers and tenners, less than one mile from the biggest train robbery in UK history. Have I forgotten anything?"

"Rose Cottage belonged to Norma Walker, who was also an ex-cop. Mounted division."

"I don't need to tell you how delicate this is. I know I can trust your team, as I trust you, but bloody hell, Simon, remind them, and then remind them again, that this *cannot* get out."

Ridley nodded his understanding.

"Right," Raeburn continued, "how can I help?"

Ridley explained, in his usual to-the-letter way, exactly what he was going to do and in what order. It was only when he mentioned the possible angle of Norma and Mike being "privately known to each other" back in 1995 that Raeburn held her hand up.

"Norma was gay. She kept it very quiet—no other option in the eighties. In '89, she was injured in the line of duty. It was serious. Her next of kin was contacted—Amelie, I think her name was. I had to liaise for a time and, well . . . You only had to see her at Norma's bedside to know they were in love. Norma spilled the beans and I said that it didn't make the blindest bit of bloody difference. Norma and Mike could still have known each other, of course. But, I have to say, I'd be very surprised if Norma had anything to do with your train robbery. I'd assume Mike's personal connections to London's lowlife are a better angle of inquiry. Follow the evidence though, Simon . . . I've been surprised before."

* * *

"That's Sam," Julia said when she returned to the conservatory with a fresh pot of tea. Jack stood by the window, watching Sam teach a younger boy how to play keepy-uppy. "He's 8 and has scars like you wouldn't believe, outside and in. His instinct is to fight anyone bigger and teach football to anyone smaller. Battling against the man he's meant to be and yearning for the kid he never was."

"He looks happy."

As Jack poured tea for them both, his mobile buzzed. A text message from Ridley:

In confidence—ID is Mike Withey. Informing family now. No private connection to Norma, as she was a lesbian.

Jack tried to hide his grin. He knew for a fact that Ridley would have agonized over whether to type the word "lesbian" or "gay." He might even have googled the most PC phrasing.

Jack handed Julia her tea and then excused himself to go to the bathroom.

He perched on the wash basin, reread the content of Ridley's text, and suddenly felt like he was definitely wasting his time with these bloody Grange women. He should be back at the nick, with his team, looking for a bunch of dodgy coppers with connections to hired hands with enough balls to do a train robbery and kill one of their own.

When Jack re-entered the conservatory, a young girl was sitting on Julia's lap, crying her heart out. Julia indicated that he should keep on with his questions while she rocked the distraught girl back to calmness.

"Do you run this place alone?" he inquired.

"I have two people helping me. I'd trust them with my life. I did have three, until the father of one of the children turned up on my doorstep demanding his son back. I knew who'd given out our address." Then Julia spoke to the girl. "Go on. Stick by Suzie for now, please. I'll come and talk to Darren in a minute."

The girl jumped off Julia's knee and headed for Suzie, who Jack hadn't noticed was waiting in the doorway. Suzie was big for such a young-looking girl and didn't seem "all there." She seemed vulnerable and timid. When the girls had left the room, Julia continued.

"Darren's a worry. He's feral. I don't mean that maliciously, it's just the best word to describe him. He lashes out so quickly."

"Self-preservation." Jack suddenly recalled another memory long buried. "A much bigger lad was after my lunch money at school—this was after I was placed with my foster parents—and as he got within reach I hit him before he could hit me. I remember that I didn't want to fight him, so I had to create a lie to tell myself . . . the lie being that I wasn't afraid."

"I have a feeling you still protect yourself in the same way," Julia teased. "You stand when I'm seated, in order to command the room. You have your hands in your pockets to show how at ease you are, you don't break eye contact showing you're no pushover, you chat to draw me in. I studied psychology as part of my doctorate, and I have to say that you are very hard to read for a copper. You're either genuine or you're one big façade, DC Warr."

Jack blew air from his nostrils as he smiled. He liked Julia very much—she sounded posh and she looked very feminine, but he didn't doubt that she was as tough as old boots.

When he asked if the isolation affected her, she said, "Isolation keeps us safe. I'm guardian to these children—that's a privilege that I don't take lightly. The truth, although they think the opposite, is that they saved my life. I owe these children everything."

* * *

Four hours later, in West London, Jack rang Angela's doorbell. She opened the door without asking who was there, and from her surprised expression it was immediately clear to him that she'd been expecting someone else.

"DC Warr," he said, holding up his warrant card.

She led him into the lounge, where she'd been re-covering a set of dining room chairs, shaking her head.

"I don't see the point in that bottom door if people hold it open for strangers—no offense. I thought you were Irene from 36—she wanted to take a picture of her chairs to show her mum. Sorry, that's not remotely interesting. What can I do for you?"

Jack explained that he wanted to ask Angela about the train robbery, even though he wasn't expecting much, having read her original statement.

"I wasn't there," she explained. "I'd taken Kathleen's kids away for the night. We got back early and The Grange was swarming with police. That's the first I knew of it. Tea?"

"No, thank you. I'm all tea'd out."

"Ask anything you like—but I'm going to keep going on these chairs. I've got a deadline!"

Jack asked question after question, most of which were answered with "I don't know, I wasn't there." It struck him as interesting that none of the women from The Grange were remotely flustered by him showing up at their homes. Surely train robbers, even 24 years on, would be a little surprised and jumpy? He got no sense of tension from any of the women, and there was precious little evidence of unexplained wealth.

Angela's flat was probably twoor three-bedroomed—the wall of photos showed numerous children, but they couldn't have all fitted in there. A toy box in the corner of the lounge contained some boys' stuff and some girls' stuff, so Jack guessed that at least two kids lived here. He also guessed the rest must be extended family. As he looked around the walls he noticed, high on a shelf, far out of the reach of sticky young fingers, were two lone toys—a small, worn teddy bear and a bright yellow teething ring. Special memories being kept safe, he supposed.

The family feel of this place was oddly similar to Julia's home, even though in other ways they were vastly different. The children in these photos had probably never known abuse, violence or anger.

Angela freely told Jack all about herself. She ran an upholstering business, earning money from family, friends and neighbors—she was bringing back the make-do-and-mend ethos in a "throwaway" society. Her husband, Rob, was doing the same with cars and bikes. Angela felt the need to digress for long enough to confirm that their businesses were legitimate and that they paid all their taxes. Unfortunately, seconds later, Irene from 36 came up to take photos of her newly covered dining chairs and took the opportunity to pay Angela in cash.

"Take it now, Ange, for God's sake, or it'll go straight back out on the 3:40 at Chepstow."

Jack smiled as Angela squirmed, trying to work out what kind of a copper he was. He laughed.

"I'm not here for anything other than a little background on the train robbery."

And to prove he wasn't going to turn her in to HMRC, he accepted the cup of tea offered when he first arrived because, as every good cop knows, sharing tea breaks down barriers.

Jack and Angela talked for a further thirty minutes about the other women at The Grange, about the failed children's home, about the death of Dolly Rawlins—and this final topic of conversation had a clear impact on Angela's mood.

"From the very second Dolly saw me, she knew I needed her. She was this old woman—old to me back then—who could suss a person out as soon as look at them. I remember I said to her once about me and her being friends or something like that, and she said, 'You don't know me, darlin'. There's lots to me no one ever knows. That's how I survive.' But I did know her. And she certainly knew me. I miss her."

"Do you visit her grave?"

"She's a good listener," Angela said with a smile. "I take fresh flowers every Wednesday. I let her down, you see. I want her to know that I'm making up for it now."

Jack inquired exactly how Angela had let Dolly down, but she didn't give much detail away; instead she spoke about how it made her feel.

"It was personal. I made a mistake . . . with a bloke. I lost a baby. And when everyone else turned their backs on me, Dolly looked me straight in the eye and told me what a stupid little bitch I'd been. She was right. And, just after she set me straight, she hugged me tighter than I'd ever been hugged in my life. That's what I mean when I say she could suss a person out as soon as look at them— she knew what I needed."

"She sounds like an amazing woman."

Angela wasn't fooled by Jack's kind words. If he'd already visited Ester, he'd know that Dolly was hated just as much as she was loved. It all depended whether or not she was on your side. As the evening drew in, Jack thanked Angela for the tea, scribbled down his mobile number in case she remembered anything else, and left her to her work. Once he'd gone, Angela went to her window and waited. Eventually, he appeared in the car park below and headed toward Kensal Green Underground.

Angela stepped up onto the arm of the sofa and took down the teddy bear and teething ring. She cried easily as she recalled the moment, twenty-four years ago, that she'd told Dolly she was pregnant. She was young and petrified and just to say the words out loud relieved so much pressure. Dolly took her to Mothercare, where she bought and paid for all of the essentials. Angela had subsequently lost the baby and, in a fit of unimaginable distress, she'd destroyed everything Dolly had bought. Except a small teddy bear and a bright yellow teething ring.

But tonight, Angela didn't cry for the loss of her baby . . . she cried for the loss of Dolly.

CHAPTER 16

After Anik's previous encounter with Susan Withey—when he mostly impressed Ridley with his approach and his questioning—he was perhaps a little too confident going into this notification of death.

Susan was in the middle of getting ready to go out, and so she didn't play by the book at all. When Anik asked her to sit, she didn't. When he asked her to listen, she continued multitasking. It was only when he started following her round the downstairs rooms that Ridley took over.

"Susan." Ridley's voice was an enviable mix of gentle and authoritative. He stood in Susan's way, put a hand on her back and steered her into the lounge, talking as he moved. "I need to be certain that I have your full attention, please." He sat down on the sofa, subliminally suggesting she do exactly the same. "We've now made a DNA identification on the body found at Rose Cottage."

And that was all Susan needed to hear, really—although Ridley went on to say the actual words, so there was no doubt in his mind that she'd fully understood.

"I'm sorry to confirm that it is your husband. It is Mike." Susan's head dipped a little, but her facial expression didn't change that much. She didn't cry. She didn't speak. "We're investigating and I'll personally keep you informed about what we discover. Where are you getting ready to go to, Susan?"

Susan, quiet and in shock, said that she was meeting a friend at the gym.

"Would you like me to ask that friend to come here instead?" Susan nodded, found her friend's name in "contacts" and handed her mobile to Ridley. He, in turn, handed it to Anik.

"Say that Susan's had some bad news and would like her to come round, please. Then put the kettle on."

Ridley reassured Susan that they'd stay with her until her friend arrived, to deal with any questions either of them might have. As Anik stepped into the kitchen to make the call, he could hear Susan ask if she could see Mike.

"There's no comfort to be found in seeing him," he replied gently. "You leave Mike to me. I'll look after him . . . so that you can look after yourself and your children."

Anik heard Susan start to cry, followed by the rustle of Ridley's jacket as he put his arm around her. When Anik returned to the lounge with a mug of sweet tea, Susan was sitting alone on the sofa and Ridley was standing in front of the fake hearth. The shoulder of his pale green jacket now showed a small dark patch, which Anik assumed was from Susan's tears. Horrible though it was, he yearned for the day that a murder victim's next of kin trusted every word that *he* said and rested their head on *his* shoulder for comfort.

* * *

It was almost seven o'clock when the team was back together in the squad room. Jack, having completed his interviews of the women from The Grange, confirmed that, in his opinion, they were nothing more than witnesses to Dolly's murder and knew nothing at all about the train robbery until after the fact. With this line of inquiry closed, Ridley focused his team on Mike Withey, Barry Cooper

LYNDA LA PLANTE | 193

and, possibly, Norma Walker. These people were connected to Rose Cottage and the money and, possibly, the robbery.

"Sir," Jack interjected. "As well as the train robbery, Mike is also connected to an earlier crime in which, again, none of the stolen property has been recovered. The diamond heist back in '84."

Ridley looked at the extensive evidence boards that had been building over the past weeks. All of the historic research Jack had insisted on including in them might just come to fruition now. The Witheys' name came up again and again, and Mike wouldn't be the first copper to get pissed off with earning ten times less than the average low-life he nicked. What if he'd changed sides? Ridley didn't want his officers to get overexcited, so he kept things calm.

"We start from today and we work backward, connecting the dots as far back as we need to in order to get the full picture. *But,*" he emphasized, "this is, first and foremost, a murder investigation. If we connect the train robbery and the diamond heist as well, that's a bonus." Then he changed the subject. "Jack, you're with me tomorrow morning. We'll go and tell Audrey about her son."

Anik buried his head in his work, trying not to look fazed by Ridley's decision to take Jack and not him on the second notification of death. Laura, as his sarge, felt she had to say something.

"Notifications are tough, Anik. Because not only are you the one who will knock them down with the news that you bring, you're also the one who will pick them back up again. That takes control."

* * *

Jack repeatedly kicked on the front door until Maggie finally turned on the hallway light.

"Darling, there's someone at the door!" she shouted up the stairs.

This was closely followed by Jack laughing from the front doorstep. Maggie opened the door, to reveal Jack laden down by a mini fridge. He staggered in and set the fridge heavily down on the bottom stair. Maggie wasn't amused.

"When some fuckwit kicks on my front door in the middle of the bloody night, I'm bound to pretend that my massive cage-fighting husband is upstairs, aren't I!"

Jack hugged Maggie and rocked her in his arms. He was so tired, he could have fallen asleep right there.

"Why have you bought a fridge?"

"For the spare room. So I can work late without waking you up by going into the kitchen."

With that, he picked up the fridge and took it upstairs. Maggie couldn't believe what she was hearing.

"I'll nick you a commode from work as well, shall I? Then you can lock yourself away for days searching for the elusive Jimmy bloody Nunn!"

Jack bounced down the stairs, grabbed her by the hand, and dragged her back up. In the spare bedroom, they both faced his ever-growing evidence wall. Jack stood behind her with his arms wrapped tightly round her waist.

"You were right, Mags. I *did* need a better reason to exhume Rawlins's first grave and now I've got it. This Rose Cottage case goes back way further than we thought . . . this far." He swept his hand through the air in front of Maggie's face, indicating every piece of evidence collected. "Right back to 1984. Back to the diamond robbery. Back to Harry Rawlins. Ridley's sold on the idea now, so all I need to do is persuade him that something relevant is hidden in that grave."

Jack couldn't see Maggie's face, but it was a combination of worry and confusion. *What the hell is he talking about?*

"The diamonds, Mags! They've never been found and they've got to be somewhere."

"Jack . . ." Maggie started.

"I know what you're going to say. But this is as relevant to the Rose Cottage case as it is to mine."

"*You* haven't got a case!" Maggie flicked her hands dismissively toward his evidence wall. "This . . . *This* is not a police investigation. This is a personal . . . God knows what!" She turned in Jack's arms to face him. "You're not supposed to be doing this and, more to the point, you don't need to be doing it. You have a dad. Why do you need another one? Especially this one, Jack—he sounds awful."

As Maggie talked, Jack looked deep into her eyes. His eyebrows were up, his eyes were wide and inviting and she could see that this was the version of her partner she'd been waiting for. He was excited. Animated. Happy. Jack was alive again.

"I'm not trying to replace anything I have now, but my past, Mags, has holes in it that you could drive a bus through. There are missing pieces and I need to find them. Jimmy's not an appealing man, you're right, but my God, he *lived*. I just want to meet him. I need to know where this restlessness comes from. I can't focus on 'now' until I do."

Maggie realized that she had to support Jack through this— whatever *this* was—and she hated that thought. But, as she smiled back at him, she also realized that this was how she'd get her husband back. The man she looked at now was the strong, driven man she'd fallen in love with back in Totnes. Their passions rose and, before she knew it, Jack was kissing her, perching her on the edge of the spare bed and pulling down her silk pajama shorts. As she unbuckled his trousers, he kissed her neck until she tightened her legs round his waist to bring him to her. She felt now as she had felt the first time they made love; she had been desperate to experience the new man in her life and, as such, it was over in minutes, but what an explosive few minutes they were. She had that same frantic feeling now. Maggie once again felt desperate to experience this "new man" in her life, but this time was better, because this time was also filled with love. Jack knew her, knew how to touch her, knew how to move her. Maggie arched her back, allowing Jack to be however he wanted to be. She loved him, she trusted him, and she wanted him.

* * *

Audrey Withey was one of those people who'd always lived life just the wrong side of the law, but never really saw it like that. She'd never declared an income, she'd not think twice about buying smuggled European fags and anything off the back of a truck was fair game. Her home was nice enough for a three-bedroomed flat, but nothing matched—clearly Audrey scooped up anything that was getting chucked out by anyone else. One man's trash . . .

Audrey was an almost skeletal 76-year-old woman who looked like she'd be blown over in a strong wind. When she took a drag on her cigarette, her face almost turned inside out and it was blatantly obvious from the smell that there was a large brandy in her coffee.

As she walked Ridley and Jack into her lounge, she didn't offer them any refreshments or, indeed, a seat. So, they both remained standing.

The décor would give lesser men a migraine. The curtains and walls were a fag-smoke tan color and, although the flat was tidy, it wasn't clean. Audrey had "gone to pot." She was an old woman, wearing old clothes, surrounded by old things, in an old flat. Her days of making an effort had long gone. There were four photo frames on the sideboard: one picture of Shirley, aged 20, in a beauty pageant sash; one of Mike, at the same age, in his army uniform; one of Greg, aged about 14, in his school uniform; the fourth frame contained a tiny pink baby bonnet and mittens. Badly knitted. Never worn. These photos showed the pinnacle of each child's life, and they were displayed with a huge amount of love and pride. They were the only things in this room not covered in dust.

Ridley sighed heavily. Shirley had been shot to death in a botched diamond raid, Greg was in prison on his fifth compulsory drug-rehab program, there was obviously a miscarriage in the mix somewhere, and he was about to tell Audrey that Mike had been bludgeoned to death and then burned beyond recognition. Sometimes Ridley hated this job—no mother should outlive one of her children, let alone three.

Ridley knew that, after the death notification, he'd lose any cooperation from Audrey; he opted to delay the bad news until he'd had the opportunity to ask a few questions.

"Mrs. Withey, back in 1995 there was a train robbery in Aylesbury, do you remember? Mike was still on the force back then, under the command of DCI Craigh—"

"We never spoke about work." Audrey shut Ridley down before he could start. "What you asking about ancient history for, when you should be looking for my boy?"

"I presumed Mike would have mentioned this particular case to you, seeing as it involved Dolly Rawlins."

Audrey pursed her sallow lips and jabbed her yellow-tipped finger at Ridley.

"You don't mention that woman's name in my house," she snarled as the instinctive, uncontrollable hatred bubbled quickly to the surface. "I only let you in 'cos you said you wanted to talk about Mike. And now you're mentioning that bitch and talking about some train robbery. Not trying to pin that on him as well, are ya?"

"As well as what, Mrs. Withey?" Ridley was annoyingly calm, making Audrey jump to her feet.

"Don't you dare talk to me like I'm thick. You're in my house! I been around the block, son, so don't try and trick me into incriminating Mike. *Yes!* I remember the train robbery—'cos it was just months before your lot booted Mike out. He served his country, home and abroad, and what did you do? You treated him like a criminal." Then Audrey smiled. "You got no clue where he is, 'ave ya? Well, good. All you want to do is use him as a scapegoat again. If he's running, good!"

"Why would he be running?"

"'Cos he knows your game. When *she* was released, we grieved all over again for our Shirl and . . ." Audrey glanced at the photos, gulped and regained composure. "The bonnet and mittens are pink 'cos I so desperately wanted it to be another girl. I'd have called her Eve—that was my Shirl's middle name, after my mum." When Audrey looked back in Ridley's direction, her eyes were red but the tears were being held back by the hatred. "Stress, the doctors said. Stress made my body neglect my unborn child and she died inside me. Dolly Rawlins did that!" She pointed to the line of four photos. "She did all of that!"

Audrey's hatred for Dolly had taken her way off track, so Ridley endeavored to pull her back to the here and now.

"Mrs. Withey, please calm down. We're not here to pin anything on Mike, nor do we think he's running. Please sit down." Audrey didn't sit, but she did calm sufficiently for Ridley to continue. "We simply need to know if you and he spoke about the '95 train robbery."

"He said one thing worth remembering in '95. He said, 'She's dead, mum.' Now I'd like you to leave."

Ridley ignored the request. He asked Audrey if Mike had ever mentioned a police officer called Norma Walker, and if she knew where his Range Rover was. All the while, Jack remained silent because this wasn't a normal notification of death. This was also a tactical interview and, with Ridley about to play the heartless bad guy, it would be useful for Jack to remain neutral in Audrey's eyes. So, for now, he played the silent, unobtrusive young DC in the corner. Audrey hardly noticed he was even there.

Ridley asked Audrey once more to sit down and, once more, she didn't. He took a step closer to her and spoke with all of the respect and kindness he could muster for such an objectionable woman.

"Mrs. Withey, I regret to inform you that, several days ago, we found the body of a man, which, via DNA evidence, we're now able to identify as your son, Mike."

He had very purposefully taken a step closer to Audrey so that, when her legs crumpled beneath her, he could catch her and sit her back in her chair. Audrey collapsed like a rag doll and howled in agony at the loss of yet another child. Jack poured her a brandy, but she didn't even notice. In the end, sheer exhaustion made her stop crying and become almost catatonic.

"Mrs. Withey." Ridley's words were met by a blank stare, but he hoped she could still hear him. "Someone took your son's life and I want to arrest that person. Mike was mixed up in something, accidentally or knowingly, I don't know yet. What I do know is that he was found in the home of Norma Walker, which was located next door to a house owned by Dolly Rawlins. And he was surrounded by evidence from a 24-year-old train robbery."

Audrey's eyes unglazed and she glared at Ridley.

"Get out," she breathed, almost inaudibly.

"Is there anyone we can call for you?"

Audrey dipped her eyes and she was gone again. Ridley moved away; Jack put the brandy down on the nest of coffee tables by her side and both men left, pulling the front door to behind them.

In the hallway of Audrey's block of flats, Ridley briefed Jack.

"Give it ten, then go back in. Apologize for me upsetting her—you be her friend. We need to know how much the villa in Spain sold for. Mike was the only one earning, so we need to know where that money came from. And see what she knows about Barry Cooper."

* * *

When Jack entered Audrey's lounge, she was seated in exactly the same position as when he left. He sat on the edge of the sofa, his body turned toward her, leaning forward into her eyeline—whether she acknowledged him or not, he wanted to be sure that she could actually see him.

"I wanted to make sure you're OK," he lied. "I don't like the idea of you being on your own. Mrs. Withey, I came back because, well, I wanted to assure you that this is a murder investigation and all we want is to find out who took your son from you. Of course we need to delve into his past, but not to discredit him in any way. We just need to track his associates, his friends . . . Barry Cooper?"

Without looking up, Audrey spoke. "How did he die?"

"Mike suffered a blow on the head. He would have died instantly, before the fire started, and wouldn't have suffered."

"Barry wouldn't do that to Mike. Brothers in arms, they were." Audrey looked like a wrung-out rag, used up and ready to be thrown away. She was a sorry sight, but Jack knew that this new vulnerability would make her more likely to talk to him. He continued to play it as though he was on her side, by handing her the brandy he'd poured earlier on. This time, Audrey took the drink and downed it in one.

"He felt so guilty for being abroad when Shirl got killed. By the time he got home, Greg was back inside an' all. How come the wrong people always get away with it, eh? And decent people are left to suffer." She handed him the empty glass and he got up to refill it. "Dolly said she'd 'do ten' for me. When she got out after blowing her husband to smithereens, she come round to *my* home and threatened to kill me too. That's the sort of animal she was."

"Why on earth would Dolly want to kill you?" Jack asked.

"I dunno . . . People like Dolly don't need an excuse to threaten and terrorize. It was just power games to keep people in their place."

Audrey spluttered nervously. There was clearly more to this slip of the tongue, as Jack knew that Dolly was wily enough not to make idle threats. He left it alone for now and changed the subject.

"Do you know where Barry is? Only he may have been the last person to see Mike, so we'd like to speak to him."

"I take it you know where he lives?"

Even now, amid so much grief, Audrey maintained her ingrained instinct to answer coppers' questions with another question, to make sure she wasn't giving away any secrets.

"He's not there. Barry's not in any trouble as far as we can make out—he may be able to help us, that's all."

Audrey necked the second glass of brandy as quickly as the first and said that she had no clue where Barry was. She also denied knowing Norma Walker, claimed to have never been to The Grange and to have only learned about the train robbery from the newspapers. When Jack took the conversation back a decade further, to 1984, her demeanor changed—she become nervous, evasive and she developed that very familiar look of a criminal desperately trying to accurately recall an old lie. Jack asked about the Strand underpass robberies, one and two. He asked about the diamond robbery—and he mentioned the names Terry Miller, Joe Pirelli, Jimmy Nunn and Harry Rawlins. Audrey leapt onto the defensive, saying that Mike was in the army when all of that went down, so why was Jack asking about them in relation to her boy's murder?

"You're going to find his killer, aren't you? He was one of yours, you owe him that much."

"I promise you, Mrs. Withey, that the moment we find out who killed Mike, I'll come back here and tell you personally."

* * *

When Rob got home from finishing the repairs to the bus, Angela was sitting in the dark, holding a glass of wine in one hand and the small, worn teddy bear in the other. He moved round the back of her and wrapped his big, warm forearms around her shoulders. The thick black hairs on his arms tickled her chin—something that normally made her smile and scratch her face—but, this time, it went unnoticed.

"The police have been round," she said calmly. Rob pushed his lips against her cheek in a long kiss to show her she had nothing to worry about. "He asked about the train robbery."

"We knew they would," Rob reasoned. "We're in good shape. Everybody knows what they have to do." He held Angela's hand, as she held the teddy bear. "I wish she could see you, Ange. Dolly would be so proud."

CHAPTER 17

DI Prescott watched a young PC stepping from foot to foot and clapping his hands together in an attempt to stay warm. Prescott smirked— the poor kid looked like he was doing a Greek dance. Prescott, on the other hand, stood statue-still by the side of the muddy Range Rover. This was a big find and would allow him to legitimately get bang up to speed on the case.

Mike's Range Rover sat in a field, tucked in close behind a tall hedgerow, about a quarter a mile back from Rose Cottage. The fuel cap was missing and the tank had been siphoned almost dry; a sample of the fuel had been taken for analysis and Prescott was confident that this was where the accelerant for the fire had come from. Police tape protected the vehicle and the messy array of footprints that surrounded it. Rain had taken most of the evidence, but between the vehicle and the hedge the ground was sheltered, and SOCOs were getting some good casts from the footprints they found right next to the open fuel cap. With no keys in the ignition and no sign of hotwiring, the immediate area was being searched— the keys could have vital fingerprints on them.

Prescott's eyes narrowed as he processed the scene in his mind and tried to figure out the sequence of events.

Had Mike siphoned his own tank with the intention of burning down Rose Cottage? Probably not—because if the fire was premeditated, he'd have been more likely to bring a siphoning hose with him and not cut a piece from the one they found in the back garden, or just siphon the petrol into a container before he got there. Unless Mike had been to Rose Cottage before and knew the hose was there. The fire somehow just seemed more likely to be a forensic countermeasure by the person Mike had fought with and was killed by. So, the killer must have known where Mike had hidden his Range Rover, because it had been a bugger to find. Maybe they'd arrived together. Or was there a second vehicle for the killer to escape in?

Prescott reached for his phone to call Ridley. It was a fair bet Mike Withey had known his killer.

* * *

"Barry Cooper." Ridley looked around at the sea of blank faces gathered in the squad room. "Where the hell is he? I know he's binned his old mobile, so that's a dead end, but there must be something. He's not a genius. Come on! Why can't we find him?"

"He is ex-army, sir," Jack offered.

Ridley snorted. "And what are we? Chopped liver? He's our main suspect. The Range Rover's on its way to the pound. The SOCOs will go over it with a fine-toothed comb. And we've got footprint casts and soil samples from the scene to compare with the soles of Barry's shoes." He turned to look at the ever-expanding evidence boards. A third board had been added and they were all overflowing with details of four crimes spanning four decades.

"All of this . . ." Ridley said calmly. "Don't let any of it distract us from the fact that we're here to solve the brutal murder of one of our own. If this is all connected, it'll come to light through the investigation of that murder, so stay focused." He paused. "However, it's looking likely that Mike *was* involved with the train robbery. Anik . . ."

Anik spoke from his desk, head down, looking at his extensive notes.

"Late eighties or early nineties, Audrey bought a villa in Spain—I still need to establish where that money came from—but in 2005 it was sold for £350,000 and Mike's family home in Weybridge was purchased for one point five million. So there's an extra million to be accounted for, too."

Anik looked up before continuing.

"When Mike left the force, he . . . Well, he pretty much fell apart. He drank, gambled, slept around. I spoke to Susan about this time in their lives. She never knew who he was having affairs with, but always assumed they were coppers or prostitutes he nicked. When he was drunk, he'd also get a bit handy with his fists. She never reported him, but her medical records tell us that he didn't hold back. Then they tried to start again in Spain—I've got bank statements from over there spanning '96 to '05—but the kids' schooling eventually brought them home. The villa was sold, the house was bought. Being back in the UK turned Mike straight back into the arsehole he used to be, so Susan finally kicked him out. That's where we came in."

As Anik spoke, Jack became increasingly frustrated by how vague his information was. Why didn't he already know where the extra money had come from? Why didn't he already know the names of Mike's mistresses? Anik had a lot to learn about manipulation. That's all interviewing really was—the manipulation of another person into revealing the things you needed to know.

"Right," said Ridley, "let's get on with it. Why isn't Barry Cooper's picture on the board yet? Why hasn't someone contacted the army, or the Passport Office or Driver and Vehicle Licensing, to get a picture of him? Why aren't you trawling Missing Persons for him as well? Mike's dead, Barry could be too. He could be our killer, but he could also be a second victim ... well, couldn't he? I want him to be alive because we've got questions that need answering and no bugger to ask. So find Barry Cooper!"

As the meeting broke up and the team started bustling about, Jack slipped out.

* * *

In the middle of Susan's lounge was a box full of items belonging to Mike: hats, shoes, underwear, toiletries. In her hand, she held one brown leather shoe.

"One shoe," she said to Jack. "How did he not realize he'd only taken one shoe?"

She dropped the shoe into the box and closed the flaps.

"I'm sorry for disturbing you again," said Jack. "I'll be as quick as I can."

"It's fine. You're a distraction from ... whatever this is. If Mike had been here, sharing my life, I'd know how to deal with that. I'd cry and mourn and help the girls to do the same. But I'd already lost Mike. I'm sad for the girls, but I'm finding it hard to muster any sadness of my own."

She went into the kitchen and Jack watched her make two mugs of tea.

"You recently spoke to my colleague about life with Mike," he said. "I have a few more questions, if you don't mind?"

He spoke gently, but was aware that he'd caught her at a point of maximum vulnerability.

Susan shrugged. "Fire away."

"You mentioned to DC Joshi that Mike—and forgive me for mentioning this, but . . . that Mike was unfaithful. Was there any specific occasion that sticks in your mind?" Susan didn't look up as she stirred the milk into the teas. "I have to ask, you see, because we need to understand what made Mike tick in those difficult years after he left the force. Understanding him is very important for us."

Inwardly he winced. Was he overdoing it?

Susan looked down at the mugs of tea. "Mike once told me he'd been part of a raid on a brothel. They went in and cleared the place out, arrested everyone they found, girls and punters. Then, in the kitchen, he found a young girl hiding underneath the sink. She was fifteen, sixteen, and she wouldn't come out. She stayed pressed against the wall, just out of his reach, crying and swearing blind that she just served drinks. Mike talked her out, took her to the station in his own car and made sure he was the one who took her statement. He didn't know if she was one of the prostitutes or not, but he said he believed her story that she was nothing more than a maid . . . so she went free. The following week, he started working late." Susan handed Jack his tea. "He did like his waifs and strays."

"Are you suggesting that Mike may have had a relationship with this girl?"

"I don't know what I'm suggesting, really. I can tell you that Mike had affairs. I can tell you that he liked to be needed. Did he sleep with a teenage girl? He's capable of it, yes. I guess she'd have done anything to avoid custody. Maybe she saw him as a 'hero' for some reason. Mike wasn't a rapist."

Just a pedophile, Jack thought, *if this story was true*. He glanced at the photos of Mike's own daughters.

While they were saying their goodbyes, Jack replayed one of Susan's comments in his head.

He didn't know if she was one of the prostitutes or not, but he said he believed her story that she was nothing more than a maid.

Was there a connection somewhere? Ester Freeman had said that Angela Dunn was a worse maid than Geoffrey . . . and Angela had claimed that she'd let Dolly down by "making a mistake" and then losing a baby. Could the raided brothel Susan mentioned have belonged to Ester? It was a long shot, he realized—but if Angela had worked for Ester as a kid, and if Mike *did* raid The Grange as a young PC, then they could all have known each other. Suddenly, the Grange women were right back in the frame.

Outside Susan's inexplicably expensive house, Jack got out his mobile. Within minutes, the HOLMES database confirmed his hunch:

Angela Dunn was named in an arrest report from September 1985. She was arrested on suspicion of solicitation during a raid at The Grange. Released without charge.

If Susan's story was true, Angela Dunn had been Mike Withey's mistress.

* * *

Back home, Jack leapt up his stairs, two at a time . . . and then stopped dead. He checked his watch—10:30. *Shit!* He was desperate to tell Maggie about his day, but that would have to wait till morning now. He sneaked into the bedroom—the bed was still neatly made and Maggie wasn't there. He quickly ran through her calendar in his head, certain she wasn't at work.

In the kitchen, Maggie nursed a glass of red and stared at her laptop screen. She looked at him like a stern mum catching her teenager sneaking in late.

"What's up, love?" Jack asked.

Maggie spun the laptop round so that he could see the screen, got up and poured a glass of red wine for him. On the screen was a photo of Charlie and Penny on the balcony of their cabin. The selfie caught half of Penny's face and all of Charlie, but it was mostly sea and sky. In the bottom left corner of the image was half of a bright orange pilot boat that had come into the deeper waters to take them ashore for a day trip.

Jack smiled. His mum was terrible at taking photos! He flicked through image after image—dozens of new memories desperately made in such a short space of time. His dad was starting to look ill and Jack was so far away.

Maggie put Jack's wine on the table.

"You missed their Skype call."

Jack's face drained and his skin went cold. His eyes began to fill and he gulped to stop himself from crying. He felt so ashamed. Maggie had reminded him in the morning before he left, and he'd promised not to forget.

What am I doing? he asked himself. He looked up at Maggie.

"Was he OK, Mags? Does he sound OK? He looks pale, doesn't he?"

Maggie knew she didn't need to say anything more and just rubbed his back as he flicked through more terribly framed selfies.

"He's having a wonderful time, Jack. He said feels fine—gets tired more quickly, but they slow down after lunch and Penny plans each day to include a nap, so they don't miss out on any of the evening cabaret shows."

"I should have been here." Jack thumped the table. "Was Mum angry? I bet she was. I'm going to stop looking for Jimmy Nunn, Mags. It's making me miss the here and now and I can't get any of this back. I can't get that Skype call back." He slumped down into the chair. "Tell me what they said again."

Maggie put Penny's photos on "slide show" and then relayed the Skype call, word for word. When she'd finished, she said, "I'll go on up to bed. You come up when you're ready."

As she left the room, she looked back to see him staring intently at the screen as the slide show went round and round.

CHAPTER 18

By morning, Jack's guilt had been replaced by an irrepressible sense of excitement at discovering a possible connection between Ester Freeman, Angela Dunn and Mike Withey. If they were linked, then the decades were linked—which suggested that the crimes could also be linked. The fact that he could now trace Ester and Angela's relationship back as far as the 1980s wasn't particularly relevant to their current investigation; but if Angela knew Mike—that was a game-changer. It might even put them in the same place at the time of the train robbery.

When Angela Dunn opened the door, she looked startled. "Oh!" she said. "You!" She recovered herself. "Come in."

It took her twice as long to make the tea as it had the last time, as if she was giving herself time to think.

"I'm making a dress today," she said as she led the way back into her sitting room.

She held it up for Jack to admire. It was stunning, if on the large side. For some reason he thought of Connie; she'd look fabulous in it.

"What can I do for you?" Angela asked, as she poured the tea.

"Further inquiries have raised a few more questions, if you don't mind, Mrs. Dunn."

Angela smiled and waved a hand. "Such as?"

Jack jumped in. "Do you know Mike Withey?"

"No."

The answer was so quick and confident that, for a moment, Jack thought he'd got it all wrong. But then it was odd she hadn't asked who Mike Withey was. Jack decided to trust his newly developed "gut."

"I think you might know him, Mrs. Dunn—although maybe you've forgotten? It was a long time ago. Do you recall working for Ester Freeman at The Grange?"

"I wasn't a prostitute!" Angela snapped. "Is that what you've come here to ask me?"

"Not at all." Jack widened his eyes. "I know you were a maid. But I know that, on one occasion, you were arrested along with everyone else and I know that PC Withey, as he was back then . . . looked after you."

Angela's face softened. "PC Withey . . . ah, yes. I'd forgotten the name, sorry. He was very good to me."

"You know," Jack went on, "'hero worship' is a common reaction in victims who are rescued from abusive environments. It's natural— it wouldn't have been your fault—but affairs are often the final outcome."

"I was fifteen! And he was married, I think. I did cling to him for a bit, I remember that, but he was always very professional. There was nothing unsavory about it, DC Warr, if that's what you're implying."

Angela was cool, all right. Every inch of Jack tingled as her words washed over him. Something wasn't right with her manner, her words, her tone; she was lying and he knew it.

"Whose baby did you lose?" he asked abruptly. "You previously told me that you put flowers on Dolly's grave because you let her down. You said you'd made a mistake and you lost a baby. This was back around 1995, when you were all living at The Grange?"

Angela glanced up at the high shelf, far out of reach of sticky young fingers, at the two lone toys in pride of place—the teddy bear and the teething ring. Jack followed her gaze. He needed to be more careful. This loss was still raw.

"It must have been awful. I'm very sorry." He paused. "Did Mike know?" he asked gently.

She rounded on him. "PC Withey was *not* the mistake I mentioned. If you insist on prying, I was attacked. I'd call it rape if I'd been sober enough to remember it actually happening. Five weeks later, I was pregnant. And I didn't lose the baby, DC Warr, I drank bleach and I killed it. My body simply couldn't keep us both alive. *That's* how I let Dolly Rawlins down. She bought the bear and teether—she loved me and, by default, she loved my baby. I took both from her that day."

Angela stared at him, strong and defiant, as if willing him to question her further.

Jack got to his feet. Even though he was certain she was telling the truth, he sensed there was something she was holding back. Nothing he could do about it for now.

"Thank you for your time, Mrs. Dunn," he said, and left.

* * *

Angela stood on the balcony, staring down as Jack Warr got into his car. As soon as he'd driven off, she went inside and picked up her mobile.

"No, no, don't worry, nothing's happened," she said. "But the police are onto something. I've just had a visit. DC Warr. He doesn't know anything yet, but he'll get there in the end. We need to meet." There was a pause. "Thursday. You OK to come here? It's just, with the kids, you know? Listen—take a breath before you call her. We're not panicking. We're doing exactly what we planned, just a little bit sooner."

When she hung up, she sat down and took a deep breath herself, letting her shoulders slump and her head fall back.

When she was ready, she sprung up from the sofa and headed out. Angela was unshakable.

* * *

In Taunton, Connie sat at her dining table with a gin in one hand and her mobile in the other.

"Breathe," she repeatedly whispered to herself. By the time she'd dialed Julia's number, she was half pissed.

Julia sounded breezy.

"Thursday's fine," she said. "Love you."

She hung up before Connie could start on all the things that could go wrong, and dialed another number.

"Darling," Ester sang. "Still gorgeous? Who's seeing to you these days? Boys or girls?"

Angela had put together the call chain. Connie was in the middle, so Angela and Julia could each do their bit to keep her calm and focused. And calling Ester was Julia's job, because she knew best how to handle the cantankerous old witch. She ignored Ester's questions.

"Can you come to Angela's on Thursday?"

"Are we leaving?"

"I doubt we're leaving yet, but we'll be planning our next move and—"

"I'm not coming all the way to London to do more talking, Julia. Call me back when we're leaving. And if our self-appointed glorious leader wants to discuss that further, she can call me her fucking self."

"When will you ever learn, Ester?" Julia wasn't angry; she spoke like a disappointed mother faced with her perpetually aggravating child. "You need people in life, you know. You need friends."

"I have Geoffrey." Ester was defiant. "He's in a dominant mood this week, so we haven't left the house since Friday. He's gone all *Gladiator* on me." Her tone shifted and she became nasty. "So, you call me when we're leaving! I've done my bit, Julia. I'm old. You do the donkey work and I'll pop up toward the end, take my share and fuck off into the sunset. I will *not* be told what to do by Angela bleedin' Dunn."

And that was the real reason for Ester's frustrations.

Angela's leadership had happened organically. Connie and Julia had never objected, but Ester hated it. In Ester's egotistical, narcissistic, petty little mind, *she* was the natural successor to Dolly Rawlins. Angela was nothing more than a stupid girl who, back in the 1980s when The Grange was a brothel, hadn't even been good enough to be a prostitute.

"That child can think she's in charge, Julia," Ester spat. "I don't give a shit—but you lot can't make a move without my say-so. And you, my darling, know me well enough to know that, if you try, I'll see you all inside. So, run along, there's a good little tart. And, as I think I've mentioned already, call me when we're leaving."

She hung up.

Julia sighed. Just then, Sam wandered into the room with blood down his shirt from a split lip.

"Darren called me a pussy and nicked my bike, so I smacked him. Do you think I'm a pussy?"

As Julia stepped toward him, Sam instinctively stepped back. He looked confused.

"Have I ever hit you?" she went on.

Sam shook his head.

"Do you respect me?" Julia softened her expression. Sam relaxed a little. "You don't earn respect by hitting out, Sam. You're better than Darren. You're stronger." She tapped his chest. "You're stronger where it matters, and that's why we have to try extra hard with Darren. He's been through a lot and you know what that's like. So, I need you to do something for me ... I need you to be smarter than this. Because, one day soon, I'm going to ask something of you and, if you're not ready, if you're not smarter than this, I won't think twice about leaving you behind."

Sam's mouth had slowly dropped open. She gently placed her forefinger underneath his chin and closed his mouth.

"Clean yourself up," she said, and kissed his cheek before leaving the room.

* * *

Dougie Marshall stank from the inside out. The smell seemed to seep from his very pores. In his eighties now, he was the only forger Angela knew. Back in the day, Dolly had spoken about him by name and reputation, and Angela had never forgotten. Not being part of the criminal fraternity, her knowledge of London forgers was not up to date—so, when her world began to get complicated, she turned to Dougie. But if he was good enough for Dolly, he was good enough for her.

Dougie and Angela sat in his small, unventilated office above Marshall's Bookmakers on the main street through Croydon. The bookie's had been there for as long as anyone could remember, and was still frequented by old men with no one to go home to. A new generation also came in to spend their hard-earned cash, in the hope of winning some easy money. Dougie's son, Gareth, now ran the shop itself, while Dougie sat upstairs in his museum of an office, and lived out his days sticking address labels onto marketing flyers.

Dougie's upstairs office was accessed by a side entrance no wider than a flight of stairs. A stairlift had been fitted recently, making the stairs hard to maneuver. Angela banged her shin on the footrest every single time she visited.

As Angela examined the passports and driving licenses, Dougie's eyes lit up with pride. It had been a long time since anyone needed his skills, his craftsmanship, his artistry. He prided himself on making his IDs look used and worn. He'd fray edges, add stains and scratches; he'd even wear down the embossed leather pattern in the bottom left-hand corner to make them look like they'd been opened by a thousand pairs of hands over the years. He'd make sure the issue date wasn't brand new and he'd add stamps from various countries. He was a true master. He was worth the money and the uncomfortable twenty minutes in his stale-smelling office.

Angela handed him three bundles of £20 notes, which he did her the courtesy of not counting.

"Good luck," Dougie said as Angela stood.

She smiled. She wouldn't be needing luck.

CHAPTER 19

By the time Ridley walked in to the squad room, one hour ahead of the rest of his team, Jack had rearranged all three evidence boards into an order that more easily supported his latest theory.

The linear timeline had gone and, instead, he'd grouped people and events together.

The picture of Mike was pinned next to one of Angela, with the other Grange women beneath her. Audrey was in the mix, as was Norma Walker. And at the heart of it all was the train robbery, closely followed by the diamond raid.

Ridley took off his coat, perched on the edge of Jack's desk, folded his arms and waited for Jack to speak.

"Angela Dunn worked for Ester Freeman back in '85," said Jack. "Mike Withey and Angela knew each other in '95. All of these women were living under the same roof in '95, so it's possible they all knew Mike, too. I think it's likely that Dolly Rawlins also knew him, because of the acrimonious history between her and Audrey, Mike's mum. I'm not sure where Audrey and Norma fit in, but I don't want to dismiss them just yet."

Jack paused for Ridley to respond, but he didn't, although he remained alert and attentive.

"Now, when Dolly Rawlins was released from prison," Jack continued, "Mike was certain she knew where the diamonds were. He claimed it was a tip-off, but what if . . . ?"

Ridley's eyebrows shot up, stopping Jack in his tracks. It was dodgy territory to be accusing a police officer of anything, but Jack plunged on regardless.

"What if Mike himself was the tip-off? His sister was murdered during the diamond robbery. Mike's mum lives in the beating heart of London's gangland. They all knew each other, sir, then and now."

Without a word, Ridley got to his feet and went into his office. In the corner was a coffee machine, and Jack could see him fiddling with the buttons. He could almost hear his boss's brain processing the evidence he'd just been presented with. All Jack wanted right now was for Ridley to accept that it was all feasible.

Ridley emerged with two Americanos and handed one to Jack. He perched on the desk again.

"So who do you think's in that first grave belonging to Harry Rawlins?"

Jack had to stop himself from smiling. Ridley's question was unexpected, but it gave him just the opportunity he wanted.

"I don't know who's in there, sir, but I'll tell you *what* I think's in that grave . . ." He took a deep breath. "The diamonds."

He blurted the words out before self-preservation could stop him from speaking. If Ridley accepted this, then Jack would soon find out if Jimmy Nunn was dead or alive. If they also found six million pounds in diamonds, that would be a bonus.

Ridley had drunk almost half of his coffee by the time he was ready to speak.

"That funeral turned into the biggest embarrassment for the Met in living memory. And, from the second we knew that Rawlins couldn't possibly be in that coffin, it became the biggest no-go area. We couldn't have ID'd the body anyway, 'cos there wasn't enough of it left—that was our excuse back then for not digging it up. And, over the years, people stopped caring who was down there."

"We can ID the body now, sir," Jack said, trying to sound casual. "We know all the players, except him. Or her. And what better place to hide the diamonds than in a grave that the police don't want to admit even exists? I've read the reports on the diamond heist. Those gems couldn't be fenced in London and there's no evidence they were taken out of the country. They have to still be here."

Jack had been agonizing for days about how he was going to suggest to Ridley that digging up a 35-year-old grave was a good idea; now, here he was, seconds away from Ridley suggesting it himself.

Easy does it, he told himself. *Don't push him. Let him decide . . . God almighty—why does Ridley think so fucking slowly?*

At last Ridley spoke. "You decided what you're doing about the sergeant's position, Jack?"

"I was going to mention that to you first thing, sir. I'm going to go for it," Jack replied earnestly. "This case . . . Something's clicked into place and there's no going back for me now. No more apathy, sir, I promise. I know what I want."

Ridley collected the two empty coffee cups and headed back to his office.

"Leave this grave thing with me," he said.

Through the window, Jack watched as Ridley picked up his phone and pressed the uppermost, right-hand, fast-dial button— the button that connected him to Superintendent Raeburn. He sat and spun his chair away from the squad room.

Jack's grin spread from ear to ear.

* * *

Pathologist William Fox was in his lab when Jack burst in.

"Foxy, you'll be getting a bag of bones in the next few days, maybe weeks, I'll give you the nod. But, when they arrive, I need you to do a DNA test for me."

Foxy and Jack had trained together for six months. They'd got on like a house on fire and had kept in touch when Jack went back to Devon. They were proper friends. The kind who, when asked for a favor, said "yes" first and asked "what is it?" second.

"I can't use stock from here, Jack," said Fox. "You'll have to provide the DNA kit."

It was that simple.

CHAPTER 20

Angela's children ran into the lounge. They were dressed in their pajamas, their hair was wet at the bottom and crazy on top from where Rob had blasted it with the hairdryer, making no attempt to brush it during the process. Aggie was 7 and Riel was 9. Aggie was still young enough to leap into her parents' arms, hugging and kissing them goodnight, whereas Riel had recently got into the habit of standing reluctantly in front of Angela and allowing her to drag him toward her body. He was still young enough to want a hug before bed, but too old to admit it.

Tonight was a nightmare for Riel—because after he'd allowed his mum a snuggle, he was steered in the direction of Aunt Connie, who squeezed him into her ample breasts. Julia then grabbed Riel, threw him onto the carpet and showered his neck with rapid-fire kisses.

"Stop it!" he yelled, but his uncontrollable giggles told a different story.

Julia threw him back onto his feet and shoved him away as though she was the one who didn't like cuddling.

"Now, get out of my sight," she said with a straight face.

Both kids ran to Rob, who was waiting in the doorway, ready to take them away and give the three women privacy.

For a few moments, the women quietly sipped their wine, enjoying being under the same roof once again.

Connie broke the silence. "He's a cutie, isn't he?" Angela and Julia giggled into their glasses. "I'm just saying. I thought Detective

Constable Jack Warr was very nice indeed. They could have sent some old wrinkly. I mentioned Lennie early on, 'cos I knew that'd make me cry. Then I gave him my very best 'Princess Diana' look, all wide-eyed and innocent through my fringe. He was putty in my hands. Then we just sat and enjoyed the view. I was sorry to see him leave, if I'm honest."

"Did he ask anything that we need to worry about?" Angela asked. "He knew about John," Connie said.

"Whatever you did or didn't get up to with John Maynard doesn't matter," Angela reassured her. "In fact it's good. He'll just have confirmed Dolly was converting The Grange into a children's home."

"He didn't ask me anything unexpected, either," said Julia. "Just mentioned he'd personal experience of the care system—said it had made him understand more about life."

"There's one thing, though," Angela sounded serious. "And it's why I've called you together. Jack Warr asked me if I knew Mike back in '95 when we were all at The Grange. He thought Mike and I were in some sort of a relationship. I denied it and I made him feel guilty for even asking."

"Fuck me, Angela!" Julia breathed. "He's not asking about Mike because you were shagging him two decades ago. He's asking because he knows Mike's the bloody body from the fire!"

She caught Connie's fearful look out of the corner of her eye.

"I think we need to assume he knows everything. To do anything less would be suicide. We are where we are," she added calmly. "We carry on. And we stick to the plan."

* * *

By eleven o'clock, Angela, Julia and Connie were well on their way. Getting drunk together was exactly what they needed as they came to terms with how far they'd come and what they were about to do next.

"Here's to Dolly Rawlins." Connie's speech was slurred. "The only woman with balls big enough to hide *twenty-seven million pounds* underneath a copper's house." She rolled backward onto the floor, slapped her hands over her eyes and snorted muffled giggles into her palms. "All those police officers! Coming and going at all hours. Wishing Norma well, doing her shopping, tidying her garden . . . right above the money they were looking for! God, if only they knew!"

* * *

Blue lights flickered through the branches of the trees as Dolly, Julia, Connie and Gloria raced away on horseback toward The Grange. Gloria's saddlebags had started to slip off one side of her horse, so she grabbed hold of them and held their weight, as best she could, away from the galloping legs. At some point, Gloria realized exactly what she was doing—she was riding a horse, for the first time in her life, onehanded, while holding on to her share of around £30 million! Gloria let out a scream of unadulterated joy. Dolly hoped to God that they were far enough away from the coppers for that not to be heard.

At The Grange, Ester was on autopilot. She had absolutely no idea whether the other women would make it back. The last time she'd seen Dolly, she was surfing a train carriage down a river embankment with Connie inside. So, Ester was blindly sticking to the plan.

She'd emptied her share of money into the skip and thrown the sacks into the lime pit, dug and filled three days ago by Gloria. As the money sacks slowly dissolved, Ester used an industrial vacuum to get the cash out of the skip and into black bin bags.

By the time the other four women rode up from the back lane and into the grounds of The Grange, Ester was ready to explode. She swore, ranted, blamed Dolly for the rain that had made the train carriage slip down the embankment, cursed her for the danger she had put them all in. Dolly knew this rage came from fear and from relief; Ester had had to return to The Grange alone, not knowing if anyone else was alive or dead, free or arrested.

Dolly ignored her. "Quick—get the money into the skip! Dissolve the sacks and all of your clothes—nothing left! Nothing! Come on! We're behind schedule!"

They emptied their cash into the skip, so that Ester could keep vacuuming it up and into bin bags.

"Not one single note can be left behind," Dolly urged. "If they find one note—it's over."

Once all of the money was re-bagged, and all of the sacks and overalls were melting in the lime pit, the skip was dragged over the top. All of the bin bags were thrown into the back of one of John Maynard's work vans, and all except Ester drove the quarter mile to Rose Cottage.

It had been Julia who had discovered the internal layout of Norma's house. Norma fancied the pants off her and Dolly had told her to get into Norma's home and, if required, her bed. The coal shaft under the cottage had a long-disused chute opening in the back garden, clearly marked with the construction date, 1841. The chute came out in Norma's kitchen but had been bricked up decades ago;

the only way of getting the cash back out of the chute once it was in was to take the kitchen wall down.

Tonight, Rose Cottage was empty. Norma was away on a police training course for four days. In the garden, Connie passed the bin bags full of money to Julia from the back of John's van, and Julia poured them down the coal chute. Ester gathered the empty bin bags, Angela checked that not one single note went astray, and Dolly kept lookout. Gloria was back at The Grange, letting the horses loose—they knew that these trail horses would head straight back to the stables just along the road where Julia had stolen them some hours earlier.

Within forty minutes of the train robbery, the five women from The Grange had been in their nightdresses and in bed. As Dolly lay back in her crisp, clean white sheets, wet hair soaking into the pillow case, she allowed what they had just achieved to sink in. She pushed her head back, opened her mouth and let out the loudest cackle she could muster. It echoed down the hallway, seeping into every other bedroom and triggering a chain of celebratory screeching and laughing. No one could believe they'd actually done it—they'd robbed a mail train!

* * *

For as long as she could remember, Dolly's life had been a series of events out of her control. It had all started when she made the mistake of leaving the diamonds with Audrey bloody Withey. Audrey had sold them for a fraction of their value, meaning that Dolly couldn't afford to open the children's home she'd dreamed of and had somehow ended up taking on responsibility for six other women. All of this had ultimately led her to the decision to rob a mail train.

Some days Dolly would reason that committing this crime had been the only way for all of the women to have the lives they needed, but on others she would admit that the opportunity had been too good to pass up. Whatever the reason, nothing would ever be good enough for Ester. She was the one person who still doubted Dolly's integrity. The one person who, after all of the risks Dolly had taken, couldn't see a future where she didn't screw them all over and leave them with nothing. Dolly didn't blame Ester for her paranoia—prison damages some people beyond repair.

* * *

It was one o'clock in Angela's flat and the women were on to their third bottle of Cava. Connie sat on the floor, propped against the sofa where Angela sat with her legs out straight. Julia was curled up into an armchair—for a tall woman, she folded up into the smallest of spaces.

The lounge was quiet, except for the far-off sounds of Rob snoring gently from the bedroom at the other end of the corridor. The main lights were off; only a tall lamp in the corner of the room, by the balcony doors, provided any light. The bulb reflected in the glass through the cheap paper shade, highlighting the children's little handprints. Out on the balcony itself, wrapped around the top railing, was a string of white lights. At Christmas they flashed on and off, but tonight they were permanently on.

Again, Connie was the one to break the silence.

"I'm glad Ester's not here. Is that horrible of me?" Julia and Angela made faces in agreement. "I think she must be very sad. She can't have many friends, can she? Not with her being such a bitch, I mean." Julia spat out a laugh. "After all, she's the reason we couldn't go anywhere near the money for 20-odd bloody years! 'You make a move without me and I'll see the lot of you inside!' Cheeky cow! She gets herself locked up for murder and we have to wait for her to get out!"

"It wasn't just her, Con," Julia pointed out. "Even after Ester got out, we couldn't get near because Norma was still alive. Who knew she had so many friends? Most nights in her house was like the Policeman's bloody Ball—coppers everywhere. I mean, we couldn't have found a more stupid fucking place to hide the money if we'd tried."

"I think it was genius," Angela countered. "Dolly couldn't have known Ester was going to lose her mind and shoot the place up."

"See!" Connie added triumphantly. "Ester's fault! Just like I said in the first place."

Angela moved on to a happier memory. "Do you remember that guided tour we went on, Julia?"

"I was gutted not to be able to come on that!" Connie screeched.

Down the hall, Aggie stirred in her bed and mumbled, "*Mummy.*" Connie slammed her hand over her mouth but Angela just smiled. Aggie could sleep through a hurricane.

"I met you at the Dog and Gun, remember, for the 'Murder and Mayhem Tour'?" Angela continued. "That young barman took us up to The Grange and started . . ." She couldn't talk for laughing.

Julia took over. "He described us as five 'wicked women,' drawn together by a thirst for mayhem and murder. The outcome was inevitable, apparently—he even suggested that we got Dolly there specifically to kill her. He claimed our debauched orgies were eye-watering! Clearly he was getting the children's home mixed up with Ester's whorehouse. I was described as a drug-addled GP, Dolly was a murderess and I think everyone else was a prostitute. That right?"

Connie was outraged. "I was an escort, not a prostitute!"

"A classy, peroxide blonde escort in crotchless knickers, singing 'boo boo be do' up against an alley wall?" said Julia. "You were a prostitute, Connie, darling. And I *was* a drug-addled GP—but look at us now. *Look* at us now! Thousands of tourists traipsed through the grounds of The Grange listening to lies and exaggerations. We're legends already—imagine if they knew the truth!"

"Twenty-four years," Angela reflected. "Twenty-four years of pandering to Ester in fear of our freedom—of waiting for poor Norma to die. You're right, Julia. Just look at us now!" Then she whispered, "Do you want to see it?"

The spare bedroom was locked from the outside. Inside, it was filled with all twenty-five of the seats from the bus Rob had bought from the auction two weeks earlier. The backs of the seats leaned against one wall and the cushions leaned against the opposite wall. In the far corner was a sheeted mound. Angela removed the sheet to reveal dozens and dozens of strong green garden waste bags.

Angela carefully untied the nearest bag, unrolled the top and opened it to expose the contents—£20 notes and £50 notes, thrown together with all the care and attention of raked leaves. These notes were "used" in the first place; now, they looked downright tatty. But to the women, they were breathtakingly beautiful.

This garden waste bag, along with the other forty-odd others, held their long-awaited, carefully nurtured dreams. Dreams that could have begun twenty-four years ago, had Ester not shot Dolly Rawlins dead in front of four police officers.

But now . . . Now it really *was* their time.

CHAPTER 21

The squad room was buzzing. Ridley wasn't late—he was never late. He was with Superintendent Raeburn, waiting to find out if they had been given their "Consent to Exhume" from the coroner.

A low hum filled the room as DC Morgan took bets. An old fossil of a man, Morgan lived in the corner of the squad room, with his own mini fridge tucked away under his desk. He was allowed this because it contained his insulin; but it also contained cans of Coke and bars of chocolate. Morgan walked that fine line between hypo and hyper—and he didn't give a shit. He was also the squad room bookie.

Morgan had a book on who would get the sergeant's job: Jack, Anik or an unknown quantity from outside. He had a book on which senior officer would suffer the next heart attack. And he had a book on the exhumation. He was certain that Raeburn would be refused the exhumation for "financial reasons," but then he was one of the few coppers still working who had been at the funeral back in August 1984. He remembered watching Dolly Rawlins bury some bloody stranger. And he knew Raeburn would be secretly praying for a refusal from the coroner, so they could all just let sleeping dogs lie.

When Ridley finally arrived, he had good news for Morgan's bet.

"Currently, there's not sufficient justification for the spend required to exhume the grave," Ridley said in a monotone. It was hard to tell whether he was pleased or frustrated by this. "On a different note," he went on, "Barry Cooper has been spotted in Essex. He's disappeared from his digs, but the local force are tracking him down. Jack, a DS Mary Fleming is going to contact you with some details."

With a wave of his hand, he disappeared into his office to answer the phone.

Jack fired up his computer and opened a message from DS Fleming of Essex Police. Laura stood behind him and, in a whisper, she read the screen out loud, which meant that Jack had to read at a slow pace as well. She leaned her hand on the desk by the side of his keyboard and, as her breathy, whispered reading warmed the back of his neck, Jack thought about making love to Maggie in the spare bedroom. He started reviewing the number of rooms they'd made love in and realized that, since moving to London and since working such opposing shifts, they'd not been anywhere near as adventurous as they used to be. Kitchen?—no. Lounge?—yes. Bathroom?—no. Outdoors?—no. Car?—no. Work?

He smiled as he recalled delivering a pizza to Maggie at the hospital during a night shift. It had been one o'clock; he'd had a particularly boring day at work and had nipped out for a pint or five on his way home. He'd ended up at a pizza place close to the hospital, and had popped in for the company. Maggie had had an arduous shift up until that point, so was lying down in the on-call room when Jack arrived. She'd asked him to hold her and he knew that she must have lost a patient. He held her as tightly as he could, nuzzled his cheek into hers and stroked her hair. Within seconds, they'd forgotten where they were and had made love in the creaky single bed.

Jack was brought crashing back down to earth by Laura leaning even further forward so that she could track the words on the screen with her finger.

"Fucking hell, Jack, look. Cooper's army record says he was a sapper! A combat engineer whose duties included breaching fortifications and demolition. He knew his way round explosives. He would have known exactly how to blow a section of train track and leave the carriage intact."

Just then, Ridley stepped from his office.

"That was DI Prescott," he called across the room. "The demolition crew at Rose Cottage have found something."

* * *

The heavy iron coal chute door had once been positioned above the kitchen at Rose Cottage. It had blown off at some point during the fire and landed in the front garden, so it had lain there unrecognized. It was only when a demolition crew, heavily supervised by officers from Thames Valley Police, were taking the cottage down brick by brick that the tunnel from the chute door down into the kitchen had been revealed.

Prescott, Ridley and Jack stood in the doorway of what used to be the kitchen.

"That far wall, behind the stove, didn't come down in the fire," Prescott explained. "Apparently it was smashed down beforehand. That back wall used to have a coal door in it, which had been shoddily bricked up at some point. So the bottom end of the chute was bricked over, but the top end was still accessible from the front garden. Very dangerous apparently. Anyway, in the crumbling brickwork halfway down the old chute, one of the demolition guys found these."

Prescott had been building to this. With an air of triumph, he handed Ridley a small, clear evidence bag containing several partly charred, crushed and ripped pieces of paper. It was perfectly clear that they were—or had been—banknotes. And along with the notes was half an old money band off a bundle of £20 notes, marked with "£1,000."

"There's easily enough room in the chute for the twenty-seven million taken in the train robbery," Prescott continued. "But once the cash was in, there was no way to get it out—"

"Without smashing down the wall." Ridley ended Prescott's sentence.

For a big man, Prescott was very animated when he was excited.

"Those robbers . . . balls of steel! Fancy shoving twenty-seven million of stolen cash into the wall of a copper's house! And they were cool enough to play the long game right from the start, because they'd have known they couldn't get the money back without taking Norma's kitchen wall down . . ."

He moved outside so that he could smoke, and Ridley went with him, followed by Jack, still holding the evidence bag of ruined money.

He listened to them as the two older men discussed theories, questioning and speculating, ruling things in or out as they chatted. The gang didn't go for the money while Norma was alive, so she probably wasn't involved. But how did they know the coal chute was there? Do all these cottages have them and, if so, is that common knowledge? And Mike . . .? It looked like he was the ringleader, with Barry as his right-hand man. But on the night they came back for the money—something went very, very wrong.

* * *

Mike stood amid the pile of bricks that used to be Norma's kitchen wall. Crumpled bundles of notes flowed over the bricks like a waterfall. He scooped them up, his hands like two shovels, and stuffed them into the green garden waste bag Ester was holding open. In front of Mike, higher on the pile of bricks and closer to the 1.5 meter square coal chute hole, Angela and Julia separated out the final bundles of £5 notes and £10 notes and threw them into the open hearth. Connie stood by the window as lookout, although Rose Cottage was so secluded that if anyone did turn up unexpectedly, they'd be on the driveway before she spotted them.

Angela slowly stood upright, working through the sharp, needle-like pain in her lower back. She looked toward Julia, hoping for sympathy, but was instead confronted with Julia's arse in the air as she stretched her own pain away with a Downward Dog yoga pose. As the final two bundles of £50 notes were dropped into a bag, Ester rolled the top of it down, squeezed out all of the air and tied the twisted corners into a knot.

"Right," Angela said, "let's load up the van."

The women picked up the garden waste bags, two by two, and took them outside, while Mike began stacking the bundles of £5 notes and £10 notes into the empty hearth—there had to be somewhere between £1.5 million and two million altogether.

"Imagine it's just paper." Angela had returned without Mike noticing. "It's not legal tender anymore. It's impossible to cash in, so it's got to go. The bag on the sofa is yours, Mike."

"Ange . . ."

Mike wanted to say so much but, in truth, he knew he had nothing to say that she wanted to hear. There was a time when Angela had looked at him like he was her superhero; now there was nothing. She was in charge and he was nothing more than a member of her crew.

"Burn it." Her words were purposely flat. "Bring Rose Cottage down— lose the coal chute, the money, every trace of us. Dump the Range Rover in the Thames. Take your cut and get on with your life, Mike."

And she was gone.

Angela knew he would do exactly as she asked, because he had just as much to lose as she did. What she didn't know was that Mike had asked his army demolition friend, Barry Cooper, to help him destroy Rose Cottage.

* * *

Ridley and Prescott walked in step, slightly ahead of Jack, back to their cars. Ridley had his hands clasped in the small of his back and his neatly pressed trousers swayed perfectly with his long strides. Prescott had his hands plunged deep into his pockets, his straight arms pushing his unironed trousers down from his hips and untucking his shirt at the back. He seemed scruffy compared with Ridley, but Jack sensed their mutual respect.

When they got to the cars, the men shook hands.

"Everything's paused again for now," Prescott said. "Site's been made safe, so I'll get the SOCOs back in to see what we might have missed. And we'll do the door-to-door again."

Ridley turned to Jack. "Get Susan and Audrey Withey brought in first thing in the morning, for further questioning," he said. He put his hand out to Prescott. "I'll keep you in the picture. There's approximately twenty-five million in stolen banknotes out there somewhere, and we both deserve to be there when it's found."

* * *

Angela and Connie sat on the floor in the lounge of Angela's flat. Angela had one of the bus seats propped on its side between her legs and she was stitching the seam closed. Connie was removing the old foam padding from inside another seat and stuffing it into a bin bag to be thrown away.

"I was reading the other day—" Connie hadn't stopped talking since she'd got up that morning—"about this commune of women. They left the fellas, took the kids and lived in this field in caravans. Nice big ones, you know, like the ones you get at beachside holiday parks. The kids all went to school and lived normal lives, they just came home to these ... static homes, they're called, aren't they, not caravans. Somewhere in the Lake District, I think it was. Or maybe the Peak District. Some 'district' anyway. They all *loved* it. Everyone was happy. No arguing. No asking for permission to do ordinary things like go for a drink with your mates. And definitely no backhanders for opening your gob at the wrong time. No men, you see, Angela. I mean, I'm sure there'd be a bit of lesbian activity going on, but so what? I often used to think that Ester and Julia had the right idea. Even though Ester was—is—a bitch, she's still not as bad as most men. What d'ya think?"

"Do I think women-only communes are a good idea? Course I do! What's not to like? Apart from the sex, which, let's face it, we could get anywhere—and from someone who wouldn't expect you to do their washing, ironing, cooking, cleaning and child-minding."

Connie giggled to herself. She knew Angela didn't mean any of that really, because Angela had a good man in Rob. A great man, in fact. She was very lucky.

Once Connie had stripped her bus seat of its old foam padding, she dragged a green sack out from behind the sofa and began layering bundles of £20 notes into the now-empty space.

"Leave a gap on top for a bit of new foam," Angela reminded her. "They need to be comfortable enough to sit on."

She'd worked out that if Connie was stuffing each coach seat with £50 notes, then it could hold around £250,000, and each seat-back could hold around £200,000. If she was stuffing the seats and backs with £20 notes, then it was more like £100,000 per seat and £75,000 per seat-back. This wasn't exactly accurate, but Connie liked it when Angela sounded definite. It made her feel safe.

* * *

PC Adam Franks and PC Tanya Daly were soaked to the skin. They were standing on the doorstep of one of the identical houses in the estate where the old Grange had once stood, waiting for the door-bell to be answered. At the window, the curtains twitched and three children pressed spotty faces against the glass. They wore pajamas and their lounge fire roared away behind them. Eventually, a woman opened the front door and stepped out onto the front porch, wrapping her cardigan round her body.

PC Franks introduced himself.

"Apologies for disturbing you again, Mrs. Stanhope. I know you and your neighbors have already been questioned about the fire—I've got your original statement—but I'm hoping that you'll look at a couple of photographs for me, please."

"Happy to help," she said. "But we'll have to talk out here. The kids have all got chicken pox."

Franks passed her the photographs of Mike Withey and Barry Cooper, but Mrs. Stanhope, like everyone else who had bothered to answer their door, didn't recognize them.

"Have you remembered anything else since you last spoke to the police?" asked PC Daly. It was a routine question.

"Nothing." Mrs. Stanhope shook her head apologetically. "I mean, when I was at Puddle Ducks—that's a swimming group for toddlers— we all had a chat about the pest control van parked at Rose Cottage on the night of the fire, but Jean said that wasn't important enough to bother you with."

Franks and Daly glanced at each other as the same thought passed through both their minds: why the hell does the general bloody public insist on deciding what's important and what's not?

Back in the patrol car, PC Daly held her hands by the air vent to thaw her fingers, while PC Franks got Prescott on the phone.

"It was parked on the grass verge apparently, sir. She saw it on her way to Puddle Ducks at 4 p.m. and it was gone when she drove back home at seven. The fire started at 8 p.m., sir . . ."

Franks held the phone up to Daly's ear so she could hear Prescott curse and rage.

"She's so stupid, it's a miracle she can get herself fucking dressed in the morning!" he ranted.

Daly stifled her laughter as Franks continued, deadpan.

"Pest control vans aren't uncommon in this part of Aylesbury, sir. Thousands of rats live in the farm buildings and come into the houses for easy food. No, sir, I don't know why I'm telling you that, sir, no, sorry. Of course she had no right to decide whether it was import—Yes, I've got the company name, sir. Daly and I are heading over there now." Then a longer pause. "It's a swimming class for toddlers, sir."

Prescott wasn't angry with Franks. He didn't even know Franks. He was angry because now he had to call Ridley and explain how his uniformed officers had not been specific enough—or persistent enough, or experienced enough—to get every little detail out of a bunch of civvies first time round. To calm himself down, Prescott got every spare PC busy watching every second of CCTV from the night of the fire. If the pest control van was parked on the grass verge, it had to have been on the main road at some point.

* * *

The pest control van pulled out of the driveway of Rose Cottage and drove away toward the Chiltern Hills. In the driving seat, Angela wore glasses, a wig of cropped brown hair and had a trendy little stubble. Her shoulders were high and tight, brimming with tension. Once the van cleared the more populated areas and headed out into the countryside, she relaxed. Green fields surrounded her, the clear road lay in front of her and there wasn't another soul for miles around. She peeled the stubble from her chin, pulled her sleeve down over her hand and rubbed her face till it was red—it was so itchy! She then pulled off her wig.

She drove for a good forty minutes toward Little Marlow, until she saw a battered old black Ford Ranger pickup truck parked at the side of the road. The only thing new about this pickup was the heavy-duty metal cover that was rolled out across the back, protecting the normally exposed flatbed space underneath. A key lock and a padlock held the cover in place.

Angela pulled over in front of the pickup, jumped out and opened the back doors of the van. Inside, Ester, Julia and Connie were perched on top of £27 million, stuffed into forty or so green waste bags. As soon as the sunlight hit her face, Ester started to shuffle on her bottom toward the doors.

"'Bout fucking time," she growled. "I'm bursting for a piss."

As Julia and Connie jumped out the back, familiar arms wrapped around Angela's waist and Rob rested his chin atop of her head. He beamed a huge smile at the women and he opened his arms for an impromptu group hug, easily enveloping them all. For a moment, no one spoke. They stood there, savoring the moment until Ester ruined it with some crude comment about foursomes. They came to their senses and set about moving the bags from the van into the back of the pickup.

"Is Mike OK?" Rob asked.

He'd known lots of men like Mike, men who needed to be part of a team to understand their role in life; the army, the police—it was all the same. This need to belong had been a useful way of keeping Mike in check . . . but not today. Today he needed to play his part on his own and Rob wasn't sure that, alone in Rose Cottage, he would keep his nerve. But there was nothing they could do about that now.

Once all of the bags were in the back of the pickup, Ester jumped into the back seat, while Rob slid the heavy-duty cover closed and doublelocked it. Ester couldn't be clearly seen through the blacked-out windows and even the driver's cab partition window was blacked so that, if Rob was stopped or caught on any cameras, none of the women would be identifiable.

Angela, Julia, Connie and Rob jumped into the pest control van and drove a few feet before going off-road and heading toward the Thames. Once they were close enough, they all got out, Rob released the handbrake and they pushed the van into the water. With all of its doors open, the van sank quickly. They then headed back to the pickup and the women climbed into the back with Ester.

Once they were all settled, Rob pulled back the partition window, winked at Angela and passed through a bottle of champagne. The shrieking and cheering coming from the back would have been deafening if there had been anyone around to hear it.

* * *

Back at Rose Cottage, Barry Cooper was staring at the bundles of £5 notes and £10 notes piled high in the hearth. He was about Mike's height and age but was a good couple of stone overweight, although he carried it well. Life had been harsh for Barry. Like Mike, the army had taught him how to survive in a group but not on his own; civvy street didn't suit him. It didn't really suit either of them.

"You gotta be fuckin' kidding me," Barry whispered in a deep, gruff smoker's growl.

Mike held open a small bag. "Two hundred thousand pounds in twenties and fifties. Untraceable. This is for you. We need to burn the fivers and tenners first, make sure they're properly gone, and then we need to take down the cottage. There's always tramps sleeping rough in here using tea lights and candles, so we can easily make it look like an accident."

Barry took the bag of money from Mike. Even though it contained more money than he'd ever had in his life, he couldn't take his eyes off the mountain of cash piled high in the hearth and he couldn't quite comprehend burning it. He looked back at the relatively small bag of cash in his hand.

"Papers said you got about thirty million. You're happy to burn a couple of million here, so you must have plenty left."

Barry turned and Mike recognized the dead stare; it was the stare Barry got when he was about to take on a job that no one else dared to do.

"I want more, Mike. You couldn't even have robbed that train if I hadn't given you the explosives to take out the track—I got 100k for doing that. Now you want me to destroy all the evidence that ties you to the train robbery and all I'm getting is 200k. I want a million."

Mike smiled nervously. "It's nowhere near that. The papers exaggerated. And in any case, I'm just one small part of a much bigger gang. They took most of the cash anyway."

But, as he spoke, his eyes flashed to the green bag sitting on the little two-seater sofa, containing his cut: £5 million in untraceable £20 and £50 notes.

Barry dived at the bag, ripping it open. And the red mist instantly descended. One punch fractured Mike's lower jaw and sent him flying onto his back. Barry knelt down by Mike's side and leaned in close.

"I thought we were brothers, Mikey. When I nicked that dynamite for you, I got sacked after the boss found it missing—remember? And you gave me a job to say 'sorry.' We had each other's backs. In the army, we looked after each other, me and you. So, why are you ripping me off now? Eh? How much is in the bag?"

As Mike opened his mouth to answer, a sickening pain shot through his jaw. Mike held up five fingers.

"Five million?" Mike nodded.

"I'd have been happy with a million, Mikey—but now I'm taking it all."

Barry got to his feet and turned his back on Mike as he stuffed the small bag of money earmarked for him inside Mike's bag.

"I'll still burn down the cottage for you, 'cos I'm not a double-crossing prick like you. I'm a man of my word. It'll look like an accident and you'll be in the clear. Course, you'll be skint but, well, there's a lesson about sharing in there somewhere."

From behind him, Barry heard a gurgle and turned to see Mike with a fire poker raised high above his head. As the poker came down, Barry raised his left arm to protect his head and his radius bone snapped. In a blind fury, he wrenched the poker from Mike's hands, sending him off balance and spinning to his left. Once again, the red mist took over and before Barry knew what he was doing, he'd hit Mike as hard as he could on the back of the head. Mike landed face down, blood pouring from the split in his skull and merging with the red and brown swirly patterns on Norma's fake Persian rug.

* * *

Ridley's mobile buzzed in his trouser pocket as he stood opposite Superintendent Raeburn, hands clenched behind his back. There was a perfectly good chair right in front of him, but Raeburn, along with every other officer who worked with Ridley, was used to him doing everything standing—even sucking up, which is what he was doing now. He'd been attentive all morning, stopping just short of obsequious, because Raeburn was getting a second answer from the coroner today, after Ridley had persuaded her to push harder.

"It's got to be low-key, Simon," Raeburn revealed eventually. Ridley hid his glee behind a well-controlled, "Thank you, ma'am."

* * *

Across in Aylesbury, Prescott squinted at the grainy CCTV image of the pest control van leaving the grounds of Rose Cottage. The driver looked alarmingly like an old-school Photofit. It gave them nothing and he knew it. His phone rang out on speaker and he prayed that Ridley wouldn't answer.

* * *

At sunrise the next day, a small ring of low-level LED lighting outlined the first grave belonging to Harry Rawlins, providing enough extra light for the JCB mini-excavator to do its job. The turf had been dug up by hand and was stacked in squares ready to be relaid later. Ridley and Raeburn watched by the graveside, while several plain-clothes PCs made sure that dog walkers and druggie teens didn't stray onto church grounds.

"The diamonds had better bloody well be in there, Simon," Raeburn whispered as she stamped from foot to foot, to keep her toes from freezing.

Ridley appeared to be far less concerned with property than people.

"It's also time we knew who he was, ma'am. He must have family. People who miss him."

Raeburn snorted. She was in no mood for sentimentality. Her predecessors had worked hard to keep this fiasco out the press all those years ago, and she didn't want to be the one now standing in front of the press explaining how they'd buried the same man twice. She needed something to distract the public. Solving a 35-year-old diamond heist and recovering the jewels would do nicely.

* * *

Angela had taken a break from sewing cash bundles into the bus seats and had brought Connie along on her weekly visit to the graveside of Dolly Rawlins. She didn't usually visit so early, but Connie needed to get out of the flat—she was missing the crisp fresh air of Taunton. Being blocked by plain-clothes police officers was the last thing they expected; if Connie had been sober, she'd have panicked. The police politely apologized for the inconvenience, before sending Angela and Connie on their way.

As they left, Connie's eyes focused on a small group of officers tucked in against the wall of the church, sheltering against the cold.

"He's here!" she gasped. "Jack Warr's here. This is to do with us, Angela. They're digging up Dolly!"

"Why on earth would they be digging up Dolly?" Angela dragged Connie away before she could be overheard. "Calm down, this doesn't have anything to do with us. I can see Dolly's grave from here and they're nowhere near it. They're round the front somewhere."

As they walked away, Angela looked back at the faint glow of portable LED lighting coming from the main churchyard. Whoever the police were digging up, they were important enough to have one of the big graves out front.

*　*　*

It took another hour to dig down as far as the coffin and hoist it out onto the grass. The brass plate on the lid read Harry Rawlins, another reminder for Raeburn of the mistake they'd made all those years ago. The coffin was put into the back of an undertaker's van, and Ridley, with Raeburn in his passenger seat, followed.

Foxy was in early so that he could open the coffin as soon as it arrived. This was the "bag of bones" Jack had spoken to him about. When he popped the lid, all that was inside the coffin was an incomplete skeleton. It was easy to see every inch of the coffin without having to move the body itself. There was nothing else. No diamonds. No bag or box that could possibly contain diamonds.

Raeburn walked away.

"What was she expecting?" Foxy asked.

Ridley headed for the door. "A promotion."

CHAPTER 22

Audrey Withey was furious about being brought into the station at 7:30 in the morning. She'd not even had time to dry her hair so, as she sat in Interview Room 1 dunking biscuits into her coffee, she complained about uncontrollable frizz.

"I'm not having my picture taken!" she shouted. "I flatly refuse!"

The female PC standing just inside the door was used to disgruntled visitors and was, therefore, perfectly able to block out the noise of Audrey's voice.

Anik's early morning knock on Audrey's front door had been designed to catch her off guard. It was an uncomfortable start to the day if you had something to hide. Audrey, with a lifetime's experience of being around criminals, was suitably wary. Her aggressive attitude and posturing came from uncertainty—perhaps even fear.

On the other hand, Susan Withey, who sat in Interview Room 2, was a naturally early riser. So, when Laura knocked on her door at 7:30, she'd already been up for a couple of hours. She was calm as she sipped her tea. She had no experience of police interview rooms and, therefore, no ingrained fears; she simply assumed that they wanted a chat about Mike.

Ridley and Anik joined Susan and offered her more tea, which she accepted and then sat down. Anik tucked his legs neatly under the table, but Ridley sat further back, giving himself the legroom to put his left ankle onto his right knee. He was relaxed, so Susan was relaxed.

"We need your help, please, Mrs. Withey," Ridley began politely. "We now have evidence that suggests Mike was involved in the Aylesbury train robbery back in '95. This isn't what either of us expected or wanted to find out, right?"

Anik hid his smile. In one sentence, Ridley had put himself firmly on the same side as Susan and they were now allies.

"Obviously, with Mike being a police officer, we want to be certain that the evidence isn't misleading us. I can't divulge the details, but if you could provide us with Mike's whereabouts on several specific dates, that would be incredibly helpful."

Anik opened his notebook in preparation for the next phase of the interview.

"DC Joshi has a list of the dates in question. He'll also be asking you about the money Mike received from the sale of the Spanish villa and the money he used to buy the house you currently occupy. I'm sorry that these are intrusive questions. They're unavoidable at this stage." ·

Ridley doubted Susan knew anything about her husband's criminal activities. If she was a victim, she needed to be treated with the respect and empathy that deserved.

When Susan spoke, it was with absolute honesty.

"My husband, DCI Ridley, was a drunk, a gambler, a womanizer and . . . and he could be a violent man. He was weak in that sense. But he loved the law. He felt terribly let down by it—his sister was murdered, his brother's locked away in a system that clearly doesn't work—but he respected it." Unconsciously, she straightened her back, raised her chin and all the love she had ever felt for Mike could be seen in her watering eyes. "I'll help you.

And I think we'll discover that Mike had nothing to do with your train robbery."

Ridley stood and smiled.

"I hope you're right, Mrs. Withey," he said as he left the room.

*   *   *

Susan's former mother-in-law, on the other hand, was a less than co-operative witness. Audrey sat back in her chair, arms folded, lips pursed, eyebrows down, totally closed off. She was on autopilot and, as soon as Jack opened his mouth to ask her if she needed anything, she'd instinctively said "no comment."

"You do know you're not under arrest, Mrs. Withey? You're helping us to find out who killed your son, and we're very grateful for that. Very grateful. I didn't know Mike, but I've heard great things. I want justice for him, as I'm sure you do . . . Do you mind if we record our chat so we're not distracted by note-taking?"

Laura was in awe. Audrey should have been putty in his hands, after that little opening speech.

But Laura was wrong.

"You're as shit as the rest of them," Audrey said, and got up and walked out.

*   *   *

On the front steps of the police station, Audrey sucked in half of her cigarette in one go, before coughing out a long plume of smoke. Behind her, Susan stepped out the main doors. As she spotted the back of Audrey's damp, frizzy head, her jaw muscles flickered and her eyes narrowed.

"I'm sorry we lost Mike."

Audrey spun round. Susan's expression was nowhere near as sympathetic as her words.

"He was on a slippery slope, Audrey, and while I was trying to hold on to him, you were giving him a big old shove."

Audrey's mouth dropped open, but no words came out.

"He needed to look to the future and you . . . You couldn't stop dragging him back into the past, could you?" Susan continued calmly. "You were so obsessed with Shirley, so focused on destroying Dolly Rawlins, that in your warped search for justice, you destroyed Mike as well. You did 'something,' Audrey, I know you did. You did 'something' and, from that moment, Mike had no chance. Losing his job, the drinking, the gambling, the aggression toward me . . . Oh yes, your boy put me in the hospital more than once."

Audrey opened her mouth.

"Be quiet!" Susan snarled as she stepped closer to Audrey. "I don't want to hear anything you have to say. My husband would be alive if his mother wasn't such an almighty fuck-up. If he robbed that train to right a wrong that you started, I swear to God, I'll see you banged up. Fuck the no-grassing code of honor, I will shout it from the rooftops!"

Tears rolled down through Audrey's deeply wrinkled cheeks. Susan didn't let up.

"Mike's dead because of you. They're all dead because of you. You're poison. So don't imagine for one second that I'll allow you to do the same to your grandchildren, because I won't. You've seen the last of them."

As Susan walked off, Audrey remained frozen to the spot. The pain welled up inside her and flooded out in a stream of long-overdue tears—but even now, Audrey was crying for herself. The world was cruel, God had forsaken her, everyone was set against her; nothing was her fault.

Watching from behind the bike rack at the corner of the police station, Jack almost felt sorry for Audrey. He'd come across many people like her. She was one of life's victims; it was all she knew. If she was ever honest enough to take responsibility for her own behavior, she would probably die from the shame.

* * *

Connie snored like a bulldozer on Angela's sofa. Aggie and Riel giggled from the lounge door, pushing their palms tight over their ears in exaggerated pain. Angela sneaked past them and placed a fry-up on the coffee table, together with a cup of tea. The fabulous smell took about three seconds to wake Connie, who sat bolt upright, almost falling out of her pajama top as the buttons strained under the pressure of her breasts. Riel gawped at Connie's cleavage for the length of time it took for Angela to usher them both out of the lounge.

"Teeth. Go!"

Angela stood by the window, looking out over her modest domain, and sipped her cup of tea.

"Don't you wake up starving after a night on the booze?" Connie asked through a mouthful of bacon and fried egg.

"I ate with the kids about an hour ago," Angela said. "They love having you for a sleepover because they get sausage sandwiches for breakfast."

"They'll love me even more when they're eating banger butties on a sunbed by a pool in 80 degree heat! We're nearly there, aren't we, Ange? We're honest-to-God nearly there!"

Angela couldn't control the grin that crept across her face.

* * *

Jack was beginning to worry about Audrey. She hadn't moved in at least ten minutes. Just as he decided to go and see if she was OK, she finally snapped out of it and lit herself another cigarette. Now Jack had stepped out of his hiding spot, he had no option but to continue toward her.

"Are you all right, Mrs. Withey?" he asked.

For a good few seconds, she said nothing. She just smoked. When she was ready, she clipped her cigarette and put the unsmoked half back into the packet.

"I got summat to say."

Jack took Audrey into the Soft Interview Room. Decorated like a sparse living room complete with sofas, lamps, coffee tables and children's toys, on the back wall was a large, plain mirror. This room was normally reserved for abuse victims and children who were giving evidence, but Jack wanted Audrey to feel like this interview was completely different from the earlier one—she could be the key to their investigation. He sat her down and then left under the pretense of making hot drinks for them both. Once outside, he asked a passing PC to put the kettle on and get Laura to come down from the squad room. He went into the observation room where, through the twoway mirror, he could see Audrey sitting on the sofa, wringing her hands, glancing around and looking generally very nervous.

When Laura came in with one tea and one coffee, Jack got her up to speed.

"Audrey never left. Something's on her mind. Can you stay here and watch?"

Moments later, he appeared in the Soft Interview Room and sat on the sofa opposite Audrey. He put the drinks down on a coffee table, and gave her time to compose herself before beginning.

* * *

In Raeburn's office, Ridley was listening politely to her rant.

"It's a can of worms!" she said furiously. "And it's impossible to shut it down now. We'll have to identify a pile of bones no one has even been looking for, and we'll have to fend off the ensuing court case that's inevitably going to come once the relatives are finally notified."

Ridley could only agree. There was little point in doing anything else.

* * *

Audrey wasn't here to do the right thing. She was broken. She was a woman with absolutely nothing to live for, so she was here for redemption before she finally curled up into a ball to die. Susan's words rang in her ears as she sipped her coffee: *Mike's dead because of you. They're all dead because of you.*

"It started with the diamonds." Audrey looked down into her mug as she spoke.

Up in the observation room, Laura breathed out an excited "*Ooohhh!*" Down in the interview room, Jack remained a picture of calm professionalism.

"I was pregnant. I was allowed to enjoy that for a whole six weeks before being told that my Shirl was dead and me old man was banged up for his part in the diamond robbery. Then I was just numb. Greg was a worry—he was already off his head from all the drugs, so I couldn't tell how he was feeling. He went out to score and, within minutes, the doorbell rang. It was her—Dolly Rawlins. First thing she said was how sorry she was to hear about Shirl— then she asked for a favor 'cos she had no one else to turn to. All in the one breath, that was."

Without taking his eyes off Audrey, Jack took out his notebook and jotted down all the questions he needed to ask. He barely knew where to begin.

"She had the diamonds with her. She actually brought those fucking diamonds into my house. She said that if I did what she wanted, I'd be taken care of for the rest of my life. She said . . ." Audrey paused as if recalling exactly what Dolly had instructed. "She said I was to take the diamonds to Jimmy Donaldson, who was already lined up to take them off her."

Jack wrote down Jimmy's name.

"Go on," he encouraged her.

"Jimmy was a trusted small-time crim who could fence anything," said Audrey. "Well—I was in shock! I'm grieving and she's waving death diamonds in my face and promising me more cash than I can spend. Like I'm gonna be bought that easy when my girl's not even been delivered to the mortuary yet?"

She sounded outraged, but her next words almost made Jack smile.

"Anyway, I took the diamonds and met Jimmy in his workshop out the back of his house. He bricked them diamonds up in his workshop wall and we went our separate ways." Audrey became more animated. "The next thing—it was in all the papers—she'd only gone and shot her fucking husband! I reckon she knew she was gonna shoot him, which is why she gave me the diamonds—to hide for her coming out." Now Audrey was visibly shaking. "Can I have another coffee? And some of them biscuits I had earlier?"

Jack headed out to the corridor, where Laura was waiting. They clutched each other in excitement like a couple of kids who'd just stumbled across a hoard of buried treasure.

"Kettle's on," Laura said before Jack could even ask. "Why's she spilling her guts all of a sudden?"

"She met Susan outside the station," Jack explained. "I wasn't close enough to hear the conversation, but she looked pretty shocked."

"Better get back in there while the mood's on her," said Laura. Restocked with coffee and biscuits, Audrey was ready to start talking again.

"With Dolly in prison, I was never gonna be taken care of for the rest of me life, was I? I was never gonna be paid for helping her. Never gonna get what I was owed." Audrey's face fell. "I was working all hours on the market, drinking too much and I had a miscarriage . . . And then one day I heard Jimmy had been arrested. I thought, Jesus Christ, he's been done for the diamonds and they'll be coming for me! Turns out he was nicked for writing bad checks, so that was OK. But now I was thinking about the diamonds and how no one but me knew they was even there."

Audrey took a break from her rambling to munch on a biscuit, and Jack worried that she was about to wise up and stop talking before she incriminated herself. She didn't.

"I went round to Jimmy's. I knew his missus from bingo—bit simple. I took her a packet of fags and offered to make her a cuppa. From her kitchen, I went into his workshop and there was the wall. Untouched." She sat bolt upright. "I swear on my life, Mike never knew anything about any of it. Write that down! I don't want you thinking that any of this is Mike's fault, 'cos it ain't. It's mine. And seeing as Mike can't defend himself, I have to."

Jack dutifully wrote down that Mike knew nothing about the diamonds being stolen or hidden, or being found again by Audrey.

She watched him do it. As though those words would keep her son's memory safe.

"Them diamonds got my Shirl murdered, so I wanted them gone. I sold 'em for a tenth of what they was worth and I built a villa in Spain. By that time, my old man had died of cancer in prison, so I told everyone it was his life insurance I was spending. But he wasn't worth nothing." Audrey took a deep breath. "Can I have a fag break?"

Outside, Audrey didn't light a cigarette. She stared into the blue sky and absorbed the freedom she was now feeling. Freedom from the burden of having lived with such secrets. Eventually, she grinned at Jack.

"The next time Dolly turned up on my doorstep, it was to ask for the diamonds back. I can still see her face when I told her I'd got half a million for 'em. Do you know how much they was really worth? Three million!"

Audrey opened her mouth and emptied her lungs in one long, foul laugh, until her skin turned blue, reveling in her warped little victory.

Jack could see just how pathetic she really was. Not only did she seem oblivious to how dangerous her world and its people were, she also seemed incapable of learning. Murdered daughter, stolen diamonds, corrupt son—would nothing make her wake up and smell the coffee?

"Dolly!" Audrey spat. "I told her how the stress had killed my baby and you know what she said? 'Small mercies.' She's stood in my house and telling me my baby was better off dead. I should have killed her where she stood but, God forgive me, I didn't. Mike would be alive now if I had. That's when I told him everything. He didn't know nothing before that and everything he did afterward was to put right the mess I'd made. If you don't believe that, I'm leaving right now." Audrey's hands began to shake in anger. "Mike's a good boy. You gotta promise that he ain't remembered as anything else."

Before Jack could stop himself, he said, "I promise."

If that turned out to be a lie, he'd cross that bridge when he got to it.

"Come on," he said, and took her elbow.

He needed her to come back inside and pour her heart out on tape—not on the steps of the police station.

With another coffee in her hand and a fresh plate of biscuits in front of her, Audrey was ready to continue.

"That debt to Dolly Rawlins put Mike in a position he couldn't get out of. If my Mike had anything to do with the train robbery, it had to be because Dolly forced him into it. Mike was a victim, not a criminal!" Each time Dolly's name was mentioned, it spat out of Audrey's mouth with venom. The tears welled. "Dolly Rawlins only got eight years for taking some gangster off the streets—who gives a shit about Harry being gunned down? But she got *nothing* for killing my Shirl, my little baby . . . and now Mike! That bitch killed my babies, but you lot never punished her for any of that."

"She was shot six times!" Jack pointed out. "Not by me! Not by *me*!"

Audrey dropped her mug, hid her face in her hands and sobbed. Years of ignoring the truth fueled her uncontrollable anguish. It was as if she finally felt responsible for something—and that something was for not killing Dolly Rawlins when she had the chance.

* * *

When Jack and Laura walked into his office and closed the door behind them, Ridley hoped it was because they had something to say that he actually wanted to hear. If they were bringing him anything less than a bloody miracle, they'd better watch out. But as Jack relayed Audrey's second interview, Ridley edged toward his seat and finally sat down on it—a rare event. Once Jack had finished, Ridley confirmed that Audrey would be arrested on suspicion of handling stolen goods, bounced back to his feet and headed out into the squad room.

"Right!" he shouted. "Everybody just listen for now, so we can put this together. Questions later."

As Ridley and Jack spoke, they shuffled evidence, moved and regrouped suspects and filled in gaps on the three overflowing evidence boards. As Anik watched Ridley and Jack leading this new charge, he could feel the sergeant's position drifting out of sight.

"Harry Rawlins's gang did the diamond heist—we know this because most of them were arrested at the scene," said Jack, looking round at his colleagues. "But the diamonds ended up with Dolly, who gave them to Audrey for safekeeping while she went inside for killing her husband . . ."

By three o'clock, he'd brought everyone up to speed and the case was up to 1995. Ridley took over.

"We know Mike drove to Rose Cottage in his Range Rover and we know someone else drove there in a pest control van—probably Barry Cooper. We know someone killed Mike, then expertly improvised the destruction of the cottage and everything in it—probably Barry Cooper. We know that the remaining cash left the scene in the pest control van. And we know Barry's on the run. He has a background in the army and in demolition. He's highly dangerous and we *have* to find him. He's the key."

Ridley looked round at his team. Everyone was gripped—except Laura, who was frowning as she stared at Jack. Ridley followed her gaze. Jack had his hand up.

"I think Barry's definitely involved, sir, but there's nothing to suggest he's a mastermind. I think we need to look again at the women. If Dolly was the woman that Audrey says she was, *she'd* have had the balls to hide twenty-seven million in the cellar of an ex-copper."

Ridley looked skeptical. "Those women have been ruled out. Twice. Once in 1995 and again by us. By you, in fact."

"There was no evidence," Jack pointed out. "But then, there was no evidence to connect Dolly to the diamond raid either, yet we now know that she was the one who walked away with everything."

"So, no evidence means they did it?"

Anik smirked and the sergeant's post drifted back into his sight.

"And," Ridley continued, "if they'd just got away with a life-changing sum of money, why the hell, two days later, are they shooting each other?"

"That was Ester," said Jack. "She's unstable, but the rest of them aren't. The diamonds have to be how Dolly bought The Grange in the first place, sir. With all due respect, you haven't met them. They're . . . I don't know, there's something about them. They're calm—like they've been hiding in plain sight."

"Or maybe they're innocent?" Anik chipped in.

Jack ignored him and kept his focus on Ridley.

"We know Angela worked for Ester and had an affair with Mike, whose family has history with Dolly. We've been slowly linking them together this whole time, and now Audrey is telling us that her son did the train robbery."

"Which I agree with, but—"

"Call it gut instinct, sir," Jack interrupted, "but I *know* we should be looking at these women."

"Your 'gut' has just spent next month's overtime budget digging up a grave for no reason," said Ridley angrily. "I'm the one who'll get daily flak on that for the foreseeable, not you. You're all right, Jack. Your newly acquired 'gut instinct' has a lot to learn. We're going after Barry Cooper and when we find him, *my* gut instinct says we'll also find the rest of the money *and* a gang of as-yet unidentified army blokes who were in on the train robbery."

* * *

Jack marched the twelve-minute walk to pathology in just under seven minutes. He was fuming. He'd finally found his passion for this thankless job and now he was being ignored. His mind raced with disjointed thoughts and then oddly settled on something he had only read in passing many weeks ago—the name of George Resnick. The entire station had mocked George when he insisted that Harry Rawlins was alive, and hadn't been blown up in the Strand underpass. Every scrap of evidence was against him, his team was against him, but he *knew* he was right. Jack recalled how he'd wanted to feel that sort of tenacity. That sort of certainty. Well, now he did. He *knew* the women from The Grange were up to their necks in this.

As he pushed through the heavy rubber doors into Foxy's outer lab, his mobile signal died and a call from Maggie was sent straight to voicemail. Jack handed a DNA testing kit he'd bought online to Foxy. One sample was already labeled and ready to go; the second would be taken from the bag of bones.

"Whose is this?" asked Foxy, pointing at the first sample.

"Mine," said Jack as he left.

Foxy stood there, shaking his head.

"And I thought I'd seen everything . . ."

*   *   *

"Hi, darling." Maggie's beautiful voice brought an almost physical relief to Jack. All he wanted to do right now was go home and slide into bed next to her. "I just got a call from your dad's estate agent. The last offer was above the reserve, so it's been accepted. They want a quick sale and have asked for the bungalow to be emptied. I know you're in the middle of a lot right now. I'll come with you, Jack, but I can't do it for you. Love you."

Jack leaned against the battleship-gray wall and texted Maggie back.

We'll go tonight.

He paused mid-text. Then,

They don't need me here.

CHAPTER 23

Ridley had been sympathetic to Jack's impending family loss and had granted him the time off to go and sort out Charlie's affairs without comment. Jack got the impression Ridley was happy to see the back of him. The feeling was mutual.

Maggie drove and Jack stared out the passenger window, his mobile on his lap. For the first half of their journey, she had attempted polite conversation but now she seemed content to mumble along to Queen songs and allow him time for his thoughts. His phone was on silent but each time it vibrated, he checked to see if it was Foxy calling with DNA results. If the bag of bones was a match to him, then his dad was dead. If it wasn't a match, then his dad could still be alive. Tony Fisher had insinuated that Jimmy Nunn could well be living it up on a beach somewhere, spending someone else's money. The thought once again popped into Jack's head that it was even possible—if he was right, and Dolly Rawlins was behind it—that she'd enlisted Jimmy Nunn in the train robbery.

Jack's gut instinct was in overdrive. What if Craigh had been right when he raided The Grange looking for guns? After all, Gloria Radford's husband, Eddie, had been an arms dealer who had weapons stashed all over London. What if Ester had seduced . . . ? No, not Ester; no one could be that desperate. Julia. What if Julia had seduced Norma into helping them? Or simply into trusting them? What if Mike and Angela had been lovers since the day he'd rescued her from Ester's brothel? Right from the very beginning, coppers like Bill Thorn had totally underestimated the women, labeling them as too physically and emotionally weak. Different snippets of evidence swam around inside Jack's skull, settling into their most likely home. If one of the robbers had been on a horse, why not all of them? That would compensate for any lack of physical strength. As for emotional strength, Jack had no doubt whatsoever that none of the women were lacking in that department.

"It's them," he whispered to himself.

And although Maggie heard this comment, she didn't ask Jack to elaborate. He wasn't speaking to her.

* * *

The tall ships in Cowes were an impressive sight. Tourists snapped away, hoping that at least one of their ten thousand holiday photos would be worthy of a frame. Waiting at the quayside, Ester looked like something out of an Agatha Christie TV drama—her sense of style had waned somewhat over the years. Today she was wearing a real fur hat.

"If you're off on the run," Geoffrey warned her, "might I suggest that a dead beaver on your head isn't the best attire? It'll only take one confrontation with an animal lover and you'll end up being arrested for disturbing the peace. They'll see your new passport and, hey presto, you'll be taken from me forever."

Geoffrey was a gibbering wreck. His entire body shook and he made strange noises as he tried to stifle his tears.

"Geoffrey! You listen to me!" Ester barked. "You can't be like this. Once I'm gone, you need to go home and set about find-ing yourself another lover straight away. Someone who will think more of you than she does of herself. You deserve the best—so don't settle for the first money-grabbing tart who knocks on your door." She smiled. "That's what you did last time and look at the mess that got you into."

Ester's feelings for Geoffrey were as shallow as they were for any other human being, but she did have the emotional capacity to understand that he loved her with all of his pathetic, overly needy little heart. Unfortunately for him, Ester was a great believer in pulling the plaster off quickly and not prolonging the pain.

"I don't love you, Geoffrey, you know that—although I have always very much liked the idea of you. Buy yourself a suit—you look lovely in a suit—and go on the prowl. Oh, and, when you do snag yourself a willing lady, make sure you hide the dildos and whips until you're sure she's on board with all of that sort of caper."

Ester took off her beaver fur hat and placed it on Geoffrey's head. It slipped down his bald head and covered his face before Ester tilted it back to reveal his weeping eyes.

"Don't think I'm coming back, will you?" she said over her shoulder as she marched off. "Because I'm not. Move on, my darling."

As she headed for the Southampton ferry, Geoffrey waved goodbye to the love of his life. And Ester never once looked back.

* * *

The electric fire had been off for so long that it now filled the living room with the stench of burning dust. Packing boxes had taken over the whole of the kitchen, half of the front room and were threatening to bury Jack in the far corner of the living room.

"You know, we could sort some of this stuff out before boxing it up, Jack," said Maggie, although she knew that Penny must be the one to decide which memories she kept and which she let go.

Behind a bookshelf in the living room, Jack found a wooden arrow covered in cobwebs. The shaft was beautifully sandpapered to a smooth finish and the metal head was made from a piece of a Coke can folded and hammered into a triangular point. Even the fletching, made of pigeon feathers, was still intact.

"Our cat never actually killed birds," Jack explained. "But it'd bring stray feathers in and give them to Dad. We made a bow and arrows in the shed one day when Mum was out. We had enough feathers to make fletching for seven arrows, I think it was. I've no idea why we thought it'd be a good idea to test it in here. Maybe it was raining. Dad hates being cold."

Jack looked up the wall. Directly above his head, just beneath the narrow cornice that ran around the edge of the ceiling, there was a deep gouge in the wallpaper.

"This one hit the wall and fell down behind the bookcase, just as Mum came back. Dad almost shit himself! He threw the bow out the window and we pretended we'd been reading."

Maggie loved the "little boy" version of Jack. His smile melted away as the depth of his impending loss dawned on him. She wrapped her arms round his neck, forcing him to dip his head and rest into her neck. She felt him breathe against her tight embrace and she didn't let go until she felt him start to move away. She would have held on to him forever if he'd wanted her to.

By early evening, Maggie and Jack were eating pizza and drinking wine in front of the fire, happy just to be with each other in this comfortable, familiar space that, after today, they'd never see again.

"I'm sorry for being a dick," Jack said, out of the blue. "With all the Jimmy Nunn stuff, I mean. I'm not after another dad, Mags. I want to know where this restlessness comes from—or if it's just me not quite knowing where I fit. Foxy's helping me find the answers I need but what I won't do, I promise, is ever again allow Jimmy Nunn to distract me from the people who are really important. We should catch up with Mum and Dad, like we said we would. Do you reckon you can get the time off work?"

Maggie knew her work rota off by heart, so knew she was owed several days—but she was more concerned about the cost of two tickets to St. Lucia, which was the next stop for the cruise ship. As she googled flight and hotel prices, Jack's phone buzzed.

Foxy's text read:

No DNA match.

In a split second, everything Jack had just said went out the window. If Jimmy Nunn wasn't the man in Harry Rawlins's first grave, then he could still be walking around somewhere. He watched Maggie's lips move, but he didn't hear a word she said. He was getting to grips with the idea that his birth dad might still be alive.

CHAPTER 24

The next morning, while Maggie lay comatose, having drunk more than her fair share of the two bottles of wine from last night, Jack was in the kitchen having a whispered phone conversation with Foxy.

"No, no, that's not what I said at all," Foxy explained. He was stuck in traffic due to an accident up ahead, and was trying hard not to take that out on Jack. "I said that there's no DNA match between *you* and the skeleton on my table. I did *not* say that the skeleton wasn't Jimmy Nunn." There was silence from Jack's end of the phone, so Foxy continued. "You told me about an old shoulder injury sustained when Jimmy fell off a fence. This was confirmed by his medical records, and the skeleton on my table has an identical injury. We don't have DNA on file for Jimmy Nunn, but his dental records, I'm certain, Jack, will show that this is him."

Still no reply from Jack. Foxy's car engine stopped and started as he crawled forward, no more than ten inches at a time.

"What does this mean for you, my friend? You thought he was— who? Your dad? I can tell you he's not." Foxy glanced out of his window. "Look, I'm just driving past a pile-up that's going to keep me busy all week, but how about a drink later? You can ask me anything you need to."

Jack left a note on the kitchen table underneath a plate of apologetic pastries:

Something urgent came up. Back by midday. Sorry. X.

He had left Maggie stranded with no car, but he also knew that driving from his parents' bungalow in Totnes to Fran's house in Burnham-on-Sea would be the quickest way for him to get back to Maggie. He'd work out how to apologize properly on the return journey.

* * *

Fran was putting the bins out when Jack pulled up. She didn't look particularly pleased to see him, but he didn't care.

"We need to talk," he said, standing over her until she had no choice but to invite him in.

Fran apologized for the mess, just as she had done the first time Jack visited. It would be have been unlucky for him to catch Fran on two terrible housework days, so he concluded that she and Clay always lived in this half-hearted squalor.

Not wanting either of them to be distracted, Jack declined a cup of tea.

"When Trudie left me with you, where did she go?"

Fran shrugged. "I've no idea."

Jack believed her. "Why did she go? Was she worried, frightened?"

"She was very upset about something. She'd got a phone call a couple days earlier and that had put her in a great mood. She took you and her suitcase and off she went—to start a new life, she said. Not a thank you, or nothing. As soon as she didn't need us anymore, it was like we never existed. But two days later she came back, tail well and truly between her legs. You were screaming, she was screaming—'The bastard! I hate him! I hate him!' We thought Jimmy had promised everything and delivered nothing again. The next day, she left you with us and disappeared for the last time."

"So, she went from starting a new life to . . . what? Being stood up?"

"That's what we assumed," Fran said as she put the kettle on. "I can't go an hour without a cuppa. You sure you don't want one?"

"No thanks."

Jack sat down and fell quiet while Fran pottered. Who on earth could have called Trudie if it wasn't Jimmy? Who was the man she was so happy to be running away with? And who had hurt her so cruelly by abandoning her and her baby?

"What was the date, Aunt Fran, can you remember?"

"Oh, good God, no. Sorry, love. It was so long ago. And it was just a normal morning really. She was sat right there, where you are now, drinking tea and reading the paper. Something snapped. One minute she was OK—I mean she was upset but OK—the next minute she was out the door. I wish I could tell you more, Jack, I really do."

Jack's mobile buzzed in his trouser pocket. He checked it in case it was Maggie wondering where he was. It was Ridley. He watched the call go to voicemail. On his screen he had three messages: "missed call," "new voicemail" and "breaking news" relating to some natural disaster across the other side of the world. But it prompted him to ask a question.

"What newspaper was she reading?"

* * *

Burnham-on-Sea Library was far bigger than Jack had expected it to be and even had a research section, including newspaper archives, which was exactly what he needed. He scrolled through old copies of the *Daily Mail*, the newspaper Fran had said Trudie was reading on the morning she left. Although Jack didn't know the exact date, he knew the approximate time of year because he was only with Fran and Clay for ten months before he went into foster care; he knew the date he went into foster care because that information was on the paperwork he'd been given by Charlie.

Jack started by scrolling through the headlines, day by day, from July 1984 onward. When he got to August 12, 1984, the four-word headline stopped him dead. He read it again and again to make absolutely certain of what he was seeing. It was a good twenty seconds before he realized that he was holding his breath. As he started to breathe again, he read the four words one last time: harry rawlins shot dead. Was *this* what had upset Trudie so much? Was Harry Rawlins the man who Trudie had gone to meet, and who hadn't shown up because he was already dead?

As Jack read the words over and over, he recalled everything he knew about Harry Rawlins. Rawlins was the one who always got away, the one who reveled in ruining Resnick's career; he was smart, controlled and controlling, fearless and ruthless—and he was the only man the Fisher brothers had ever feared. Was Harry Rawlins the man his mum loved? Jack recalled Foxy's text about Jimmy Nunn:

No DNA match.

Was Harry Rawlins Jack's dad?

CHAPTER 25

Jack's detour to the library meant that he didn't get back to Maggie until well after lunch. As he pulled into the driveway, he could see that boxes were now stacked higher than the living room windowsill. In the kitchen, most of the pastries had gone. Jack didn't know what he felt more strongly—guilt or hunger. He was nibbling on a cinnamon swirl when Maggie came into the kitchen carrying a box labeled "Penny's knick-knacks."

"Everywhere's done apart from the stuff we're still using in here. I've taken the bed and wardrobe apart in their room and the bed in your room. I can't see how your wardrobe comes apart. Did you put it together? I think it's glued. I've still got to box up the bathroom cabinets and I've left the shed for you 'cos there'll be stuff in there that's too heavy for me. Put the kettle on and I'll finish the bathroom."

Maggie put the box down, picked up a smaller empty box and disappeared toward the bathroom. She sounded like nothing was wrong, but Jack knew that this was worse than if she'd been shouting at him.

* * *

The drive home was excruciating. Queen were playing again, just loud enough to stifle conversation. Jack knew that staying quiet was making things worse but he didn't know what to say—certainly not, "My dad's not Jimmy Nunn after all, Mags. In fact it might turn out to be Harry Rawlins. You know, that notorious old-school gangster?"

He had to have absolute proof before he shared his news with Maggie.

Maggie dropped him off outside the police station, not bothering even to pause the music for a loving "goodbye." As he got out, Jack turned back to say how sorry he was for leaving her alone all morning with no explanation and no car, but before he could open his mouth, she'd driven off.

* * *

Meet me outside the garages.

When Laura got Jack's text message her heart did an involuntary little flutter and her face flushed. Once she'd actually had a second to think, she realized it was probably work-related, probably something Jack wanted kept from Ridley. She was right.

* * *

The bus seats had now all been smuggled back inside the bus, and no one would ever know that the value of this second-hand vehicle had just increased from £3,700 to around £25,003,700.

Angela was very proud of all the wine-fueled hard work they'd put in.

"I can feel it," Ester complained as she bounced up and down on her seat.

"No one's going to be bouncing that violently," Angela pointed out. She was having none of it. "Perhaps the lumps you can feel is the cellulite in your arse."

"Talking of cellulite," Ester continued, "I hear Connie's put on a pound or two. Where is the old slapper?"

"Connie's sorting out her B&B. She'll be back the day after tomorrow." Angela changed the subject. "Where are you staying, Ester? You've not used your own name, have you?"

"You don't have to worry about anything I do, Angela darling," Ester replied loftily. "I was outsmarting the Filth before you were a twitch in your daddy's underpants."

Angela was tempted to point out that for someone skilled in outsmarting the Filth, Ester had spent a lot of her adult life behind bars, but it wasn't worth it. She behaved as long as she thought she had the upper hand. And behave was all Angela actually needed her to do.

"So, what's the cover story for four middle-aged women heading to Europe in a 25-seater coach?"

"There'll be Rob and my kids as well," said Angela. "So I imagine we'll look like friends going on holiday, if you can manage to smile."

In fact Julia was also planning to bring three kids from the home, but they would keep that quiet until the final second before they were due to leave, so that Ester had no option but to accept it. Sam, Darren and Suzie were unrelated orphans who would never in a million years be successfully fostered—they were too damaged for ordinary people to love. They were exactly the sort of kids Dolly would have wholeheartedly embraced if The Grange had ever been successfully transformed into a children's home. Julia adored each one of them. They were very difficult in their own ways but the rewards, when they came, were heartwarming. She wouldn't dream of leaving them behind.

* * *

Laura thanked the custody sergeant as he let Jack into Audrey's cell.

"Five minutes, Jack, OK?"

Inside, Jack handed Audrey a cup of coffee she hadn't asked for, which confused her, until she glanced to the top right-hand corner of her cell, at the CCTV camera pointing down at her. Her blood ran cold and the penny dropped: Jack didn't have a legitimate reason for being in her cell. He was covering his back so this little visit wouldn't come back and bite him in the arse. Their conversation would appear cordial to anyone watching, but even Audrey, who wasn't the sharpest tool in the box, could see that the man standing in front of her now wasn't the same kind man who'd earlier plied her with coffee and biscuits.

"Tell me about Harry Rawlins." Jack's tone was calm but cold.

"I never met the man," Audrey said. "I know he was a big noise back in the day. I mean, he even put the willies up the Fishers and no one did that."

"Go on," he prompted.

"I don't understand what you want me to say," she whined. "I never met him, like I said."

"You lived in his world, Audrey, so tell me about him."

Audrey shuffled on her thin, plastic-covered mattress.

"Well, he lived out in Potter's Bar. Married to Dolly—you know that bit. No kids. I don't know much about him. I didn't live in his world at all, DC Warr, I only skirted round it."

"DC Warr?" Jack knew he had Audrey on the back foot. She was uneasy and she was scared, and she was compliant.

"He was like a myth, you know?" she went on. "My Shirl told me she'd met him once and I was properly worried. I didn't want her near him. We was the sort of people that Harry Rawlins would use up and spit out. I mean, those poor men who got blown up in the armed raid were meant to be his friends and he left them behind quick enough. Just imagine what he'd do to someone he didn't care about. I'm really sorry, I'm just guessing what you might want to hear. I don't know him."

In the short silence that followed, Laura, listening from outside, racked her brains trying to think how Harry Rawlins might be linked to their current investigation. But then Jack had followed the Fishers as a lead when no one else made a connection, so perhaps Harry Rawlins was integral in some way.

"What family does Harry have?" Jack kept his voice monotone.

"I don't know anything about Harry's family," insisted Audrey.

Jack moved to lean on the wall near the foot of her bed.

"You do know," he continued coldly. "Think about it and you'll remember. Harry Rawlins must have had family. Cousins, nephews. He'd have had a crew that he always used. Who hung around in that group?" Audrey's gormless face was starting to annoy him. "*Think*, Audrey!"

"I dunno. I'm sorry that I don't, but I don't."

Laura heard a movement from inside the cell and before she'd made a conscious decision, she had opened the door. Jack was now standing next to Audrey and she was leaning away from him.

Laura spoke quickly. "We're done."

Jack walked off, leaving Laura to thank the custody sergeant for his discretion. When she caught him up, she had to physically grab his arm to make him stop and listen to her.

"I don't know what's wrong with you, Jack, but . . . Look, I'm on your side but this isn't you. You're acting like you have another agenda that you're not telling anyone about. You can talk to me, you know."

"I'm really sorry, Laura. I just spent yesterday clearing Dad's cottage ready for sale and . . ."

Jack dipped his head in shame. He was actually using his dying dad as a lie to explain away his unprofessional behavior. Laura interpreted the head-dip as sadness and put her hand on his shoulder.

"Go home," she said. "I'll cover for you with Ridley."

Jack put his hand on top of hers and stroked his thumb back and forth. He looked into her dark blue eyes and told her how grateful he was. He couldn't find the will to care about her feelings at all. All he wanted was to find out whether Harry Rawlins was his dad and if those fucking Grange women had committed the biggest train robbery in living memory.

Knowing these two things would make everything fall into place. Then, for the first time in his life, maybe he'd feel whole.

CHAPTER 26

Jack was desperate to find someone who had known Harry Rawlins and, more importantly, who knew a living member of the Rawlins family. As things were, he didn't even really know what Harry looked like. Every photo he'd been able to find of Rawlins was blurred, or his face was partly covered, or showed him side on to the camera. He seemed to be a dab hand at remaining incognito.

As Jack trawled through old files and new databases, he came across numerous names who could have helped if they hadn't been dead. So much time had passed. At this rate, he was going to have to convince Ridley to dig up Harry's second grave.

After an hour of searching, Jack settled on the name of DS Alex Fuller, mainly because he was one of only a handful of people from the eighties who was still breathing. Fuller had been Resnick's right-hand man and, at times, his biggest critic. One report from Fuller caught Jack's eye. In it, he expressed concern to the then superintendent about Resnick's emotional stability and requested a transfer out of Resnick's team. Fuller's report showed him to be an honest, ambitious man who didn't want his own career to be hindered or tainted by the unfounded obsessions of his boss. Jack felt an immediate affinity. Right now, he, too, thought his boss was on the wrong track. He called Fuller.

* * *

Alex Fuller was a stout man in his mid-60s. He had been handsome in his day and the years had been kind to him. He had a full head of white hair and he carried his once muscular physique well. He'd still be a handful if he ever got into a brawl.

"It's good of you to see me, Mr. Fuller," said Jack.

"Alex. And I'm happy to help." Fuller didn't ask what Jack would like to drink, he just got on with making a pot of tea for them both. "Fire away, son. I'm listening."

"I'm interested in Harry Rawlins."

Fuller let out a belly laugh. "Fuck me, that name never goes away, does it? What's he done now? Risen from the grave and robbed a bank? He's not the missing man on the Hatton Garden job, is he?"

"I read your case files today. Rawlins was certainly notorious."

"That's one word for him. So, you think he's connected somehow to a new case?"

"We're exploring a variety of avenues."

Fuller grinned at Jack's use of such a stock phrase when talking to an ex-copper. He must be new to this.

"You wrote about an occasion in 1984, when you raided the home of Trudie Nunn. She was hysterical apparently, screaming, 'He's gone, he's gone!' At the time, you assumed she was talking about Jimmy Nunn."

Fuller bowed his head as he recalled the moment.

"The only assumption that ever mattered was that Harry Rawlins died in the explosion in the Strand underpass. From that moment on, it was all smoke and mirrors and the only person who knew it for a fact was George Resnick. I remember the raid on Trudie Nunn's flat ... So you think the 'he' she was talking about was Harry Rawlins? I think you're right."

Jack told Fuller about the exhumation, and how one of the few remaining teeth from the jigsaw puzzle skeleton was currently being tested against Jimmy Nunn's dental records. Fuller nodded, as if that all made sense.

"Look—for most of his career, Resnick taught me nothing at all about the art of being a copper. He was a cantankerous old prick, resentful and fucking hard to like, meaning no one wanted to work for him. But he was an exceptional policeman. He had commendations coming out of his ears, he'd put more bad 'uns away than anyone I've ever worked with and his gut instinct was to die for. It was only when the force couldn't keep up with him that things went off track. Unfortunately, that's when I knew him. I wish I'd known him when he was younger." Fuller looked directly at Jack. "You're standing there with the same look in your eyes as Resnick back in the day. Like you're about to ask me to believe in something, based on nothing more than gut instinct. I let him down on that score so many times and that weighs heavy. So, ask what you came to ask."

"I need to find a close relative of Harry Rawlins to check his DNA for a familial match."

"The only one I can think of is his cousin, Eddie, but I don't know if he's dead or alive."

Fuller handed Jack a mug of tea, and he took it gratefully. He was exhausted and let his mind wander as Fuller rambled on about villains in the old days. But when Fuller mentioned Dolly Rawlins, he was all attention.

"She was a stony-faced old cow. At least, that's the face she showed everyone. She was afforded a huge amount of respect because she was Harry's wife, but, in truth, she earned it. She was smart. I mean, she gave us the runaround for months—we were chasing our tails and she was watching. And Harry didn't spend a single day behind bars in his life. That's not down to luck, that's down to a loyal wife. People said Dolly was lucky to have Harry—but I think it was the other way round."

* * *

Connie sat on the benches in front of her B&B, eating fish and chips out of paper and drinking stout from the bottle. She looked out over the Blackdown Hills and cried. It was a stunning view: plots of undulating light green land cut into squares by dark green hedges; horses, sheep and rabbits grazed together; the occasional walker made their respectful way along the designated paths that cut through Connie's little piece of paradise. She didn't want to leave the comfort of her safe haven, but she knew—she hoped—that her brand new life would be bigger and better than anything she'd ever dreamed of. The excitement of the train robbery flooded back—the vision of millions of pounds shooting up the nozzle of an industrial vacuum and then, moments later, down into the coal shaft of Rose Cottage. Connie giggled through the tears. It had been the most wonderful night of her entire life. The night she knew her life was worth fighting for.

* * *

The shift was drawing to an end in the squad room when Anik took the call from Essex. Barry Cooper had been found. The local force had him under covert observation while they waited for two Armed Response Vehicles to be rallied, briefed and arrive at the address. Ridley's team had time to join them if they fancied being in on the showdown. It was their case, after all.

As Ridley swept through the squad room and headed for the car park, he didn't even bother to ask where Jack was.

*   *   *

Jack listened to generic acoustic music as he waited for Maggie to come to the phone. He stood, fixed to the spot, looking across the road of a dustbin-lined terraced street, at one specific house which had the lounge light on and a TV flickering away in the far corner of the room. All around him dogs barked, men shouted at a football match on TV, women talked loudly in various languages and the wonderful aroma of foreign cooking filled the air. This part of Whitechapel had been up and coming for a while but it felt as if it still had a way to go.

"I have two minutes," Maggie said.

"I'm sorry, Mags. I'm so sorry for walking out on you at Mum and Dad's. I can't explain what happened. Not yet. I just . . . Please be patient with me, because I'm nearly there. Honestly."

Maggie was economical with her words. She had two minutes and she wasn't joking.

"I love you, Jack Warr, and I will always be here for you. Tomorrow morning, when I get home, I want breakfast in bed and a cuddle regardless of how bad I smell. And when you get home in the evening, you're taking me out because I've got tomorrow night off. Now I have to go."

Jack smiled as he put his phone away and headed toward the house he'd been watching.

Eddie Rawlins opened his front door like someone not to be messed with. Tall and with a broad set of shoulders for a man in his late 70s, he had a furrowed face from a lifetime of too many frowns and too few smiles. His deep resonating voice—"What?"—completed the picture of an old East End ex-con who'd earned his stripes.

But when Eddie focused on Jack's face, all of his bravado vanished. His shoulders slumped and he stepped back, suddenly diminished. His face drained to white, his mouth gaped, his eyebrows shot up and his eyes nearly popped out of his head.

"S-sorry, sorry," Eddie stuttered as he forced a quivering smile. "For a minute there, I thought you was . . . Well, you reminded me of a man I used to know."

CHAPTER 27

Eddie refilled his whisky glass and poured one for Jack. As they silently sipped their single malt, Jack felt something he'd never really felt before. He felt feared. Eddie feared him. Not strictly true, of course—Eddie feared the man he thought he saw for a moment standing at his front door, before he remembered that Harry Rawlins was dead.

"I want to talk to you about Harry Rawlins," Jack said.

"I bet you do." Eddie downed his whisky and poured himself another. "Let me guess—you want to know if old Harry knew your mum, 30-odd years ago." He eyed Jack. "I'd say he did."

Jack had expected to have to pry information out of Eddie, then beg for a DNA sample to test against. But here he was, inadvertently terrifying an old man by his very presence. Imagine, then, how Harry must have felt back in the day—strutting into a room and having every fearful eye on him. Imagine having that power over half of the gangsters in London, over Tony bloody Fisher, over any woman he set eyes on.

Jack realized he was staring at Eddie and, in response, Eddie was sweating and fidgeting. My God, he felt like he was Harry's boy! However, the same gene pool had allegedly produced the wimp sitting in front him, so Jack wanted to be sure. He looked around the room, which looked like it hadn't been redecorated since the eighties, and his eyes fixed on a photo of two boys in their mid to late teens. He went over and picked it up. One was blond and blue eyed, the other was dark haired with brown eyes and a heavy brow. The second boy didn't look unlike Jack when he was a teen.

"The blond is Liam—he's our oldest—the dark one is Jason. Strong genes, our Harry." Eddie moved to Jack's side and took the photo from him. "I loved Jason like my own."

"Jason is Harry's?"

"Liam's a microbiologist in Edinburgh. Married, second kid on the way. The house he's in now is the house he'll die in, I expect." Eddie glanced around his own lounge. "Jason, on the other hand, never sat still. Got his first motorbike at 16."

"Where's Jason now?" Jack asked.

"Knocked off his bike eleven years ago," said Eddie. "Dragged a quarter mile under the wheels of a tri-axle truck. Couldn't stop fast enough 'cos of the rainwater on the road. He died pretty much straight away. That's what they told me anyway. Said I shouldn't see him . . . so . . . that was that."

Eddie put the photo back in exactly the same place, at exactly the same skewed angle. When he sat back down, Jack could now see that the photo was pointing directly at Eddie's armchair.

"I don't know your name," Eddie said.

"Jack. Jack Nunn." He had no idea why he'd said this.

"You're Trudie's boy! Of course you are! Poor Jimmy . . ." Eddie shook his head as he poured himself another whisky. "Why are you here, Jack? What do you need to know?"

"I want a DNA sample, so I can be sure."

"I'm sure, lad. As soon as I saw you, I was sure. It's the eyes." Eddie glanced at the photo of his two sons again. "My Jackie left me for a biker called Harvey Rintle. He bought Jason the bike that killed him. I'll never forgive that man till the day I die, but Harry . . . I forgive Harry. Harry gave my boy something I never could. He gave Jason 'spark.' People can see strength and that gets you respect. I love Liam to bits, but he's not excited about life. He'll always be loved, but he'll never be . . ." Eddie brought his hands to his stomach and made a welling motion like a volcano coming from the pit of his belly. "No, I don't need a DNA match to tell me who you belong to, Jack."

* * *

The next two hours were spent drinking Eddie's single malt. Jack put Eddie at ease by mentioning people like Ken Moore, Jimmy Nunn's old racing buddy, and Tony and Arnie Fisher. He made out that he knew snippets about Harry's criminal past and how that didn't bother him at all. He never mentioned once that he was a police officer.

"After the underpass raid Harry hid out here with me for a time." Eddie was now drunk and so relaxed that he forgot to edit himself. He was out to impress, bigging up his role. "I know he always looked down on me, but when the shit hits the fan, family's family. It was awful watching Dolly go through what she did. The police showed her Harry's watch, 'cos there was no body to identify. The driver was Jimmy, not Harry. Harry was here with me, drinking single malt like this." Eddie took another sip. "I'll give you a DNA sample if you think you need one," he said. "But your eyes, Jack—dark, like stones. They're Jason's eyes, Harry's eyes."

Jack looked over again at the smiling picture of Liam and Jason. Did Jason miss out by not having Harry in his life? Or was he happier with his adopted dad, just like Jack had been with Charlie?

"Did Harry know Jason was his?" Jack asked.

A smile came over Eddie's face. "The only thing I ever had in my life, that Harry didn't, was a son to be proud of. So, no, I didn't tell him. Jason came along just after Dolly's first miscarriage. Harry got a man with a van to come round here with everything from their nursery. Gave it all to me. He just needed it out of his house. No baby, no memories, move on—that was Harry. It tore Dolly apart to see it all go, but she put his pain above hers and let him do what he needed to. By their third miscarriage, he was numb to it all, but Dolly . . . Her pain was just as deep and just as cruel. That's why, when they both said 'no more,' she left that nursery like a shrine to all the little ones they could have had. So, there he was, on my doorstep, supervising a couple of grands' worth of baby stuff being unloaded and brought in here for mine—oblivious to the fact that he was actually providing a new nursery for his own." There was that smile again. "Can you imagine what he'd have done to me if he'd known? He'd have torn my heart out with his bare hands. See, Harry could father kids—as we know— but what he never had was a boy to teach about life. A legacy."

Jack stared at Eddie, not really knowing how to respond to any of what he was hearing. What Eddie had done sounded so cruel, and yet, he seemed so proud of it.

"You sound as if you hated Harry."

"No, no, no. I loved him. But he was a selfish man. Harry would have ruined Jason, like he would have ruined you. Let me put you straight. Harry Rawlins fucked my wife, Jack. Fucked her with no regard for me. When he was on the run, he went to my Jackie for help—clean clothes, money and the like—so don't judge me for taking what was his, 'cos he took what was mine first!"

The whisky was making Eddie brave, but Jack didn't mind. He'd come here for some back story on his birth dad and he was certainly getting it.

Eddie glazed over for a while as he gazed at his dead son's photograph. During the silence, Jack thought about Charlie. Eddie was still suffering such a great loss—was this what grief was? Was it something you never, ever got over as long as you lived?

"Jackie never actually told me that Jason was Harry's and I never asked," Eddie continued, wiping his eye. "Then one day—Jason would have been around five—I said he couldn't have something, and he looked at me like he'd cut me down if he could. That's when I knew for certain he was Harry's. Harry was dead by then, so . . ." He stood up, as if to clear his head. "Jason was taller than you, tall like Harry.

You got Trudie's height." Eddie cackled as he gauged with his hand how tall he thought Trudie had been. By the looks of things, she was somewhere in between his knee and his shoulder. "Course, I might be remembering her kneeling down . . ." Another cackle of laughter. "No, no, I'm joking. She was a good sort, your mum."

As Eddie rocked and laughed at his little joke, Jack frowned, and the deep vertical line in between his eyebrows became more prominent. When Eddie looked up and saw his expression of distaste, his laughter stopped as quickly as it had started.

"S-sorry," he stuttered. "I didn't mean nothing by that."

Jack just nodded. "What about the rest of Harry's family?"

He might as well get everything out of Eddie while he was on the back foot.

"My dad and Harry's dad were brothers. Harry's dad was a tough businessman, buying and selling antiques in a relatively legit business, while also running with some heavy-duty villains. Harry's dad got sent away for armed robbery around the same time as mine died from lung cancer—so Harry's mum, Iris, made sure me and my mum had enough money to get by. Iris wasn't to be messed with. She became the head of the family, took over the business, trained Harry to be the man he was—and me to be the man I am, I suppose. She loved him with all of her cold, hard heart."

Eddie sat back down in his chair and gave a soft laugh.

"When Harry was just 13, Iris would make him memorize every hallmark in her little black book. When he'd got that learned, she'd have Ezra come round—he was a jeweler . . . No, not Ezra—Eli. Eli Jacobson. Dead now. Anyway, she'd have him come round with his briefcase filled with his precious metals. Harry had to value them, find the fakes, all that caper." Eddie was relaxed again now and happy to talk about this new subject. "I remember one time, she laid out three diamonds and told Harry to pick the one worth 500, then the one worth 1,000, then the one worth ten shillings. If he got it right, she'd give him fifty quid. That was a hell of a lot of money in them days!"

"And did he get it right?" Jack asked.

Eddie just grinned. "Harry was a teenager and was walking round with wads of money in his pocket. He was very generous with it, mind you, but, at the same time, he enjoyed taunting people with it. Me, usually. He had it, I needed it. He learned that from Iris . . . He learned to not only know his own worth, but also the worth of others. After my dad died, it took Harry all of two seconds to work out that I could be bought for the price of a monthly food bill."

As time went on, Eddie reveled vicariously in Harry's good fortune as a young man—the E-Type Jags, the tailored suits from

Shepherds, the handmade shirts, the women. Jack could see how a young boy with all of that genuine talent and charm could grow into an arrogant man who'd be feared and loved in equal measures.

"Iris had very high hopes for her boy—so when Harry turned up one evening with Dolly, Iris had a fucking *fit*. There was no way her son was going to marry an East End trollop!"

Eddie got up, crossed to a bureau and opened a drawer. He took out a large photo album, hugged it to his chest and, on wobbly old legs, returned to his seat.

"When Dolly found out that Harry had betrayed her by making her think he'd died in that underpass raid, she burned every photo of him she had."

Jack leaned forward, eyes wide, eager. Was he about to see a proper photo of Harry Rawlins? He moved to the seat next to Eddie; both of them perched on the edge of their worn cushions, legs wide, elbows on knees. Eddie stared at Jack and tears welled in his red, drunken eyes. Jack knew exactly what he was thinking. He was wishing it was Jason sitting by his side—and not a stranger called Jack who just happened to have the same eyes. Jack smiled, which didn't help at all. As Eddie began sobbing, Jack took the album from him and rested it on his own knee.

Eddie wiped his nose on his shirtsleeve and slid the album across so they could share it. The contents were as Jack expected: Eddie and Harry as boys, then teens, then adults together with their respective families. Eddie was finding it difficult to talk. He just kept tapping photos; some of them meant nothing to Jack, some meant everything. The protective cover on each page had done its job well over the passing years and the images were still in pristine condition: Eddie's mum and dad, their old homes, Harry's parents. There was a photo of Harry on a bicycle with drop handlebars.

"He gave me that bike. He got a new one every year . . . so, I did too." Page after page of Jack's history. "This is his wedding."

Harry was wearing a Tommy Nutter suit that he'd had made for him. Beside him, Dolly looked pale-faced, wearing a neat suit and carrying a small bouquet of flowers. There was page after page of Eddie's wife Jackie, of Liam and Jason. As the boys grew, most of the photos became about Jason; he was usually in leathers on the back of a motorbike, giving a smoldering look to the camera. Eddie closed the album.

"When I drove Dolly to Harry's funeral, and I knew she was burying someone else's charred, broken bones, I remember feeling the same as when I buried Jason. I looked down at both coffins and thought, 'It's OK, Eddie, lad. There's no one in there that you know.' My whole life, I've been thinking Jason or Harry could walk back in through that door at any moment . . . and here you are, Jack. A bit of both of 'em. Who'd believe it, eh?"

Jack got up to return the album to the bureau. By the time he'd walked the length of the room, one photo of Harry Rawlins had made its way into his pocket.

"Harry Rawlins was a man amongst men, Jack," Eddie said as he shuffled to the front door to see Jack out. "He had the ability to make you not only trust him but want to protect him. He rarely smiled, but when he did, those dark eyes of his would light up. That made me proud to be close to him. I wish you'd known him at his best."

*　*　*

Back in the street, Jack's heart was beating out of his chest. Why? Why was he excited his father was a man who walked all over people? Why was he excited he was a man who didn't seem capable of loving anyone for long? Jack was not callous and cruel. Jack was not in this world to take what he wanted and fuck the consequences. But there was something that he yearned for—a space deep in his very soul that needed to be filled. For the first time in a very long time, Jack felt like he'd stumbled on a world he belonged in. It wasn't the lawlessness, it was the excitement. Jason had lived a short, vibrant life with no regrets, whereas Liam would live a long, predictable life. Which was best?

Jack looked at his mobile. *Shit!* There was a voicemail from Laura. He'd been so engrossed in his conversation with Eddie, he hadn't even felt it vibrate. Barry Cooper was about to be taken down in a synchronized raid from two Armed Response Units and Ridley's team were all heading there to make the arrest. All except Jack.

CHAPTER 28

Barry was squatting in the corner of the kitchen, feeding a tiny tortoiseshell cat. His forearm was in a cast and the plaster was covered in penned obscenities, mainly drawings, from various army mates. Four kittens lay in a cut-down crisp box under the workbench and when the mother climbed back into the box, three of the little kittens smelt their way straight to her and fed like there was no tomorrow— but the smallest didn't stir. Barry picked this little one up, took it out of the back door and, moments later, came back empty-handed. The mother cat didn't even look up.

This property was a ground floor flat in a four-story terraced house. From the outside, it looked rather opulent, but this part of Essex had recently been reclaimed by the council to create housing for soldiers. One of Barry's army buddies, Topper, lived there in between deployments but, today, Topper had gone to Colchester Garrison for a stint at training the Army Reserve. He'd be away for three days and had said that Barry could lie low until whatever shit he was in had passed.

Barry made himself a cuppa and went into the front room. A camp bed stood upright against the wall in the corner of the room and, behind the armchair, were two khaki rucksacks—one small, one large. Barry was trying to take up as little living space as possible. As he settled down to watch a movie from Topper's extensive horror collection, he was oblivious to the vast number of eyes on him.

* * *

Ridley wasn't part of the Armed Response Unit briefing, but he knew that he'd get the nod when the time was right. He and his team would follow at a distance and, when Barry was disarmed and prone on the ground, they'd move in for the arrest. Intelligence had confirmed that Barry had no army-issue weapons in his possession, but Ridley was taking no chances with someone who had been part of the armed gang from the 1995 train robbery.

* * *

Jack raced toward Essex, suffering a bit from the effects of the whisky. Ridley had rallied his team without even asking where Jack was. He'd stopped caring. So, Laura wasn't exactly going against any orders by guiding Jack to their location via a series of text messages.

The terraced building had a shared stairwell, so the Armed Response Units had to be very careful to cut off all routes to the other properties. If Barry made it into a neighboring flat, the shit would really hit the fan. So, one ARU would block his route upstairs and out the front, while a second unit headed round the back to block the rear. Barry would have nowhere to run.

What the police didn't know was that the third floor flat was also occupied by soldiers on leave.

Barry's mobile buzzed:

Armed cops out front. Back clear for now.

He grabbed the smaller of the two rucksacks and put it securely on his back. He then pulled two handguns from under the cushion on the chair where he sat, tucking the Webley Mk IV .38 caliber into his waistband at the small of his back; this gun had seen his dad safely through World War II and was now Barry's lucky charm. Holding the street-bought Glock 9 mm, Barry walked quietly through the kitchen. The tortoiseshell cat looked up at him through sleepy eyes, while her three remaining kittens, now with full bellies, slept soundly.

In the backyard, Barry glanced up at the third floor, where a silhouetted figure signaled that five armed officers were approaching from the west. Barry signaled his thanks and headed east, toward the rural stretch of track running between Colchester and Hythe railway stations.

* * *

The ARUs entered Barry's flat on a simultaneous command. They cleared each room they passed through and met in the middle. Nothing. In the lounge, a furious Ridley found the large rucksack down the side of the armchair, with the words "Pte Cooper" sewn into the inner lining. The clothes inside were used as a scent reference for the second wave deployment: the Dog Unit.

* * *

Barry was making his way along the trackside, under Brook Street pedestrian bridge and on toward Hythe. Anik and Laura were moving in sync with the ARU up ahead, keeping the designated distance—no more, no less. Ridley, on the other hand, was discovering that his brown patent leather brogues were not cut out for muddy terrain—he'd not actually chased anyone in years, and he hadn't expected to be doing it today. He'd planned to have Barry

Cooper handed to him on a plate, after which he'd give up the names of his crew in exchange for a lighter prison sentence. No such luck.

As the dogs dragged the lead ARU at a pace behind Barry, Ridley prayed that he didn't divert up the embankment at any point and into populated areas. As Laura ran, she just managed to text Jack to give him an update. Jack immediately turned off the A134 and got onto a dirt road running parallel to and above the train tracks. As soon as he heard the police dogs, he pulled over, jumped out and followed the sound of the sniffer dog choking itself with excitement at the end of its own lead. Jack was a good fifteen feet above the tracks on a dirt road and he very quickly realized that there was no way down. The embankment was almost sheer, loosely fenced off with barbed wire tied to staggered fenceposts. He resigned himself. Ridley was probably going to boil over if Jack ended up watching events unfold from above.

* * *

Barry was tiring. He kept slipping in the deep layer of small stones that ran along the side of the railway track; each time he stumbled to his hands and knees, he'd take longer to get back up. He could feel the stones through the soles of his sneakers, whereas the dog handlers were wearing boots. The dogs, with no protection for their feet, opted to run higher on the embankment in the wet and muddy grass, the steep gradient being no problem for them.

As Barry ran, he tried to remember what was ahead of him in order to plan an escape. He needed to think of a way to explain the five million pounds on his back, while also thinking of a way to

LYNDA LA PLANTE | 303

explain his decision to set fire to Mike's dead body. But he had no answers to anything.

* * *

Barry looked down at Mike's body and watched the blood slowly stop pouring out of the gaping head wound. After a moment, the pain from his broken left forearm hit him and Barry slumped onto the small horsehair sofa. He controlled his instinct to scream, swallowing again and again to stop the sound from coming out.

He scanned the room, desperate to find something he could use as a sling. Using his knife, he managed to cut off Mike's T-shirt and tie the ends together, before slipping the improvised sling over his head and under the broken bone. He quickly stepped into the back garden to get some fresh air so he didn't pass out, and to try to straighten out his head. The stars looked amazing above the undulating horizon and Barry was soon in control of the pain and calm in his mind. Although he'd seen and done worse in wartime, the only way to think straight now was to distance himself from the fact that he'd just killed one of his best friends. From this second on, Mikey was just another corpse and Barry knew how they burned.

Barry took his time. If he made one mistake, he'd be caught. He stood on the garden hose, feet apart, holding it firmly on the ground, and used his knife to cut clean through it, before making a second cut to give himself a decent length of hose. He put the hose into a bucket, popped back inside to retrieve Mike's Range Rover keys from his pocket and set off into the pitch-black night. Walking to the Range Rover, siphoning the petrol and walking back took Barry less than twenty minutes.

By the time he was ready to move the body, the blood in Mike's hair had congealed, sticking his head and the side of his face to the carpet like red glue. Barry grabbed a handful of hair from the top of Mike's head and peeled his face clear. Then he used all his strength to drag Mike's body one-handed across the carpet and up onto the short, two-seater sofa, finally curling his legs up into the fetal position. Barry then used anything flammable to create a bonfire around him.

He poured the siphoned petrol all over the sofa and splashed the remains onto the stacks of £5 and £10 notes in the hearth. He then picked up the green garden waste bag, stepped outside into the front garden and lit himself a cigarette. The roses were doing well against the cold nights and, although they'd been left to their own devices, they still bloomed. Barry took in the silence and, once content that there was no one for miles around, he flicked his cigarette into Rose Cottage, picked up his green bag and headed back over the hills, on foot, the way he'd arrived.

* * *

Barry knew that, if he dared to look around, he'd see the dogs and the armed police hot on his tail. The weight of his small rucksack was slowing him down, but there was no way he was leaving it behind. As he ran, his Glock was clearly visible in his hand, although his dad's Webley was hidden beneath his jumper.

With Barry actually in sight ahead of them, the dog handler pulled back and the ARU took the lead. The dog strained at the end of its leash and barked loudly in protest at being taken off the job before he'd caught his prey.

"*Barry Cooper! Armed police! Stop running!*"

Barry ran on as he cycled through his options. There were only two . . . live or die.

"*Stop and throw down your weapon!*"

And then, from up ahead, the sound of a train approaching.

For the lead Armed Response Officer, time slowed as he processed all of the possibilities in a split second. Barry Cooper was so desperate to escape, he reckoned he'd definitely attempt to cross in front of the train. And he'd not think twice about firing his weapon to make the situation even more dangerous. The lead officer instructed two of his men to cross the track and shouted out again.

"*Barry Cooper! Throw down your weapon!*"

The last thing he wanted was for some poor train driver to be faced with a shoot-out and then kill a civilian with his engine.

Barry, knowing the parameters in which ARUs worked, threw his Glock up onto the embankment. As far as his pursuers were aware, they were now chasing an unarmed man and would be far more reluctant to use deadly force.

From further behind, the lead officer heard Ridley shout "*Gun safe!*," scooping up the discarded Glock as he ran past. Ahead of them, the train's headlights were getting closer.

"*Barry*, do *not* attempt to cross the tracks! We have armed officers on both sides! Stop running!"

When the train came round the bend and into view, the headlights were blinding—which was exactly what Barry was hoping for.

He left everything to the very last second. As he turned ninety degrees and darted across the track, he pulled the Webley from his waistband and shot one of the Armed Response officers who'd crossed the track. Before he could shoot the second officer, five bullets from five weapons entered Barry's torso, hurling him backward, straight into the path of the oncoming train.

It took forever for the train to pass. Once it had gone, the lead officer ran to his man down and radioed for help. Ridley, Laura and Anik didn't move; they just watched and prayed that the only dead person on this railway track was Barry Cooper.

The man down was alive, releasing Ridley and his team to find whatever was left of Barry. They looked up the track in the same direction as the train . . . and there he was. As Ridley led the way, he forced his eyes to focus in the darkness. What was lying there was definitely too small to be all of Barry, but looked like it could be a significant portion. Laura and Anik silently followed. And along the top of the embankment, a shadowy figure walked with them. Jack had had a bird's-eye view of Barry's death—it was a vision that was now burned into his brain and would stay with him for as long as he lived.

Both of Barry Cooper's lower legs had gone with a relatively clean cut, but his left arm had been ripped out of the shoulder joint high up, next to the ear; the rest of his body had been tossed and turned a dozen times as it passed underneath the length of the train and was now a broken pile of bones and bloody flesh. Ridley got out his mobile and turned on the torch. Laura and Anik followed suit.

"Forget the legs," Ridley said. "I want the rucksack."

The three of them spread out across the train track and walked slowly back toward the Armed Response officers on the ground. The noise had now turned to a strangely calm silence, in which only scurrying foxes could be heard as they ventured out to see if they could find a small enough piece of Barry to sneak off with.

Laura's mobile torch glanced over one of Barry's missing legs but, as per Ridley's instructions, she ignored it in favor of finding the rucksack. When Anik froze, hand in the air, unable to speak, Ridley and Laura knew that he'd found something. The rucksack was still on the shoulder of Barry's missing arm. Ridley opened it up and the only thing inside was money—£20 and £50 notes. All in bundles held by the same style of money wrap as the one they had found deep inside the coal chute at Rose Cottage.

Jack looked down the top of the embankment. Below him, the contents of Barry's rucksack were lit by three mobile torches.

Shit! Jack thought to himself. *This is all Ridley will need to put Barry and Mike at the heart of the train robbery.*

Any chance he'd had of convincing anyone that The Grange women were the real culprits had just been totally crushed, along with Barry Cooper.

CHAPTER 29

When Maggie got in from work, breakfast was on a tray in the middle of the kitchen table, along with a single red rose and a hand-written note. On the upside, the tea and toast were still warm—on the downside, Maggie knew that the rose had been stolen from their neighbors' hanging basket as there was still soil on the stem; the note just said "sorry x."

Maggie recalled her ultimatum . . . *Tomorrow morning, when I get home, I want breakfast in bed and a cuddle regardless of how bad I smell.*

Jack had failed.

* * *

Jack was waiting for Foxy when he pulled into the police station car park.

"You want to know if you're related to any more dead people?" Foxy quipped. Then he saw the serious look on Jack's face. "Shit, really? Barry Cooper's not your long-lost brother, is he?"

Jack handed Foxy a battered old baseball cap, sporting the Isle of Man TT Motorcycle race logo, complete with the three legs of man—although time had taken its toll on the embroidered stitching and the iconic symbol now only had two legs. Foxy took the cap and headed indoors.

"You owe me several pints, Jack. Don't die before I can collect them."

* * *

Jack was sitting at his desk when Ridley walked in. Ridley ignored him and went straight into his office. Jack sat silently at his desk and waited for everyone else to arrive.

Ridley led the briefing.

"Barry Cooper died yesterday, as you all know. In his rucksack was just short of five million in twenties and fifties from the '95 train robbery. We know this because of the information on the bands used to hold the bundles of cash together. The shoe print found at the side of Mike's Range Rover, from where the petrol was siphoned, has been matched to the sneakers Cooper was wearing when he died."

Ridley looked at the jam-packed evidence boards and, without hesitation, removed the photos of Angela Dunn, Julia Lawson, Connie Stephens and Ester Freeman. He replaced them with pictures of Mike Withey and Barry Cooper.

"Barry's initials were written in Mike's diary, identifying the person he was meeting at Rose Cottage on the night he was murdered. Thomas Kurts, otherwise known as Topper. Rashid Wassan, otherwise known as Stan, as in 'Paki-Stan.' And Dennis Marchant, otherwise known as Dennie. These three are wanted for questioning in connection with aiding and abetting a fugitive and likely for a connection to the train robbery. They're physically capable, they have the skills, the organization, the weapons experience and the track record for this kind of crime. We have Topper, 'cos he was Reserve training at Colchester Garrison. But we don't yet know where the others are. I want you to work with the Essex Police to locate them. Check their military records to get their whereabouts for the night of the robbery—I don't want to discover any unbreakable alibis later than today. Barry's death is currently being withheld from the public so as not to scare his accomplices into running. Get to work. Find them before they get spooked and disappear."

As everyone knuckled down to their computer screens, Jack stared at the pile of four photos that Ridley had removed from the evidence board. Dolly's picture was on top. Once again, he thought, the police had got it wrong. The women ticked all the same boxes as the army gang: they were physically strong enough if they used horses; they were gun-savvy because of Gloria; and they were definitely capable of facing off against a couple of male train guards and winning. These women had been surviving in a man's world their entire lives. Underestimating them now would be Ridley's downfall.

*　*　*

Julia held Suzie's hand as they moved down to the edge of the river Dee and then east along the footpath toward the pre-arranged meeting place. Julia was walking at a brisk pace and Suzie was running to keep up, her second-hand Shawn Mendes rucksack bouncing up and down and rhythmically hitting her in the back of the head. Up ahead, Sam was dribbling a football around his backpack, which he'd thoughtlessly dropped without looking to see how muddy the ground was. The expanse of mud-free waste ground that he could have been playing on was currently empty. They were early.

"Where we going then?" Sam shouted, as soon as Julia came into view. "The beach, is it? I ain't ever played football on sand!"

"Where's Darren?" Julia was trying to remain calm.

Sam shrugged. He didn't know or care where stupid Darren was and nor did Suzie, but Julia knew that he had no chance of surviving without her.

"Sam. A bus is arriving to pick us up, OK? There'll be a black guy driving—that's Rob. And Angela's the one in charge, so you do exactly what she tells you, all right? I mean it, Sam! What did I say?"

"Black dude driving. Angela's the boss. I got it." "Suzie, you don't leave Sam's side. You promise me."

Suzie nodded frantically, as confused as she was excited. As Julia headed off to find Darren, Sam made Suzie drop her rucksack to make goalposts and then get in goal, so he could hammer the ball at her. All Julia could hear as she ran back up toward the house was, "Don't kick it too hard, Sam. *Sam*, that's too hard!"

What was she doing taking these three misfits on the bloody run with her?

Darren was cycling as fast as his legs could pedal, but the bike he was on wasn't his and, with each push of the pedal, he wobbled and almost fell off. His rucksack was only over one shoulder, which wasn't helping his balance at all. As soon as Julia saw him, she knew what he'd done—she was devastated. Darren had been going on about having a bike of his own for so long and now, with the prospect of going away, he'd bloody well stolen himself one! Darren looked up, saw Julia and, with all the pride in the world, he beamed the biggest smile, took both hands off the handlebars and waved in triumph.

Suddenly, two coppers raced round the corner on foot into the quiet road ahead of Darren, sending him swerving toward the sidewalk. He tried to right himself, but now he'd slowed to the same speed as the coppers and, in a pincer movement, they closed in, dragged Darren off the bike and plonked him face down on the road. Julia hid, pushing her back flat against the wall. She screwed her eyes closed as she listened to Darren cursing the coppers and fighting for his life. She heard the police car arrive; she heard the coppers call Darren a "waste of skin" and an "unwanted stray." Julia clenched her fists so tight that her nails dug into her palms, burying the shame she felt as she abandoned Darren to his fate. What kind of mother was she?

When Julia opened her eyes, she could see Sam and Suzie holding hands in the distance. This was the kind of mother she had to be now. Sam was pointing back toward the waste ground. It was time to go, but Julia couldn't peel herself off the wall.

From her hiding place, she could hear as Darren screamed profanities and fought like a maniac. He never once shouted for Julia and he never once gave away her position. Once the police car had driven off, she walked back to Sam and Suzie.

Sam saw Julia's tears and, with all the understanding and sensitivity of a grown-up, he tapped his finger on her chest.

"He ain't strong in here. And he ain't smart."

He took Julia by the hand and together the three of them walked to the bus.

* * *

By the time the bus was on the A1 toward Newcastle upon Tyne, Sam was teaching Riel and Aggie dirty versions of pop songs, much to Connie's amusement. Ester, as expected, wasn't happy.

"I've spent my entire life avoiding the fucking North, Angela. What's wrong with Dover? It's cleaner and it's closer to Switzerland."

Angela had explained the escape plan a dozen times, so she knew that Ester wasn't really asking a genuine question, she was just whining. If they'd been in a gold-plated private cruiser, Ester would have complained about the color.

Julia sat alone, staring out the window at the Yorkshire Dales flashing by and trying not to cry. In the reflection of the window, she watched Angela approach and pause next to her. As Angela spoke, Julia could almost hear Dolly's voice.

"We were never going to get everyone out."

* * *

The squad room was buzzing. Fibers of horsehair found on Barry's severed trouser leg were being compared to any furnishings that survived from the Rose Cottage carnage—and the cash had traces of accelerant on it that matched the petrol from Mike's Range Rover.

Anik had worked with Essex Police to create a timeline for Barry since leaving the army. He had been lead foremen at a demolition company for three years, until he was sacked for "misplacing" four sticks of dynamite, just two weeks before the mail train was blown off its tracks and robbed. Mike Withey then employed Barry at his security firm. It seemed that Barry had also used his industry connections to make several discreet phone calls to the company due to demolish Rose Cottage, asking to know schedules and time frames for starting work. This was vital information, because if the cottage had been sealed off and become a building site before the cash was removed, the demolition company would have been the ones to tear down the kitchen wall.

Ridley was in his element as every officer worked toward the same goal. He could smell success. Anik could smell promotion. Jack could smell bullshit. And Ridley had fallen for it hook, line and sinker.

Jack's mobile screen lit up:

Reminder: dinner with Maggie.

This was, in fact, the second reminder and so he now only had ten minutes to travel halfway across London. Jack couldn't listen to Ridley any longer—this great man, who Jack had always looked up to, was now so far down the wrong road. Jack had bet his reputation on the guilt of the women from The Grange and he'd had it thrown back in his face. Just when he'd finally started caring about this thankless job, no one was listening.

All he wanted right now . . . was Maggie.

CHAPTER 30

The bus was in a lengthy queue waiting to embark on the ferry from Newcastle to Amsterdam. The kids were exhausted and were trying to sleep, and Ester was being more obnoxious than usual, having drunk the contents of one of her hip flasks. She had two more tucked away in various pockets of her clothing.

"It looks like a floating skip!" she said scathingly, as she caught sight of the ferry.

Ester took any and every opportunity to undermine Angela's escape plan; it was as though she wanted it to fail just so she could laugh in Angela's face and mock how the "little tart" from all those years ago should have stayed on the lowest rung of the ladder, where she belonged, and made no attempt to climb. Ester's penchant for selfdestruction was well known, so they'd already agreed to keep her sweet for another week or two because after that they'd never have to see her again.

"We're staying in Hyatt House in Düsseldorf tomorrow night, Ester." Rob's deep, velvety voice from the driving seat made Ester go weak at the knees and he knew it. "Google it, darlin'. It's stunning."

Ester obediently got out her mobile and, as she scrolled through the photos of the double-staircase, gold and winding up three floors, she beamed and opened her second hip flask.

Angela put her hand inside Rob's, as they inched closer and closer to the first test of their new passports. She was nervous; she was so excited for what lay ahead of them, and terrified of losing it at the final turn. Rob's huge hand enveloped Angela's. She loved the rough callouses at the base of each of his fingers, just above his palm. They were comforting. Her man knew what hard work was and that made him appreciate everything he had. He could take on anything, because he knew what life was about. His life, anyway.

The front wheels of the bus hesitated on the lip of the ramp, rolled back a little, then went for it. They were aboard.

A man in a yellow safety vest waved them into a parking space and Rob turned the engine off. For a few seconds, they all nervously looked out their nearest window for . . . what?

Connie was the first to grin, which she quickly followed with a shriek that scared Suzie. Riel and Aggie were used to Connie's oddness, so ignored her; Sam, out of boredom, was using his penknife to snag stitches out of the seat he was sitting on.

Angela, Julia and Connie, quite unprompted, came together in the center of the bus and hugged. They then forced themselves into Ester's two-seater space and hugged her too, which she pretended to object to.

"Gerroff me! You stink! Gerroff, I'm going to the bar." Ester struggled to her feet. "Come and get me when we're there."

Connie curtsied and off Ester went. "Right, kids!" Julia turned.

Sam was holding up a £50 note. She dived to the back of the bus and snatched it from his hand. She didn't have to say anything, she just glared. Between Sam's legs, the stitching in the front of his seat was open about half an inch, exposing one of the stacks of cash. He closed his legs, covering the damage he'd done. She read the "I won't tell a soul" in his eyes. Julia pushed the £50 note back through the hole in the seat and stroked Sam's hair. Even though he was only eight, and inquisitive as a puppy, she trusted him completely.

"I can sew that." Julia spun round to see Angela right behind her. "Maybe you should take the knife though, eh? For safekeeping."

Then, to show Sam that she too trusted him, she said, "Rob, would you take the kids to look around? Sam's going to be your wingman."

Sam handed his penknife to Julia and left the bus with the other kids, Rob, Connie and Julia.

As the ferry pulled away from the terminal, Angela sat in the driver's seat and looked out to sea. Then, quite unexpectedly, she began to cry. She tried to control it, but she couldn't; the tears flooded out from pure relief. Angela gasped in the stale air smelling of petrol fumes, to try and calm herself down. She opened the glovebox and there, sitting on top of all of Rob's junk, were a small, worn teddy bear and a bright yellow teething ring. She thought back to Dolly Rawlins and their impromptu shopping trip to Mothercare all those years ago.

You're a good girl. Dolly's voice was as clear as day. *Stay strong and, most of all, stay happy. If you're not happy, you're not anything really.*

It was only now that Angela recognized how sad Dolly had been when she'd said those words. Dolly had lost her own babies, she'd lost the man she loved more than life itself and she was hopelessly sad. Even if she had lived, she'd never have been happy again. Angela moved the little bear to one side and took out her sewing kit.

* * *

Maggie had been sitting in the restaurant for twenty minutes. She was drinking faster than usual, embarrassed to be sitting by herself at a table clearly set for two people. And if that wasn't enough, she was dressed to kill, with her 40-minute hair and her 30-minute make-up— triple the time she normally gave herself to get ready for a night out.

That morning, Jack had promised her breakfast in bed and a cuddle and he'd failed to deliver either. This evening, he had promised her a night out—which he was failing to deliver. Maggie wasn't annoyed; she was deeply upset. She could feel everything slipping away because of Jack's crazy obsession with finding his birth father, in the hope of finding himself. She knew he was grieving for Charlie, so she was being as supportive as possible—but he wasn't making it easy. She looked at the bottle of white in front of her—one glass left. She swigged the last mouthful from her glass and then emptied the bottle. The sommelier dived across the restaurant, but he was far too slow. He removed the empty bottle and, with a patronizing tone and a tilt of the head, asked Maggie if she'd like some bread while she waited for her companion. She wanted to tell him to fuck off, but instead she smiled and said, "No, thank you."

Maggie spent the next five minutes watching a spot of white wine, which she'd dripped onto the tablecloth from the now-empty bottle, dry slowly. She glanced at the clock on the wall. She'd been sitting alone for thirty-five minutes; she was starving and pissed. When the restaurant door next opened, she had to look twice at the man who entered before she recognized him. Jack was dressed as he was always dressed, but he looked different. Maggie had rehearsed what she was going to say when he finally walked in, all apologetic and eager to make amends, but this wasn't the man she'd expected. This man looked her straight in the eyes and smiled, as though he'd done nothing at all wrong. He looked handsome, confident, powerful. He looked like a man who knew that he was worth waiting for. Maggie couldn't take her eyes off him.

Jack didn't apologize for being late and Maggie didn't shout at him as she'd planned to. He simply sat opposite her, stared deep into her soul with his smiling brown eyes and told her how much he loved her.

CHAPTER 31

Colchester Police Station was a square, tan-colored new-build on the A134 with a green courtyard right in the center. It blended well into the surrounding area, making it seem unobtrusive and non-threatening, regardless of what went on inside. This is where Anik was heading, although he was currently stuck behind a stalled student driver on the roundabout just twenty yards away. Ridley was in the passenger seat, reading the police files on Thomas Kurts, Rashid Wassan and Dennis Marchant; Laura, who also had a copy of the files, was frowning as she read, having been relegated to the back seat. Anik was reveling in his "promotion" to driver, but this was because Ridley knew that he couldn't read in cars without being sick.

"The suspects have all had specialist training," Ridley continued. "Marchant's a munitions expert who we now know was at the birth of his brother's second child on the night of the train robbery. His brother had lost his license one week earlier, so Marchant had stepped up as the designated baby taxi. He's in all the photos. But we're still going to interview him—not being there doesn't mean he wasn't involved. Wassan, no such alibi, was a sapper alongside Barry Cooper. Dangerous men. These interviews will probably be 'no comment.' They'll be good under pressure, so won't bat an eye. This will more than likely come down to evidence, not confessions. It's a longer road, but that's fine. We're smart, methodical and we're patient . . . and Anik, if you don't overtake that stalled learner right now, I'm getting out and walking."

* * *

Jack stared at Foxy, waiting to hear words that he understood.

"Using the Y-chromosome DNA haplogroups as a sort of road map, my biologist friend told me—and I'm sorry to break it to you like this—but shoddy dress sense does indeed run in your family. You share patrilineal lineage with the owner of this very distasteful Isle of Man baseball cap."

Foxy could see that Jack hadn't really understood a word. He went on.

"In layman's terms, you and the owner of this cap have the same dad. Is that what you expected to hear? Is it what you wanted to hear?"

Jack said nothing as he absorbed the information.

"How's Charlie?" Foxy asked suddenly.

Jack snapped out of his trance. "You sure?"

"I'm sure." Foxy threw Jack a look. Eddie's words came to mind: *We are who we are. Can't be anyone else.*

"Charlie's fine," Jack said. "Holding on, you know."

"So—you going to tell me who you'll be sending a Father's Day card to next year?"

Jack managed a smile; he loved Foxy dearly, but he could be a tactless bastard at times. Charlie wasn't even dead yet and he was making jokes.

*   *   *

Maggie sat at Jack's desk in the squad room, watching Morgan injecting insulin into his belly. Once that was done, he stood up, tucked his shirt back in and left the room without a word. He wasn't the most sociable of men. Maggie looked around the mostly empty squad room. The evidence boards were a complex array of photos, single words that meant little to her, dates and times, plans of action. Some of the photos here were the same as the photos on the wall in her spare bedroom; she didn't recognize the soldiers.

As soon as Jack came back into the squad room, Maggie stood to meet him. But Jack sat her back down, pulled up a chair next to her, opened his desk drawer and took out the battered old file given to him by Charlie. Inside the file were all the photos and paperwork that Maggie had already seen, plus the photo Jack had stolen from Eddie's album.

"This is Harry Rawlins. He was one of the biggest criminal names in the eighties."

Jack was whispering. This conversation, in the middle of the squad room, was for her ears only. Even though Maggie knew who Harry Rawlins was, she could see that he needed to say the most important bits again.

"He was respected—reluctantly by some—but people who knew him couldn't help but respect him. Even the copper who spent his entire career trying to catch Harry respected him. Dolly loved him— even though he had so many affairs. His cousin, Eddie, loved him—even though his youngest son belongs to Harry. Harry could do that . . . He could shit on people and they'd still love him."

Jack covered his desk with newspaper cuttings from one day back in August, 1984, the funeral of "Harry Rawlins."

"Hundreds of people, from both sides of the law, turned up to see Harry off—or to make sure the bastard was dead, I don't know, but look at them, Mags. Look how many people are there. He was infamous. He was *Harry Rawlins* . . . He was my dad."

Maggie tipped her head to one side, her eyebrows raised and her eyes filled with sympathy.

"Don't do that," Jack said gently. "Don't look at me like I'm making a mistake 'cos I'm grieving. I had a DNA test done."

For the first time since Jack had started on his strange journey of self-discovery, Maggie started taking him seriously. She pulled her chair tight under Jack's desk and read through the newspaper cuttings in front of her. Jack looked around the squad room—every person here was a stranger. His immediate team was currently in Essex without him, being led by a man who had lost faith in him, if he'd ever really had any faith in him in the first place. Jack picked up one of the old, blurred, black and white newspaper images of Harry's funeral.

"Charlie won't leave this kind of mark. There'll be a handful of old builders and some of Mum's friends to have a sherry with her at the wake afterward. Then, nothing. He won't be remembered nearly forty years from now."

Maggie took Jack's hand, and pressed it to make him stop. She almost felt sick.

"Listen to yourself ! This man—this terrible, horrible man—is no one to be proud of. Charlie, or 'Dad' as you used to call him, will be dearly missed by good, hard-working people—whether there's ten or ten thousand of them. Jack, please, this isn't you!"

"This *is* me!" he snapped, making Maggie jump.

He was desperate to explain how he felt, but he didn't understand it himself. He repeated something Eddie had said to him.

"'People can see strength and that gets you respect.' It was never the job, or moving to London that was wrong, Mags—it was me. I'm not planning on changing sides, but I am going to start being the man I'm meant to be. I *will* be heard. And Ridley *will* start treating me with the respect I deserve."

CHAPTER 32

It was almost forty-eight hours since Kurts, Wassan and Marchant had been escorted back to London and, just as Ridley had predicted, they'd all been "no comment" the entire time. Kurts could be charged with perverting the course of justice, because Barry had been hiding in his flat—but they still needed to prove he knew Barry was there. Wassan was just hours away from being released. And Marchant was waiting for his lift back to Essex, after his good deed of playing chauffeur to his brother had finally exonerated him from any involvement in the train robbery.

Jack was head-down, checking numerous family statements supporting the fact that Marchant had never left the hospital at any point during his sister-in-law's 27-hour labor. It wasn't his aim to undermine Ridley or make him feel stupid; all Jack wanted was to be taken seriously.

Ridley sat at his desk, door open, and looked through the army service records of every man and woman who'd ever crossed paths with either Barry Cooper or Mike Withey. There were so many possibilities, but, as the hours ticked by, his gut got louder and louder. He was on the wrong track. He looked up to see Jack in the doorway.

"Rashid Wassan's solicitor's saying we either charge him or let him go, sir."

"Release him," Ridley said. He had no option.

When Jack returned to the squad room, Ridley was standing by the evidence board. He'd added the photos of Marchant and

Wassan to the discarded evidence pile, so that only Mike Withey, Barry Cooper and Thomas Kurts remained on the board, in pride of place, staring him dead in the eyes and challenging him to solve a 24-year-old train robbery and a brand new murder.

"Once you eliminate the impossible . . ." Ridley muttered. He sifted through the discarded evidence, picked up the photo of Dolly Rawlins and stuck it next to Mike Withey before completing the quotation. "Whatever remains, however improbable, must be the truth."

He let out a long sigh. He beckoned to Jack. The two men stood side by side, hands in pockets, looking at the women from The Grange. Laura and Anik could hardly believe what they were seeing.

"Can we justify search warrants?" Ridley asked.

"We wouldn't find anything, sir," Jack said, with an absolute certainty that made Ridley turn to look at him. "They're smarter than that. Always have been. They hid in plain sight, then and now. They looked like a bunch of women opening a kids' home, so that's all we saw."

Jack tapped the photo of Dolly Rawlins as he started to speak, and he swept a hand to include all of the other photos as he continued.

"Dolly Rawlins, the grief-stricken wife of a criminal master-mind driven to murder because of marital betrayal. Ester Freeman, a two-bit madam running her own brothel. Connie Stephens, a dumb prostitute. Julia Lawson, a drug-addled ex-doctor who turned to dealing to survive. Gloria Radford, the downtrodden wife of a gunrunning husband. Angela Dunn, nobody of consequence. And Mike Withey, burned-out drunk. Individually, they're easy to ignore—but together . . ." Ridley and Jack looked at all seven photos, side by side. "Leader, second in command, horsewoman, gun expert, seductress, inside man, and a babysitter to keep Kathleen's kids out of harm's way. Ester's insane decision to shoot Dolly was something no one could have predicted and it was what pushed them into this waiting game. They had to wait for Ester to get out or she'd have grassed them all up. They had to wait for the local pub landlord to stop making cash on the side by traipsing hundreds of tourists through what quickly became a notorious murder scene. And they had to wait for Norma to die. When the coast was finally clear, Mike made the mistake of asking Barry to help burn down Rose Cottage. The only time two blokes were left to do a job, and they fucked it up!"

"Sounds like you admire these women, Jack."

"I do, sir. They watched us underestimate them back in 1995 and they watched us do it again now. *Me*, sir. They watched *me* underestimate them."

Ridley removed the photos of Dolly Rawlins, Gloria Radford and Mike Withey—leaving Ester, Julia, Connie and Angela. "So, who's the mastermind now?"

"Not Ester. They don't like her, don't trust her and, anyway, she was out of the loop for too long. Not Connie—she's not capable. Julia or Angela. They're both smart and organized enough to juggle families and jobs. Angela's my guess—she was Dolly's protégée and she still puts flowers on Dolly's grave."

Ridley stood, arms folded, legs apart, temples pulsing as the tension flickered through his facial muscles. He nodded.

"Let's bring her in."

* * *

The drive to Angela's flat in West London was short and silent. Ridley was driving faster than normal, which was an indication of how annoyed he was. From the car park beneath Angela's third floor window, they looked up to see the flat in darkness. It seemed that Angela, Rob and the kids had gone. Within minutes, Ridley was requesting search warrants and coordinating simultaneous entries into Ester's home on the Isle of Wight, Julia's care home in Chester and Connie's B&B in Taunton. Ridley wanted to be the one to search Angela's flat; if she was the ringleader, as Jack suspected, then she'd be the one with all the answers.

* * *

The Chester police arrived in force, expecting to have to herd unwanted children into the back of a police van just to stop them from scattering like rats, but what they actually found was an English lesson in midflow. Julia's two helpers, who she "trusted with her life," kept the children entertained while the police searched the three adjoining houses. The female helper escorted the police while the male helper, Daniel, continued the class as though nothing untoward was happening at all.

Daniel spoke as if he was reading a quote from a textbook.

"The police burst in through the door, all red-faced and sweaty. *Burst.*"

A sea of tiny hands shot into the air and Daniel pointed to a young Asian lad, who was dressed in clothes at least three sizes too big for him.

"Verb!" the boy shouted with pride.

"Brilliant!"

Daniel caught a glimpse of the overweight PC in the corner of the room scowling at the children, as though they were not worth the effort Daniel was putting in.

"*Sweaty*," Daniel continued.

Again, tiny hands reached for the ceiling. Daniel nodded his head toward the PC and asked if he knew what sort of word "sweaty" was. All the while, the children's hands strained into the air, begging to be chosen. The PC flushed with embarrassment as a girl, no more than 6 years old, explained to him what an adjective was.

There was nothing suspicious at Julia's. Her paperwork was meticulous, there were no drugs or alcohol on the premises and the kids were well looked after. The sergeant questioned everyone to try and ascertain where Julia was, but no one knew a thing.

* * *

The bleached blonde at The Grange B&B in Taunton told the local police that Connie had probably "nipped to the shops."

"Well, I dunno, do I? I'm up at five to do the breakfasts, then it's the bedrooms, then packed lunches for the walkers, then general stuff, then the dinner prep! I'm sure I saw Connie yesterday on the third floor. Maybe I didn't. We sometimes don't see each other for days and we're in the same building! She's gone then, has she? Where to?"

She was still gibbering away to herself when the police left.

* * *

On the Isle of Wight, Sergeant Henderson knocked on Ester's front door for a fourth time before deciding to send his accompanying PC round the back to try and find an alternative way in. They had the paperwork to force entry, but an open window would be the best solution seeing as no one was home.

Through the kitchen window, the PC was faced with Geoffrey pinned flat against the side of the fridge-freezer, his eyes screwed tight shut. He had taken Ester's advice about hiding his fetishes in order to bag himself a nice woman, so was dressed in blue jeans, a white T-shirt, a black V-neck jumper and black brogues. He looked good. But the smart clothes couldn't hide the fact that he was a broken man. The PC tapped gently on the window, so as not to frighten him further.

Like a greyhound out of the starting gate, Geoffrey bolted for the front door, raced outside and barreled straight into Sergeant Henderson. Once Geoffrey was down, he stayed there. He lay on his back, his arms wrapped around his face, sobbing, "I miss her! I miss her! I miss her!"

Henderson got to his feet and dialed a number in his mobile.

* * *

Ridley looked out of Angela's balcony window, across the gray, rainfilled skies of West London, and tried to maintain his trademark calm demeanor—but his fist was clenched tight around his mobile phone as if he was about to explode. It wasn't something Jack had ever seen before, and it wouldn't last long, he was sure of that. Next to Ridley was Angela's stack of transparent plastic sewing boxes, neatly labeled by client name. The stack stood seven boxes tall and when Ridley kicked out at the third one up, he sent the top four flying across the lounge. He then returned to the balcony window. His shoulders were tense beneath his coat and they moved rhythmically up and down as he took deep, controlled breaths.

While Jack waited for Ridley to calm down, something made him glance upward at the high shelf, out of reach of sticky fingers. The worn teddy bear and yellow teething ring had gone. Jack smiled in admiration for what the women had managed to achieve. The patience, the mutual trust, the mutual love, the organization that lay behind this was staggering. Of course Jack was frustrated at always being several steps behind them but, my God, what special women they were!

"Geoffrey Porter-Lewis is being escorted across to us," Ridley said when he finally spoke. "He's all we've got. You've met him, Jack—will he give us the women?"

"He won't know anything, sir. Geoffrey will snap like a twig and Ester would know that."

"I'm going to send you some uniforms. Tear this place apart. And when Geoffrey arrives I want you to interview him."

And Ridley left without another word.

Jack pushed his hands deep into his pockets and took his place by the balcony window. On the balcony, next to a child's bike, a bunch of flowers stood in a bucket. Jack could see the handwritten label in its plastic pocket on the side of the wrapping: TO DOLLY. NEVER FORGOTTEN. X.

The rain started to fall just as Ridley stepped outside, forcing him to jog across the car park to his BMW. Jack felt sorry for him, even though his own arrogance—no, not arrogance; Ridley wasn't arrogant—his own blinkered self-belief was responsible for this monumental mistake. Ridley was an excellent officer, but he played by the rules and the truth was that anyone can learn them. And once you learn the rules you can predict what someone might do. The women had predicted Ridley, move by move, and *that's* why he'd failed. Jack was different. Jack, for the first time in his career, was thinking outside the box . . . He was thinking like them.

CHAPTER 33

The squad room was a hive of activity. Fourteen officers were all backtracking several weeks, retracing steps, re-investigating, reinterviewing, rereading, reversing through everything they knew, back to the moment the women were first mentioned.

They knew that they would not be traveling on their own passports, and that their mobiles had all been left behind at their respective homes. They knew that the school Angela's children attended was under the impression that the Dunn family had gone on holiday to Greece; Riel and Aggie had been practicing *yassas* and *efcharisto* for days. They guessed that Angela would have lied to her children about where they were going, but they had to explore the possibility of them being in Greece regardless. They also knew that Ester's parole officer was a total waste of space. He hadn't even known she'd left the Isle of Wight.

* * *

Jack watched three PCs systematically work their way through Angela's flat, expecting to uncover a clue. What did they think they'd find? Flight information jotted on a notepad perhaps, together with the name of the hotel they'd be staying in? Jack knew that the flat would be clean, because he knew Angela was smart. He paced the lounge, thinking. Not only did these women have to disappear without a trace, they had to disappear with £27 million. Jack had a sudden flash of inspiration and bolted for the front do

Irene at number 36 remembered Jack from his last visit, and excitedly showed off the dining chairs Angela had re-covered, now sitting around her family-sized dining table.

"I wanted to ask you about Rob." Jack showed his ID and Irene looked confused. "He's done nothing wrong. I'd just like to ask you about his business. He does up cars, doesn't he?"

Irene didn't know how to answer in case she got Rob into trouble.

"Irene, I just need to know if their flat has a private garage."

* * *

Rob's double garage was also his workspace but it was sparsely kitted out now—as though the best tools had disappeared along with his family. Half-empty shelves lined two of the walls, and different sized hooks lined a third. Some of the tools left behind dated back decades; Jack could loosely date them because Charlie owned similar ones. Rob, like Charlie, was a man who liked quality and remained loyal to his old work tools through the passing years. He was probably an ordinary man, dragged into an extraordinary world by the woman he loved. Jack knew that he'd do exactly the same for Maggie.

He scrabbled about in oil-stained filing cabinets and chests of drawers. He sifted through stray nuts and bolts, spare parts and mislaid drill bits but found nothing of significance. After about twenty minutes of pointless searching through the neatest garage ~~ seen, Jack stepped out into the fresh air. Boys on bikes ~~ de, looking over his shoulder to see if the garage ~~ ing worth stealing.

~~ of car was in here last?"

The biggest kid got £5 out of Jack before telling him about the bus. Once he'd paid up, Jack pinched the brow of his nose, waiting for a recent memory to come back to him; then he headed at a jog back toward the entrance to the flats. To the left of the main door was a narrow space where five large bins were stored—four black, one blue. Behind the black bins was a sheltered dry spot of ground being used by at least two homeless people. Blankets and sleeping bags were rolled up against the wall, together with a rucksack and a pile of tatty, ripped old foam squares that Jack expected would be laid out into a mattress at night. These foam squares were the memory he was searching for—he'd seen them in Connie's house.

Jack flipped the lid on the bins to reveal more squares of foam—dirtier, smaller, more torn. The rough sleepers had certainly salvaged the best ones. He took out his mobile and snapped some photos before racing back to Rob's garage. He'd left the door wide open and the gannet children were swarming.

Back in Angela's flat, Jack called Ridley. He was cautious about going to him with another hunch, but a hunch was all he had. He requested that someone check into a bus purchase made by Robert Chuke, and he told Ridley about the foam squares. He'd already googled different types of vehicle seat stuffing, and his theory was that if the women had emptied the seats, then it had to be because they were putting something else in. He had no idea if twenty-five seats would hold £27 million, but Angela was a talented seamstress, so it could fit. These women weren't criminals who'd be escaping on a private jet; they were ordinary people who would use their innate skills to their best advantage—driving out the country in a second-hand bus with a couple of kids in tow seemed typically "them."

In the time it took Ridley to say "leave it to me," Jack had had another thought.

"Sir, did the Chester police get a list of the kids at Julia's place?"

When Jack came off the phone from Ridley, he went back into the flat.

"This doesn't look like a search," he said to the uniforms as he looked around the lounge. "This looks like you've ransacked the place! Someone lives here! Tidy it up."

He stepped back out onto the balcony and logged into HOL-MES, scrolling through the list of kids found to be living at Julia's. He wasn't certain what he was looking for but when he'd thought about Angela absconding with her children, even taking the memories of her dead baby, he'd remembered Julia saying she'd die for those kids . . . and yet she'd just left them all behind?

He thought of Sam. An unwanted scallywag who occupied a soft spot in Julia's heart. His name was not on the list of children present at the care home. He thought of Suzie, the gentle giant of a girl who'd helped Julia protect a waif from Darren, the bully—and her name was not on the list, either. Darren's name had been added in red by the police; he was in a secure children's home as of a week ago, having been arrested in possession of a stolen bike and a rucksack full of his own clothes. They'd assumed he was running away—and not for the first time.

Most of these will never know where they're from, so it's vital for them to know where they're going. Do you know where you're from?

Julia's words spun round in Jack's head. She was doing so much for so many kids who, without her, would be abused, corrupted or even murdered. Jack could have been just like Sam if he'd not been rescued by Charlie and Penny. He didn't feel he was chasing hardened criminals who deserved to be in prison. He didn't feel he was making the streets a safer place for ordinary people to live in. He felt like he'd be making the world a worse place by removing these women from it. What harm were they actually doing by taking long-forgotten money and starting life again?

* * *

Darren had been in three fights during his short stay in the children's home and had won all of them. His position in the hierarchy was strong and the older lads were already looking to recruit him to their gang. He'd prove useful on the outside, seeing as he was only eleven and, therefore, highly unlikely to get nicked for anything and definitely not in danger of getting prosecuted.

Daniel, Julia's helper from her care home, had been to see Darren on the day he was arrested. Darren had attacked him, scratching his neck and punching him in the balls so hard that his eyes had streamed for at least a minute. Today, Darren was calm, but silent. He was a terrifyingly self-destructive mixture of depression, helplessness and fury. He didn't listen to a word Daniel said; he hardly blinked and the tears flowed unashamedly. Darren was broken.

As Daniel walked out, Jack walked in. Having never met, they passed each other in the corridor with nothing more than a tight smile and a nod.

The Quiet Room, where Darren had been put in order to meet Jack, was very similar to the police station's Soft Interview Room. It was plainly pleasant, with comfy sofas and a two-way mirror. Jack knew that, behind the mirror, there'd be a camera set to record this meeting. And the man standing just inside the door was there to make sure they didn't need anything.

Jack decided not to treat Darren like a kid.

"I know she was taking you away," he said. "And I know you screwed up by nicking a bike. I expect you thought she could just hide it for you underneath the bus." Darren's eyes flicked from the floor to Jack, but his face betrayed nothing. "Your rucksack was full of summer clothes, so I guess you were off to a sunny country in Europe. What was your new name going to be? If I could start again and choose any name in the world, I think I'd be called . . ." The first name to pop into Jack's head was "Harry," but he didn't finish his sentence. "Listen, Darren, I know you like Julia. I like her too. But she's making a mistake that will get her into a lot of trouble and I'm trying to help her before it's too late."

Darren rolled his eyes at Jack's lie. He didn't know what Julia had done, but he knew that she was the strongest and most loving adult that had ever passed through his life. If she was running to another country then she'd not just made a mistake, she'd done something to change her life. And there was no way he was going to mess that up for her.

Once Jack reached his dead end, he sat back and relaxed. "So what do you want to be when you're older?"

Darren looked at Jack as if he was stupid. His hard eyes seemed to say *I ain't getting older.*

Jack slipped to the edge of his seat and leaned toward Darren. The man by the door tensed as he readied himself for a potential assault.

"When I was adopted—" Jack's words made Darren's eyes widen—"I was saved from experiencing any of this. You've not been lucky so far, Darren, but what happens next is up to you. You either join a gang—being protected and feeling like you belong somewhere. Or you stay on your own and, in the end, be better than all of them. A respected man doesn't shout and throw his weight around, Darren. A respected man is quiet and calm ... and terrifying. Because you never quite know what he's capable of. Be that man. Smile ... and they will never see you coming."

Jack smiled, his eyes crinkling to prove he was being genuine.

He stood quickly, making Darren jump a little. Then he held his hand out for Darren to shake. Darren stood, and shook Jack's hand. Jack held on.

"DC Jack Warr. Remember the name. You ever need anything, you let me know."

By the time Jack left the room, Darren was a different person.

*   *   *

Jack walked the battleship-gray corridor toward the squad room, thinking through everything they had. Laura would have sourced an image of the bus and a license plate by now, although that would more than likely have been changed. And based on the time of day Darren was arrested, Jack's latest hunch was that Julia and the bus were probably heading north to get to Europe, rather than using Dover. Jack was buzzing—he'd single-handedly worked out how and where the women were traveling, and how they were transporting the money. Now what they needed were the false names the women were traveling under—then they'd have them. Then they'd have solved the biggest train robbery in history.

Jack entered the squad room with an uncharacteristic spring in his step and came to an abrupt halt. Maggie was sitting in Ridley's office. She should have been in bed, resting before her night shift. Jack slowed to a snail's pace.

Maggie stood to meet him. "Penny called."

She was looking at Jack in exactly the same way he imagined she looked at the relatives of dying patients, with an air of professionalism that allowed her to speak without becoming emotional.

"Charlie's in the hospital in St. Lucia. DCI Ridley knows and he's agreed to let you go."

CHAPTER 34

On the interview table in front of Geoffrey was a pile of tissues, and Ridley was seriously considering whether to send Laura for a second box. Normally, an interviewee would get upset when asked a specific question, or when reminded of details that were worrying them, or just before they were charged with something. But Geoffrey was simply mourning the woman he loved with all of his heart and soul. He had been a client of Ester's since the mid-eighties and, when she got out of prison for the murder of Dolly Rawlins, he had volunteered to take her in. He hadn't been the most exciting man in the world, personality or sexuality wise, but he'd been a very fast learner and, in the end, Ester and Geoffrey had made a formidable team. Between them, they'd alienated half of the Isle of Wight with their elaborate antics—Ester had once taken Geoffrey to the post office on a diamante dog leash. They'd thought it was the funniest thing in the world.

"What can we do to help you, Mr. Porter-Lewis?" Ridley asked. "Would you like a drink?"

"Sparkling water, please," Geoffrey whispered.

Ridley rolled his eyes and sent Laura to the canteen.

"You know you're not in any trouble, right? We don't think Ester revealed her plans to you, so all we really want to know is whether you have any idea where she was heading after Southampton."

Geoffrey shook his head in a series of short, sharp movements. "She never loved me," he sniffled, blowing spit bubbles as he endeavored to smile. "I gave her half of my life and all of the love I had, but she never loved me back. I was OK with that because she liked me—and Ester never liked anyone." He paused long enough for Ridley to inch toward the door. "Love would have been an awfully big adventure, if only she'd allowed me to show her the way."

It was the most Geoffrey had said since arriving at the station. He seemed to want Ridley to stay; Ridley would have done if he'd thought for one second he'd get something remotely useful from him at the end of all that dribbling. But that wasn't going to happen.

* * *

The flight to St. Lucia was long. Jack was silent and Maggie didn't push him for conversation. He was in a world of his own, so all she did was hold his hand as a sign that she was there for him when he needed her. She glanced to her left every now and then to see if his furrowed brow had lifted, but it hadn't. In all of their time together, Jack had never lost anyone close; she imagined he'd now be flicking through the memories of his life with Charlie, and longing for those unrepeatable years gone by.

In fact, Jack was wondering how a bunch of old-school women, who'd learned their tricks and cons back in the eighties and nineties, would go about getting new passports more than twenty years later. He was convinced that, since the train robbery in '95, they'd have had no connection with the criminal world at all—Ester went to prison and the others went straight. What Ridley and his team should be doing now is looking back at forgers from twenty years ago. Eddie Rawlins would know exactly whose door to knock on. God, he wished he wasn't flying to St. Lucia! He glanced to his right and saw Maggie's face. He softened his brow and squeezed her hand.

"We'll get him home," she whispered. "I've boxed up your 'evidence wall' and put up some old family photos for them. I'm sure your mum and dad don't want to lie in bed looking at ex-cons and crime scene photos."

Jack forced a smile. "You've done exactly the right thing," he said. "And I'm sorry for leaving it all to you."

"I know this case is important to you. I know it's revealed some unexpected things from your past but, Jack, all of that can wait. Ridley has the case in hand, and as for your revelation about Harry Rawlins, well . . . he's not going anywhere, is he?" Maggie's face lost some of its empathy. "I can't see how he's a man to be proud of, Jack. Charlie's a man to be proud of. The next few days will be so important for you as a family, so don't let anything distract you."

"Days?"

Jack suddenly looked like a little boy coming to terms with the loss of his very first loved one—it didn't matter how much you explained about the cycle of life, the hurt would be overwhelming and it would be Maggie's job to rock him to sleep when the end had come and gone.

Maggie leaned her head on his shoulder.

"Life goes on." Her words were oddly upbeat. "What do you mean?" asked Jack.

"Nothing," she said.

But he could see how her eyes sparkled.

"This is completely the wrong moment," Maggie went on, floundering. Jack let out a laugh.

"You're pregnant!" he shouted, so loud the whole cabin could hear. "It's exactly the right moment," he said, showering Maggie with rapidfire kisses. "Marry me!"

Jack blurted the words out, and they were as much of a shock to him as they were to her. Marriage had been mentioned in the past, but they always said they'd wait to be more settled, more financially comfortable, more secure. It was nonsense. They'd been doing things in order and now, 35,000 feet above the North Atlantic Ocean, everything was suddenly out of order. Charlie was dying, Maggie was pregnant and Jack was proposing. The world was turning, however painful that might be, and they had no option but to turn with it. The entire cabin had heard the question, and although Maggie whispered the answer only to Jack, the instant round of applause showed they thought she must have given the right answer.

Maggie's words swam around in Jack's head: the pregnancy; boxing up his "evidence wall"; accepting his proposal; Harry not being a dad to be proud of; Charlie only having days left.

Thinking of Charlie made Jack feel comfortable and safe; thinking of Harry made him feel edgy and excited. Men wanted to be like Harry and women wanted to be with Harry. It must be amazing for someone to have such an impact on those around him. But would Harry fly for nine hours to collect his dad and then care for him until the day he died? Would he feel this much weight in his heart at the thought of losing the man who'd taught him to ride a bike, chat up girls, make a bow and arrow, and appreciate the beauty of the English countryside? Had Harry ever really loved anyone? Jack was proud to belong to Charlie Warr. And he hoped that his child would be proud to belong to him.

* * *

Robert Chuke's face was now on the evidence board, alongside Angela's. Ridley had just got off the phone to Police Captain Gallatos of the Hellenic Gendarmerie in Greece, who had said categorically that the bus they were searching for had not crossed his borders.

"Right!" Ridley barked as he emerged from his office. "We're going to focus on Angela and Robert Chuke. She's the youngest. She went from being a maid in a brothel, to being a housewife and mother. She wasn't even trusted to be at The Grange on the night of the train robbery—she was off somewhere babysitting Kathleen O'Reilly's kids. And she wouldn't have had the smarts to lie to her own kids about going to Greece, so I still think that's where they've headed. Maybe they dumped the bus. But she's our weak link. We find her, we find them all."

"Sir?" In Jack's absence, Laura felt she had to remind Ridley how much Jack rated the intelligence of the women. "These women have stayed under the radar for so long because we underestimated them. They're relying on it. They hid guns from Craigh, they hid their involvement in the train robbery from Newman and Thorn. With all due respect, sir, I don't think we can dismiss any one of them as being a weak link."

"So what do you suggest?" asked Ridley.

"It's all smoke and mirrors, and misdirection," she said. "Angela was banking on the kids mentioning their holiday, so we'd assume that's where they were heading. But if you ask me, I think Greece is the only European country they're definitely *not* in."

* * *

Laura sat alone in the squad room. All the desk lights were off, apart from hers. Behind her, Ridley's door was open, meaning he must be in Superintendent Raeburn's office. She had demanded daily updates since the dead-end accusations thrown at Barry Cooper's army buddies.

They didn't know the exact day the women had left the country, but they did know that it had to be after Darren's arrest, so Laura had put out an "all ports" warning requesting CCTV spanning three days. Now, she was watching CCTV footage of a bus matching the one Rob had bought in London, pulling off the Amsterdam ferry and heading south along the N236. Thirty minutes later, the N236 split into the N238 and the A28, and a faulty intersection camera resulted in Laura losing sight of the bus.

Ridley walked in at that precise moment and sat down at Jack's desk.

"Pick a road to follow," he said. "I'll take the other one." And together, they worked into the early hours.

* * *

By 11 p.m., Maggie and Jack had arrived at Victoria Hospital in St. Lucia. Charlie was asleep in a private room, and Penny was at his bedside, struggling to sew a rip in the knee of his jeans.

"Hello, Mum," said Jack, and she burst into tears, running into his arms and putting her head on his chest. He held her there for what seemed like an age. "It'll be fine," he murmured, knowing that wasn't true.

While he comforted her, Maggie unpicked the mess Penny had made of Charlie's jeans.

"He ripped the knee when he fell," Penny wept. "I tried to catch him, but he was too heavy. Oh, Jack, I thought I'd lost him. I thought I'd lost him!"

"Where are you staying, Penny?" Maggie asked. There was no reply. "You're meant to be aboard ship tonight, so I've booked you in with us."

Penny nodded, but Maggie could see she hadn't really taken it in. And even though Charlie was sedated, they had to prise her away from the hospital on the promise that they'd come back the next morning at eight o'clock. It was well before visiting hours, but the rules had been set aside for them.

"They're so kind," Penny said between sobs, but Maggie knew that it was because they didn't think Charlie had long left to live.

The Le Haut Resort was only three stars, but it had a swimming pool and almost all the rooms had a beach view. Jack didn't care where they stayed as long as he and Maggie could snuggle down together. As they lay there, with one thin sheet pushed down over their naked bodies by the powerful draft from the ceiling fan, they could hear Penny crying in the bedroom next door.

"Since moving to London, I've seen Dad three times. And the second time was the day he told me he was dying." There was so much guilt in Jack's whispered voice. "I thought I didn't need to see him all the time, because he wasn't going anywhere. I wish—"

"Don't wish for things you can't change, Jack. Just love him while you can."

Jack watched a yellow and green gecko crawl along the ceiling directly above his head.

"Mags," he whispered, and the movement of her fingers in his chest hair told him that she was awake and listening. "How far gone are you?"

"A few months already," she said. "But I only just found out."

They went on to have a whispered conversation about practical things such as maternity leave, pay drops, the price of nappies and whether they'd need to move from the flat. They both knew that money was tight now, so when the baby came, it'd be even worse. Maggie pointed out that Charlie would never have got medical insurance, being terminally ill, so their pensions and money from the sale of the bungalow would disappear if they didn't get him home quickly. She wasn't begrudging the way Jack's parents had spent their life savings; she was pointing out that Penny would probably be left with little or no money of her own and so would need looking after financially. Maggie and Jack would soon go from having no dependents, to having two.

At last, as a gentle snoring came through the paper-thin walls, Maggie and Jack allowed themselves to relax and drifted off to sleep.

* * *

The next morning, Maggie dealt with all of the medical notes and the medication they needed to take back to the UK with them, while Penny sat in the chair by Charlie's bedside, watching the two most important men in her life play dominoes. She smiled as she recalled the days when Charlie would allow Jack to win; now it was Jack allowing his dad to win. By the time the first game was halfway through, Penny's head was nodding and her eyes were closing. Charlie and Jack exchanged glances. Neither of them needed to mention the terrible stress Penny was under; they just allowed her to sleep.

The German police had found the bus, torn it apart and found nothing. No money, no sign of the women. However, under the guidance of Ridley, they had discovered that the front edge of each seat and the top edge of each seat-back had all been recently re-sewn.

Jack's hunch about the seats being stuffed full of the stolen cash was right. Unfortunately for Ridley, it seemed that the staff at Hyatt House had "lost" the women's booking information—and the bus parking around the back was not covered by working CCTV. The women had switched from the bus to a new vehicle or vehicles, unseen, and Ridley had no idea what sort of transport he was now looking for or the pseudonyms the women were using. So far, no known forger of passports and ID documentation had been connected to the women. Ridley was stumped. And for the first time in this entire investigation, he wished that Jack was there.

* * *

In West London, Angela's neighbor Irene from number 36 had been worrying ever since she'd directed DC Warr to Rob's garage. Unable to bear it any longer, she opened a secret drawer in her bureau and took out a mobile phone which had one number stored in it. She sent a WhatsApp message:

> Jack Warr knows about Rob's garage and the bus. Sniffed about the bins too. Dining chairs were admired by all at afternoon tea on Monday! Love to the kids. Irene.

Then she took out the SIM card and flushed it down the toilet. She watched the water settle, made sure the card had gone, then put the kettle on.

CHAPTER 35

Jack couldn't believe how beautifully Maggie had transformed their spare bedroom for Charlie and Penny. There was bedding he'd never seen before and framed photos he'd not seen in years. The effect was spoiled slightly by the commode and the stash of cardboard urine bottles underneath the bed, which Maggie must have snatched from the hospital the second she got the call from St. Lucia.

One of the photos on the wall was of Jack on Charlie's shoulders, aged about 5. Charlie's arms were raised, his huge builder's hands lying gently on Jack's thighs, holding him safe. His triceps and biceps—even the muscles on top of his shoulders and down his sides—stood out through his tight white T-shirt. The gentle giant.

Jack pulled open the spare bedroom door as the puffing and panting coming along the hallway got closer. Charlie was now a skinny gray man, with too much skin to cover his non-existent muscles. Jack felt a swell of emotion come from deep inside, but it wasn't sadness, it was anger. How *dare* the man who'd held Jack high enough to touch the sky be leaning so heavily on two women because walking ten feet is too much for him? How dare this be happening to his dad when the world was full of bastards like Tony Fisher, who refuse to fucking die? How *dare* this hard-working, generous, gentle man be taken from people who needed him in their lives?

As if he could tell what his son was thinking, Charlie put his arm around Jack's shoulder. The effort of lifting it made what was left of his bicep shake.

"You were 5 in that pic. It was the first year we had you. I took you to work, showing you off. Been doing the same ever since."

Jack put his arm around Charlie's thin waist and pulled him close, allowing the old man to lean on him and rest where he stood. Jack's mobile rang, disturbing the moment.

"I'll leave it, Dad," said Jack.

"Answer it," Charlie insisted. "I'm so proud of everything you do, lad, and the thought of me holding you back would kill me quicker than any cancer. Do what makes you happy."

* * *

Ridley was the kind of officer who understood that you have to go down a dozen dead-ends before you find a way through to the next stage of an investigation. But today, he sounded as close to defeated as Jack had ever heard; he made no bones about the fact that he'd called Jack in for a brainstorming session.

"We've shifted tack to try and trace them beyond Düsseldorf. They've got to launder the money, so we're looking into European countries where that's most easily done. And they might have more than one new identity each, because the women who entered Germany in that bus certainly haven't left across any official border. No luck yet on who might have made new passports for them."

"I may have an idea about that, sir," said Jack. "I'll make a quick stop before I head in and see what I can find out."

"My best wishes to your dad," said Ridley. "And Jack—Superintendent Raeburn wants to see you in her office as soon as you arrive."

Jack had put in for his sergeant's exam not long back and he assumed that Raeburn wanted to see him about that. Ridley had told him that he was not going to approve Anik's request for the same promotion, so Jack figured it was all pretty much in the bag. He felt no swell of excitement, no anticipation, no nerves, just a simple, practical need for a pay rise because of Penny and Charlie, and because of the baby.

He went back into the spare bedroom. Charlie was sitting on the bed by himself. He knew that what he was about to say wasn't entirely true, but it was entirely necessary. Jack needed his dad to die knowing that his boy's life was complete—even though it wasn't yet.

"Can you keep a secret, Dad?" he asked.

And Jack told him about the impending promotion, the baby and the marriage proposal. Charlie cried, loud and proud, and Jack held him tighter than he'd ever done before in his life.

* * *

Eddie Rawlins was pleasantly surprised to see Jack on his doorstep. "Come in, come in," he said.

Neither man noticed, as the front door closed, a figure watching from across the road, in the shadow of a tree.

Eddie was already on the whisky. It seemed more like a habit, to numb the dullness of his life, than any attempt to get drunk. Jack got straight to the point.

"Who would you go to for fake passports? Not me, you understand, Eddie—*you*. Where would an old-timer like you go?"

"You in trouble, son?"

"I need to trace some people who've been around since your day. I don't think they'd trust new blood—I think they'd dig up an old faithful."

Suspicion crossed Eddie's face and he sat down to stop himself jittering from foot to foot.

"You're starting to sound like Old Bill," he joked.

"I am," said Jack, raising his chin and introducing himself—prematurely—as "Detective Sergeant Jack Warr."

Eddie slammed his hands on the arms of his chair and attempted to leap up in indignation—although all he actually managed was a bunny-hop to the edge of the chair until his hips were far enough forward for him to throw himself into a standing position. The effect was somewhat spoiled by the time it took him to stand up, but he still managed to sound pissed off when he spoke.

"He'd be ashamed of you! You hear me? You come in here under false pretenses, get all cozy and then think I'm gonna spill the beans just 'cos you're Harry's boy? Get out and don't come back. You ain't welcome."

According to the law, Jack knew he had to leave as Eddie had demanded. Ridley would have done it. But Ridley was a copper through and through and Jack ... well, Jack was evolving into something else. As he frowned at Eddie and listened to the barrage of insults, Jack wanted to punch him. It dawned on him that Eddie wasn't scared of Jack, the policeman—but he *was* scared of Jack, the son of Harry Rawlins.

Jack took a step forward and got in Eddie's face.

"I *am* Harry Rawlins's boy," he whispered menacingly, and watched as fear flushed through Eddie's face. "But I'm also Charlie Warr's boy. And you know what that adds up to? The best of both worlds, Eddie. I know you *and* I know how to get to you. So, I want the names of any old-school forgers in London that are still alive, and that anyone would dare go to. If you give me names, I won't take you in."

Jack stepped forward again, forcing Eddie to shuffle backward until he toppled back onto his seat. He leaned his hands on the arms of Eddie's chair and gave him one final nudge.

"Believe this, Eddie, Harry's got nothing on me."

The stench of Eddie's whisky breath blew hot in Jack's face, but he didn't back off.

"They'll all be dead now." Eddie trembled as he spoke. "I can't think of no one—I swear I can't."

Jack sat himself next to Eddie, just as he'd done when they flicked through the photo album together, and smiled.

"You take your time," he told Eddie. "I'm going to make us both a nice cup of tea."

* * *

Ridley had updated Interpol and now half the police forces in the bloody world were looking for four women, buying and selling high-end goods at a pace. Monaco, Rio, Zurich, Monte Carlo: anywhere known for its rich visitors was being looked into. The waiting was almost painful.

Jack and Laura sat together at her desk as he fed her names of forgers from the eighties and she checked them on the system.

Marcia Armante—dead. Thomas Sykes—alive: Alzheimer's. Scott Hughes—dead. Dougie Marshall—alive: care home. Rachel Yarborough—alive: glaucoma.

Laura couldn't believe they were looking at such decrepit old relics. But Jack was encouraged. Eddie had mentioned that Dolly knew Dougie and Marcia very well, because they'd both worked closely with Harry. They were his go-to forgers.

"Once you got involved with Harry," Eddie had said, "he never let you go. Treated you right, mind, as long as he got it back tenfold."

Eddie had explained that, after the first underpass raid went so badly wrong, Harry had been nursed back to health by Trudie. He'd suffered minor burns in the explosion and bits of him were all wrapped up like a mummy. Trudie had been sent to get him a new passport—Eddie didn't know which forger he'd chosen, but it had to have been Dougie or Marcia. And seeing as Marcia was dead, Dougie was top of Jack's list.

As Jack pulled his coat on, Ridley came out of his office for an update. His every instinct screamed *What the fuck are you doing, chasing a pensioner in a care home?* But he didn't say anything, because he also knew that his every instinct had let him down recently.

* * *

The care home had directed Jack to Marshall's Bookmakers, in Croydon, Dougie went in every day to help his son, Gareth, run the family business.

Jack entered through a side door and up a dirty, stained staircase, half-blocked by a stairlift. There was so little room that he had to slide along the wall as he climbed. On the landing, he passed an old bathroom with a few remaining dark green tiles clinging on to their old grout for dear life. There was a dirty towel hanging over the rail, a stained tub and a toilet that Jack could smell from the corridor. It was truly horrible.

There was a closed door at the end of the corridor. There was no sign, and the paint had seen far better days, but this had to be Dougie's office. Jack knocked lightly, pushed down on the handle and swung the door open.

Dougie Marshall was sitting at his desk behind a plume of noxious cigar smoke when Jack walked in uninvited. He wore a wide, shoulderpadded, pale blue and pink tweed jacket with a yellow shirt and mismatched tie. He was obese, with a flushed complexion and a bulbous red nose. There was a cigar clamped between his yellow teeth, which were almost the same color as the final few strands of hair that had been combed over his otherwise bald head. In front of Dougie and to his left was a stack of promotional flyers for the bookies, and to his right were some sticky labels showing their new web address. Dougie was sticking one label on each flyer and then creating a third stack ready for distribution in the street, no doubt by spotty teens wanting to earn pocket money.

Jack flashed his ID and got straight to the point.

"I want to talk to you about Angela Dunn."

"It would be my absolute pleasure to talk about such a lovely girl."

Dougie started to waffle on about how it had taken her just two weeks to produce the office curtains and four matching cushions—he couldn't recommend her highly enough.

Jack smiled at the cheek of him.

"I'm actually talking about the fake passports you made for her," he said.

"Well, you're a very rude policeman, aren't you?" Dougie scoffed. "As you can see, my job is nowhere near as exciting as you seem to think."

"I know you provided the—" Jack started.

"You don't know anything!" Dougie snapped. "I, PC Plod or whatever your name is, did *not* make any fake anything for anyone."

Jack wondered if Eddie had called Dougie to give him a heads-up, but decided that Eddie wouldn't have the guts.

"Now," Dougie continued, "is there anything else?"

Jack pulled the chair opposite Dougie away from the smoke cloud and sat down.

Dougie smirked. "You remind me of someone. It'll come to me."

Jack looked around. On a high shelf, running the circumference of the room, mixed up with other junk, were old inks, paints, brushes, an old washing mangle and an artist's drying rack. All items used by oldschool forgers, all in pride of place. Dougie followed Jack's eyes—he wasn't worried. Jack could look all he liked; it was all just memories. A row of short, locked filing cabinets stood underneath the window sill. One lone print of Constable's *Hay Wain* hung on the wall above Dougie's head. A drinks cabinet occupied one corner of the room and a small, worn armchair occupied the other.

"Angela Dunn is no criminal, if that's what you think. She's a survivor. As are you, I'd wager. Except you're also a lucky boy and don't have to fight quite so hard for the things you have."

"You like fakes?" Jack asked casually as he headed around Dougie's desk and removed the *Hay Wain* from the wall, revealing a safe.

"2698. But you'll need a warrant to open it."

Jack replaced the painting and, as he straightened it, he thought of Harry Rawlins, and a story Eddie had told him about how he'd steal original paintings to be copied, along with their provenance, so that he'd end up with several "legitimate" works of art. Jack wondered if this *Hay Wain* was Harry's work.

Jack pushed his hands deep into his pockets and moved slowly round the room, looking carefully around because Dougie was quite right to say he couldn't do anything without a search warrant. Dougie never took his eyes off him. Never blinked. As Jack headed toward the worn armchair, Dougie suddenly dragged himself to his feet.

"I'm bored of you now, son!" Jack hadn't seen but, as he stood, Dougie had pushed a small button underneath the lip of his desk. Dougie grabbed his walking frame. "If you wanna waste any more of my time, you get a warrant. For now, fuck off!"

Jack stood in the center of the room as Dougie shuffled toward him.

"You're a disrespectful little shit!" he shouted.

Dougie's arms were doing far more work than his legs—they shuffled forward an inch or two at a time, unable to bend at the knees or ankles. Stairs would be impossible now for him.

As Jack was trying to work out what he'd actually done to cause such a change in mood, the door swung open.

"You all right, Dad?"

Gareth was a large man in his forties, good looking in a battered sort of way, with the flattened nose of a boxer. He was fashionably dressed in a three-piece suit, pristine shirt and coordinated tie— the exact opposite of his dad. Gareth clearly wasn't remotely happy to see Jack in his dad's office.

"Who the fuck are you?" Gareth guided Dougie to the old armchair as he spoke more gently. "What've I told you about leaving that side door open, Dad? You got to lock it when you arrive."

Once Dougie was safely seated, Gareth's focus returned to Jack.

"I was just asking your dad about Angela Dunn, Mr.—?"

"Don't fucking 'Mr.' me. You ain't after no upholstery review."

"No. I'm after information on how she might have obtained a passport at short notice."

Gareth took a step toward Jack. Jack quickly took his hands from his pockets in case he needed to defend himself. He instantly regretted this move, as it told Gareth that he was on edge and very aware of his own comparatively small stature. Dougie grinned from the comfort of the armchair. His boy had this!

"Oh, no, no, no—you ain't talking to my old man about that bollocks. He's fucking 84! He's got angina. He's a sick man, not your go-to snout. He ain't well enough to be ambushed by some half-arsed copper. That is what you are, right? You're a copper."

"I'm not pressuring your father into anything—" Jack began.

Dougie interrupted. "He wanted to look in my safe without a warrant, son. I told him to leave but he wouldn't. I didn't want to disturb you by pressing the emergency button, but it got so I was scared to be up here on me own with him."

As Gareth moved forward, Jack moved back, toward the door. He wasn't scared, although Gareth did look like a handful, but he couldn't afford to get into a fight with a civilian after he'd already been asked to leave their property.

"I'm going, I'm going," Jack sang. "Don't put a hand on me, all right? I'm going."

"Move faster, then!"

Gareth walked at Jack, chest first, like an immaculately dressed, expensive smelling brick wall that was impossible to argue with. Jack backed off in time with Gareth, went out the door and down the hallway, toward the stairs. He'd completely forgotten about the stairlift, so when he turned to head down the stairs, he tripped over the footrest sending the top half of his body down the steps before his legs could untangle. He grabbed out in a vain attempt to save himself, caught the start button with his elbow and tumbled head first down the filthy stairs, all the way to the shitty doormat at the bottom. With his nose pressed into the floor and his eyes screwed tight shut, all Jack could hear was Gareth cackling and the slow whirr of the stairlift heading down to meet him.

"Don't worry. You got at least twenty seconds to get out of its way!" Gareth howled.

* * *

Maggie stood in between Jack's legs, pressing around his nose and cheekbones. He sat with his head back, gripping the arms of their dining chair and desperately trying not to push her away because of the pain he was in. His eyes were blackening and wouldn't stop watering, and his nose was swollen and wouldn't stop bleeding.

"I don't think it's broken." Maggie glared down at him as though he was the one who'd done something wrong. "You've reported them, right? You can't let them get away with attacking you. We get so many police come into the ER, and paramedics now as well. It's disgusting, Jack. You have to take a stand against this sort of violence."

Jack put his hands on Maggie's hips, in an attempt to reassure her.

"It was my fault, Mags," he said.

She misinterpreted his meaning. "Oh, don't tell me this is down to your newly discovered past! Did you go in all gung-ho, all 'Harry Rawlins'?"

Jack stood up. "No, I didn't!" he protested.

She didn't believe him. "Jack, you don't belong in that world. You're a good, kind man—not a gangster. They survive by having no heart, nothing to lose. You . . . You have so much to lose." Maggie instinctively put her hand to her belly. "Please, Jack, I can't stand the thought of you putting yourself in danger. You're not a fighter, you're a smart man who's always used words rather than fists. I don't want you coming home like this ever again, you hear me? No more fights, Jack, please."

Jack couldn't stand any more of this.

"I tripped over a stairlift!" Maggie stopped talking. "And I fell down a flight of stairs. Nobody hit me. I'd rather you'd think I'm an idiot than a thug—but if you repeat what I just said to anyone else, I'll leave you."

She burst into giggles.

* * *

The next morning, Jack looked at his face in the wing mirror of a parked car. His nose was still very painful. Even the breeze blowing in his face made him wince. He called Laura.

"How did you get on with Dougie?" she asked.

"It's not him. I'm about to go and see Rachel Yarborough—"

Laura laughed. "She's blind," she reminded him. "She can't possibly be our forger."

Jack corrected her. "She's got glaucoma. I asked Mags and she said that, if it's not too far developed, she'd be perfectly capable of close work."

* * *

Within seconds of being inside Rachel's home, however, it was obvious that her glaucoma was seriously bad. Her furniture was sparse so as not to cause an obstacle course, the décor clean and her TV was like a cinema screen.

"If I have the contrast right up, I can see some things. Not details. Tea?"

Jack declined, not wanting to put her out, but she insisted.

"I'm not useless, Mr. Warr." As she made the drinks, she talked. "Dougie Marshall, eh? How is the old bastard?"

Jack watched in awe as Rachel made a pot using a push-button kettle that poured exactly the right amount of hot water, and mugs with talking sensors attached to the sides. To see her wander about her home, you'd never guess that she was partially sighted. In fact, if it wasn't for the living room clock announcing the time on the quarter hour, Jack would never have guessed this home had been modified at all.

"He was a genius back in the day. Sharp as a tack, wily as a fox—that was our Dougie. The only time he ever went inside was when that stupid kid of his was caught forging betting slips. Dougie owned up to that one for him, thinking they'd never send a dying old man down. Got three years. You can't get a license to run a betting shop if you've got a criminal record, see, so Dougie had to go down for Gareth, in order to secure both their futures. Dougie didn't mind prison— within a week, he'd forged a medical referral and got a cushy time in the hospital wing. What he *did* mind was people thinking he'd forged Gareth's terrible bloody betting slips—very shoddy workmanship. Gareth's got no style. You met him?"

"Briefly," Jack said. "Mrs. Yarborough, I'm wondering if you can suggest any old-time forgers who might still be active in the area."

"If by 'old-time' you mean anyone mine and Dougie's age, then no. We're the last ones. I gave it all up years ago, way before my eyes started to let me down, on account of being a terrible liar. If I ever got questioned by the police, I was bound to give myself away, so I quit while I was ahead. Dougie worked a good twenty years longer than me. *Great* liar, he was. That's why all the big names trusted him."

"Names like Harry Rawlins?"

"There's a blast from the past! He did do a bit of work with Dougie, yes." Rachel smiled as she remembered Harry. "He was a master. And we were his willing servants. If you did right by Harry, he did right by you. He liked Dougie because he didn't look like a genius. He hid in plain sight. What the coppers saw was a fat fucker in a betting shop—what Harry saw was an artist." Then Rachel said something quite unexpected. "Can I touch your face?"

"I wouldn't mind," Jack said when he'd got over his initial surprise, "but my nose is a little sensitive at the moment."

* * *

Jack fitted right in at the hospital; no one gave his face a second look. It was 6:30 p.m. and Maggie was thirty minutes away from starting her night shift. Jack was enjoying doing nothing except eating a beef sandwich and watching Maggie eat a tuna salad. All he wanted to do was sit, relax and enjoy the company of his lovely, beautiful, pregnant, soon-to-be wife. Maggie had other ideas.

The Antenatal Unit was, of course, empty, but Maggie's pass got her into any area of the hospital. She opened a wardrobe at the back of the room and got out an ugly, tan-colored vest with a padded front. She held it up for Jack to put on. Maggie zipped him in.

"Comfy?"

"Not remotely." He scowled.

"That's what it feels like to be seven months pregnant."

"Jeez, Mags. How are you going to carry this lump round?"

Jack put his hands in the small of his back and pushed his hips forward, arching. He puffed out his cheeks and then blew, making his lips ripple in a silent raspberry. He started to walk around the room. He bent his knees, widened his feet and waddled.

"Look, Mags, I'm you!"

As Jack moved with more and more exaggerated waddles, Maggie ran at him, laughing, calling him a cheeky bastard. He dodged her a couple of times, but the weight of the vest became too much and eventually he collapsed onto a yoga mat, exhausted. Maggie sat astride him and strained to lean down over his padded belly to kiss him. She couldn't get anywhere near his mouth, which made them both laugh.

Sitting astride Jack, looking down at him in his pregnancy vest, with his two black eyes and swollen nose, Maggie had never felt so happy.

"I love you, Jack Warr. I can't wait to be Maggie Warr." Then her hormones took over and she started to cry. "Me and you know so much about pain, Jack. Promise me we'll protect our baby from it."

As Maggie wept, Jack unzipped the vest and sat up. He wrapped his arms tight around her body, let her gibber on about silly things and tried not to make it obvious that he was laughing at her.

"Promise me we'll teach it only about happiness. Promise me we'll play sleeping lions, and hide and seek, and at Easter we'll hide eggs and play the hot and cold game."

"I promise you all those things," Jack whispered.

And in this tenderest of impromptu moments, he found himself thinking about Dougie Marshall's grotty little office.

Hot and cold, he said to himself. *I put the painting back over the safe and I walked round the room, looking at his forging paraphernalia. I passed his filing cabinets—not a flinch. Then his drinks cabinet. I even spotted an old £5 printing plate under a bottle of single malt, and that didn't worry him. Where was I heading that made him jumpy? What made him call for backup?*

Jack visualized the layout of the room, and all he could see in front of him, in the moment Dougie panicked, was the worn old chair.

That's *what was "hot."*

That's what Dougie didn't want him to look at.

Jack decided, there and then, that Dougie was the man they were after. A "wily fox" Rachel had called him. Jack would go back tonight and discover exactly what Dougie Marshall was hiding in his armchair.

Maggie pulled away from Jack and wiped her tears on his T-shirt. "Put it in the wash when you get home. It'll be nice for you to have an evening in with your parents, just the three of you. Get a takeaway."

She stood up, picked up the vest and went to hang it back in the wardrobe. Jack sat on the floor, trying to work out whether chicken fried rice with Charlie was more important than breaking into Dougie's office and finding proof that he'd helped the women escape the UK.

CHAPTER 36

The night bus back to Croydon was full of the dregs of society. A man sat on the back seat with his head back and mouth open, seemingly comatose. Two lads up front rolled themselves a spliff. An old couple, probably homeless, slept against each other's shoulders. Jack sat in the middle of the bus, and as the driver braked the sleeping man on the back seat suddenly gave a loud groan and a woman got up from the floor in front of him, where she'd been invisible till now. The man zipped himself up and they both got off the bus. Jack closed his eyes for a second. *That's an image that'll take a long while to get rid of*, he thought.

The entrance to Dougie's back stairs was slightly set back from the street, so once Jack had stepped into the little recess, he wasn't visible to passers-by or to CCTV. From the shadows, Jack donned gloves and a balaclava, then got out a lock-picking kit—surprisingly cheap from Amazon—although he did already know how to pick a lock from his school days, when a precocious classmate had taught him . . .

The day before they were due to start in sixth form, he and his mates had broken into the staff room and the sixth form common room and swapped all of the furniture. They started life as sixth formers with sofas, a telly, a coffee machine, and a microwave. It hadn't lasted long but they'd made the most of it while it did.

The stench of the bathroom was almost overpowered by the stench of bleach. Jack got an instant headache and his eyes stung through the holes in his balaclava. Using the thin beam from the torch on his phone, Jack moved straight to the worn old chair and flipped the seat up, revealing a crudely placed piece of hardboard cut slightly bigger than the hole it was covering. Underneath it was what looked like £50,000, in five bundles, each wrapped with the now familiar band from the train robbery money, empty passport covers, old and new, inks, gold leaf and all the other paraphernalia needed to forge passports and other IDs. Under all of that, Jack found a little black notebook.

Inside the notebook was a list of names—Elaine Fortescue, Joanne Lewis, Anita Davidson, Reginald Davidson, Claire Simeon. Textbook: using the same initials as people's real names often made for an easier transition into a new life. More names—Steven Kirkwood, aged 11. That passport must be for Sam. David Stainer, aged 11. That one would have been for Darren if he'd made it. And Suzie was to become Sharon Whittaker, aged 10. Angela's kids would have to get used to being called Abbi and Raul—risky, as they were so close to the children's actual names, but he guessed that Angela wanted them to be as comfortable as possible in their new lives.

The notebook shook in Jack's hand. This was the case breaker. All he had to do was walk into the station and hand the book to Ridley; he'd call Interpol and the women would become instantly visible. Within half a day, they'd be back in the UK. Train robbery solved; murder solved. Jack sat down at Dougie's desk, his breath dampening the inside of his balaclava. He stared at the list. He couldn't take it in. Jack suddenly spat out a burst of laughter as he read the date of birth of "Elaine Fortescue"—it would have made her 62! How the fuck did Ester think she was going to get away with *that*?

* * *

Jack sat alone in an all-night café drinking tea from a giant, stained mug, enjoying the privacy and silence. He flicked through the other pages of Dougie's notebook, reckoning it might help them track down some other missing villains as well. "Villains." He didn't like that word in relation to the women. He knew it was what they were but after all, Jack had broken into Dougie's office to get this notebook. So, what did that make him? He liked to think of himself as a copper using his ingenuity, but, in truth, there was no way he could take this notebook to Ridley—not considering the way he'd acquired it.

For a moment, Jack felt ashamed that he'd crossed a line. Then he felt more ashamed that he could make or break the lives of nine people who, in the big scheme of things, hadn't done much wrong other than collect a hoard of cash, more than two decades old, that nobody else even knew existed. As he recognized the magnitude of what he was holding, and the lives he could bring down with it, he suddenly felt immensely powerful. His heart pounded and his eyes narrowed—he wanted the "kill" like never before. He was being too soft: these women had stolen the money in the first place. They'd outsmarted him, embarrassed him and he wanted to *win*. Again, and without any prompting, Jack thought about Harry.

And then he thought about the only person who really mattered—Maggie. He thought about the lower maternity pay, all of the stuff they'd need for the baby, Penny possibly moving in with them, his promotion to sergeant. Jack needed this. He needed to sacrifice the women and their kids in favor of his newly shaped family. Every man for himself. The women selfishly wanted to better themselves . . . Well—now it was Jack's turn.

He dialed a number.

"Sarge, do me a favor, please. First thing, I need DCI Ridley to be told that Dougie Marshall is our forger. A raid on his son's bookies will confirm everything. I'm going to send him an email shortly with more information, but I'm 100 percent certain. Can you pass that on? I'll be in at eight."

Across the road from the café, the shadowy figure from outside Eddie's flat was, once again, following Jack's every move.

* * *

Jack drove into the police station car park bang on 7:30—half an hour early for their raid on Marshall's bookies. Ridley had called Jack back last night, the instant he'd received the email. They'd chatted through how Jack had got Dougie's name from an unofficial, rather impromptu "informant"—and how Rachel Yarborough had confirmed the old man's reputation. Jack described the office, highlighting all of the forgery equipment and how he thought Dougie's age was irrelevant; he was more than capable of giving the best of today's forgers a run for their money. He ended by reiterating that he was certain a search of the property would come up trumps. It was Jack's intention to "find" the notebook while on this morning's raid.

Jack sat in his car for a second, preparing for the impending praise he was about to get from Ridley. He checked the small rucksack by his side—the notebook was on the top, in pride of place. Jack took it out and put it into his glovebox. He then checked his mobile. In his photo album was a picture of every page in Dougie's notebook . . . just in case he ever needed it in the future. He didn't know quite what he might need it for, but he was certain that it was something Harry would have done.

The battleship-gray corridor looked oddly bright and cheerful this morning. Jack entered the squad room to a chorus of friendly "well done"s and, less cordially, the odd "jammy wanker." Then, as they took a closer look at him: "What the hell have you done to your face?"

From behind his desk, Ridley stood to meet Jack and, for the first time since his interview, he offered Jack his hand to shake. Jack took it with pride—his broad smile was making his nose ache.

"Was that in the line of duty?" Ridley asked.

"No, sir. Just a fall. It's not as bad as it looks."

"Well . . . you were bang on the money."

Jack's smile dropped. What did Ridley mean, he *was* bang on the money?

Ridley reached into his out-tray and dropped £5,000 in an evidence bag onto his desk.

"Anik argued a case for moving the raid to seven, so we went with that. He said he'd called you to let you know. That'll teach you to start picking up your bloody voicemails, won't it?"

Jack was furious. What the hell was he going to do now? He could hardly claim to have found the notebook in the raid, if he wasn't on the fucking raid! He daren't turn round in case seeing Anik's stupid face made him snap and rip the little shit's throat out. All of his plans were ruined in a split second of selfish, petulant jealousy.

"We've got Gareth downstairs," said Ridley. "He's waiting on his solicitor, so we can't interview him yet."

"What about Dougie?" Jack asked.

"Dead." Jack couldn't hide his shock. "According to Gareth, someone saying they were a policeman barged into his dad's office yesterday, and scared the crap out of him. He had a massive angina attack later that night and ... Well, he wasn't strong enough to come back from it. There's no CCTV, but Gareth says he'd recognize the man if he saw him again. But we've got them, Jack! We found passport sleeves, driving licenses, and £5 k from the train robbery. Gareth will talk. And then we've got them!"

CHAPTER 37

Jack leaned heavily on the edge of the sink in the men's loo, water dripping from his face. He stared at his reflection; his eyebrows were down, the furrow between his eyes was deep, his cheek muscles flinched. Who was this angry man? Jack tried to change his expression, but he couldn't. Anik's betrayal was impossible to forget. Ridley's pathetic, thoughtless, disrespectful decision to leave an immature prick like Anik to contact Jack with such vitally important information as a change of time to the raid was unforgivable. Jack didn't know how to feel about this side of the law anymore. Were they really worth his time, his skills, his dedication?

Behind Jack, a stall door opened and Anik emerged. He knew enough to freeze as Jack's eyes stared him down in the mirror. Jack said nothing. Anik said nothing. Jack stood statue-still, his prey in his sights, toying with the poor defenseless weasel. Anik sidestepped out of his stall and left without washing his hands.

* * *

Jack's demeanor on entering the interview room had not yet improved. Gareth sat alone, back from the table, legs crossed, sipping a cup of coffee. He was still waiting for his solicitor, so there was no camera or tape on yet. Gareth scowled at the sight of Jack.

"*You!* You got a whole heap of shit coming down on you, copper," Gareth growled.

Jack was unfazed.

"Your old man's dead, meaning you're suddenly very rich. You want to stay free to spend your money? Or am I gonna put you away for aiding and abetting four of the UK's most wanted, and for nicking the other £45 k that I know was in that chair? Your choice. 'Cos this is all just a game, Gareth—you run with your gang, I run with mine, and every now and then we cross paths. Sometimes there has to be a winner and a loser, but not today. Today, you get to go home if you do the smart thing."

As the blood drained from Gareth's face, he swore blind that he didn't know what his dad had been up to.

"Doesn't matter," Jack said. "All that matters is what my boss believes."

And, right now, Jack could tell Ridley that the sky was green and he'd believe it.

Jack's mobile rang. He left the room to answer it.

The warden from the secure children's home, which was the temporary stopgap for Darren, said that Darren had just received a call from abroad and he'd thought Jack might like to know. Even if the phone was a burner, they'd still be able to trace the country of origin. So now, Jack not only knew the aliases of the women, he could also find out exactly which country Julia was in right now. He thanked the warden for his vigilance and hung up.

Once again, Jack was in possession of information vital to Ridley's tracking of the women, especially as he knew they were about to get nothing of use out of Gareth. But he felt so betrayed by those who should be on the side of justice that he just couldn't bring himself to hand over more key information for no reward, no appreciation and no acknowledgment. Ridley shaking his hand meant nothing! He'd been kept out of the raid, and he was being treated like a dog that you pat on the head every now and then, placate and keep in line. He *still* wasn't being taken seriously. And he wasn't going to stand for it any longer.

Jack left the station and headed home, leaving his car in the car park. He'd jump on the Underground eventually, but right now, he needed to walk. He needed fresh air. And he needed to think.

CHAPTER 38

Gareth spoke freely and confidently, making Anik feel like he was racing down the final straight of their lengthy investigation. But, for Ridley, nothing felt right. Why wasn't he just "no comment"? The answer to that was because Gareth was streetwise enough to give them plenty so he could be noted as co-operating, but nothing of importance. For now, Ridley allowed the interview to continue in the hope that Gareth might slip up.

"Dad drank with some of his buddies from the bad old days, but they was even more past it than he was. I mean, as in, 'doolally.' Dad was all there in the head—it was his body that let him down. I never knew anything about him still forging, on my life I didn't. I thought he was up there, sticking labels on flyers!" Gareth smirked. "Makes me kinda proud of the old bastard."

"Tell me about Angela Dunn."

Anik's tone was serious and to the point. Ridley would have been impressed if he hadn't already decided that this interview was going to be a waste of everyone's time.

"She used to clean for my parents. When Mum died and Dad went into the care home, Ange still popped round every now and then—had a cuppa with him, chatted about Mum. Ange knew Mum better than me in truth, so I liked her visiting. She made curtains. Cushions, that sort of thing. I don't know what else I can say about her." Then, Gareth very cleverly turned the tables. "You can't really think that little girl had anything to do with that train robbery?"

Ridley rolled his eyes, but Anik was being sucked in.

"Hard to believe." Gareth shook his head. "I mean, Dad and his mates were guessing left, right and center about who it could be. Someone even thought old Buster had snuck back, done the job, and buggered off again."

"On the night your dad died, you said he was visited by a man claiming to be a policeman . . ."

"That's right. Big fella. Dark hair. Bit smaller than me. We don't have CCTV on them back stairs, so I can't tell you much more than that, really. Dad was a very sick man in those final months. Anything could have caused an angina attack at any moment. But, well, he had a massive stroke on top of it, so . . . no chance. I'm sorry I can't help you any more than that, I really am."

* * *

"*Death of a Salesman!*" Penny shrieked.

Maggie moved on to miming the last word in *War of the Worlds* and wondered how the hell this game of charades was ever going to end. Jack watched Charlie sleep. He was in a recliner, feet up, blanket over his knees. The heating was on full blast, but Charlie really felt the cold now. His head had lolled to one side, and the skin on the lower side of his face seemed to have slid down his skull—he just had no muscles left to hold it all up.

"*Planet of the Apes!*"

Maggie screamed "*Yes!*," gave Penny a round of applause, said how incredibly clever she was, and they swapped places.

Jack laughed under his breath as Maggie slid down the arm of the chair he was sitting in. He squished up a little, but this chair wasn't wide enough for the two of them. They didn't care. They watched Penny stomp around the lounge, mouthing the word

"*Godzilla.*" She was so bad at games! By eight o'clock, Penny was snoozing on the sofa, Charlie was in bed, and Maggie and Jack were in the kitchen tidying up after dinner.

Jack opened the fridge to put the butter away and his attention was caught by the shelf full of high-protein, high-vitamin, high-mineral, life-prolonging milkshakes.

"Thanks, Maggie," he whispered.

"What for?"

"For buying a month's supply of these. Imagine if you'd bought a week's worth. Imagine what that would have been like for Mum to see." Maggie turned him round and he was crying. "I couldn't do this without you."

"You don't have to do anything without me. Ever. And Penny will stay with us for as long as she needs."

"They're in the nursery . . ." he said half to himself.

This thought had come from him trying to work out how they were all going to fit into a two-bedroom flat; but it instantly turned into a much more disturbing thought.

"He's going to die in the nursery, Mags. You hear, don't you, of babies and kids sensing stuff that's gone on before them. What if Dad—?"

Maggie hugged Jack. "Your dad is a loving man with a beautiful soul. A room is a room, but *if* Charlie hangs around . . . I think we'd be blessed to have him looking over our little one."

Jack began laughing at his irrational thoughts. As Maggie hugged him, she couldn't tell where the giggling ended and the crying began, nor did she care. When Jack was ready, he pulled away.

"We do need three rooms, though. When the time's right, I'll ask Mum what's left from their pensions and the sale of the bungalow— and I'm up for promotion."

"As long as we're all happy," Maggie said, "everything will work out." Jack loved her impractical take on finances, but one of them had to be sensible.

* * *

Jack walked the last few miles back to the police station to collect the car. It was just getting dark, and the streets were alive with a mix of commuters and drinkers. He used this time to talk himself into giving the women up, getting his promotion and living happily ever after with Maggie. He liked them, but he loved Maggie and that's all that really mattered in the end. Telling Ridley about the phone call from Julia to Darren would be simple. But he'd need to work out how to get the women's new names into the mix. He'd need to lie about how he got his hands on the notebook, and why it wasn't found in the raid. He'd pretty much decided to make Gareth hand it in and pretend to have found it in his dad's bedroom at the care home. That would work.

As Jack rounded the corner toward the police station car park, he suddenly stopped dead. By the passenger door of his car, a shadowy figure was trying to break in.

Jack didn't shout out; he just ran, full pelt, in the hope that his gaining momentum would give him a good enough head start to catch the would-be thief before they even saw him coming. All Jack could think about was the notebook in the glovebox. And then he thought about how old the car was and how easy it was to bloody well break into.

Just as the passenger door finally gave way, Jack launched himself at the thief and they both hit the ground hard. The man's shoulder hit him in the face and a piercing pain shot through his nose, rendering him useless for long enough to allow the man to scrabble to his feet and run. The chase was on.

His target was hefty and slower than Jack—but Jack reckoned he'd be handy when caught, so he'd have to get the upper hand quickly. He swiftly gained ground and the second they turned onto a street with a grass verge, Jack dived at the man's legs, taking them both down onto the soft turf. Jack grabbed the man's right arm with the intention of twisting it up his back, but he was too strong and shrugged Jack off like a rag doll. The man, unable to get to his feet more quickly than Jack, flipped onto his back so when Jack came in again, he got a fist to the side of his jaw, sending him spinning across the pavement. Now the man had time to stand up and make a break for it again while Jack was still on his hands and knees, trying to make sense of where he was. He shook the dizziness away, stood, stumbled into a tree trunk, righted himself, focused on the running figure through his streaming eyes, and powered after him.

Jack rounded a corner just seconds after the man and, out of the blue, was sucker-punched to the ground. It was like running into an iron bar. The pain was sickening. Jack flipped onto his hands and knees and vomited on the pavement. His nose dripped bright red blood onto the gray concrete and his eyes watered in sympathy.

The man stood over Jack. As Jack's head spun and he tried to stop himself from vomiting again, he heard a few words.

". . . not stealing, you prick . . . a gift."

Jack's head became too heavy to hold up. He lay down on the hard, cold pavement and looked straight into the light on top of the lamppost above his head. He could feel the blood running down his throat, so he rolled onto his side and spat it out. From this position, Jack watched the man's dirty white sneakers walk away.

A moment later, a Yorkshire terrier sniffed its way along the blood trail and licked at Jack's face, bringing him back to himself. As he clambered back to his feet, using the wall for balance, the pain in his face had subsided just enough for the pain in his arm to take over. It was excruciating and, although he had never broken a bone in his life, it felt like it must be broken. Jack pushed his aching body upright, fell back against the wall, pushed himself vertical again and spread his legs in the hope of being steadier on a wider base. He wobbled on the spot while the elderly woman in front of him, the terrier now tucked under her arm, came into focus and asked if he needed an ambulance. Jack shook his head and started back toward the police station.

The car's passenger-side door was still open. And on the seat was a bag he didn't recognize. He reached over this bag to check the notebook was still in the glovebox—it was. Jack kneeled heavily onto the edge of the footwell.

. . . *not stealing, you prick . . . a gift.*

Using his uninjured arm, Jack unzipped the bag. Inside were one hundred bundles of fifty-pound notes. Jack picked up one of the bundles and, with bloodied fingers, leafed through it: fifty notes. Fifty notes per bundle, one hundred bundles; the bag contained a quarter of a million pounds.

Jack's mobile rang. Unknown number. Jack slid onto the ground.

"You OK?" Angela Dunn sounded like she was right by his side. "He wasn't meant to fight with you, just . . . I'm sorry. He's called an ambulance, so they'll be with you in a few minutes. He's one of

Julia's misfits from years ago. He knows the darkness better than you, so you'll not find him."

Jack listened. He didn't know what on earth to say.

"If I've learned anything at all over the past 24 years, Jack, it's patience. Good things come to those who deserve it, and we deserve this."

"I know where you are . . . Anita Davidson," Jack managed.

Angela remained silent for what seemed like an age. When she spoke again, she wasn't flustered, she was calm. Her words were exact, purposeful and brilliant.

"It sounds like you have the power to take away all of the good we've managed to scrape together. I honestly can't tell you how it all started, and I definitely can't tell you how it'll end. That's up to you, it seems . . . This money is not a bribe, Jack, it's a thank you. Thank you for taking the time to know us better than anyone, because knowing us is the only way this will turn out the way we want it to. We're not bad people and we had nothing to do with Mike's death. We're just trying to do the best we can for those we love. You know what that's like."

"Don't talk about my family!" Jack snapped.

"I'm sorry," said Angela. "Whatever you decide to do, the money is yours to keep. I want to start living, Jack," she went on. She sounded so strong. "I'm sick of just getting by. I'm better than that. I'm more than that. We all are. I was born into a terrible life, but I'm damned if I'm going to die in it. I don't know what else to say really, except . . . I hope you're happy in the end. It gets easier once you've decided who you are . . . No, not who you are—who you need to be."

In the distance, sirens began faintly and gradually grew louder.

"I can hear help arriving," she said. "Take very good care, Jack, and if we ever do meet again, I hope it's as friends."

The second his mobile went dead, Jack dropped it onto the ground and struggled round onto his knees, desperately trying not to use his broken arm. He zipped the bag, stuffed it underneath the passenger seat, grimacing through the pain, and then he collapsed onto his back, panting for breath. He finally let go, and allowed himself the painless joy of passing out.

CHAPTER 39

Jack was in awe of the sheer number of cars bringing more and more mourners to Totnes Crematorium. Hundreds of people he'd never even met—from the building trade, from the pub, from Charlie's Labour Club, from Penny's bridge club. The driveway was a sea of slow-moving people and vehicles.

Maggie linked her arm through Jack's plaster cast. His good arm was inside his newly dry-cleaned sergeant's uniform and his broken arm was in a sling underneath it.

"Remember when you said your dad wouldn't be remembered by as many people as Harry Rawlins? I don't think this lot would agree with you."

Jack did recall saying it. He'd been looking at news articles from Harry's funeral; half of London's gangsters and half of London's coppers stood shoulder to shoulder. It had been an impressive sight that he thought would never be matched by Charlie. But this was better. Because all of these mourners actually loved Charlie.

Ridley cut an impressive figure as he walked up the driveway in his black suit. Even though he was a good few inches shorter and narrower than Charlie's tradesman mates who surrounded him, he stood out as being a man to be reckoned with.

"Condolences." He shook Jack's hand. "The uniform looks good on you. Impressive turnout, your dad was clearly much loved."

"Thank you, sir. And thank you for stepping in. The arm's not healing quick enough and Mum didn't want strangers doing it."

"It's an honor to be asked, Jack." Ridley kissed Maggie on the cheek. "It's been a tough time for you both."

Five strapping older men, probably in their sixties or even seventies, approached and introduced themselves to Jack and Ridley as the other pallbearers. Maggie took this as her cue to stand by Penny's side, put her arm tightly round her waist and help her to put one foot in front of the other. That's all Penny had to do today. Tomorrow would be tackled when it arrived.

Penny was taking deep breaths, trying to maintain dignity in the face of such unimaginable tragedy. But Maggie's touch immediately broke through all her defenses and the tears came.

"Sorry," Maggie whispered. "I didn't mean to make you cry."

"Jack looks handsome in his uniform, doesn't he?" Penny's words were barely audible. "He was the same as a Scout—uniforms suit him. I was so disappointed when he got kicked out, because they wouldn't let me keep his smart little shirt."

"Why was Jack was kicked out of the Scouts?" Maggie asked, keen to keep the conversation light.

"He was a bit on the naughty side. When all the other boys were lining up or sitting in a circle, he'd be off doing his own thing. Not very good with authority, they said. And when he was finally tracked down and the Scoutmaster asked what he'd been up to, he'd come up with some fairy story about playing cops and robbers. Not sure which one he was."

Penny chattered on, hanging on to the past for dear life because she had no clue how to cope with the present or the future.

"He lived in a fantasy world at times—'always looking for excitement,' I used to say. More exciting things than we could give him. No surprise to me that he became a policeman." She managed a laugh. "He could be a little fibber, though. For the first two weeks he was with you, he told us he'd got shift work in a local pub."

Penny could see that Maggie had taken this the wrong way. "Oh—he was never ashamed of you! He wanted to keep you all to himself, Maggie. That's what it was . . . Look at him now. My beautiful boy walking beside my beautiful man one last time."

Music began to play from inside the chapel and Penny's grip on Maggie's arm tightened. The five burly men and Ridley stepped up to the back doors of the hearse and formed two lines of three, opposite each other. The funeral director pulled the coffin far enough out for everyone to take up position on either side. Maneuvering the weighty box up onto everyone's shoulders was a jittery affair, but they all soon settled. The funeral director then led the way inside. Jack walked directly behind his dad. It took twenty minutes for everyone to file into the crematorium and find their seats. The walls were lined with standing friends, two deep. It was a wonderful sight.

The only person in the room who had no clue who Charlie Warr was was the Humanist celebrant. He started to read the prepared words dictated by Penny and redrafted by Maggie into something that at least sounded spontaneous.

Maggie glanced at Jack. He had his good arm tightly around Penny's shoulder and he was listening, but there was a distance in his eyes. Maggie gripped his hand and brought him back to them.

"Be with Charlie," she whispered in his ear. "You can never do today again, so *be here*."

As she spoke, she stroked the back of Jack's hand to lessen the impact of her words.

And he knew, that although she loved him with all her heart, she wasn't going to stand for any of his nonsense. Not today.

AUGUST 12, 2019

Jack laid a fresh bunch of flowers on Dolly's grave. The card, written in Jack's handwriting, read, LOVE FROM ANGELA X. He then poured two glasses of whisky from his hip flask and placed one glass on top of the small stone wedge of the grave next to Dolly. Jack downed his whisky.

"Here's to your first grandkid, Dad."

Back at the car, Maggie leaned against the bonnet, waiting. As Jack got close with the second glass of whisky in his hand, she grabbed his wrist and inhaled the deep peaty vapors. She closed her eyes and imagined the taste.

"Four months and counting," she sighed.

Jack moved his hand across her stomach and leaned in to kiss her cold mouth.

"Let's get you home before you freeze," Jack whispered, his lips still on hers. "I'll finish painting the nursery and you order the takeaway. Mum likes chow mein."

*   *   *

"A live-in babysitter! Heaven!"

The decision to move from a flat to a house with an annex for Penny wasn't hard after Jack's surprise announcement that he'd won £250,000 on an impulsive, one-off lottery ticket. Maggie was pleased to be moving somewhere they could finally call home, but of course she didn't believe Jack's story about where the money had come from for a second, and when the time was right, she would make him tell her the truth. She liked her new husband with his new-found sense of his place in the world, but she wasn't about to let lies become part of their relationship.

Jack Warr was no longer lost. He finally knew where he came from. With the best of Harry and the best of Charlie flowing through his veins—nature and nurture—he was now a man who effortlessly straddled two worlds: crime and punishment.

For most people, those worlds would be polar opposites, but Jack knew better—they complemented each other, like light and shade. And Jack knew he had to live in both in order to finally be the man he was always destined to be.

Acknowledgements

I would like to thank all the staff at my publisher, Bonnier Books UK, particularly Kate Parkin and, of course, Bill Massey for his edits.

In Australia and New Zealand, the team at Allen and Unwin. It is an absolute pleasure working with them.

In South Africa, all the staff at Jonathan Ball. I hope to see you all soon.

In Ireland, Simon Hess and Declan Heeney, for all their hard work in selling and publicizing my books. I always love my trips to Dublin.

Cass and Ann Sutherland for their continued assistance in getting the police and forensic procedures correct.

Neil Granville for his help in researching the fire.

Everyone at La Plante Global: Nigel Stoneman, Tory Macdonald and Veronica Goldstein.

A huge thank you to my readers, who always support me and give me such great encouragement. It makes me want to continue writing.

Also thank you to Debbie Owen in working with me to hopefully bring my vision of *Buried* to the screen.

Lynda La Plante
Readers' Club

If you enjoyed *Buried*, why not join the
LYNDA LA PLANTE READERS' CLUB by visiting
by visiting www.bit.ly/LyndaLaPlanteClub?

A MESSAGE FROM LYNDA LA PLANTE . . .

Dear Reader,

Thank you very much for picking up *Buried*, the first book in my brand-new series, and one I'm very excited about. Jack Warr is a character who has really taken hold of my imagination and I've loved writing about him. He is a complex character: charming, slightly lost and searching for answers, and the road that he finds himself on was a fascinating one to explore. I also loved dipping my toe back into the world of *Widows*, but in a contemporary setting and with a new cast of characters, as well as a few old favourites. I hope you enjoyed reading the book as much as I enjoyed writing it.

My fans will know that I am a stickler for accuracy in my forensics and police research, which is out of respect for those that give me such valuable advice. The eagle-eyed amongst my readers may have noticed that there is a bit of a discrepancy when it comes to the stolen bank notes in *Buried*. The Bank of England regularly take notes out of circulation, which in this case would mean that the ill-gotten gains from the train robbery would have no value in the present day. I decided, therefore, to use my license as a novelist and have the £20 and £50 notes as legal tender, even though in reality they would not have been.

If you enjoyed *Buried*, then please do look out for the second book to feature Jack Warr, which will be published in 2021. And in the meantime, this Autumn sees the publication of the next book in my Jane Tennison series, *Blunt Force*, in which Jane finds herself reunited with old friend, Spencer Gibbs, and the two must navigate the salacious world of showbusiness to solve the brutal murder of a famous theatrical agent.

The first five novels in the series, *Tennison*, *Hidden Killers*, *Good Friday*, *Murder Mile and The Dirty Dozen* are all available in paperback, ebook and audio now. I've been so pleased by the response I've had from the many readers who have been curious about the beginnings of Jane's police career. It's been great fun for me to explore how she became the woman we know in middle and later life from the *Prime Suspect* series.

If you would like more information on what I'm working on, about the new series or about the Jane Tennison thriller series, you can visit www.bit.ly/LyndaLaPlanteClub where you can join My Readers' Club. It only takes a few moments to sign up, there are no catches or costs and new members will automatically receive an exclusive message from me. Zaffre will keep your data private and confidential, and it will never be passed on to a third party. We won't spam you with loads of emails, just get in touch now and again with news about my books, and you can unsubscribe any time you want. And if you would like to get involved in a wider conversation about my books, please do review *Buried* on Amazon, on GoodReads, on any other e-store, on your own blog and social media accounts, or talk about it with friends, family or reader groups! Sharing your thoughts helps other readers, and I always enjoy hearing about what people experience from my writing.

With many thanks again for reading *Buried*, and I hope you'll return for the second in the series.

With my very best wishes,

Lynda

Want more DC Jack Warr?

Keep reading for an exclusive extract
from the next thriller in the series

Judas Horse

Some killers can't be tamed...

Coming April 2021

**Available to pre-order in hardback,
eBook & audio now**

CHAPTER ONE

The Cleveland Nature Reserve was a cluster of lakes situated between Cirencester to the north and Swindon to the south. The reserve was just a small section of the Cotswold Water Park, which consisted of hundreds of lakes intercut with cycle paths, farms, fishing sites, water sports and walking routes. Home to thousands of species of flora and fauna, it was only marred by the presence of the occasional, unexpected area of quicksand – proving that even the most beautiful things are highly accomplished at hiding their dangerous side.

Jamie and Mark often cycled along Spine Road, which, as the name suggested, ran through the centre of this cluster of lakes. They'd go fishing, watch the jet skis and beg free cans of pop from the Waterside Café. Today, they were distracted by a strange sight in one of the lakes: dozens of crows on the surface of the water. The brothers, aged twelve and thirteen, didn't know much about anything yet, but they did know that crows could not land on water. Each time the wind blew tiny waves across whatever they were standing on, the birds panicked and took flight, creating a cloud of flapping black wings. But they didn't fly away. Something was keeping them there in the middle of the lake, on their strange, out-of-place platform.

Twenty minutes later, Jamie and Mark had cycled round to a small rowboat that they'd hidden away many months ago, tied to the low, overhanging branches of an old tree. They pushed the boat into the water. Mark, being older and stronger, always did the rowing.

As they got closer to the mass of birds, it became clear that the crows were standing on a submerged horsebox, the roof of which sat just above the surface of the water by no more than an inch. The birds began to shriek and flap in a unified show of force – a desperate endeavour to keep their prize, whatever it was. They were clearly focussed on a six-inch tear in the metal roof.

'Climb up, then,' Mark instructed Jamie. Then he swung one of the oars through the air and the crows flew away, creating such a foul smelling down-draft that the boys screwed up their faces and pinched their noses. Jamie almost puked. He said he didn't want to climb on top because he was scared that the horsebox would sink, but Mark assured him that it must already be sitting on the bottom, so couldn't possibly sink any further. Jamie took off his t-shirt and tied it round his face like a mask, before tentatively climbing onto the roof. He shuffled towards the six-inch hole and peered down into the pitch-dark water.

'Nah, there's nothing,' Jamie quickly declared, desperate to get back to dry land, or at least the safety of the rowboat. But Mark wasn't prepared to give up that easily. He told Jamie to push the metal tear with his foot and make the hole bigger. Above them, the crows circled and cawed angrily.

Jamie pushed his toe into the hole, trying not to get his trainers wet. But that didn't work. Egged on by his brother, he began stamping down hard on the ripped edge, again and again and again. Finally, it gave way by another inch or two, sending a bubble of old, trapped air up into Jamie's face. The stench was so rancid that he immediately puked into the lake, and his foot slipped through the hole, filling his trainer with icy water. Mark couldn't stop laughing. Jamie did not see the funny side.

'I only just got these trainers for my birthday!' Jamie said. 'I'm coming back, this is stupid.'

'You're wet now anyway,' Mark giggled. 'Stamp on it, go on. Make the hole big enough to see inside. Go on, Jamie! Don't be a baby!' Mark knew exactly what to say to rile his younger brother. Jamie angrily jumped up and down on the roof of the horsebox, each jump splashing Mark in the process. Soon they were both soaked, but it didn't matter – *now* they were having fun.

With each jump, Jamie brought his knees up to his chest, getting as much height as he could. And each time he landed the hole opened up a little more. Until, after one jump too many, the roof finally split and completely gave way beneath his weight.

To Mark's horror, Jamie plunged into the lake and disappeared beneath the surface. The next five seconds seemed to last forever. Mark didn't dare shout his brother's name in case someone heard and saw what they were doing. He just held his breath, as though he was underwater too.

Finally, Jamie bobbed back up, gasping and slapping the surface of the water with his palms. He dragged air into his lungs and stomach, then burped it back out. He waved his hands around, trying to find the oar being waved above his head. Mark guided it into Jamie's hands and pulled his little brother to the wall of the horsebox. Jamie draped his armpits over the top of the wall, wiped his face and gradually let the wonderful realisation sink in: he wasn't going to die.

Mark was as white as a sheet, as the horror of what-could-have-been spun round and round in his head. Jamie, knowing that he'd now earned enough cool points to last a lifetime, began to laugh, which gave Mark permission to relax. The boys giggled and snorted, coughed and burped. Mark's hysteria, fuelled by relief and adrenalin, was brought to an abrupt end when something broke the surface of the water behind Jamie.

Mark couldn't see what it was at first, but gradually the thing bobbing about – just inches away from the back of Jamie's head – turned and twisted in the water and, from a new angle, it took shape. The human skull still had some flesh attached, but not much; and the rest of the skeleton looked like it was only being held together by the black clothes it wore. In the sky above, the carrion crows went wild, driven crazy by being so close and yet so far away from such a feast.

Jamie, oblivious, was still giggling away to himself.

'Jamie ...' The serious tone of Mark's voice made him stop laughing and pay attention. 'Grab the oar. I'll pull you over the wall, then you swim to the boat.' The old, rotted corpse bobbed back and forth as Jamie kicked his legs, and the drag of the water lapping against the inside of the horsebox pushed it closer towards him. '*Now* Jamie. Get out of the horsebox and into the lake! Quick!'

Jamie had no idea why his brother was panicking. He followed Mark's eyeline and slowly turned his head. 'No! Don't turn around! Keep looking at me!' But it was too late.

The scream that came from Jamie scared the crows from the sky and the distant fishermen from their deckchairs.